Hélène Aldeguer

After
the spring

A Story of Tunisian Youth

Facebook: **facebook.com/idwpublishing**
Twitter: **@idwpublishing**
YouTube: **youtube.com/idwpublishing**
Tumblr: **tumblr.idwpublishing.com**
Instagram: **instagram.com/idwpublishing**

ISBN: 978-1-68405-546-3   22 21 20 19   1 2 3 4

Translation by **Edward Gauvin**

Lettering by **Frank Cvetkovic**

Edits by **Justin Eisinger**
and **Alonzo Simon**

Design by **Ron Estevez**

Originally published by Futuropolis as Aprés le printemps: Une
jeunesse tunisienne.

Chris Ryall, President, Publisher, & CCO
John Barber, Editor-In-Chief
Cara Morrison, Chief Financial Officer
Matt Ruzicka, Chief Accounting Officer
David Hedgecock, Associate Publisher
Jerry Bennington, VP of New Product Development
Lorelei Bunjes, VP of Digital Services
Justin Eisinger, Editorial Director, Graphic Novels & Collections
Eric Moss, Senior Director, Licensing and Business Development

Ted Adams and Robbie Robbins, IDW Founders

I would like to thank

the crew at the independent blog Nawaat for giving me
such a warm welcome, Ali for his help and advice, and
Aymen, without whom this comic would not exist.

My thanks to Virginie Jourdain and Paulette Smets
from the Leblanc Foundation and the members of
the prize jury: Jean-David Morvan, Gauthier Van
Meerbeeck, Frédéric Ronsse, Daniel Couvreur, and
Thierry Tinlot, as well as my wonderful editor Sébastien
Gnaedig, who gave me the chance to be published!

*This book received the Raymond Leblanc Prize for young comics
creators. With the support of the IMPS and the Brussels Comics
Festival, and participation from the newspaper Le Soir and the
MOOF Museum (Museum of Original Figurines).*

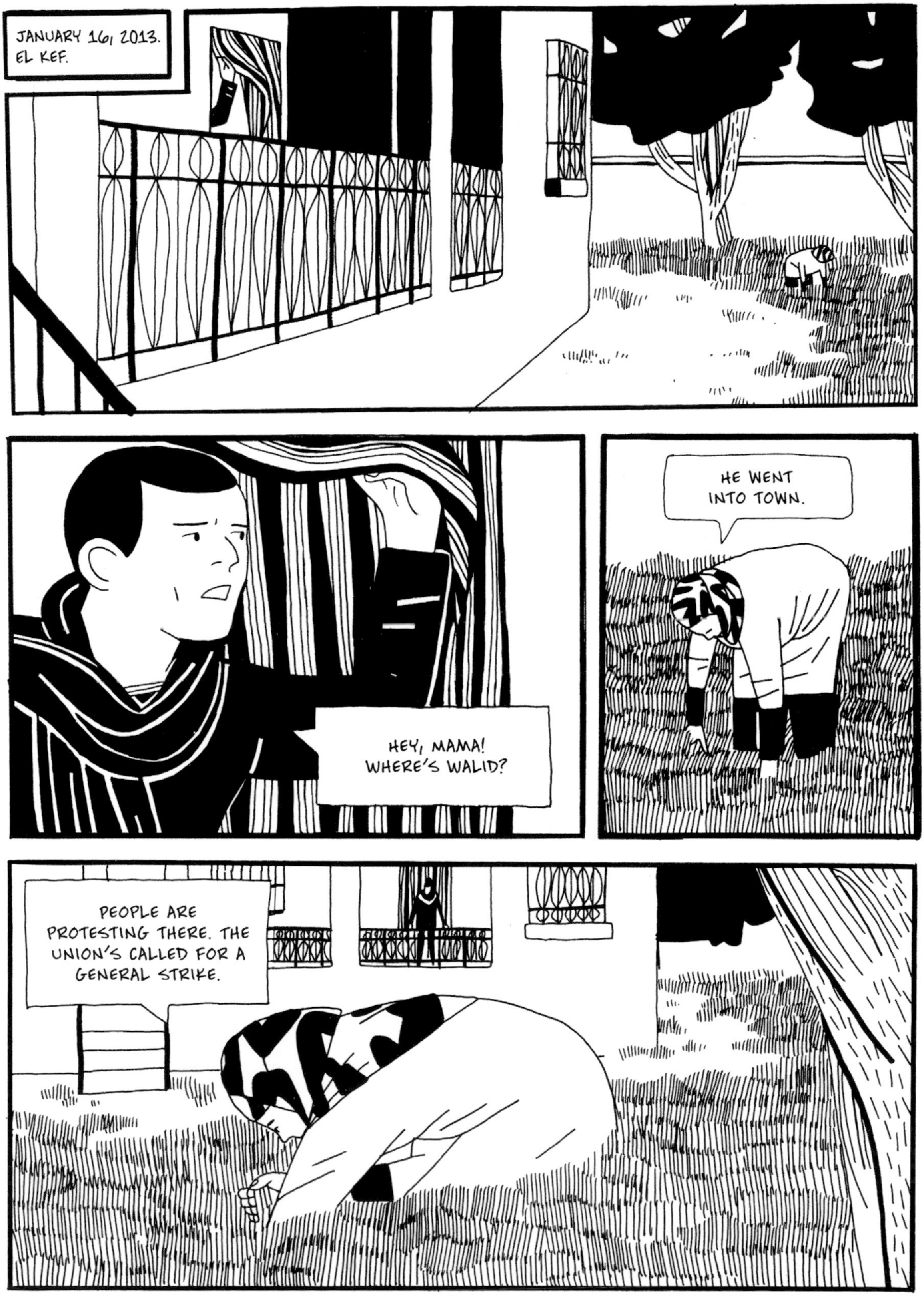
JANUARY 16, 2013.
EL KEF.
HEY, MAMA! WHERE'S WALID?
HE WENT INTO TOWN.
PEOPLE ARE PROTESTING THERE. THE UNION'S CALLED FOR A GENERAL STRIKE.

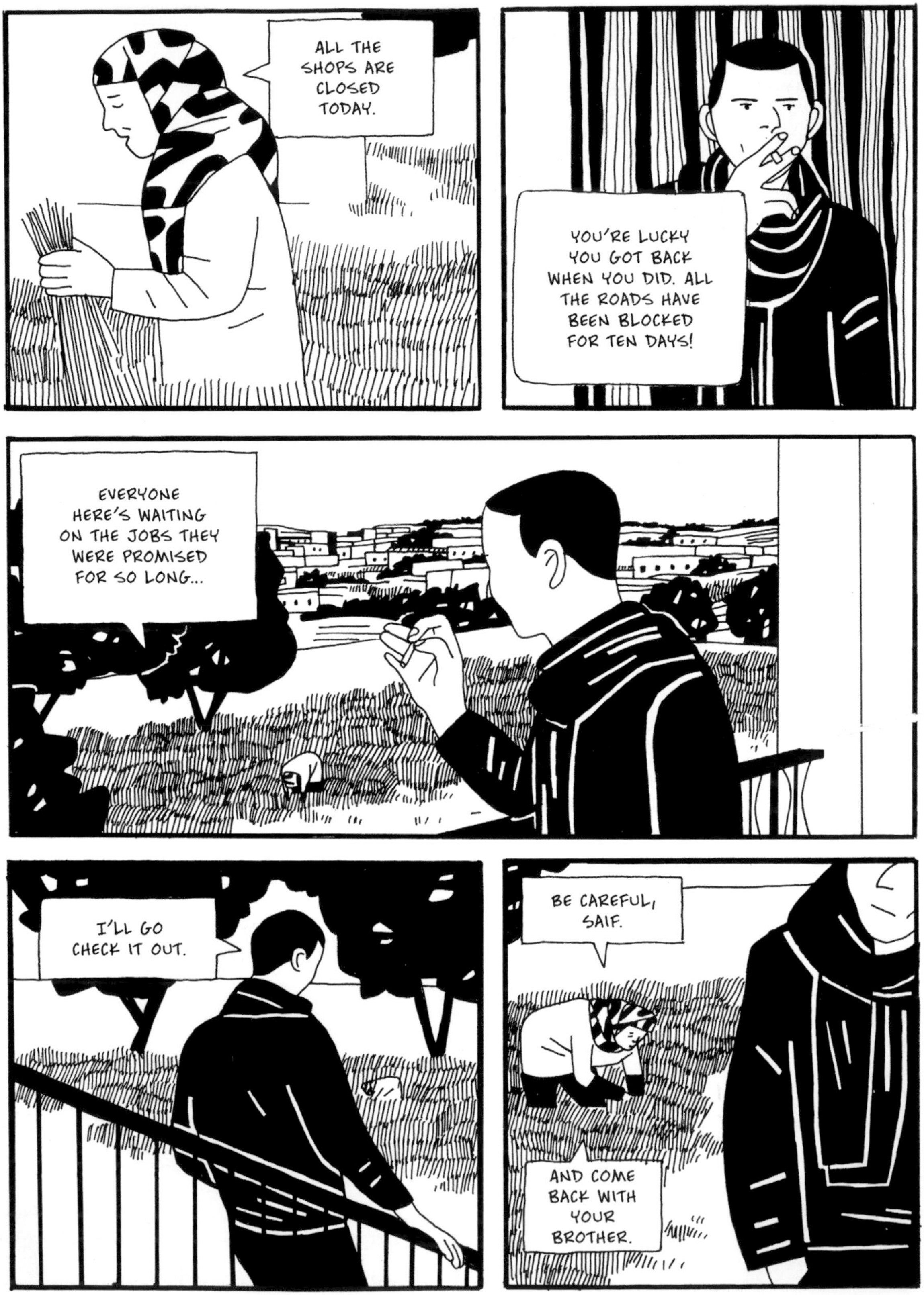
ALL THE SHOPS ARE CLOSED TODAY.
YOU'RE LUCKY YOU GOT BACK WHEN YOU DID. ALL THE ROADS HAVE BEEN BLOCKED FOR TEN DAYS!
EVERYONE HERE'S WAITING ON THE JOBS THEY WERE PROMISED FOR SO LONG...
I'LL GO CHECK IT OUT.
BE CAREFUL, SAIF.
AND COME BACK WITH YOUR BROTHER.

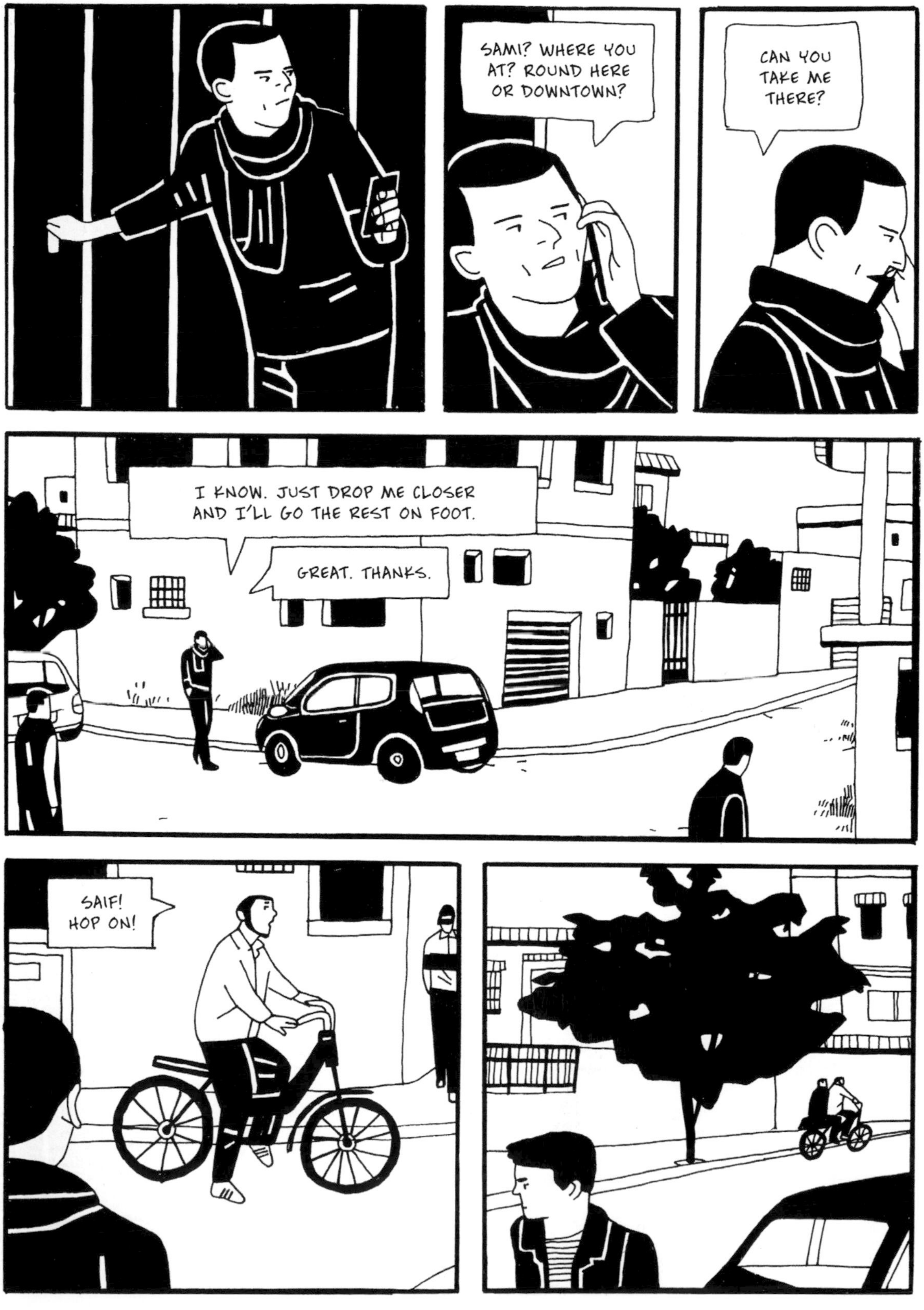
SAMI? WHERE YOU AT? ROUND HERE OR DOWNTOWN?
CAN YOU TAKE ME THERE?
I KNOW. JUST DROP ME CLOSER AND I'LL GO THE REST ON FOOT.
GREAT. THANKS.
SAIF! HOP ON!

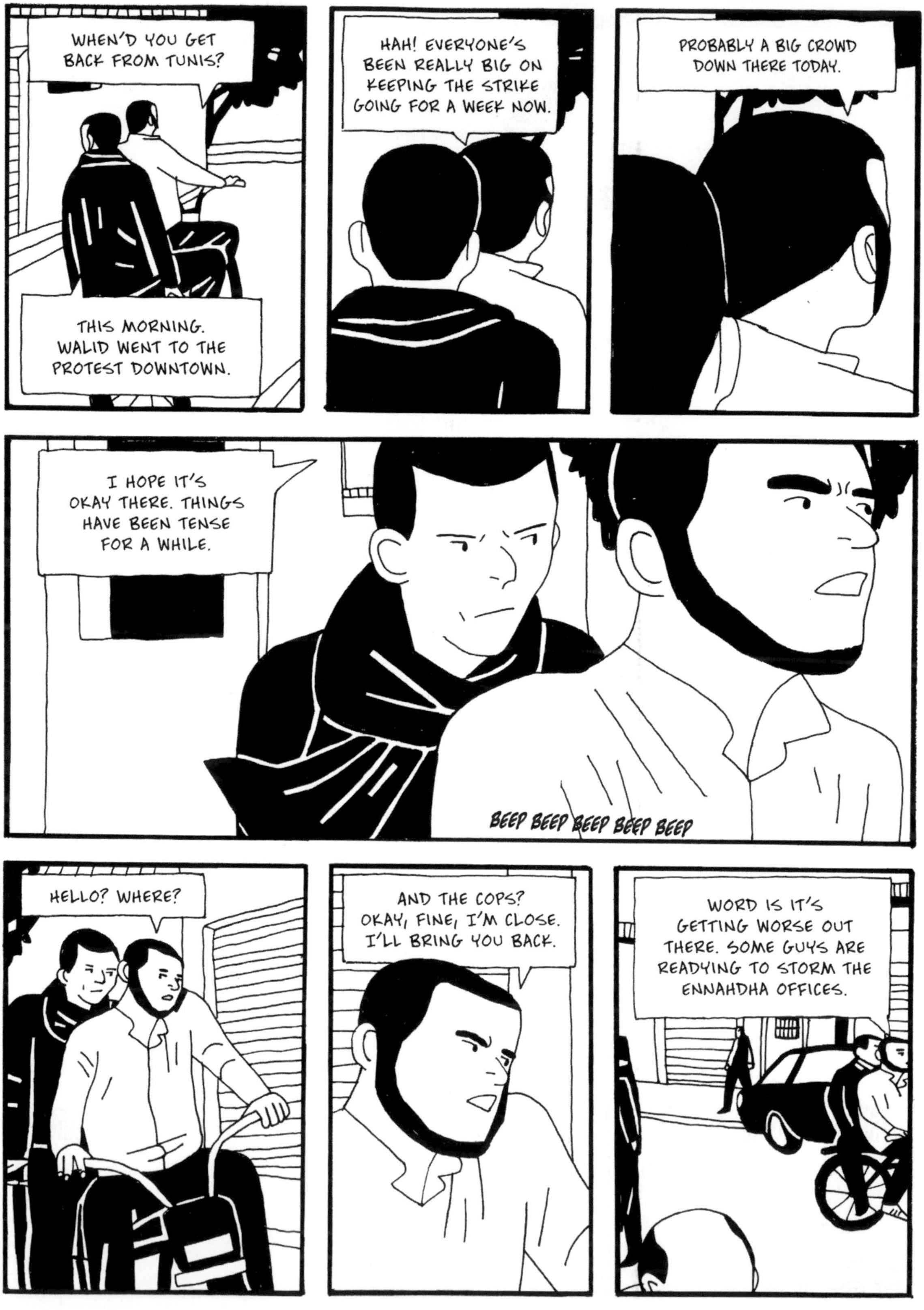
WHEN'D YOU GET BACK FROM TUNIS?
THIS MORNING. WALID WENT TO THE PROTEST DOWNTOWN.
HAH! EVERYONE'S BEEN REALLY BIG ON KEEPING THE STRIKE GOING FOR A WEEK NOW.
PROBABLY A BIG CROWD DOWN THERE TODAY.
I HOPE IT'S OKAY THERE. THINGS HAVE BEEN TENSE FOR A WHILE.
BEEP BEEP BEEP BEEP BEEP
HELLO? WHERE?
AND THE COPS? OKAY, FINE, I'M CLOSE. I'LL BRING YOU BACK.
WORD IS IT'S GETTING WORSE OUT THERE. SOME GUYS ARE READYING TO STORM THE ENNAHDHA OFFICES.

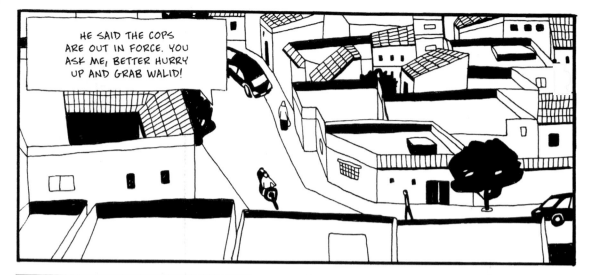

HE SAID THE COPS ARE OUT IN FORCE. YOU ASK ME, BETTER HURRY UP AND GRAB WALID!

THEY'LL BE LOOKING TO LOCK PEOPLE UP.

FUCK...

TWO DAYS I'VE BEEN BACK, AND HE'S OUT THERE STIRRING SHIT UP ALREADY.

GO EASY ON HIM. THINGS ARE SHITTY ALL OVER. YOU LEFT FOR THE CAPITAL...

...AND YOU WERE RIGHT TO. THERE'S NO FUTURE HERE. NO ONE GIVES A SHIT ABOUT US. WHERE ARE ALL THOSE JOBS THEY WERE TALKING ABOUT?

THAT SO-CALLED AGREE-MENT WAS JUST HOT AIR...

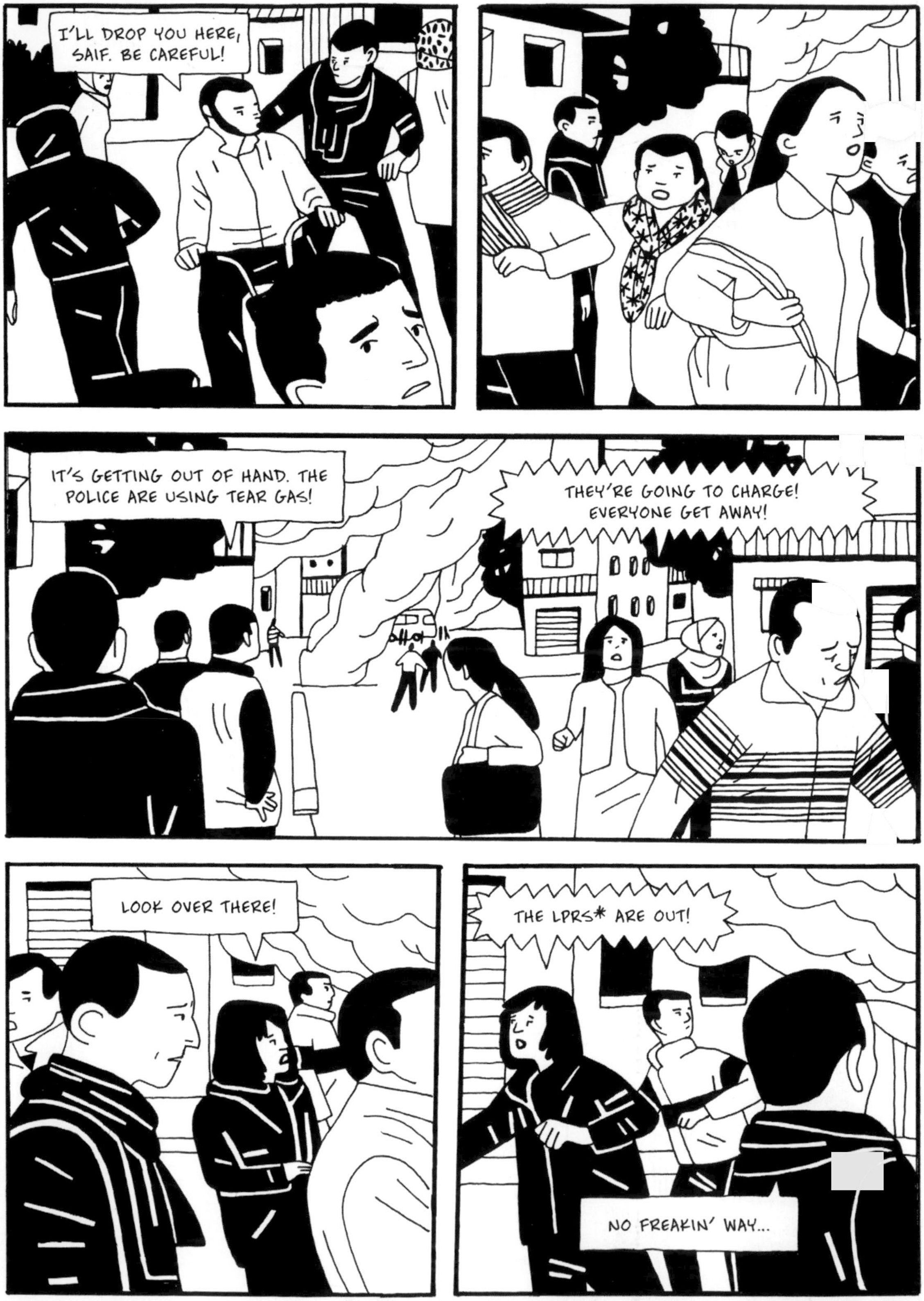
I'LL DROP YOU HERE, SAIF. BE CAREFUL!
IT'S GETTING OUT OF HAND. THE POLICE ARE USING TEAR GAS!
THEY'RE GOING TO CHARGE! EVERYONE GET AWAY!
LOOK OVER THERE!
THE LPRS* ARE OUT!
NO FREAKIN' WAY...

* LEAGUES FOR THE PROTECTION OF THE TUNISIAN REVOLUTION: ORGANIZATIONS SYMPATHETIC TO ENNAHDHA, "THE MOVEMENT OF ISLAMIC TENDENCY," A RELIGIOUSLY CONSERVATIVE MUSLIM DEMOCRATIC PARTY

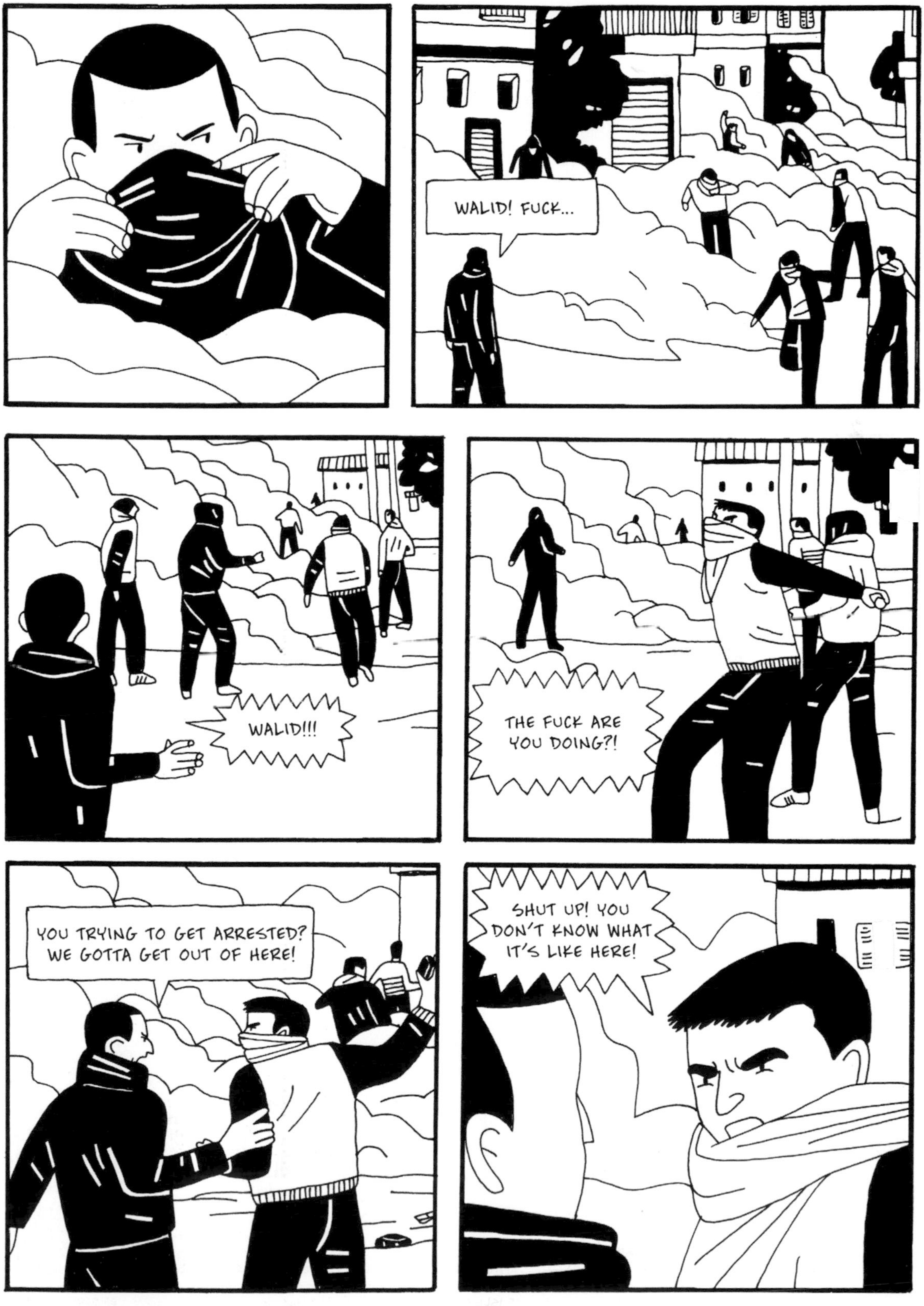
WALID! FUCK...
WALID!!!
THE FUCK ARE YOU DOING?!
YOU TRYING TO GET ARRESTED? WE GOTTA GET OUT OF HERE!
SHUT UP! YOU DON'T KNOW WHAT IT'S LIKE HERE!

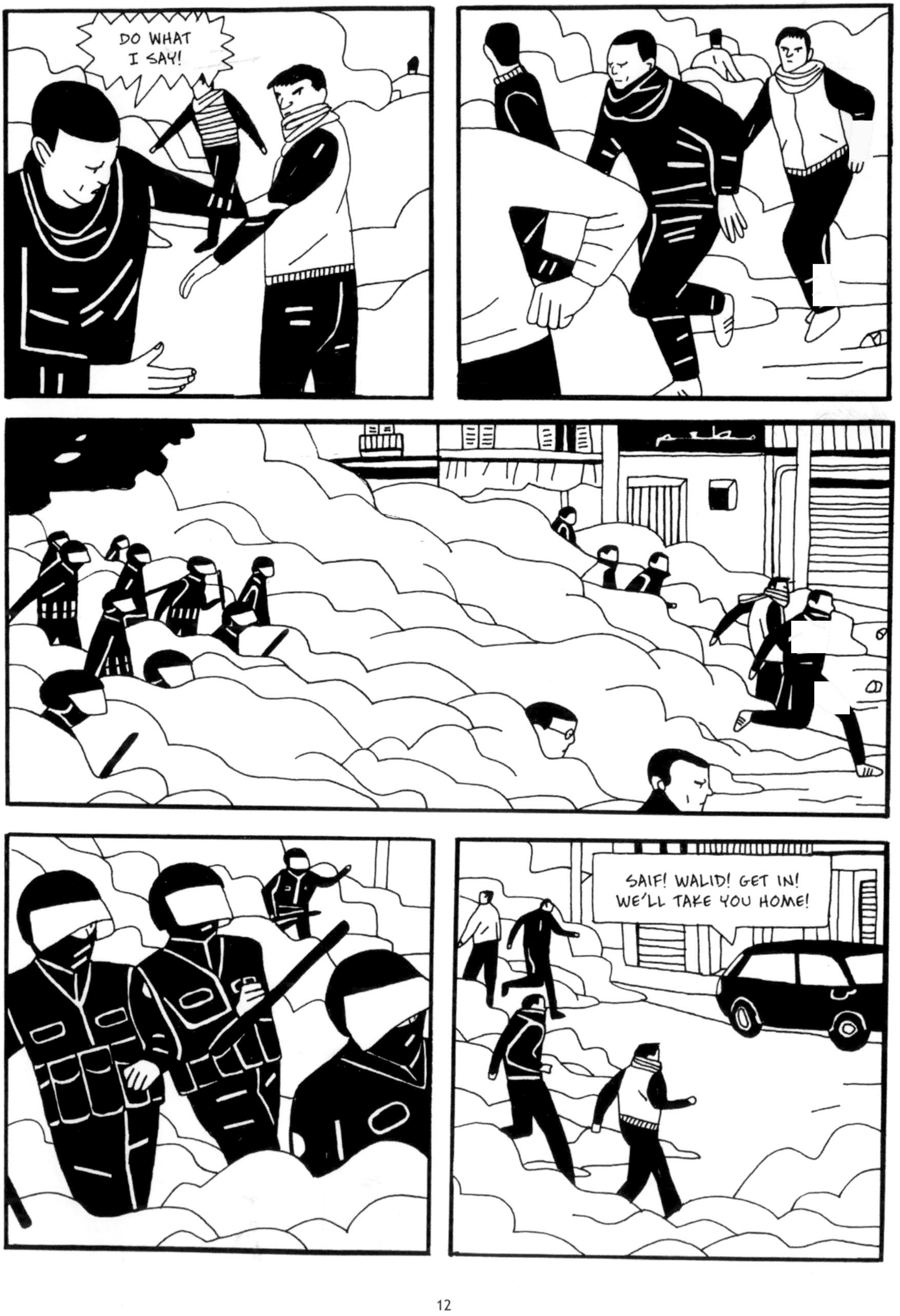
DO WHAT I SAY!
SAIF! WALID! GET IN! WE'LL TAKE YOU HOME!

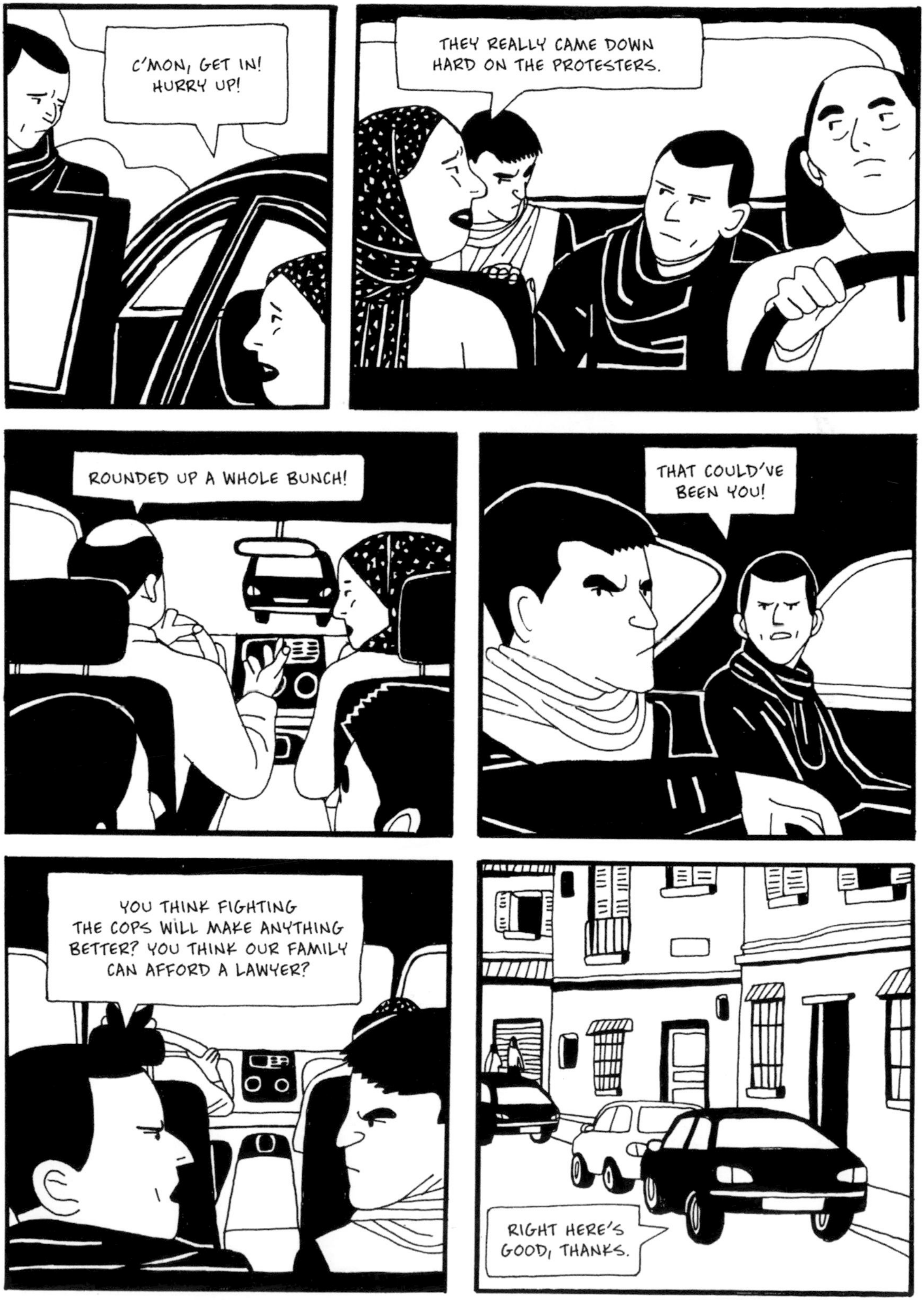
C'MON, GET IN! HURRY UP!
THEY REALLY CAME DOWN HARD ON THE PROTESTERS.
ROUNDED UP A WHOLE BUNCH!
THAT COULD'VE BEEN YOU!
YOU THINK FIGHTING THE COPS WILL MAKE ANYTHING BETTER? YOU THINK OUR FAMILY CAN AFFORD A LAWYER?
RIGHT HERE'S GOOD, THANKS.

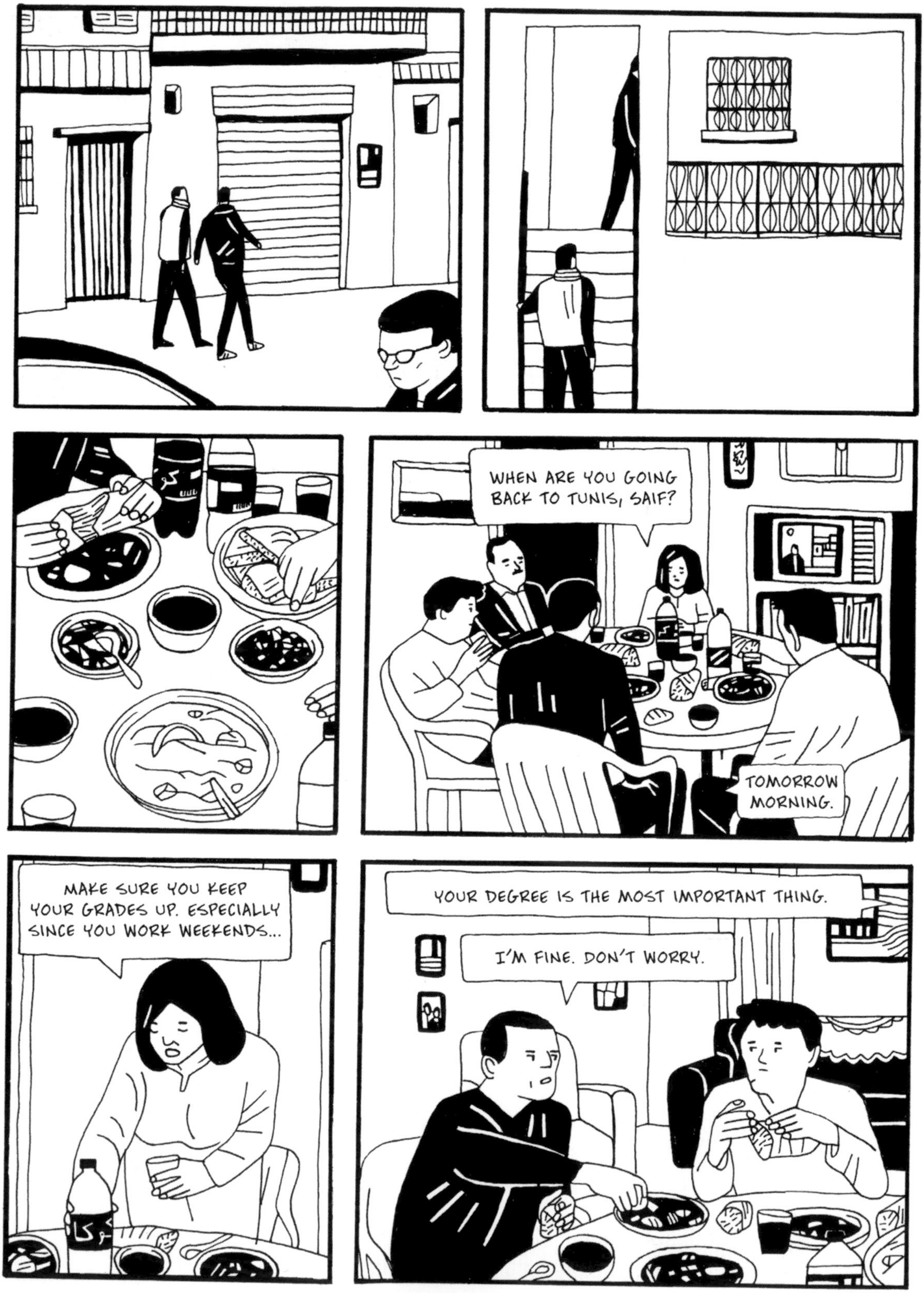
WHEN ARE YOU GOING BACK TO TUNIS, SAIF?
TOMORROW MORNING.
MAKE SURE YOU KEEP YOUR GRADES UP. ESPECIALLY SINCE YOU WORK WEEKENDS...
YOUR DEGREE IS THE MOST IMPORTANT THING.
I'M FINE. DON'T WORRY.

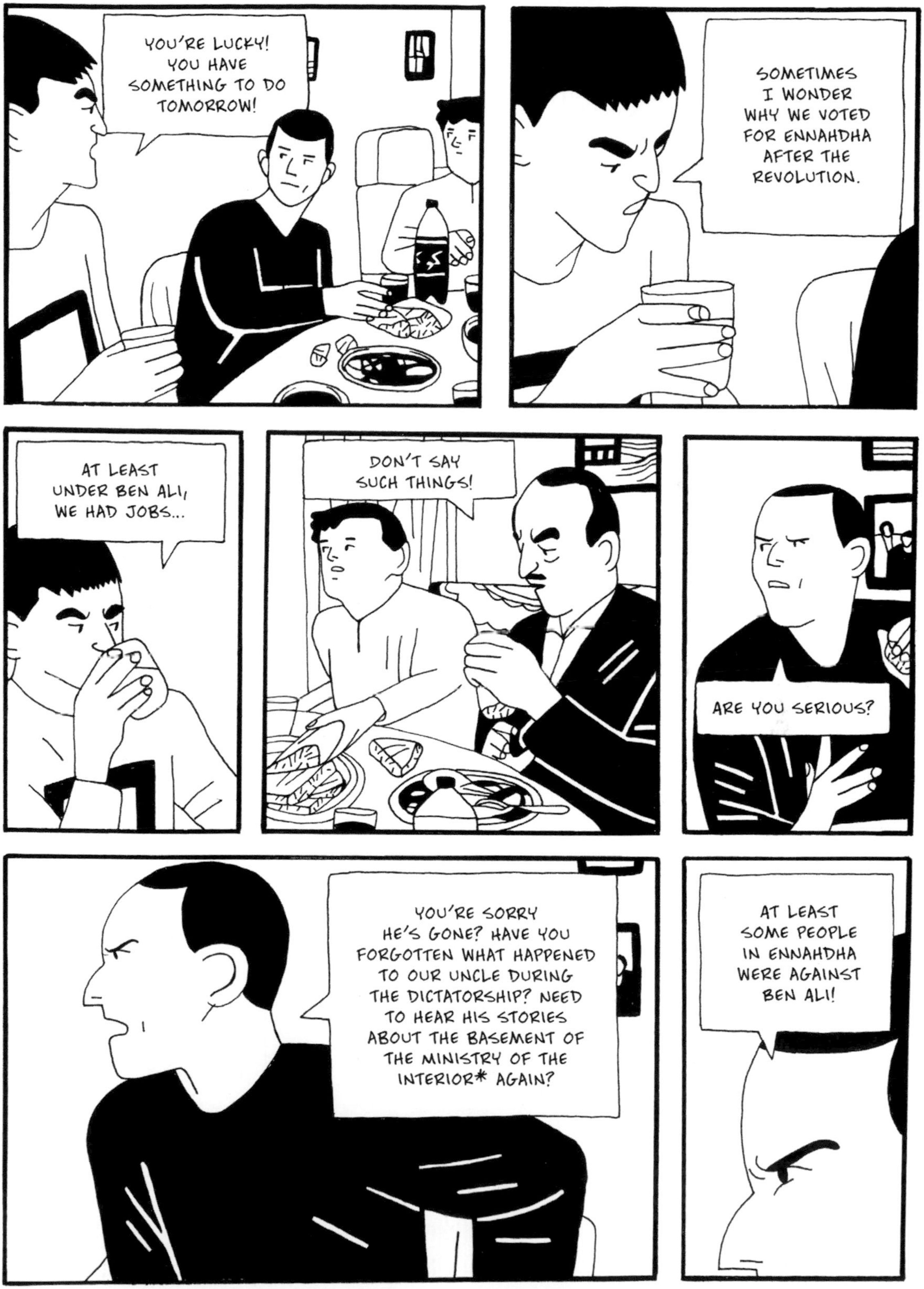
YOU'RE LUCKY! YOU HAVE SOMETHING TO DO TOMORROW!
SOMETIMES I WONDER WHY WE VOTED FOR ENNAHDHA AFTER THE REVOLUTION.
AT LEAST UNDER BEN ALI, WE HAD JOBS...
DON'T SAY SUCH THINGS!
ARE YOU SERIOUS?
YOU'RE SORRY HE'S GONE? HAVE YOU FORGOTTEN WHAT HAPPENED TO OUR UNCLE DURING THE DICTATORSHIP? NEED TO HEAR HIS STORIES ABOUT THE BASEMENT OF THE MINISTRY OF THE INTERIOR* AGAIN?
AT LEAST SOME PEOPLE IN ENNAHDHA WERE AGAINST BEN ALI!

* A PLACE WHERE PEOPLE WERE TORTURED

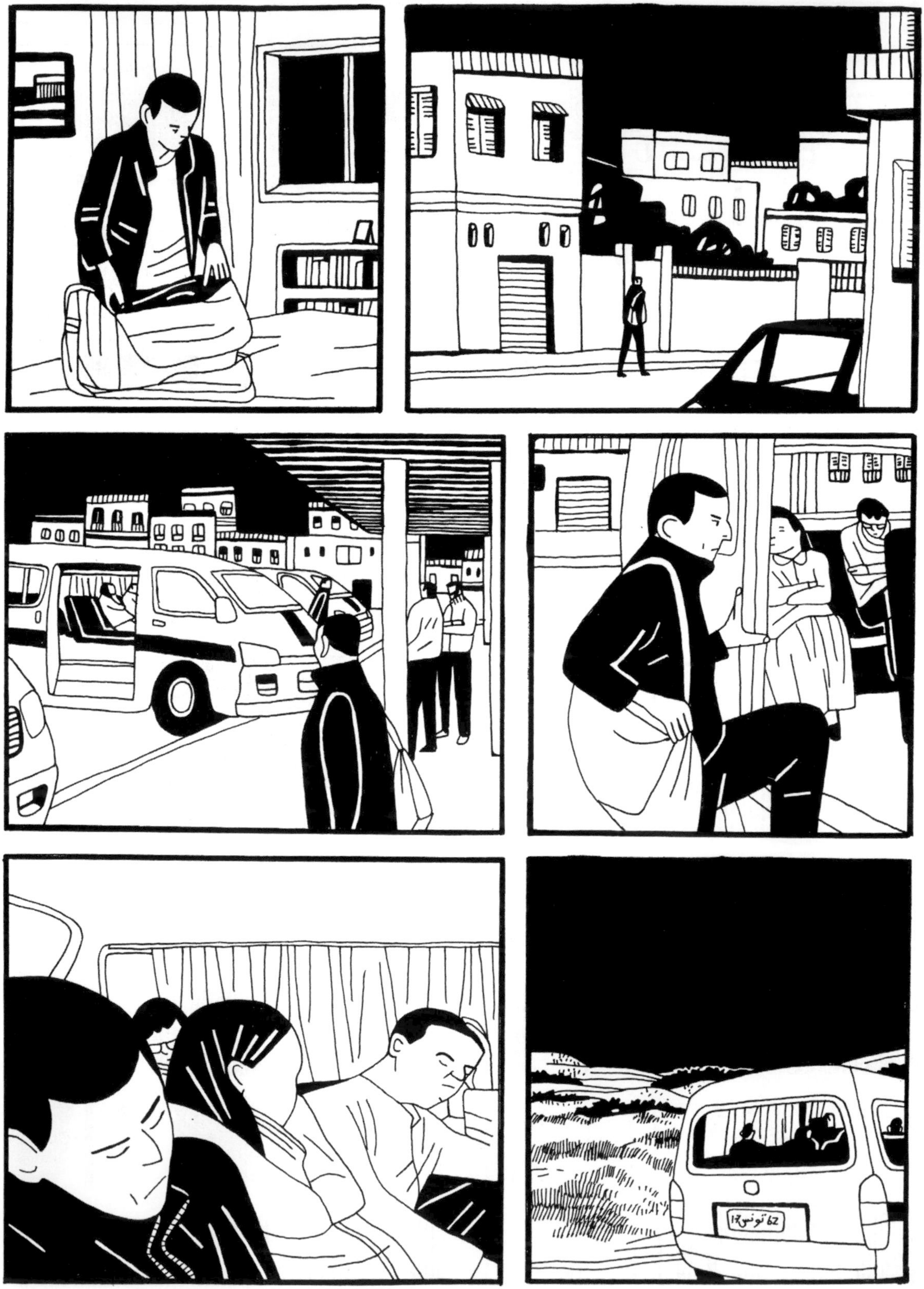
تونس

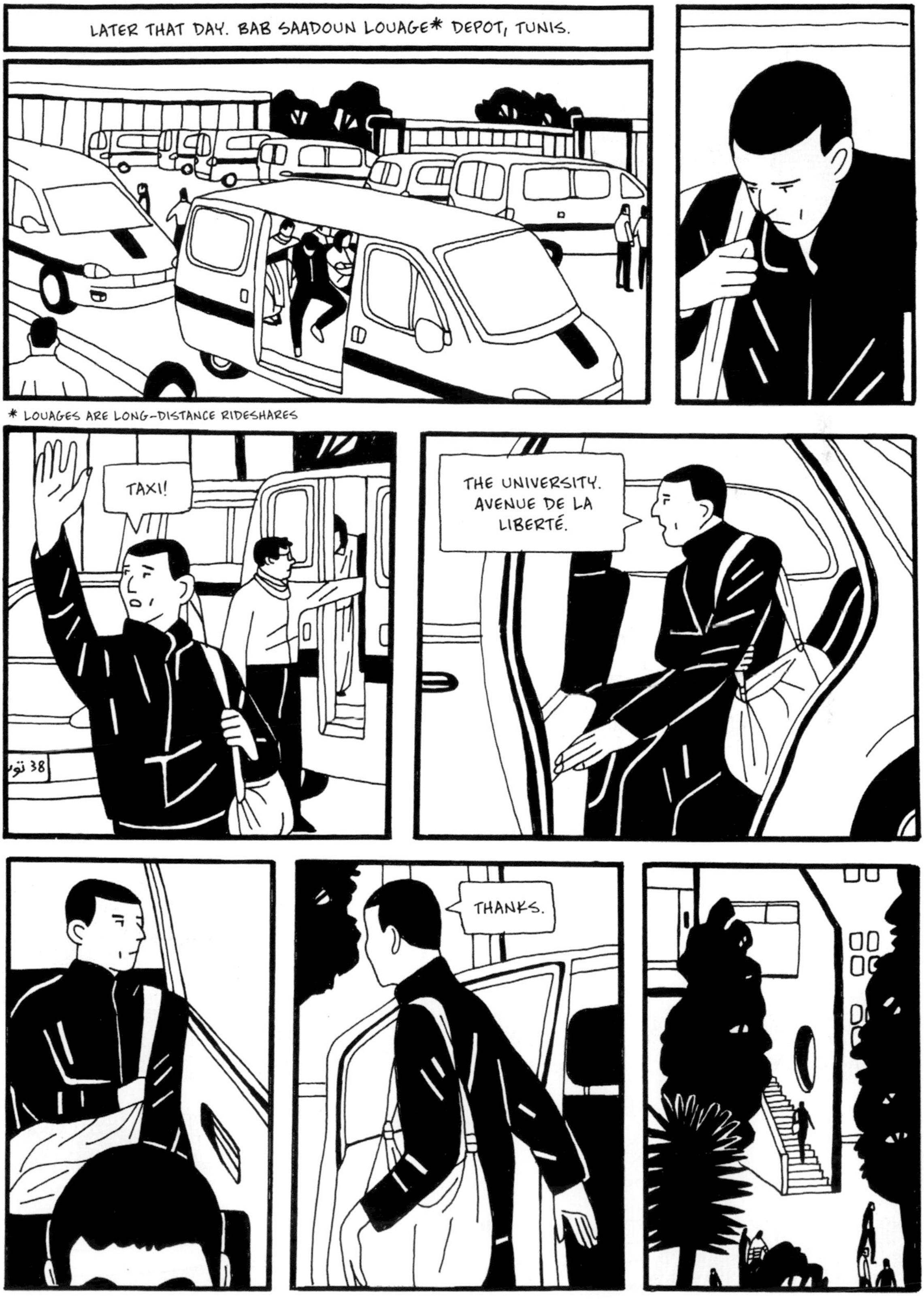
LATER THAT DAY. BAB SAADOUN LOUAGE* DEPOT, TUNIS.
* LOUAGES ARE LONG-DISTANCE RIDESHARES
TAXI!
38 تونس
THE UNIVERSITY. AVENUE DE LA LIBERTÉ.
THANKS.

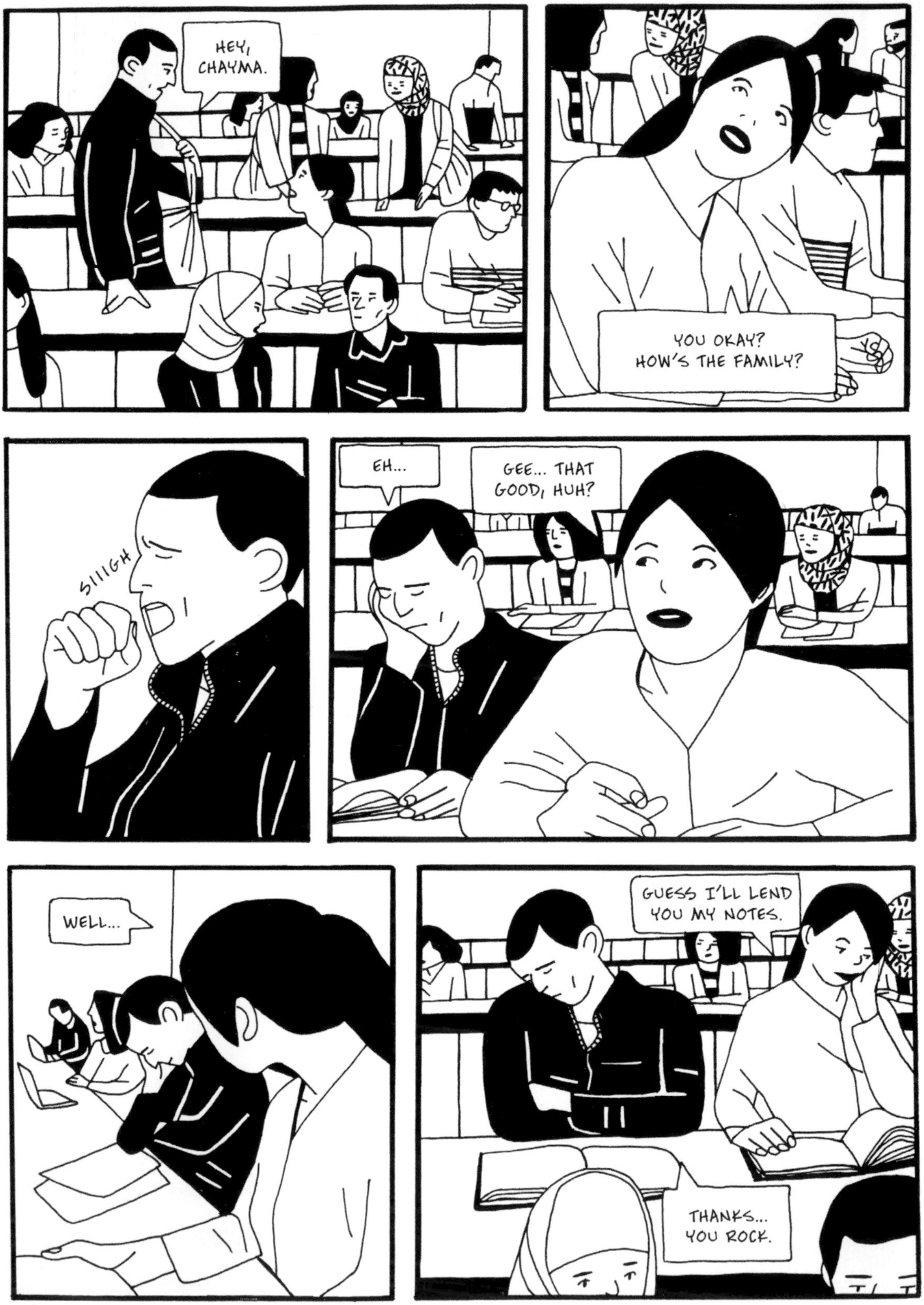
HEY, CHAYMA.
YOU OKAY? HOW'S THE FAMILY?
SIIIGH
EH...
GEE... THAT GOOD, HUH?
WELL...
GUESS I'LL LEND YOU MY NOTES.
THANKS... YOU ROCK.

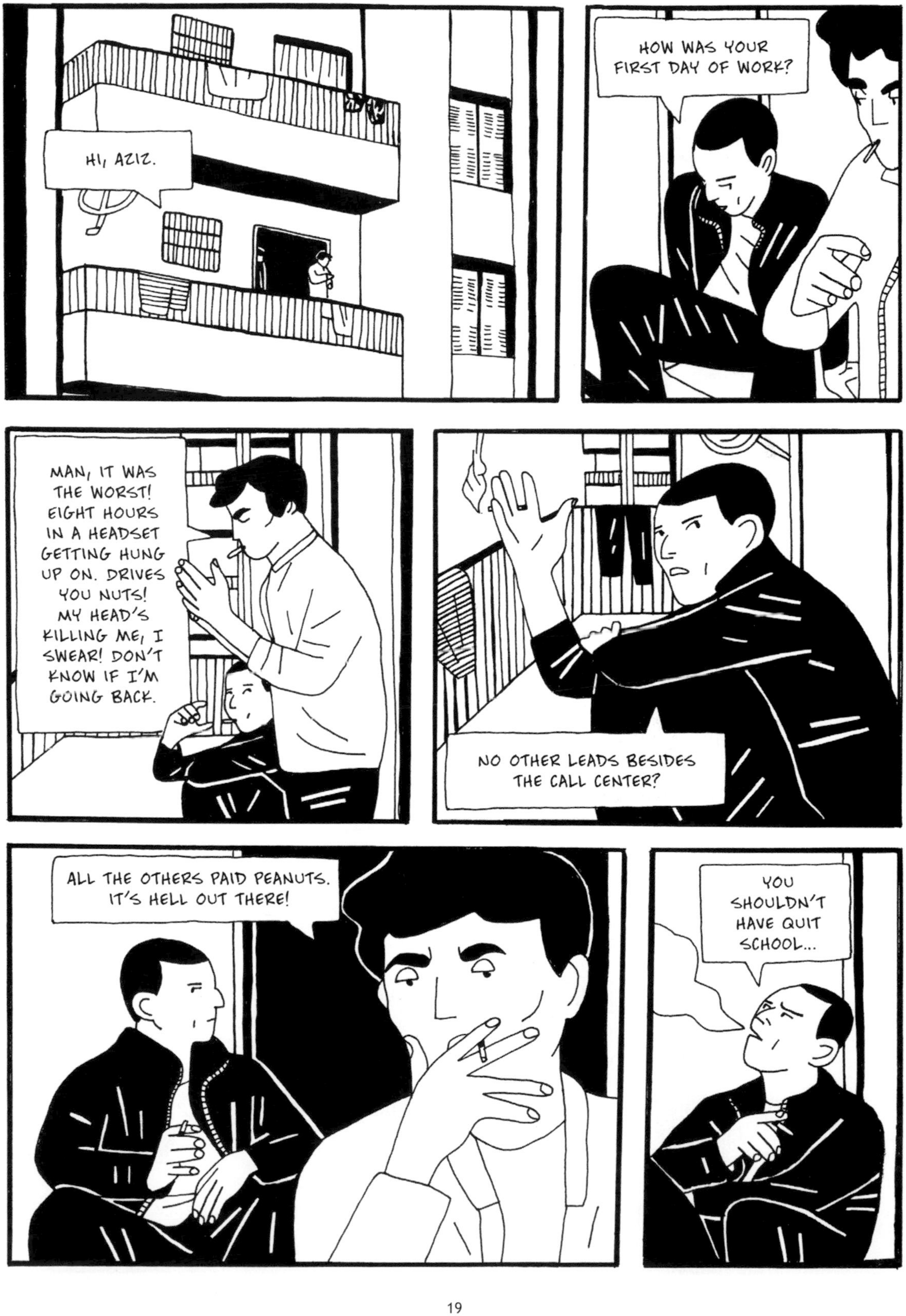
HI, AZIZ.
HOW WAS YOUR FIRST DAY OF WORK?
MAN, IT WAS THE WORST! EIGHT HOURS IN A HEADSET GETTING HUNG UP ON. DRIVES YOU NUTS! MY HEAD'S KILLING ME, I SWEAR! DON'T KNOW IF I'M GOING BACK.
NO OTHER LEADS BESIDES THE CALL CENTER?
ALL THE OTHERS PAID PEANUTS. IT'S HELL OUT THERE!
YOU SHOULDN'T HAVE QUIT SCHOOL...

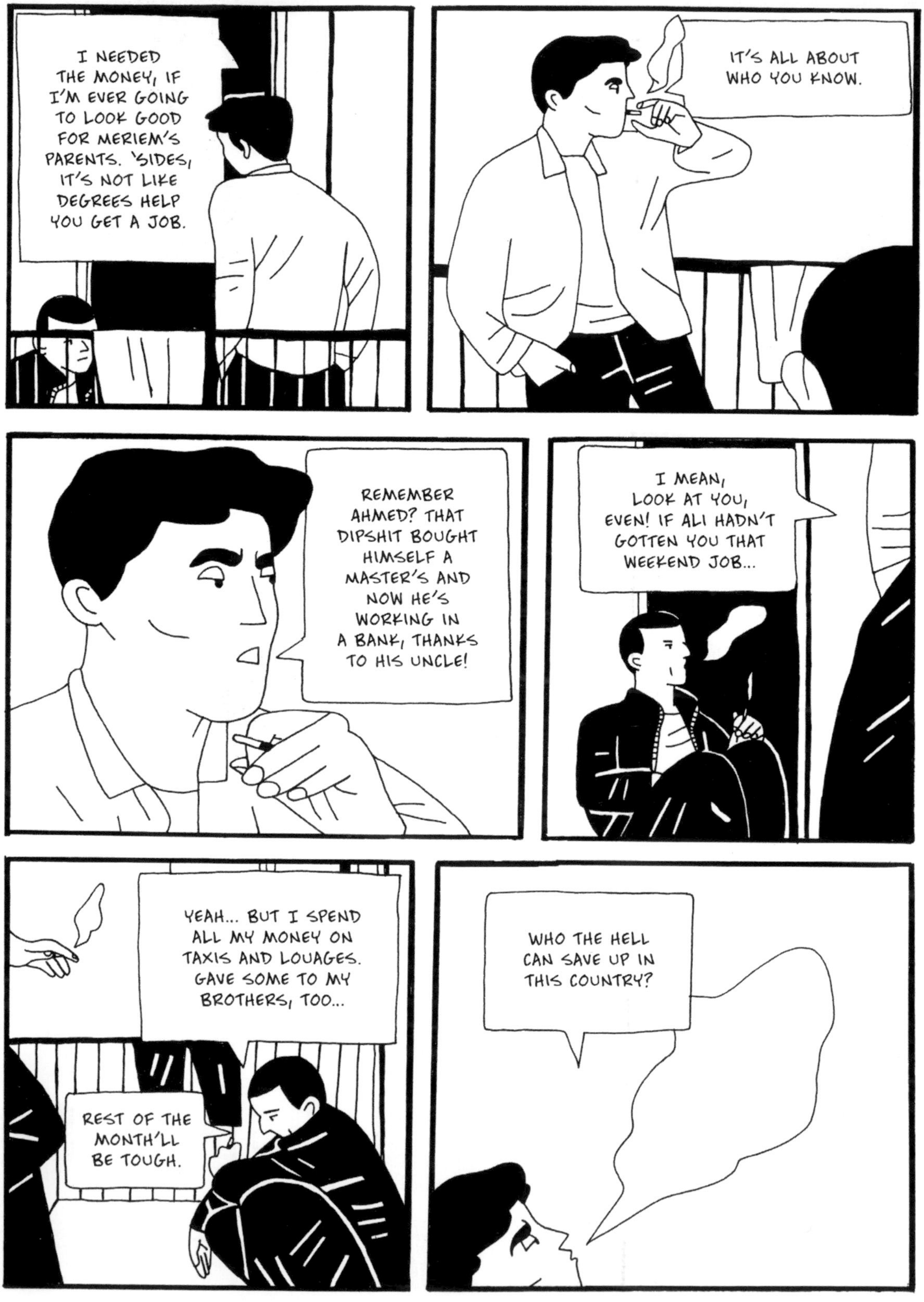
I NEEDED THE MONEY, IF I'M EVER GOING TO LOOK GOOD FOR MERIEM'S PARENTS. 'SIDES, IT'S NOT LIKE DEGREES HELP YOU GET A JOB.
IT'S ALL ABOUT WHO YOU KNOW.
REMEMBER AHMED? THAT DIPSHIT BOUGHT HIMSELF A MASTER'S AND NOW HE'S WORKING IN A BANK, THANKS TO HIS UNCLE!
I MEAN, LOOK AT YOU, EVEN! IF ALI HADN'T GOTTEN YOU THAT WEEKEND JOB...
YEAH... BUT I SPEND ALL MY MONEY ON TAXIS AND LOUAGES. GAVE SOME TO MY BROTHERS, TOO...
REST OF THE MONTH'LL BE TOUGH.
WHO THE HELL CAN SAVE UP IN THIS COUNTRY?

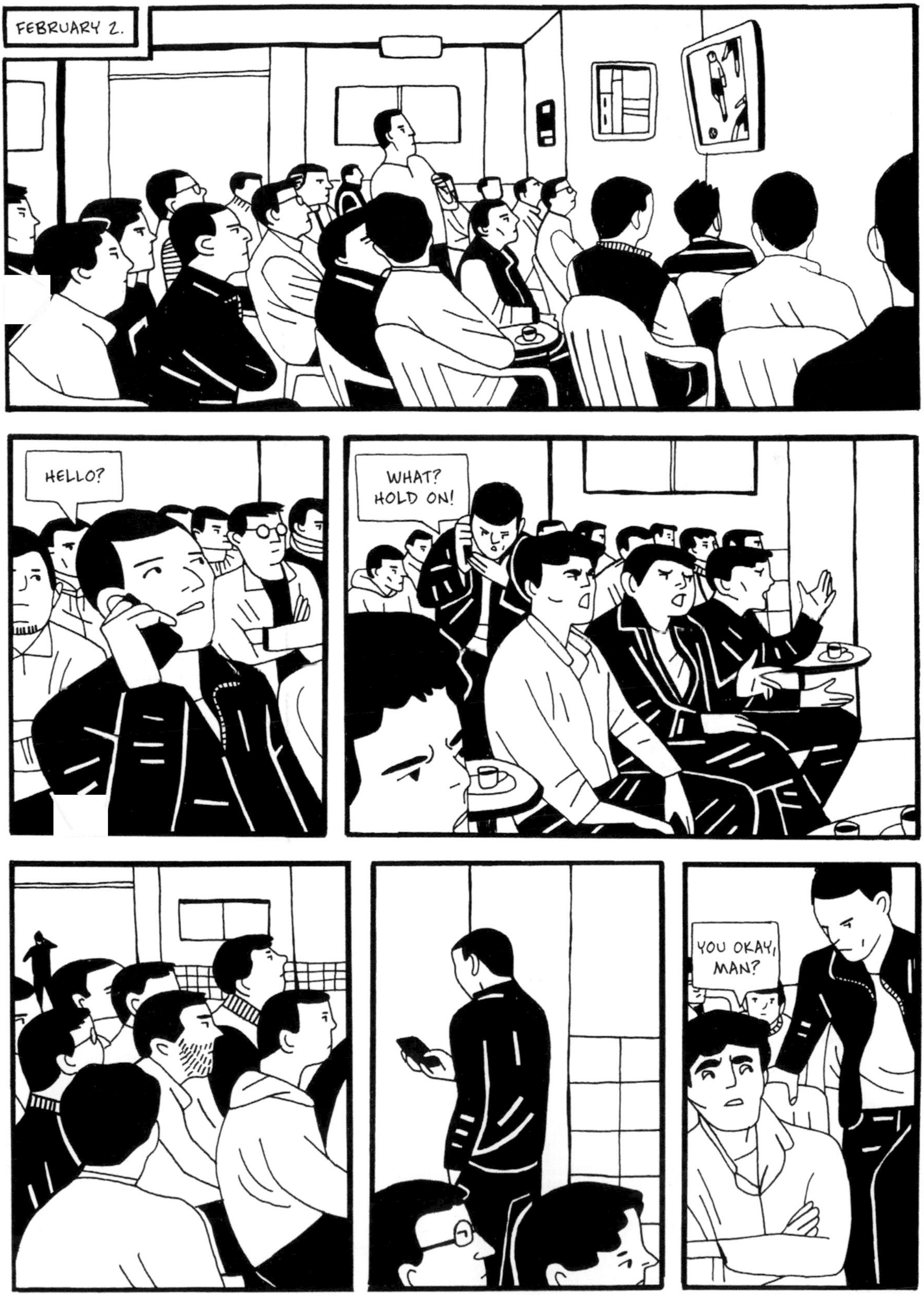
FEBRUARY 2.
HELLO?
WHAT? HOLD ON!
YOU OKAY, MAN?

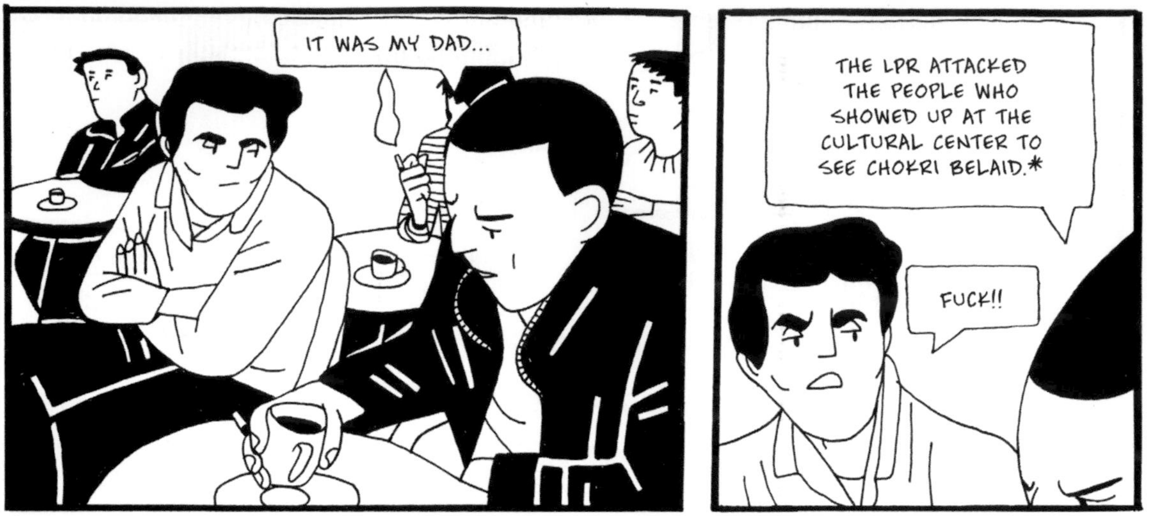
IT WAS MY DAD...
THE LPR ATTACKED THE PEOPLE WHO SHOWED UP AT THE CULTURAL CENTER TO SEE CHOKRI BELAID.*
FUCK!!

* CHOKRI BELAID, TUNISIAN LAWYER AND AN OPPOSITION LEADER WITH THE LEFT-SECULAR DEMOCRATIC PATRIOTS' UNIFIED PARTY

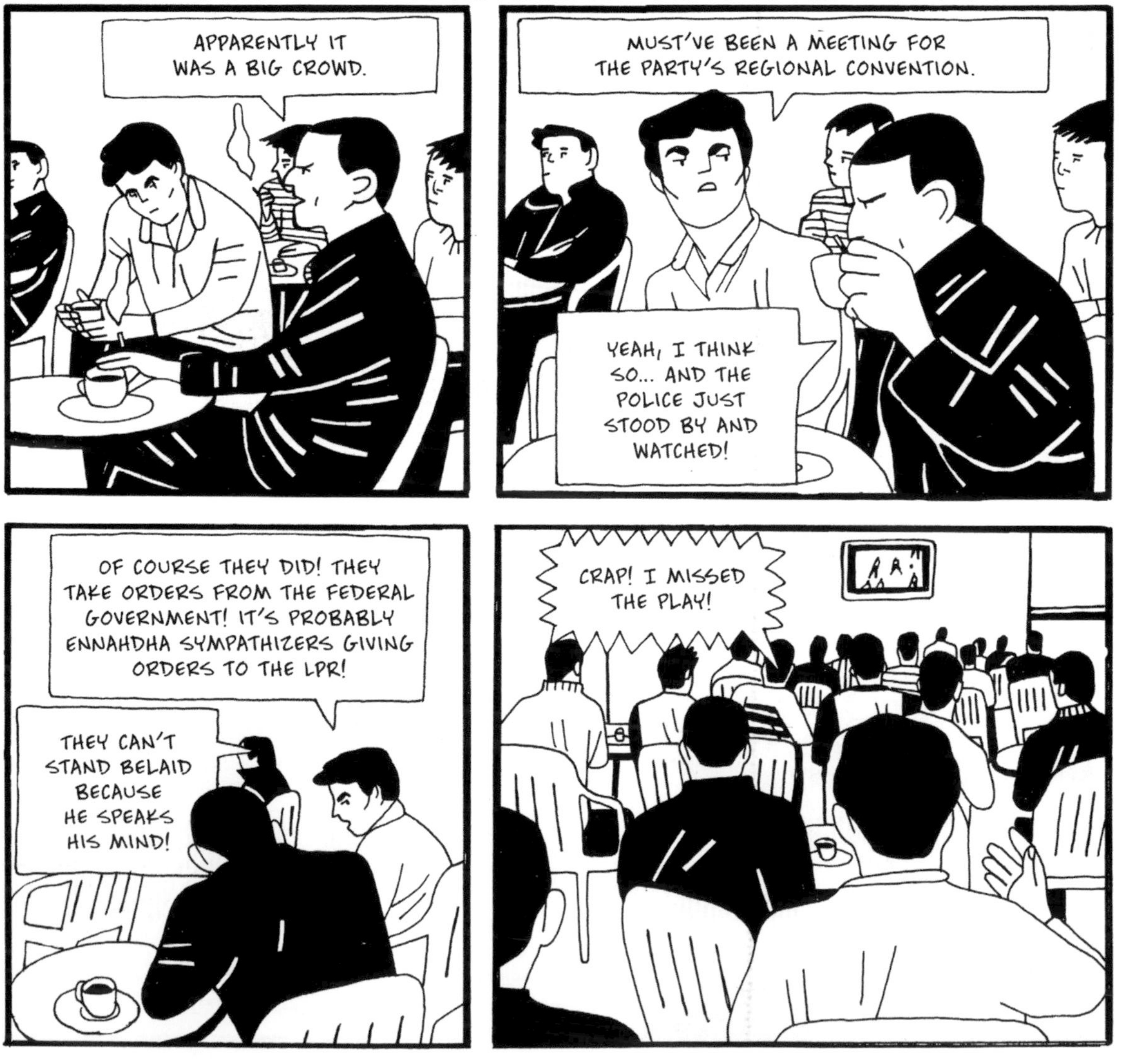
APPARENTLY IT WAS A BIG CROWD.
MUST'VE BEEN A MEETING FOR THE PARTY'S REGIONAL CONVENTION.
YEAH, I THINK SO... AND THE POLICE JUST STOOD BY AND WATCHED!
OF COURSE THEY DID! THEY TAKE ORDERS FROM THE FEDERAL GOVERNMENT! IT'S PROBABLY ENNAHDHA SYMPATHIZERS GIVING ORDERS TO THE LPR!
THEY CAN'T STAND BELAID BECAUSE HE SPEAKS HIS MIND!
CRAP! I MISSED THE PLAY!

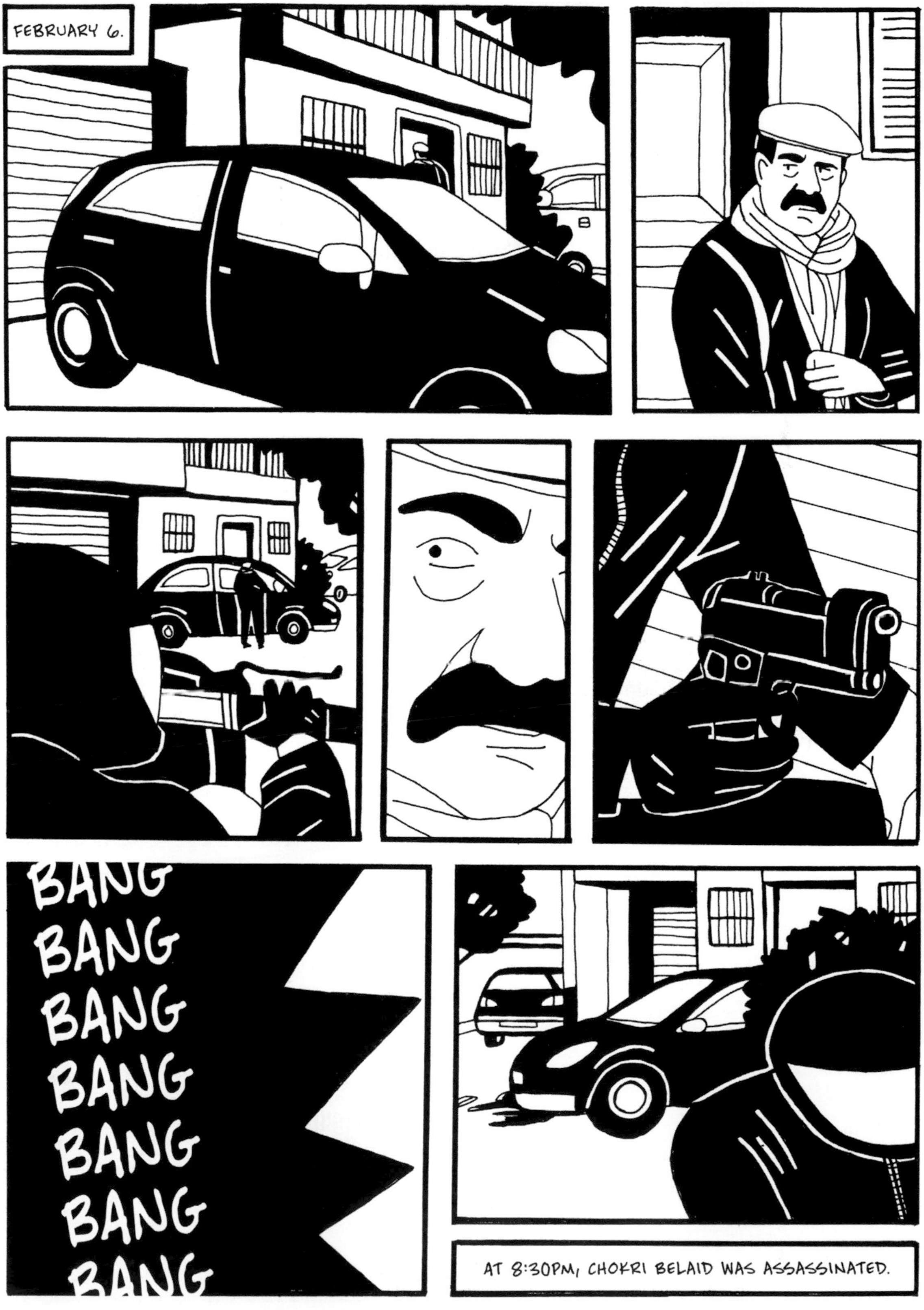
FEBRUARY 6.
BANG
BANG
BANG
BANG
BANG
BANG
BANG
AT 8:30PM, CHOKRI BELAID WAS ASSASSINATED.

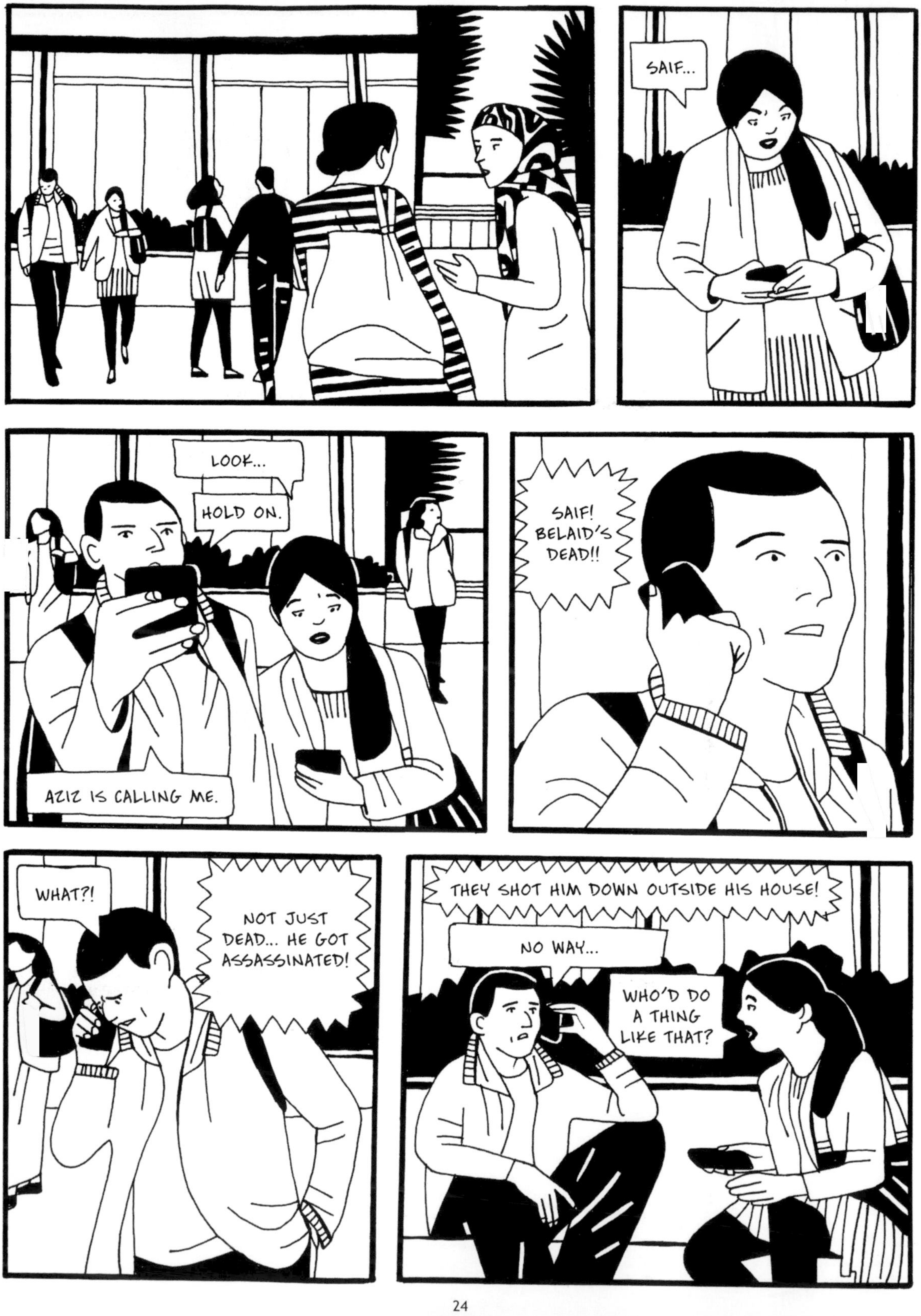
SAIF...
LOOK...
HOLD ON.
AZIZ IS CALLING ME.
SAIF! BELAID'S DEAD!!
WHAT?!
NOT JUST DEAD... HE GOT ASSASSINATED!
THEY SHOT HIM DOWN OUTSIDE HIS HOUSE!
NO WAY...
WHO'D DO A THING LIKE THAT?

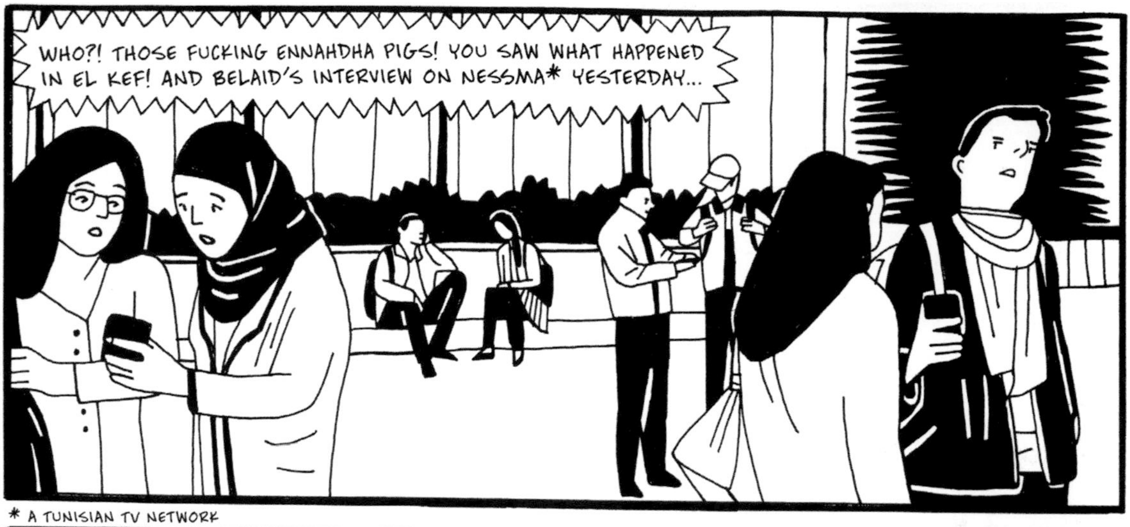
WHO?! THOSE FUCKING ENNAHDHA PIGS! YOU SAW WHAT HAPPENED IN EL KEF! AND BELAID'S INTERVIEW ON NESSMA* YESTERDAY...

* A TUNISIAN TV NETWORK

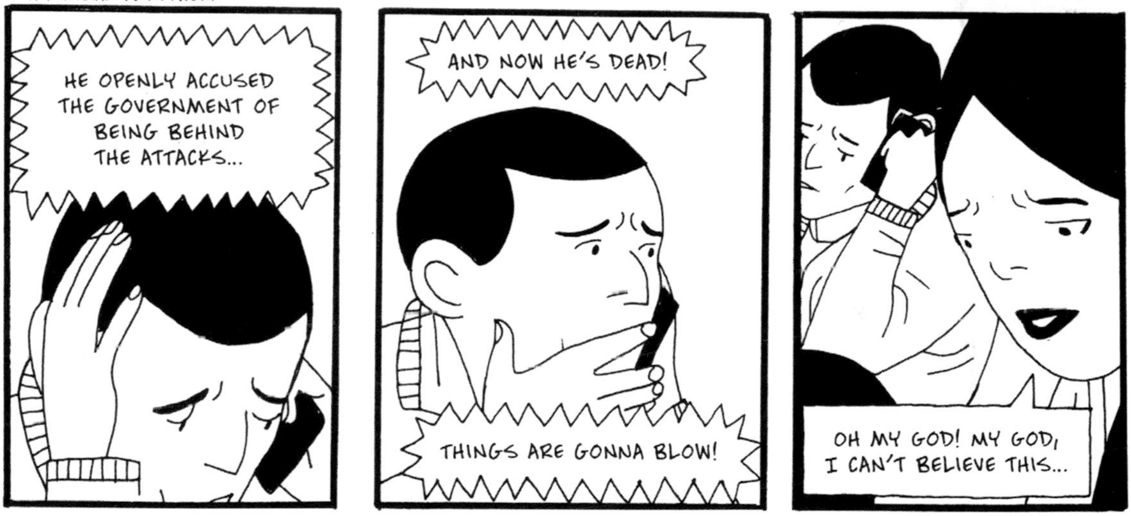
HE OPENLY ACCUSED THE GOVERNMENT OF BEING BEHIND THE ATTACKS...
AND NOW HE'S DEAD!
THINGS ARE GONNA BLOW!
OH MY GOD! MY GOD, I CAN'T BELIEVE THIS...

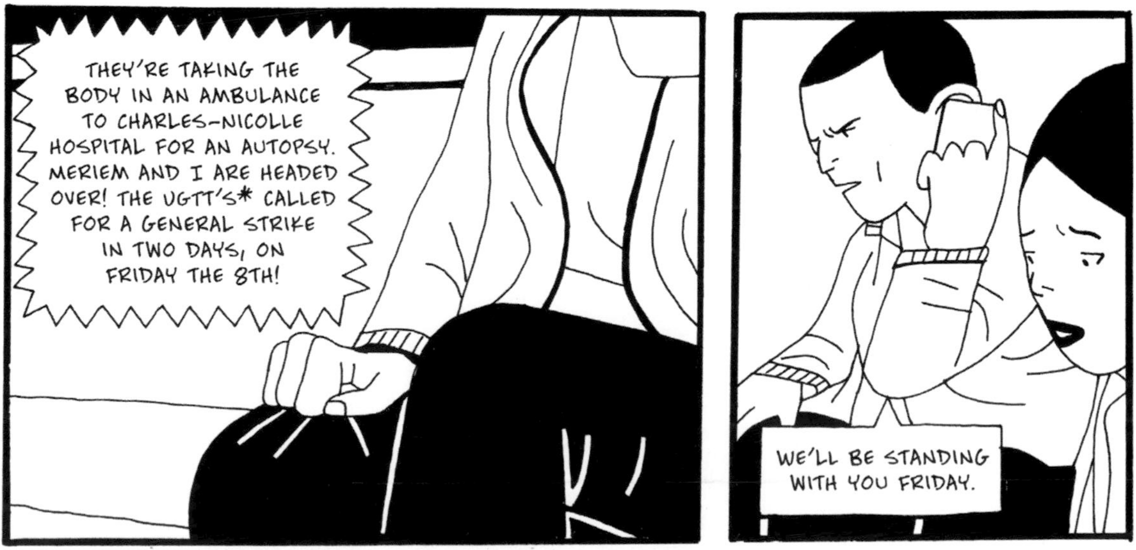
THEY'RE TAKING THE BODY IN AN AMBULANCE TO CHARLES-NICOLLE HOSPITAL FOR AN AUTOPSY. MERIEM AND I ARE HEADED OVER! THE UGTT'S* CALLED FOR A GENERAL STRIKE IN TWO DAYS, ON FRIDAY THE 8TH!
WE'LL BE STANDING WITH YOU FRIDAY.

* TUNISIAN GENERAL LABOUR UNION

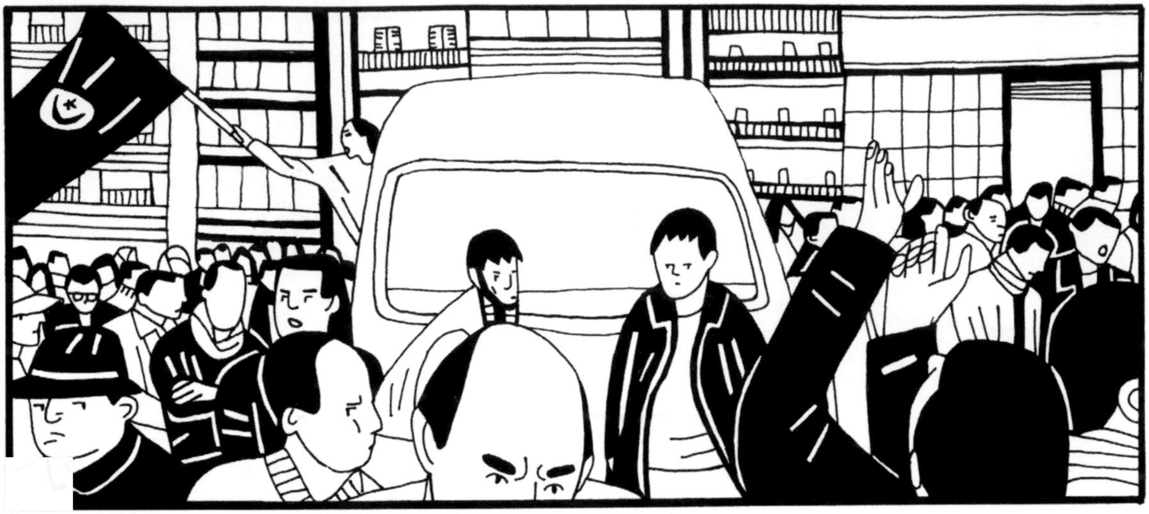

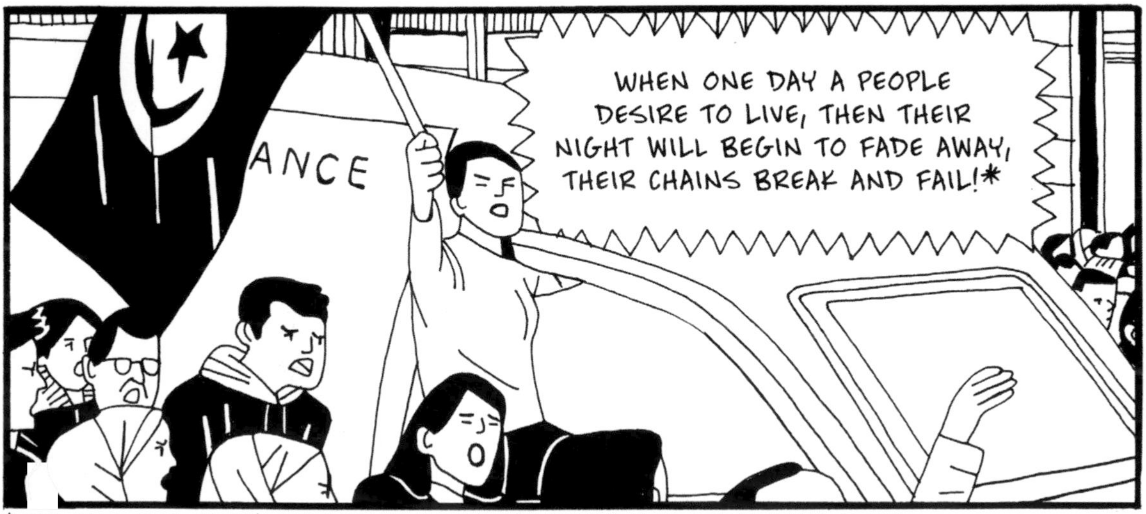
WHEN ONE DAY A PEOPLE DESIRE TO LIVE, THEN THEIR NIGHT WILL BEGIN TO FADE AWAY, THEIR CHAINS BREAK AND FAIL!*
ANCE

* FROM ABOUL-QACEM ECHEBBI'S POEM "THE WILL TO LIVE," LATER APPENDED TO THE NATIONAL ANTHEM IN 1955

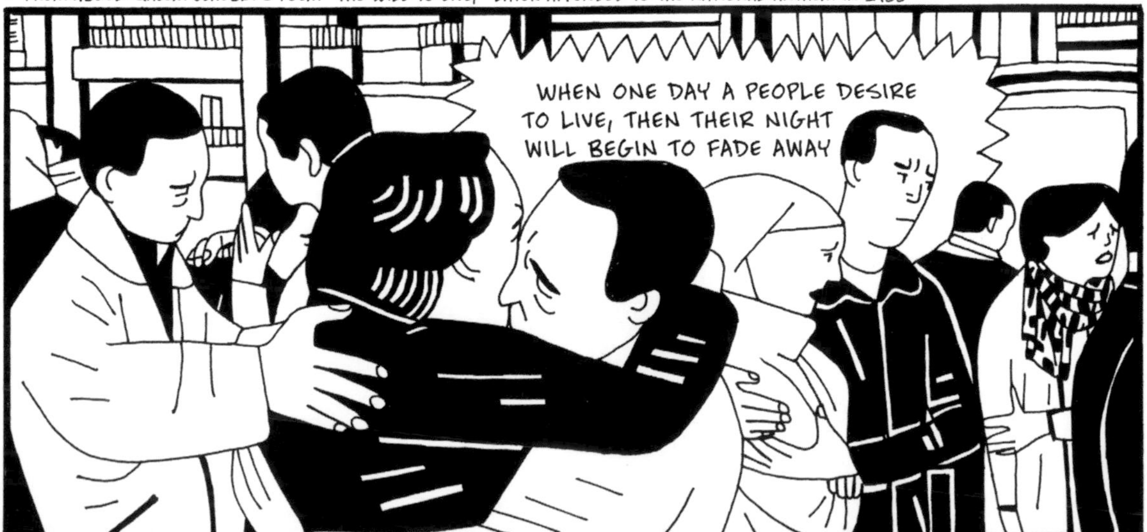
WHEN ONE DAY A PEOPLE DESIRE TO LIVE, THEN THEIR NIGHT WILL BEGIN TO FADE AWAY

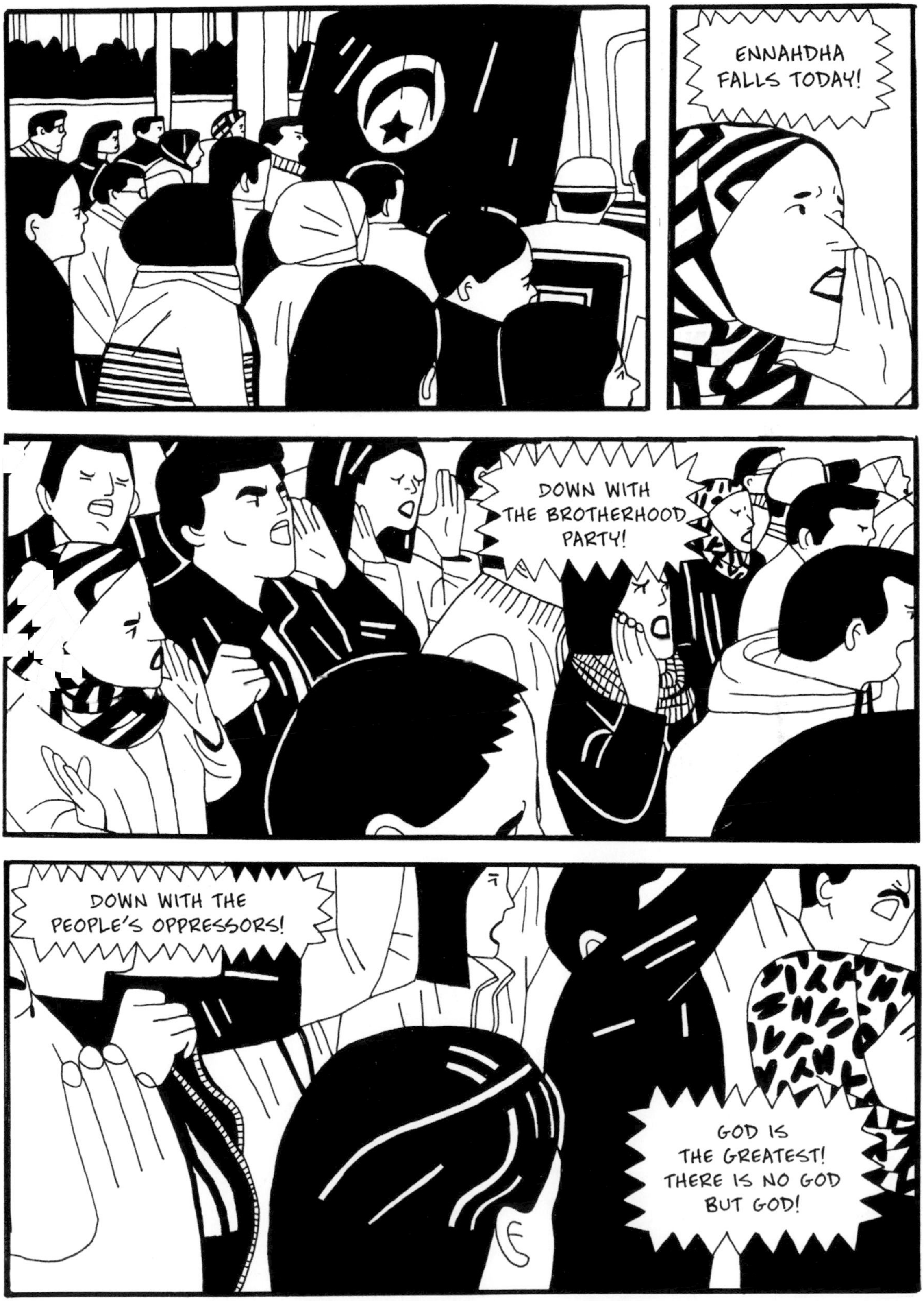
ENNAHDHA FALLS TODAY!
DOWN WITH THE BROTHERHOOD PARTY!
DOWN WITH THE PEOPLE'S OPPRESSORS!
GOD IS THE GREATEST! THERE IS NO GOD BUT GOD!

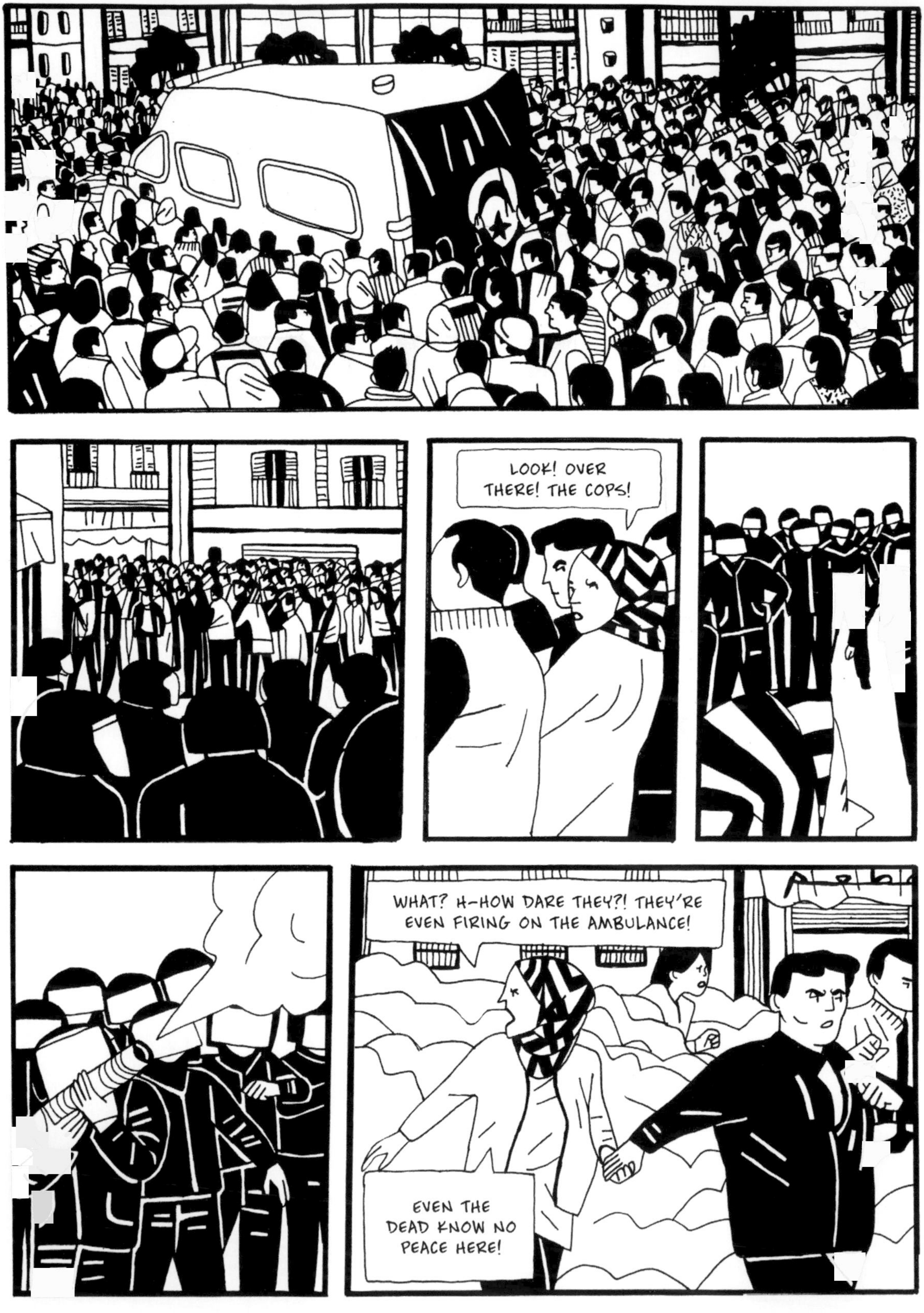
LOOK! OVER THERE! THE COPS!
WHAT? H-HOW DARE THEY?! THEY'RE EVEN FIRING ON THE AMBULANCE!
EVEN THE DEAD KNOW NO PEACE HERE!

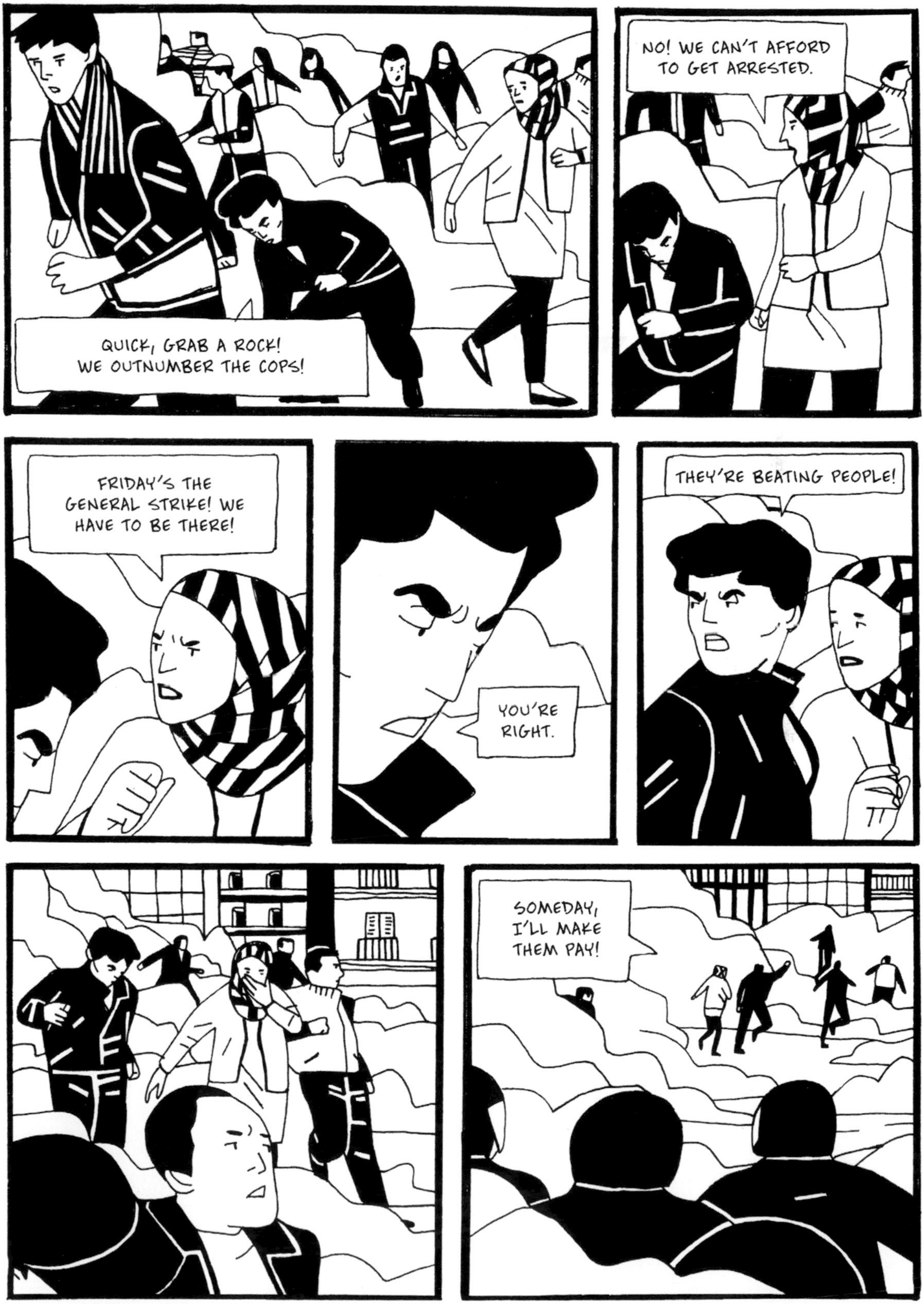
QUICK, GRAB A ROCK! WE OUTNUMBER THE COPS!
NO! WE CAN'T AFFORD TO GET ARRESTED.
FRIDAY'S THE GENERAL STRIKE! WE HAVE TO BE THERE!
YOU'RE RIGHT.
THEY'RE BEATING PEOPLE!
SOMEDAY, I'LL MAKE THEM PAY!

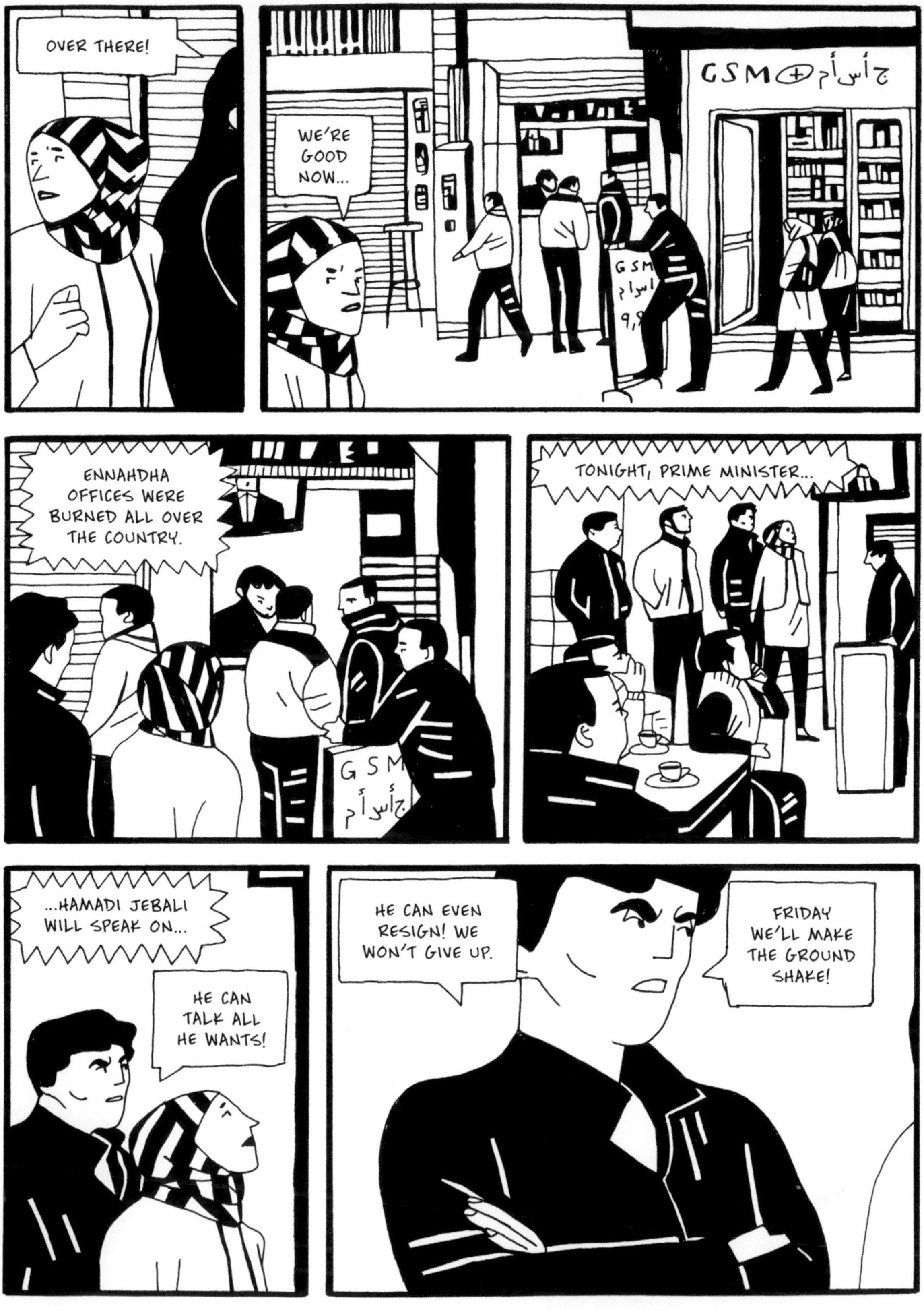
OVER THERE!
WE'RE GOOD NOW...
GSM جاس أم
ENNAHDHA OFFICES WERE BURNED ALL OVER THE COUNTRY.
TONIGHT, PRIME MINISTER...
...HAMADI JEBALI WILL SPEAK ON...
HE CAN TALK ALL HE WANTS!
HE CAN EVEN RESIGN! WE WON'T GIVE UP.
FRIDAY WE'LL MAKE THE GROUND SHAKE!

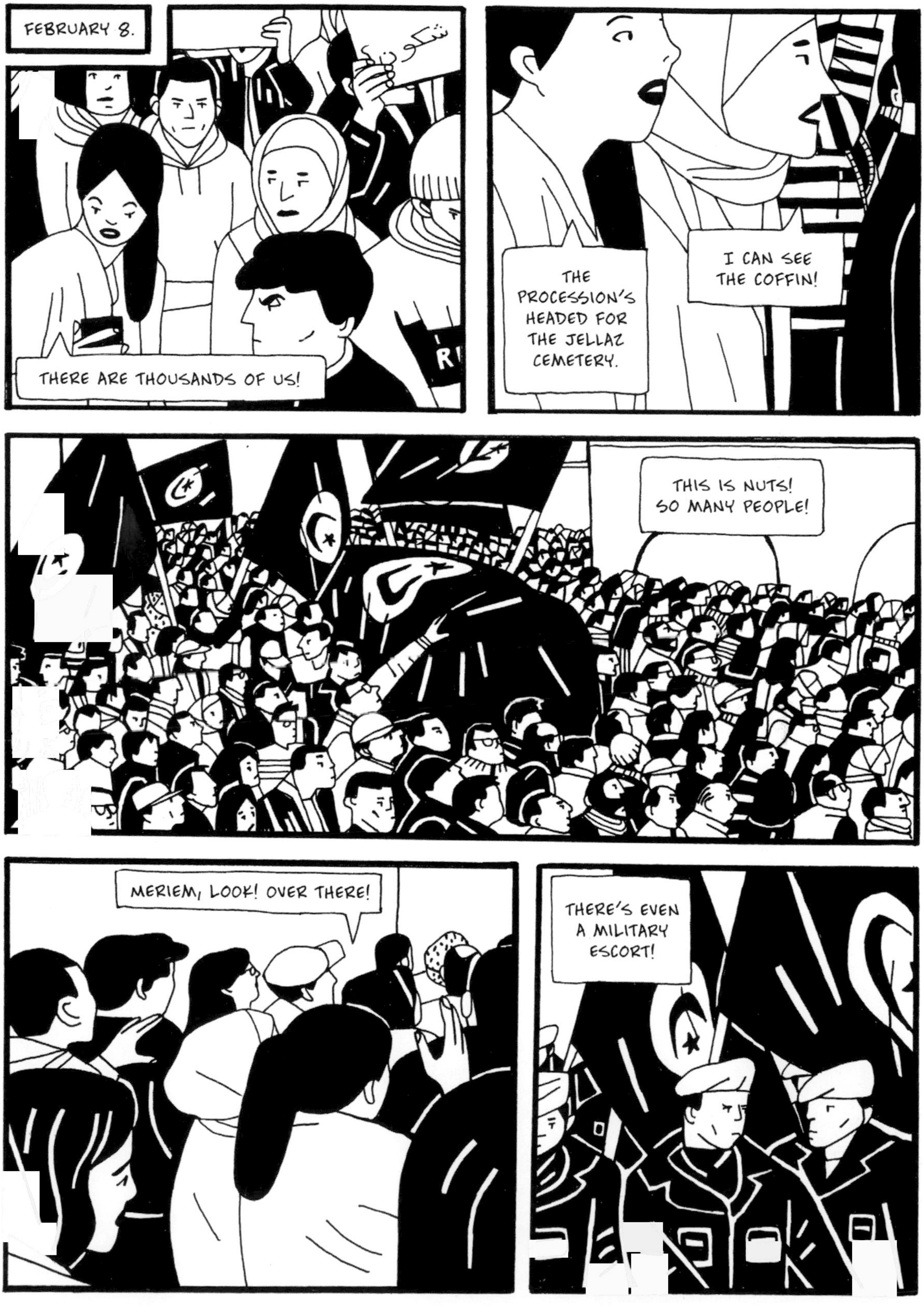

FEBRUARY 8.
THERE ARE THOUSANDS OF US!
THE PROCESSION'S HEADED FOR THE JELLAZ CEMETERY.
I CAN SEE THE COFFIN!
THIS IS NUTS! SO MANY PEOPLE!
MERIEM, LOOK! OVER THERE!
THERE'S EVEN A MILITARY ESCORT!

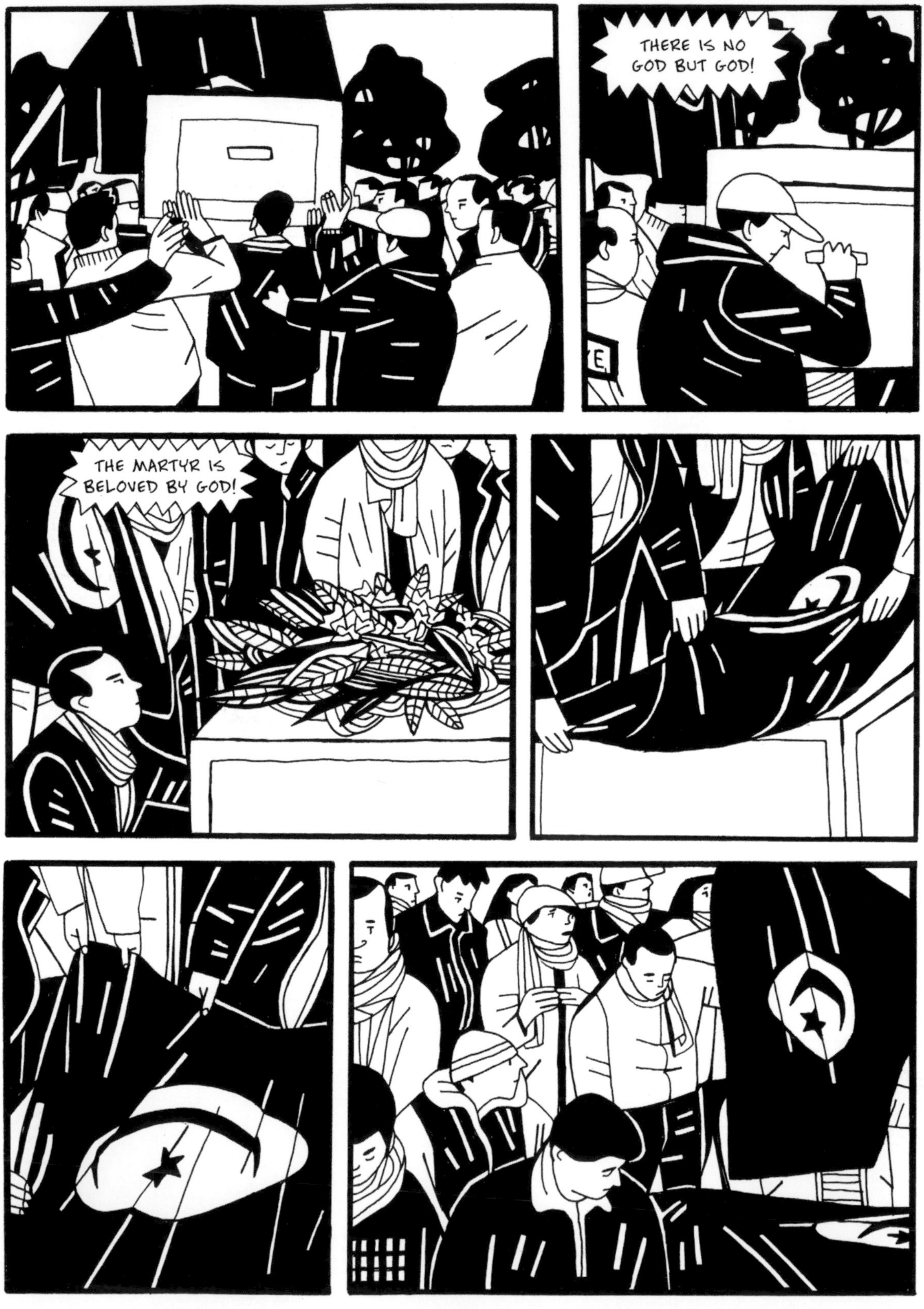
THERE IS NO GOD BUT GOD!
THE MARTYR IS BELOVED BY GOD!

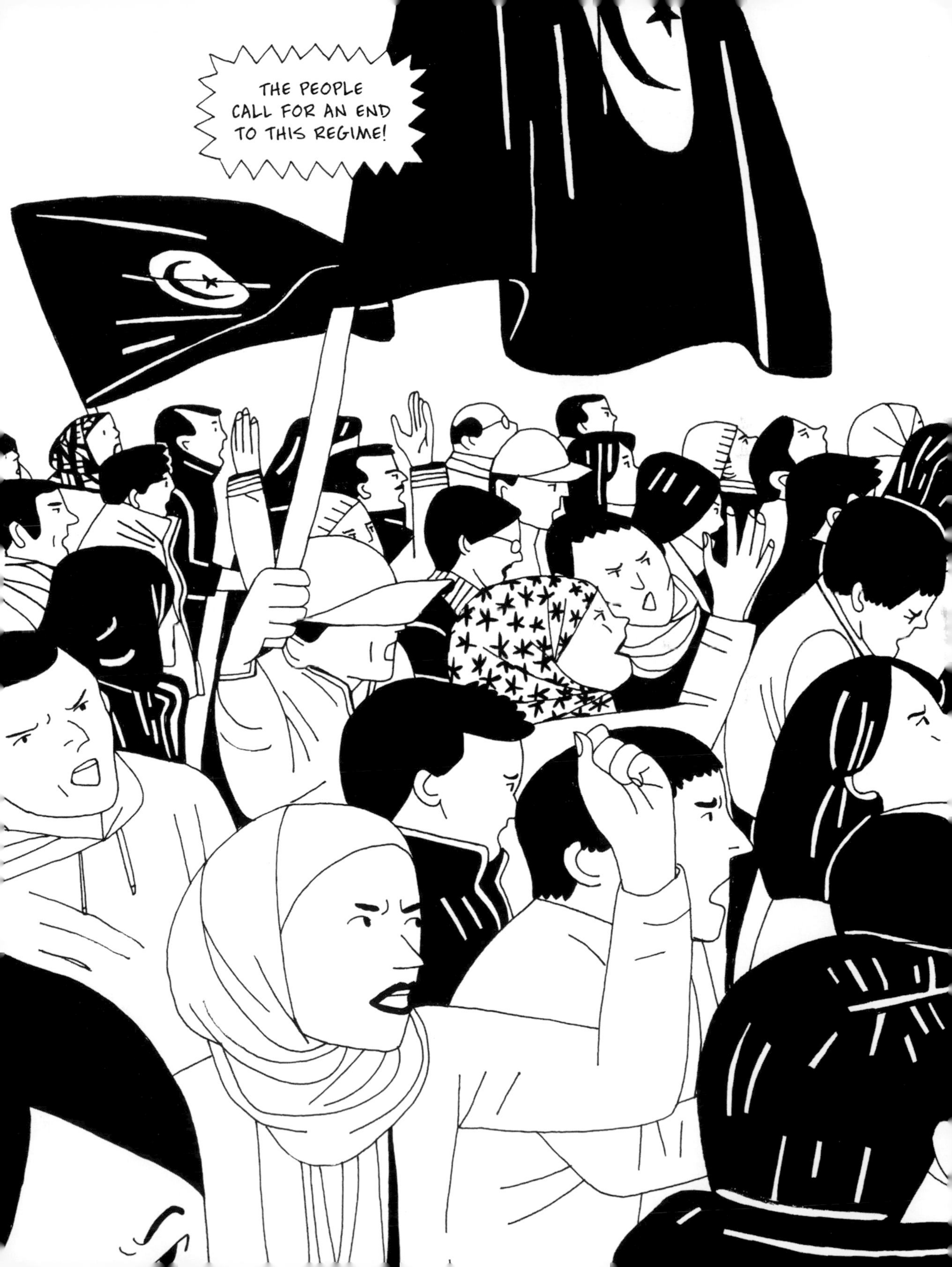
THE PEOPLE CALL FOR AN END TO THIS REGIME!

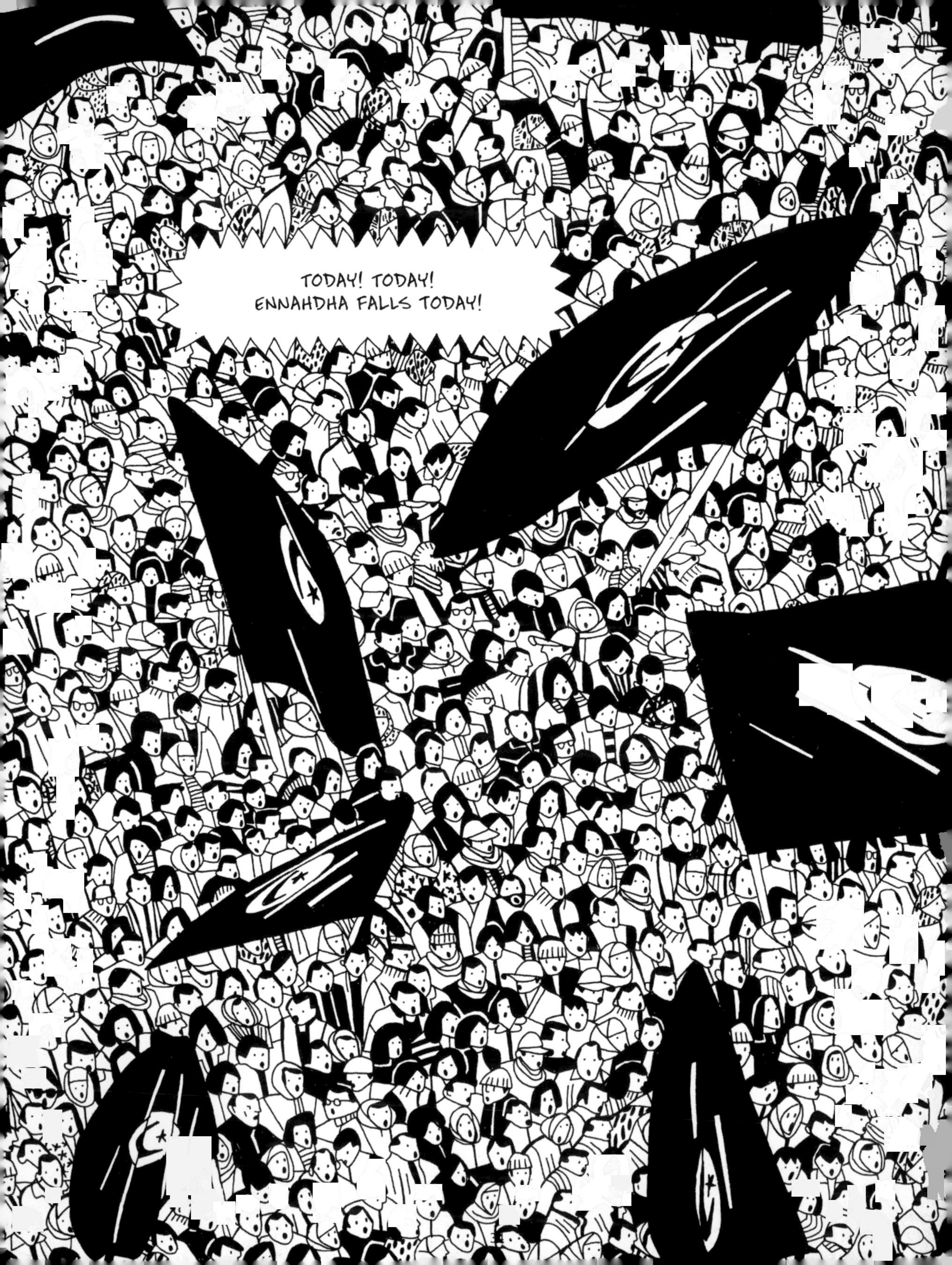
TODAY! TODAY!
ENNAHDHA FALLS TODAY!

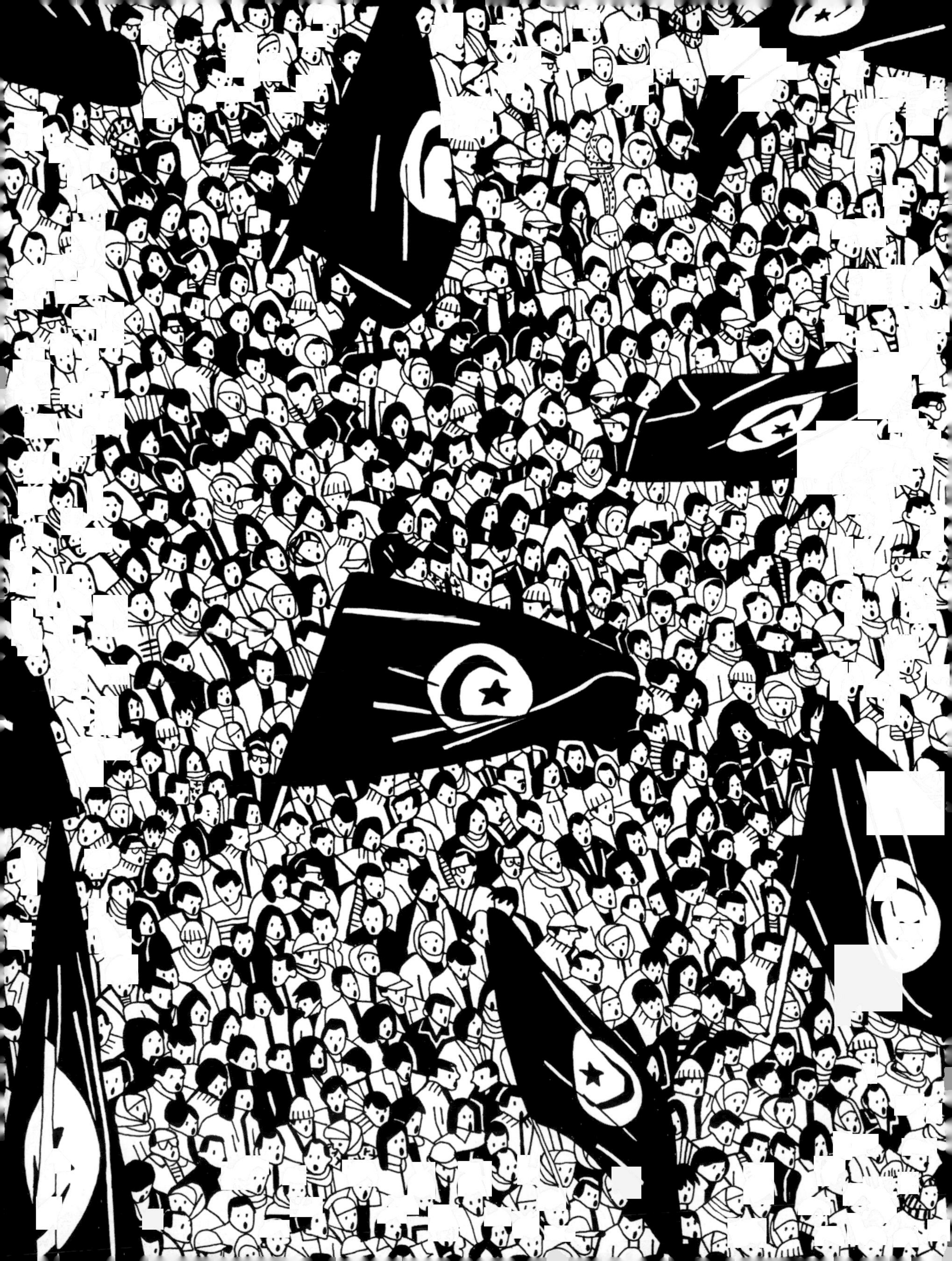

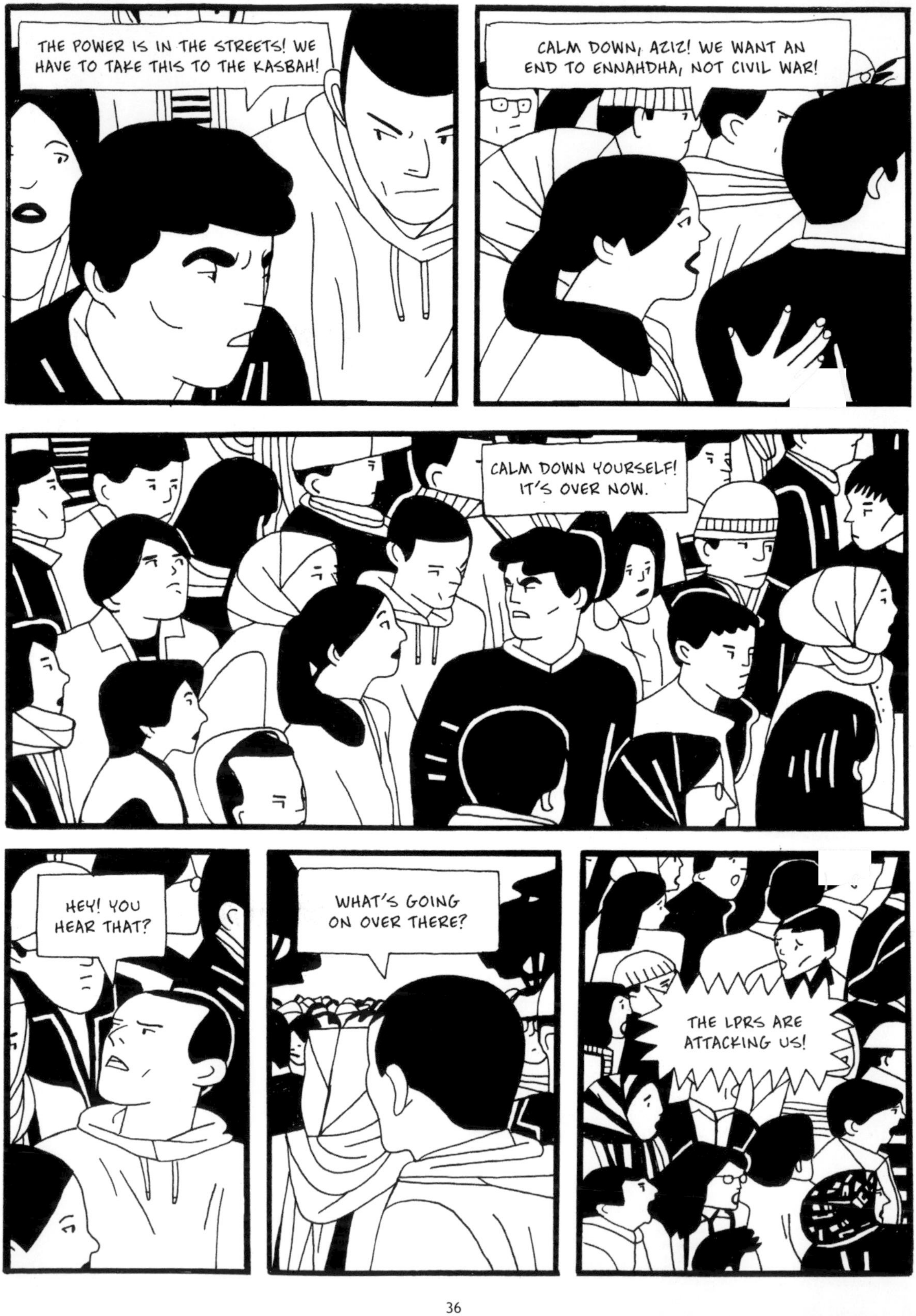
THE POWER IS IN THE STREETS! WE HAVE TO TAKE THIS TO THE KASBAH!
CALM DOWN, AZIZ! WE WANT AN END TO ENNAHDHA, NOT CIVIL WAR!
CALM DOWN YOURSELF! IT'S OVER NOW.
HEY! YOU HEAR THAT?
WHAT'S GOING ON OVER THERE?
THE LPRS ARE ATTACKING US!

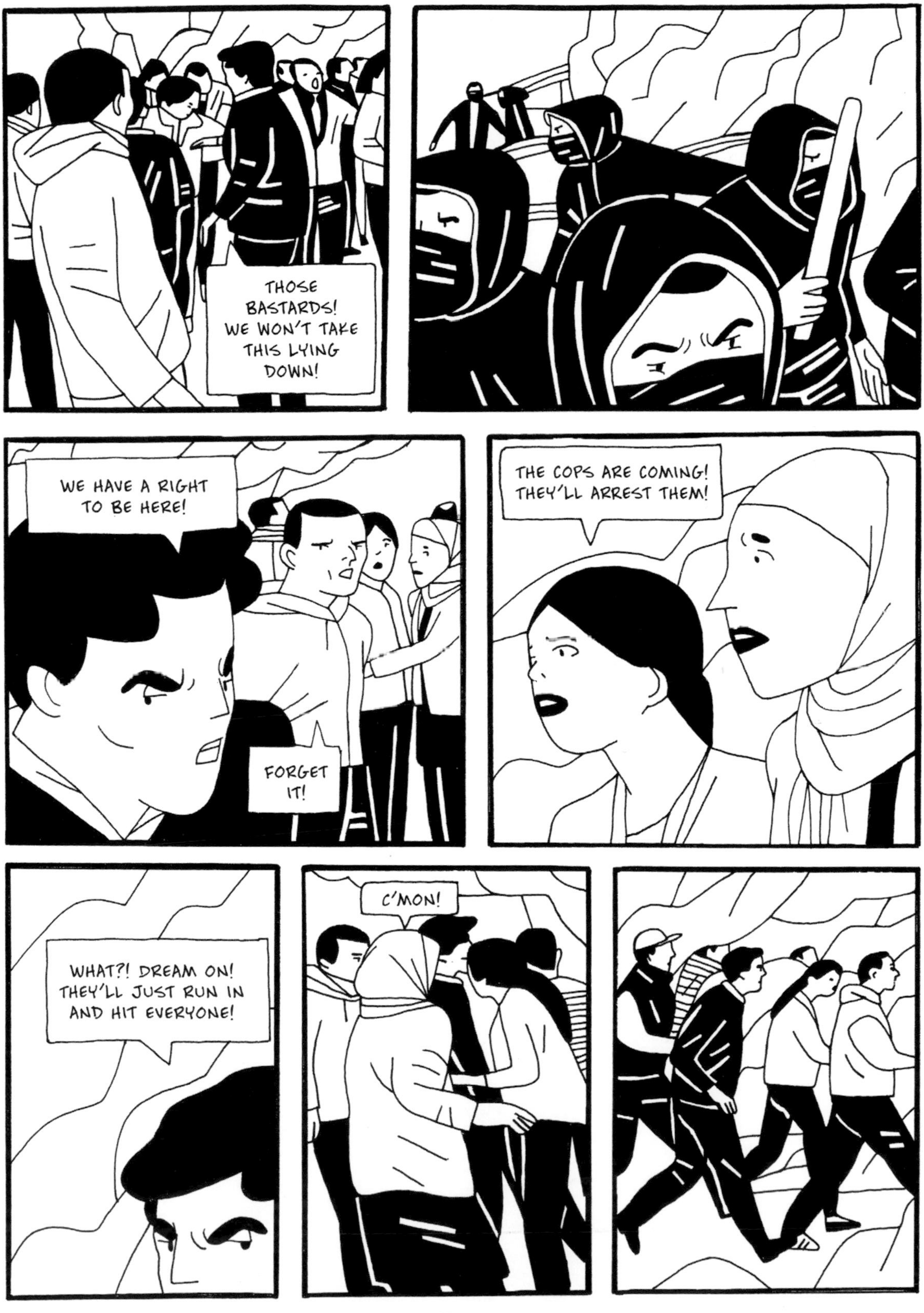

THOSE BASTARDS! WE WON'T TAKE THIS LYING DOWN!
WE HAVE A RIGHT TO BE HERE!
FORGET IT!
THE COPS ARE COMING! THEY'LL ARREST THEM!
WHAT?! DREAM ON! THEY'LL JUST RUN IN AND HIT EVERYONE!
C'MON!

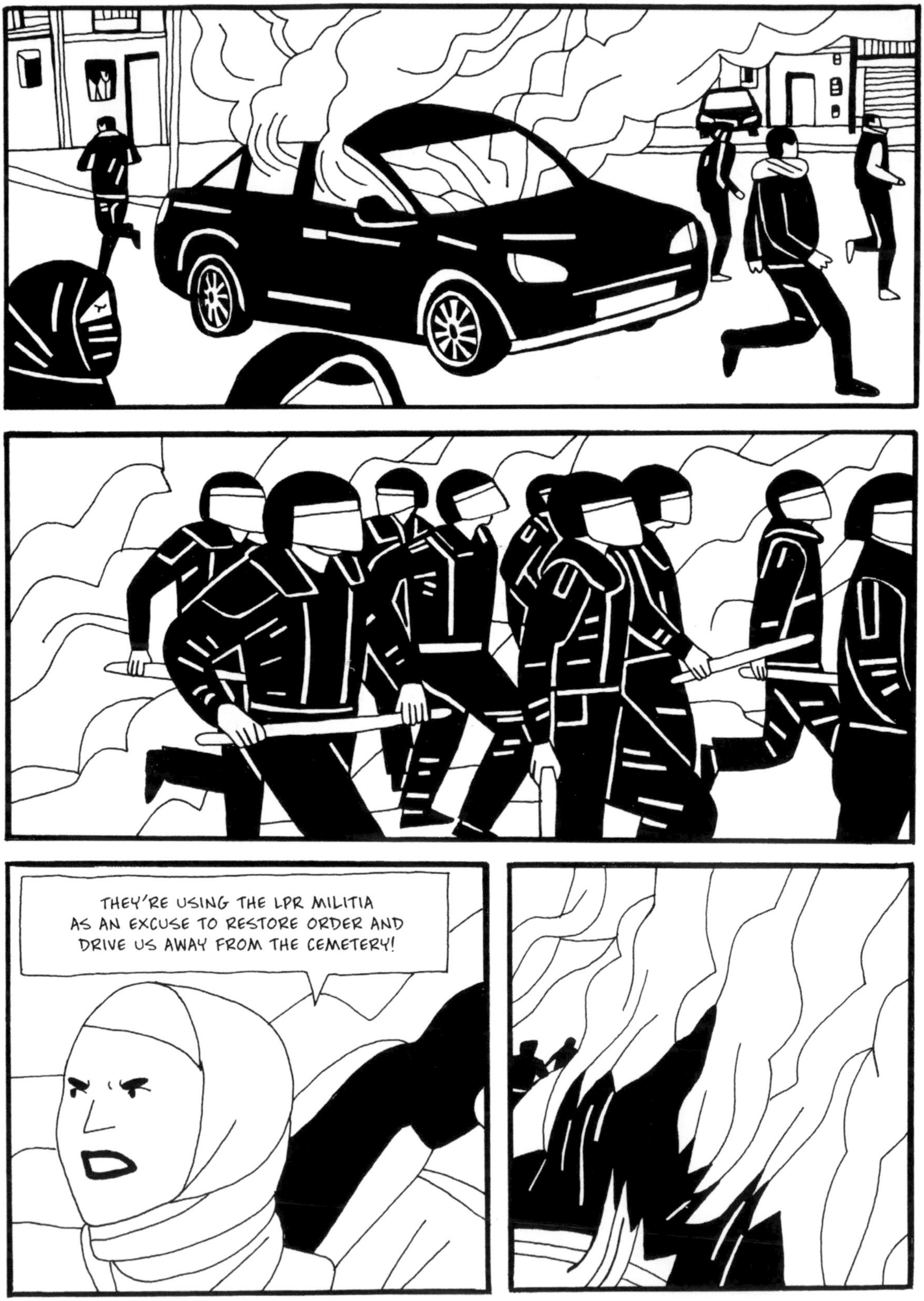
THEY'RE USING THE LPR MILITIA AS AN EXCUSE TO RESTORE ORDER AND DRIVE US AWAY FROM THE CEMETERY!

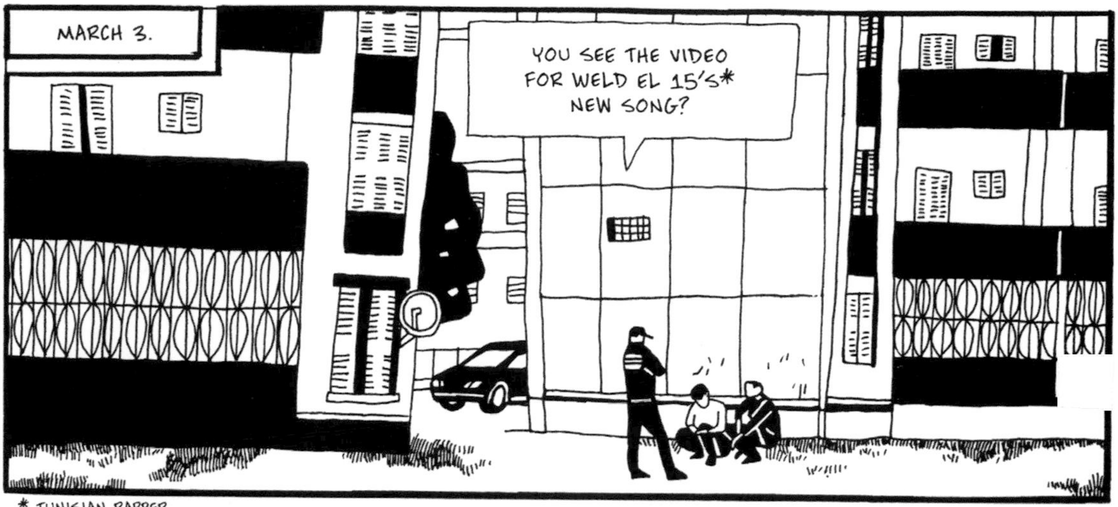
MARCH 3.
YOU SEE THE VIDEO FOR WELD EL 15'S* NEW SONG?

* TUNISIAN RAPPER

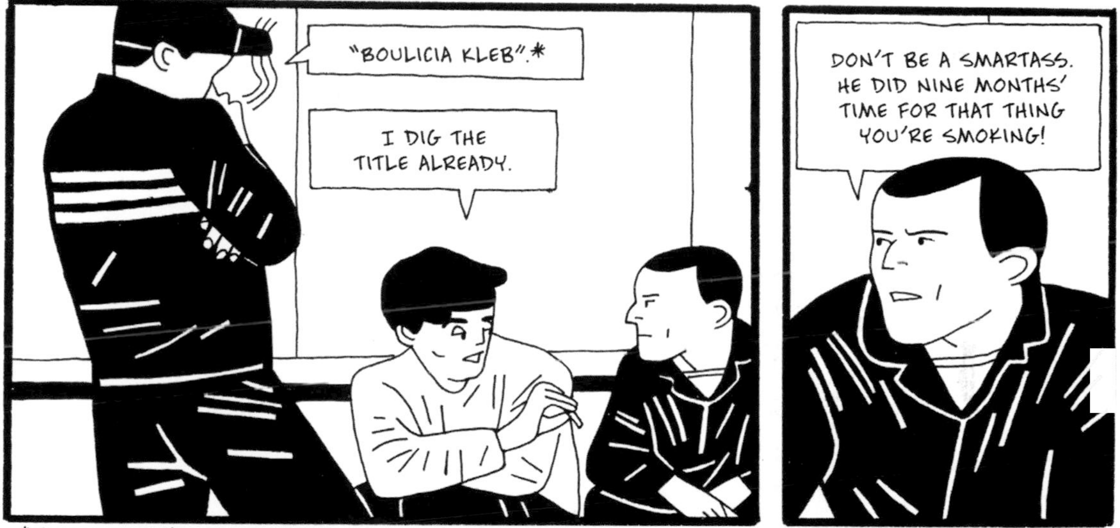
"BOULICIA KLEB".*
I DIG THE TITLE ALREADY.
DON'T BE A SMARTASS. HE DID NINE MONTHS' TIME FOR THAT THING YOU'RE SMOKING!

* "COPS ARE DOGS"

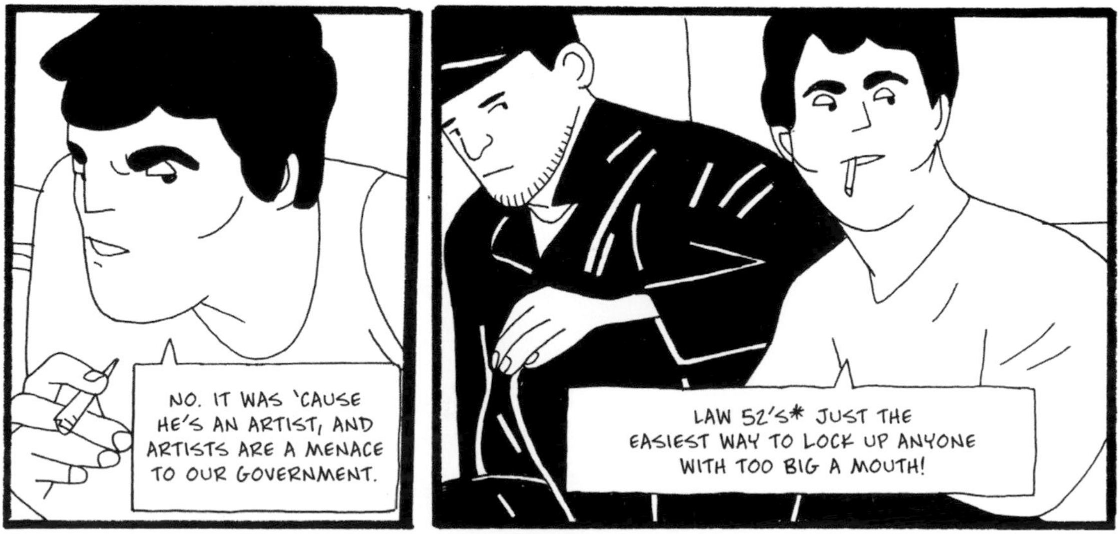
NO. IT WAS 'CAUSE HE'S AN ARTIST, AND ARTISTS ARE A MENACE TO OUR GOVERNMENT.
LAW 52'S* JUST THE EASIEST WAY TO LOCK UP ANYONE WITH TOO BIG A MOUTH!

* A DRUG LAW IMPOSING A MINIMUM MANDATORY SENTENCE OF A YEAR IN PRISON FOR ANYONE WHO USES OR POSSESSES EVEN A SMALL QUANTITY OF AN ILLEGAL DRUG

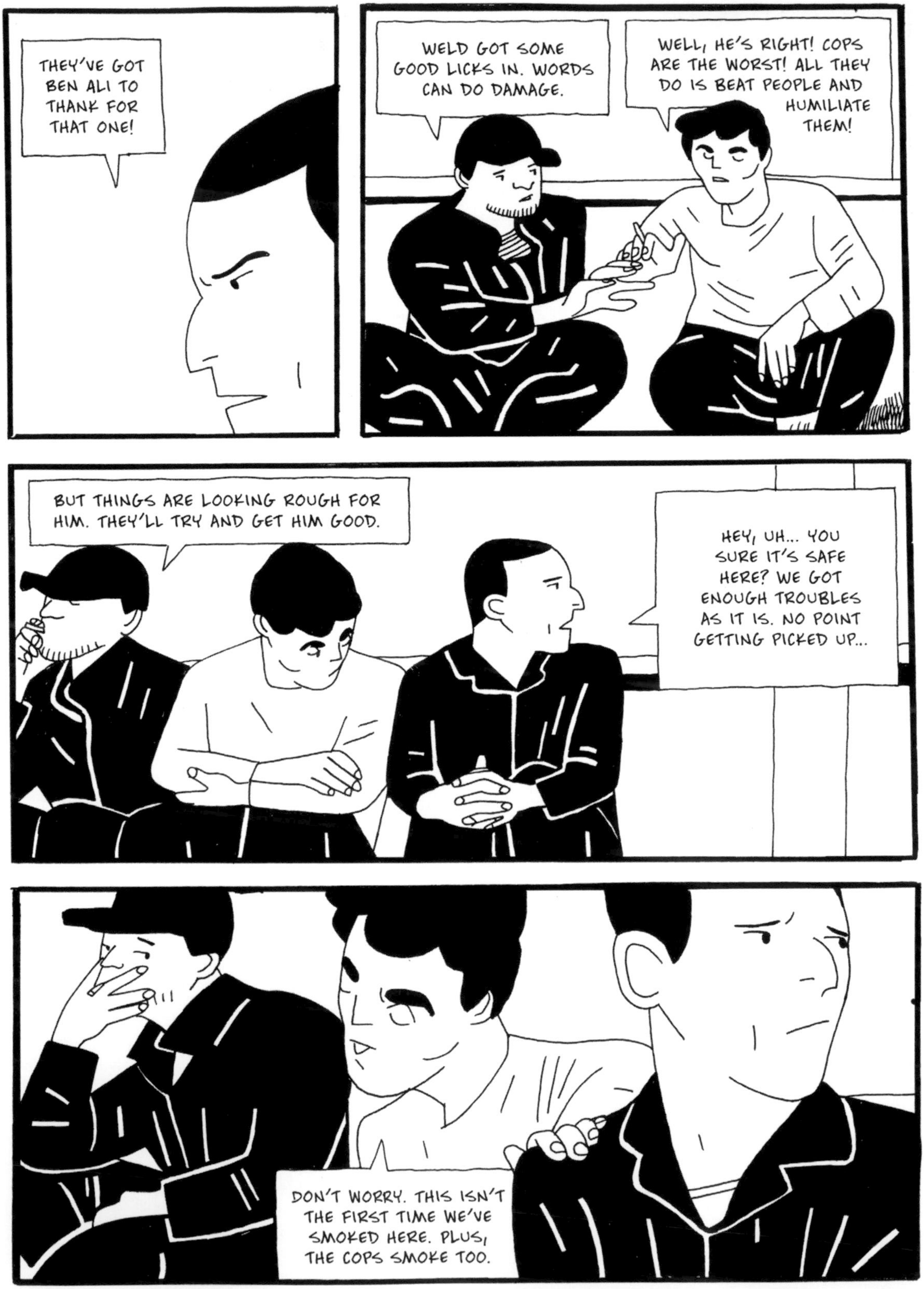
THEY'VE GOT BEN ALI TO THANK FOR THAT ONE!
WELD GOT SOME GOOD LICKS IN. WORDS CAN DO DAMAGE.
WELL, HE'S RIGHT! COPS ARE THE WORST! ALL THEY DO IS BEAT PEOPLE AND HUMILIATE THEM!
BUT THINGS ARE LOOKING ROUGH FOR HIM. THEY'LL TRY AND GET HIM GOOD.
HEY, UH... YOU SURE IT'S SAFE HERE? WE GOT ENOUGH TROUBLES AS IT IS. NO POINT GETTING PICKED UP...
DON'T WORRY. THIS ISN'T THE FIRST TIME WE'VE SMOKED HERE. PLUS, THE COPS SMOKE TOO.

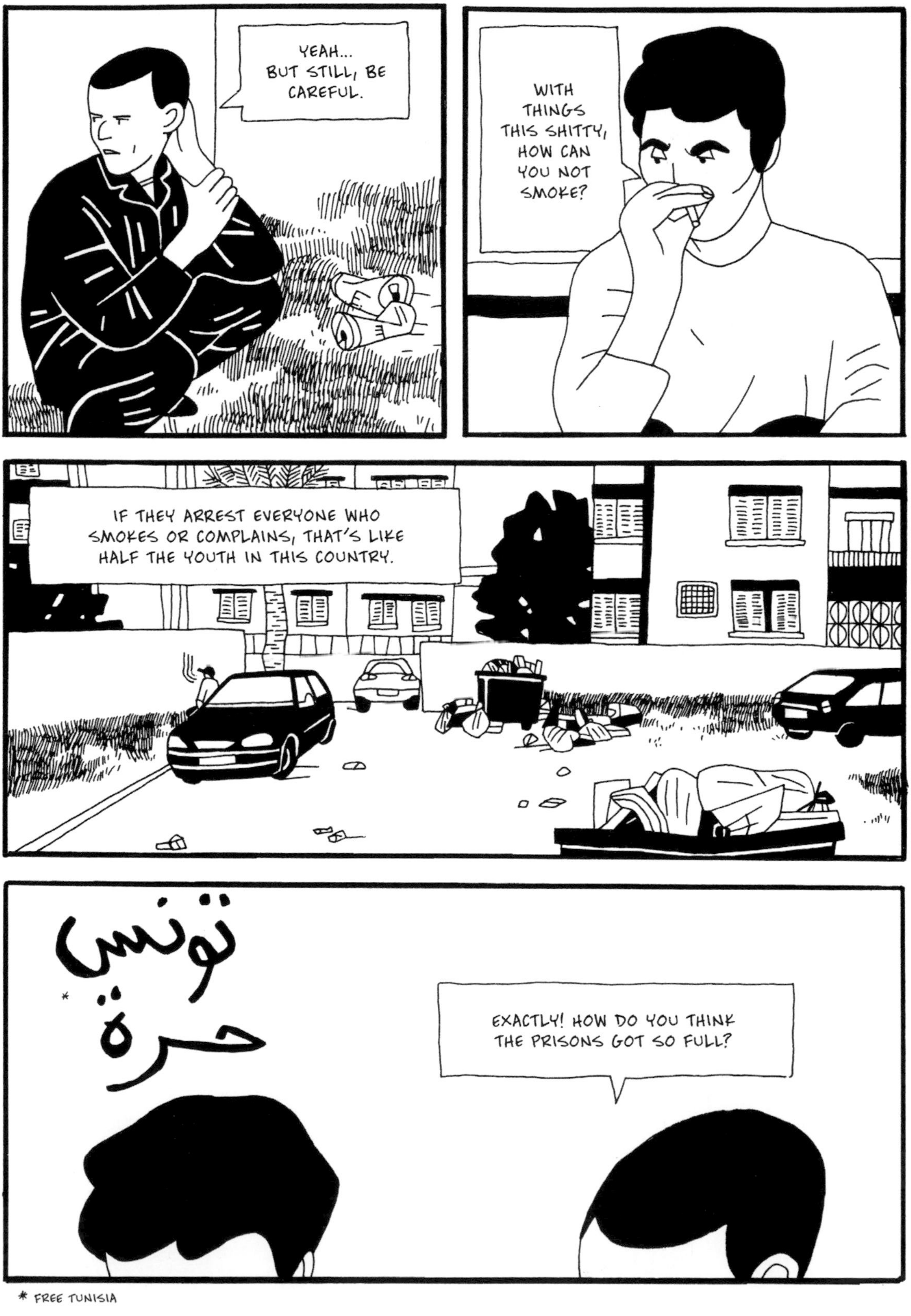
YEAH... BUT STILL, BE CAREFUL.
WITH THINGS THIS SHITTY, HOW CAN YOU NOT SMOKE?
IF THEY ARREST EVERYONE WHO SMOKES OR COMPLAINS, THAT'S LIKE HALF THE YOUTH IN THIS COUNTRY.
تونس حرة*
EXACTLY! HOW DO YOU THINK THE PRISONS GOT SO FULL?

* FREE TUNISIA

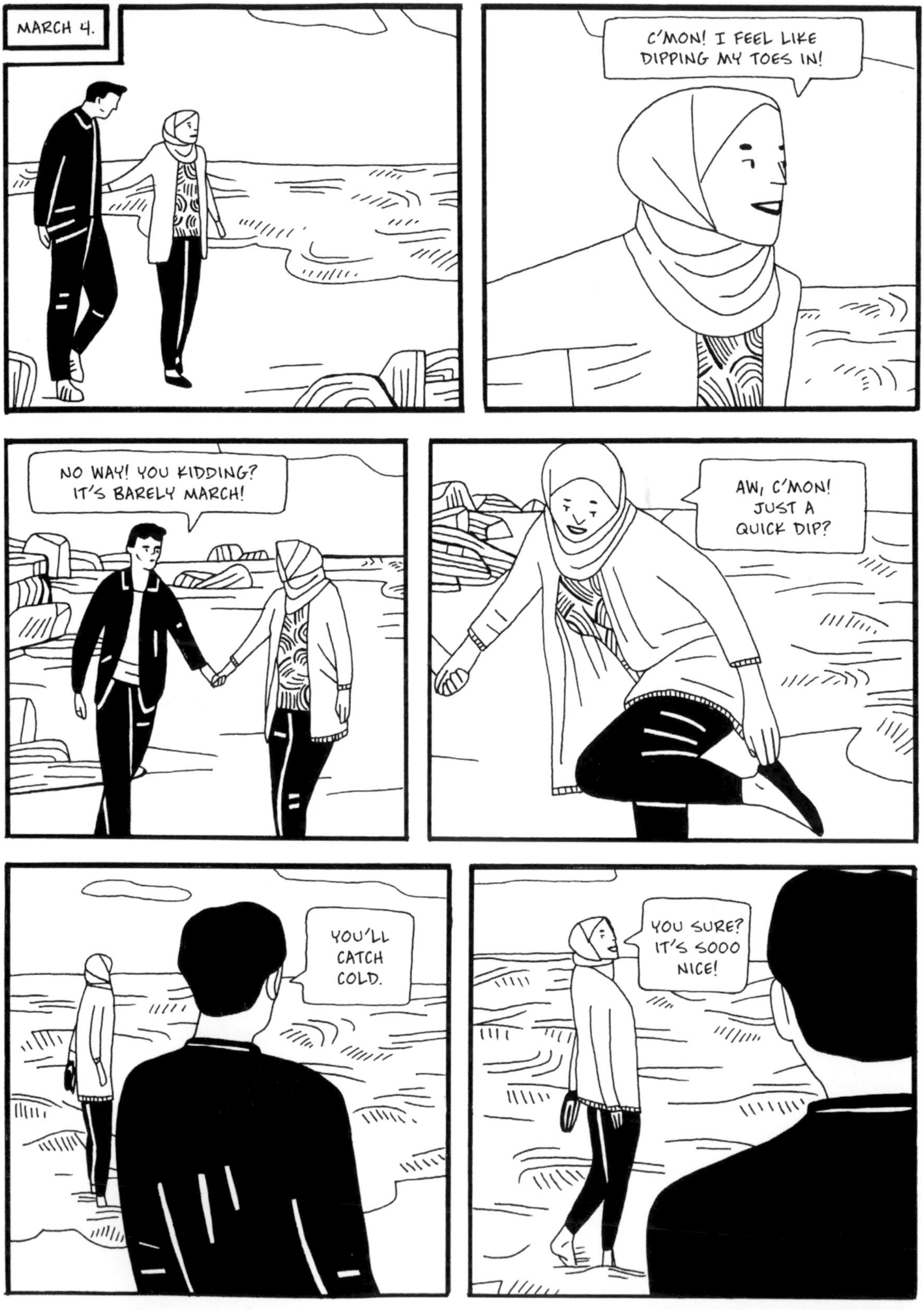
MARCH 4.
C'MON! I FEEL LIKE DIPPING MY TOES IN!
NO WAY! YOU KIDDING? IT'S BARELY MARCH!
AW, C'MON! JUST A QUICK DIP?
YOU'LL CATCH COLD.
YOU SURE? IT'S SOOO NICE!

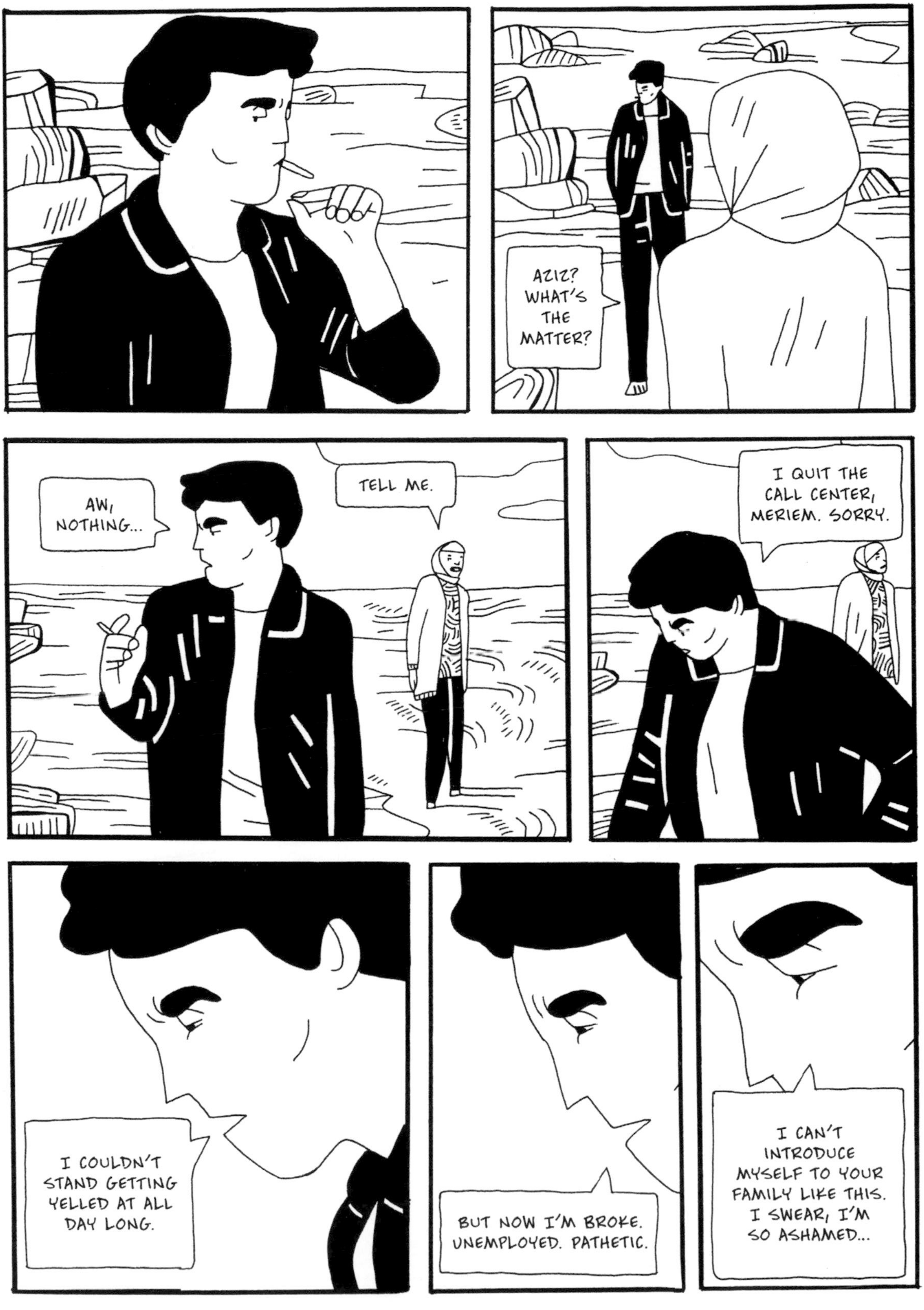
AZIZ? WHAT'S THE MATTER?
AW, NOTHING...
TELL ME.
I QUIT THE CALL CENTER, MERIEM. SORRY.
I COULDN'T STAND GETTING YELLED AT ALL DAY LONG.
BUT NOW I'M BROKE. UNEMPLOYED. PATHETIC.
I CAN'T INTRODUCE MYSELF TO YOUR FAMILY LIKE THIS. I SWEAR, I'M SO ASHAMED...

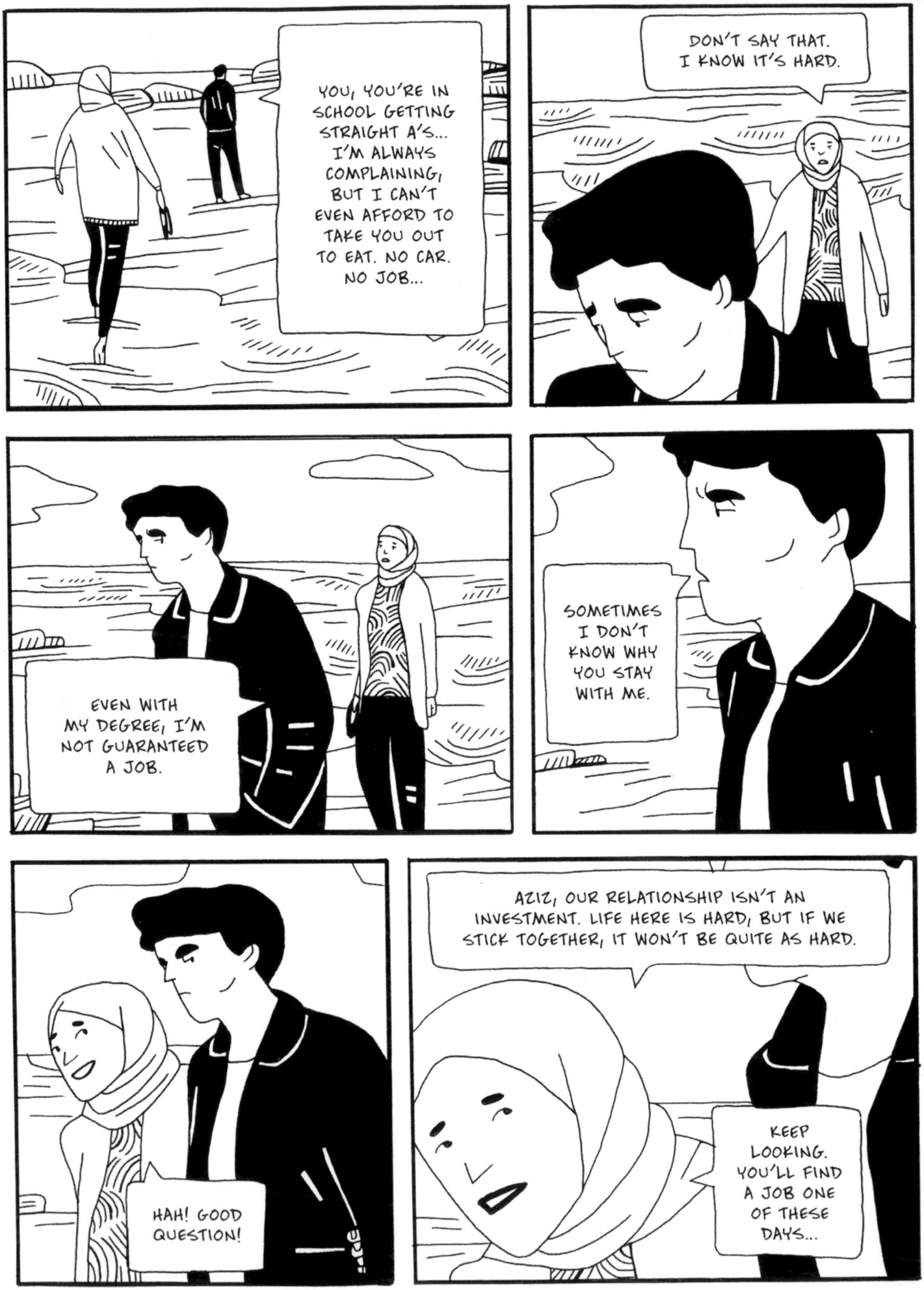
YOU, YOU'RE IN SCHOOL GETTING STRAIGHT A'S... I'M ALWAYS COMPLAINING, BUT I CAN'T EVEN AFFORD TO TAKE YOU OUT TO EAT. NO CAR. NO JOB...
DON'T SAY THAT. I KNOW IT'S HARD.
EVEN WITH MY DEGREE, I'M NOT GUARANTEED A JOB.
SOMETIMES I DON'T KNOW WHY YOU STAY WITH ME.
HAH! GOOD QUESTION!
AZIZ, OUR RELATIONSHIP ISN'T AN INVESTMENT. LIFE HERE IS HARD, BUT IF WE STICK TOGETHER, IT WON'T BE QUITE AS HARD.
KEEP LOOKING. YOU'LL FIND A JOB ONE OF THESE DAYS...

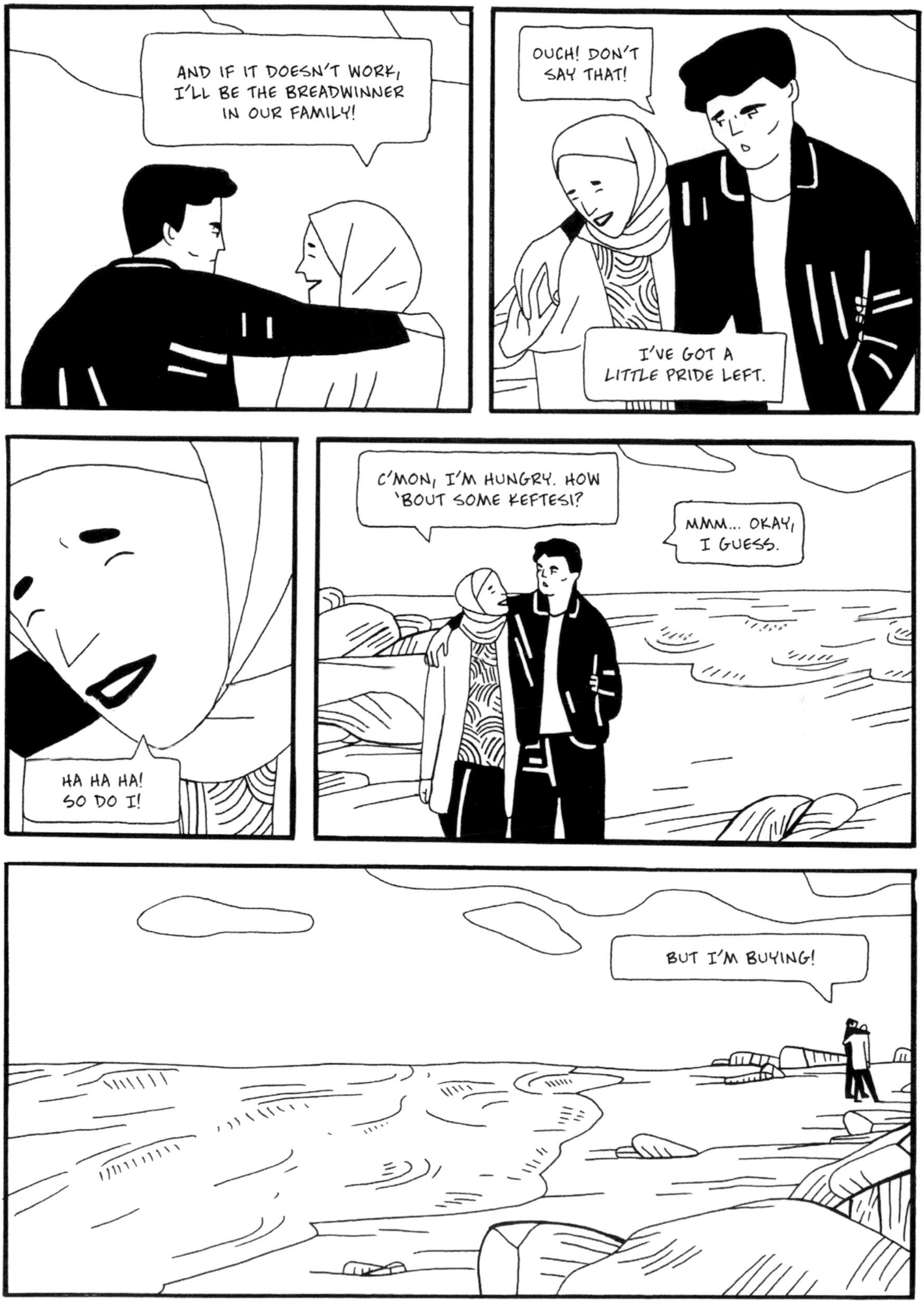
AND IF IT DOESN'T WORK, I'LL BE THE BREADWINNER IN OUR FAMILY!
OUCH! DON'T SAY THAT!
I'VE GOT A LITTLE PRIDE LEFT.
HA HA HA! SO DO I!
C'MON, I'M HUNGRY. HOW 'BOUT SOME KEFTESI?
MMM... OKAY, I GUESS.
BUT I'M BUYING!

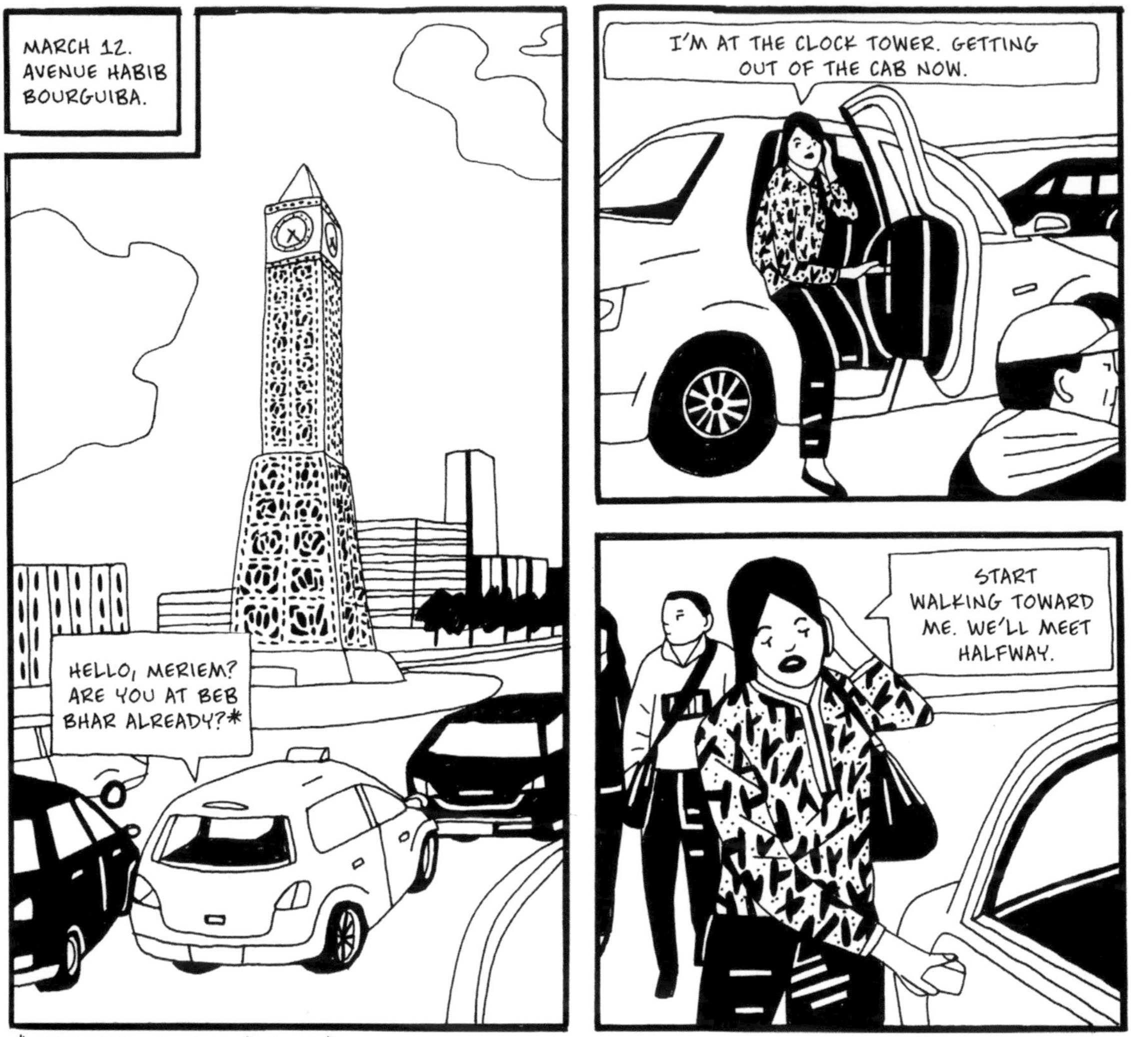
MARCH 12. AVENUE HABIB BOURGUIBA.
HELLO, MERIEM? ARE YOU AT BEB BHAR ALREADY?*
I'M AT THE CLOCK TOWER. GETTING OUT OF THE CAB NOW.
START WALKING TOWARD ME. WE'LL MEET HALFWAY.

* PORTE DE LA MER, OR THE "SEA GATE" AT THE OTHER END OF THE AVENUE

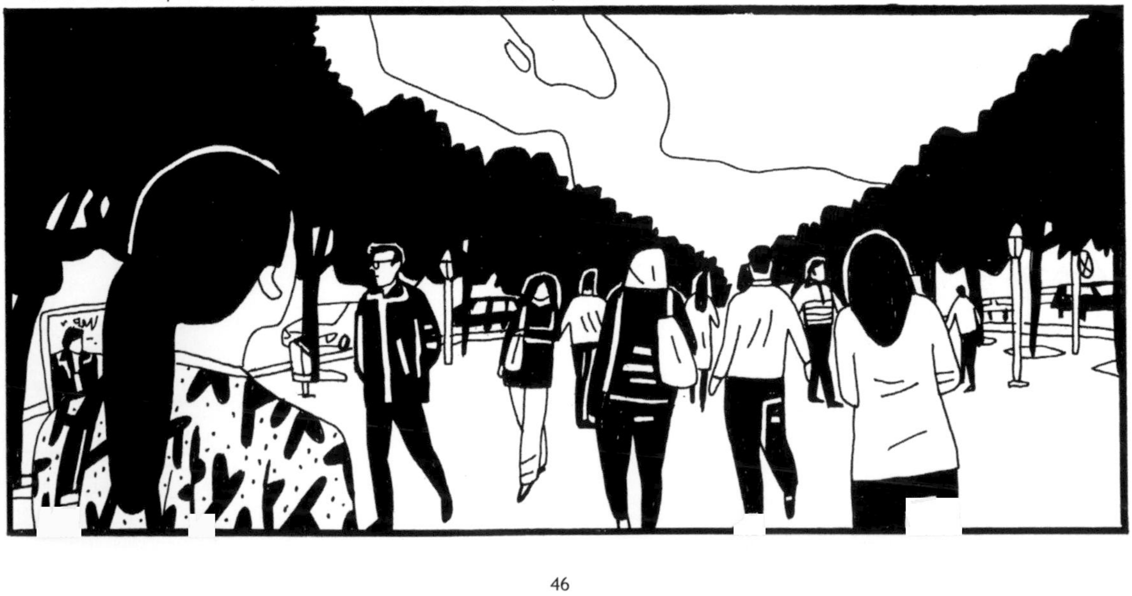

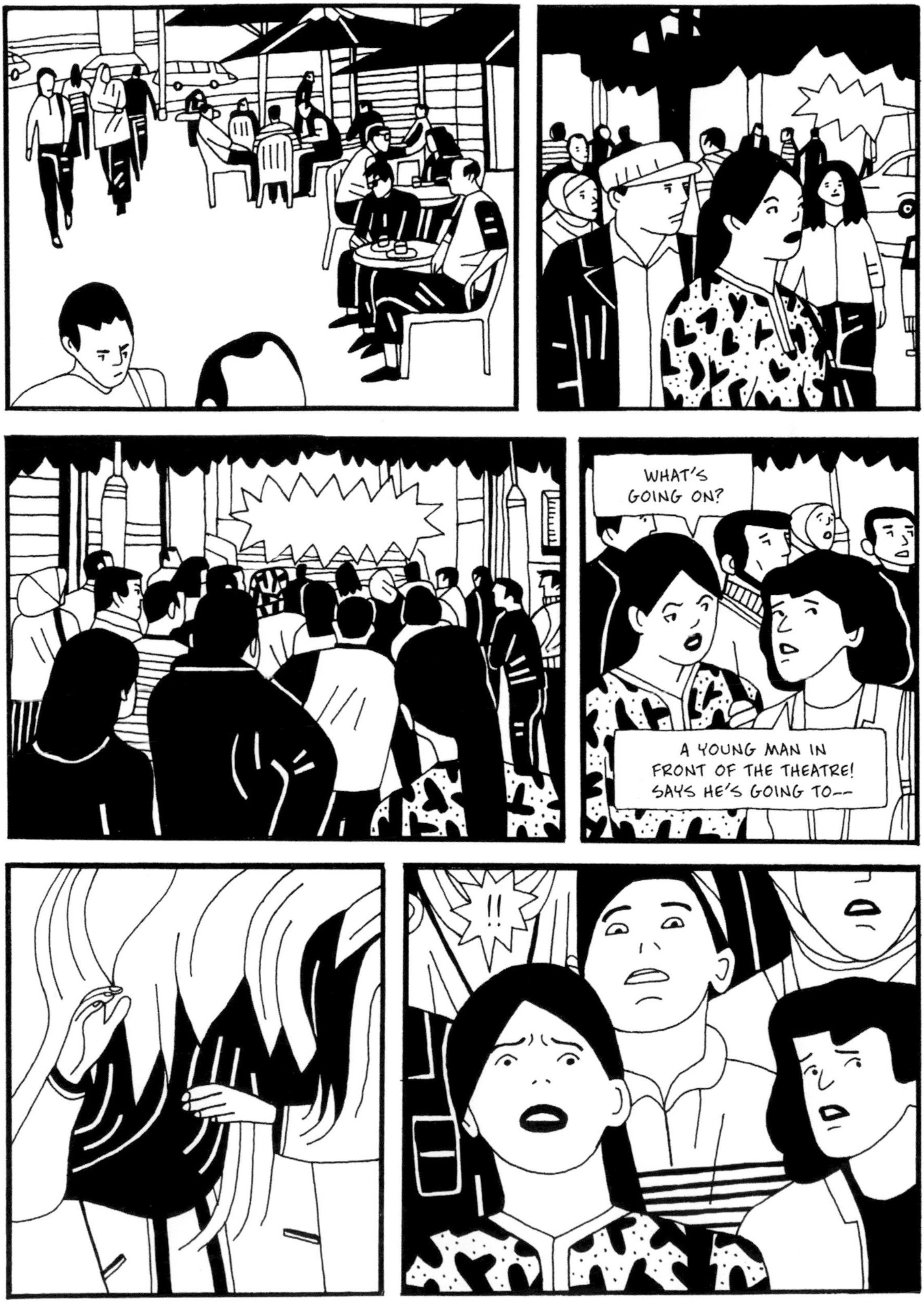
WHAT'S GOING ON?
A YOUNG MAN IN FRONT OF THE THEATRE! SAYS HE'S GOING TO--
!!

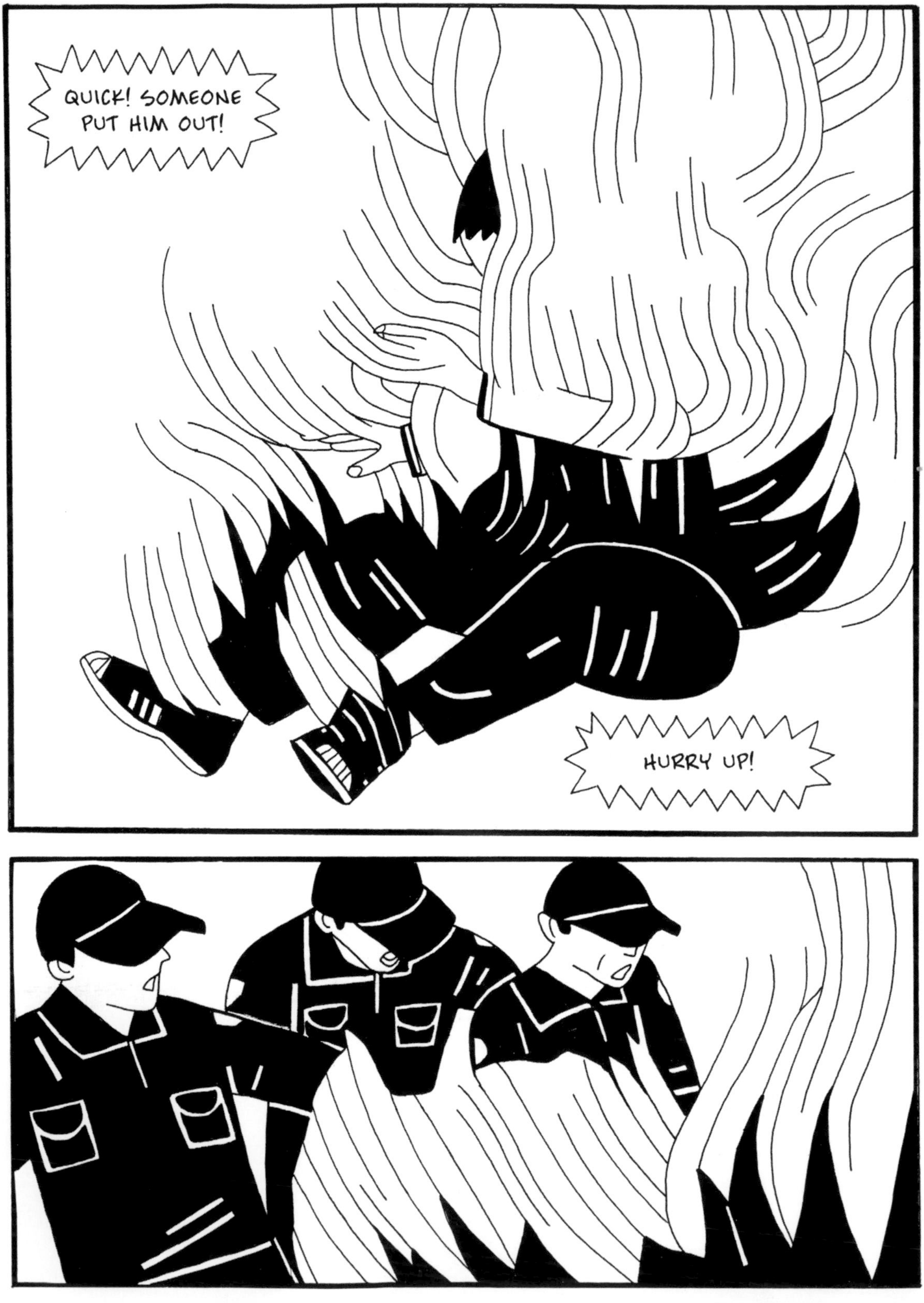
QUICK! SOMEONE PUT HIM OUT!
HURRY UP!

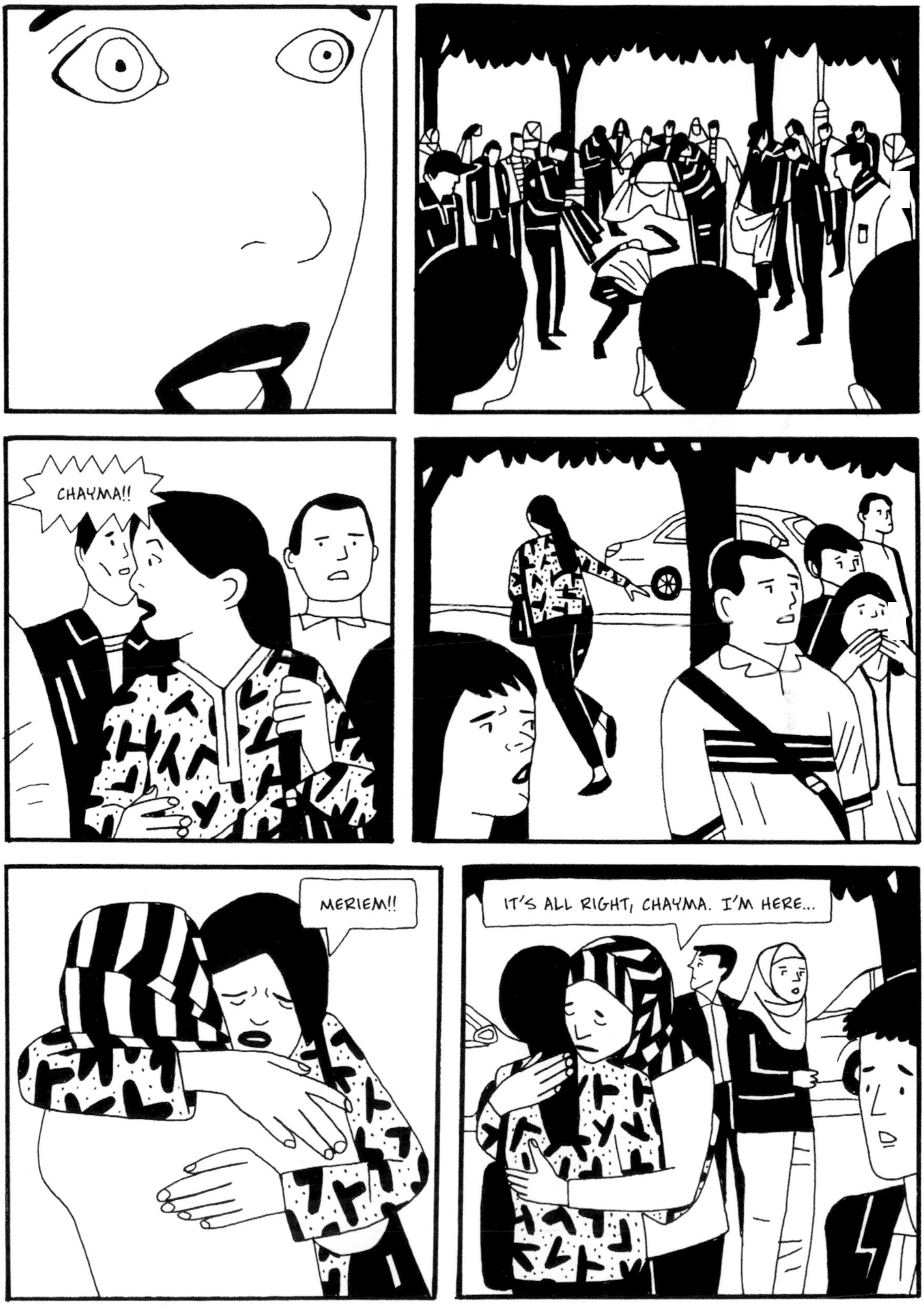
CHAYMA!!
MERIEM!!
IT'S ALL RIGHT, CHAYMA. I'M HERE...

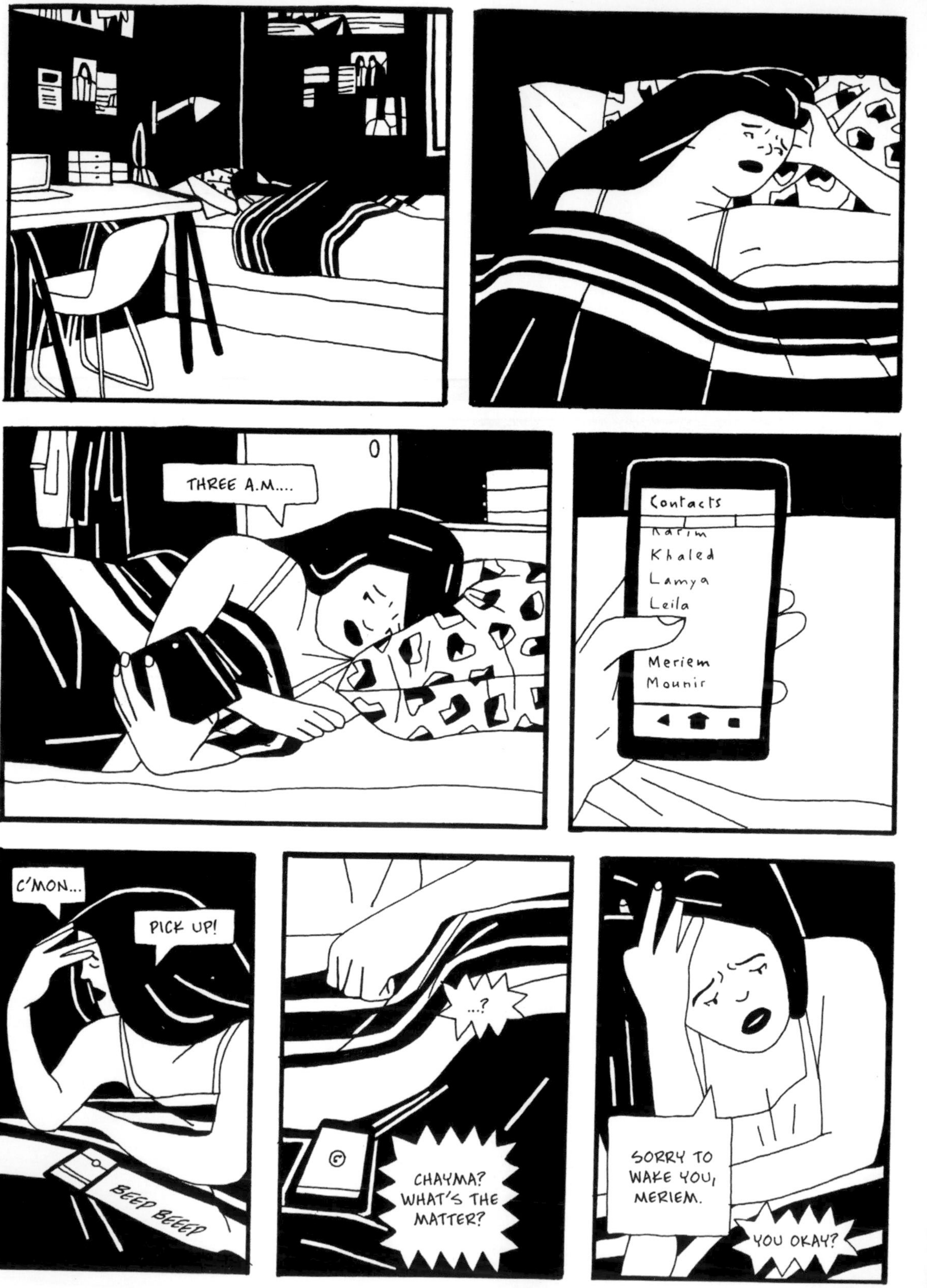
THREE A.M....
Contacts
Khaled
Lamya
Leila
Meriem
Mounir
C'MON...
PICK UP!
BEEP BEEEP
...?
CHAYMA? WHAT'S THE MATTER?
SORRY TO WAKE YOU, MERIEM.
YOU OKAY?

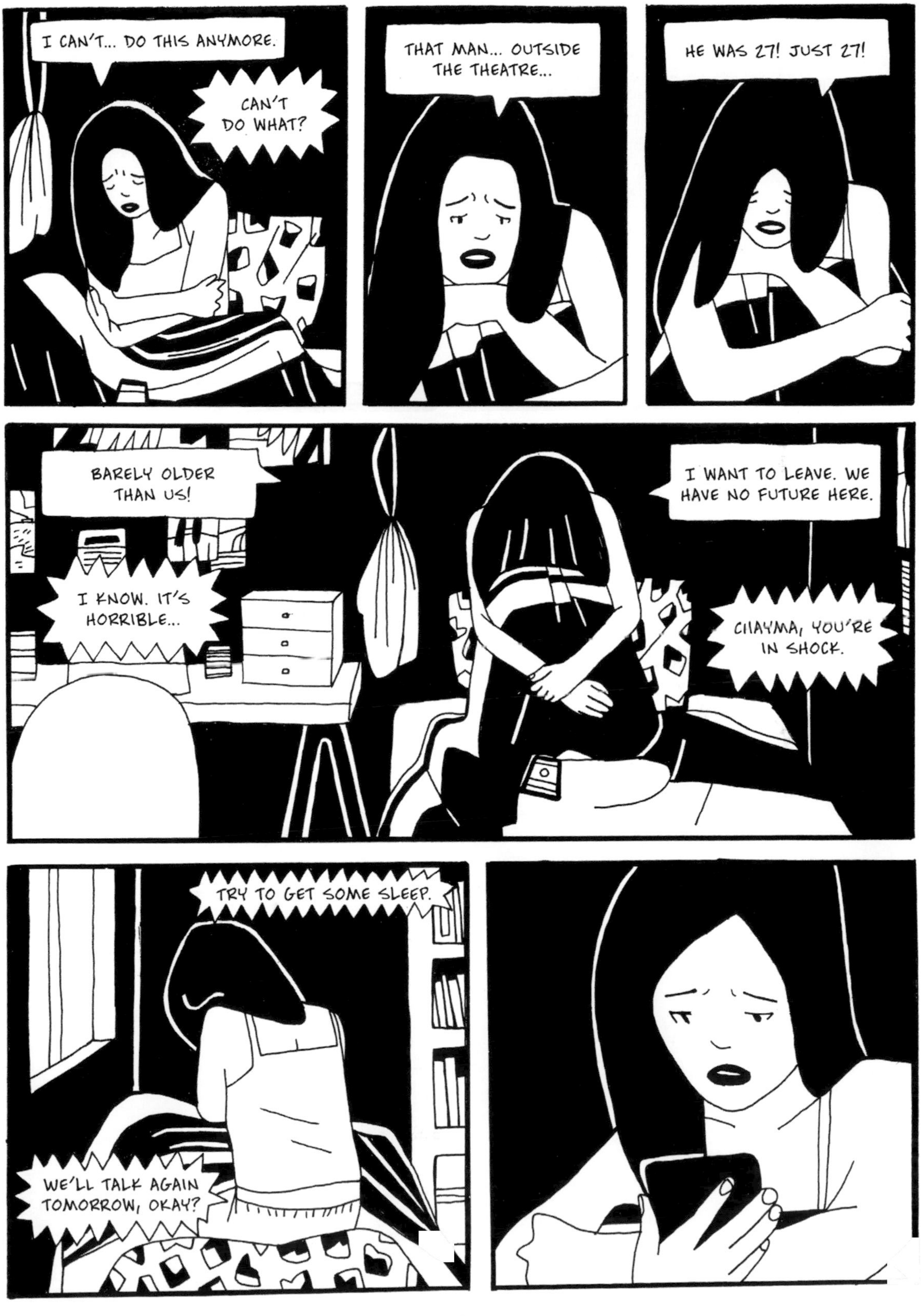

I CAN'T... DO THIS ANYMORE.
CAN'T DO WHAT?
THAT MAN... OUTSIDE THE THEATRE...
HE WAS 27! JUST 27!
BARELY OLDER THAN US!
I KNOW. IT'S HORRIBLE...
I WANT TO LEAVE. WE HAVE NO FUTURE HERE.
CHAYMA, YOU'RE IN SHOCK.
TRY TO GET SOME SLEEP.
WE'LL TALK AGAIN TOMORROW, OKAY?

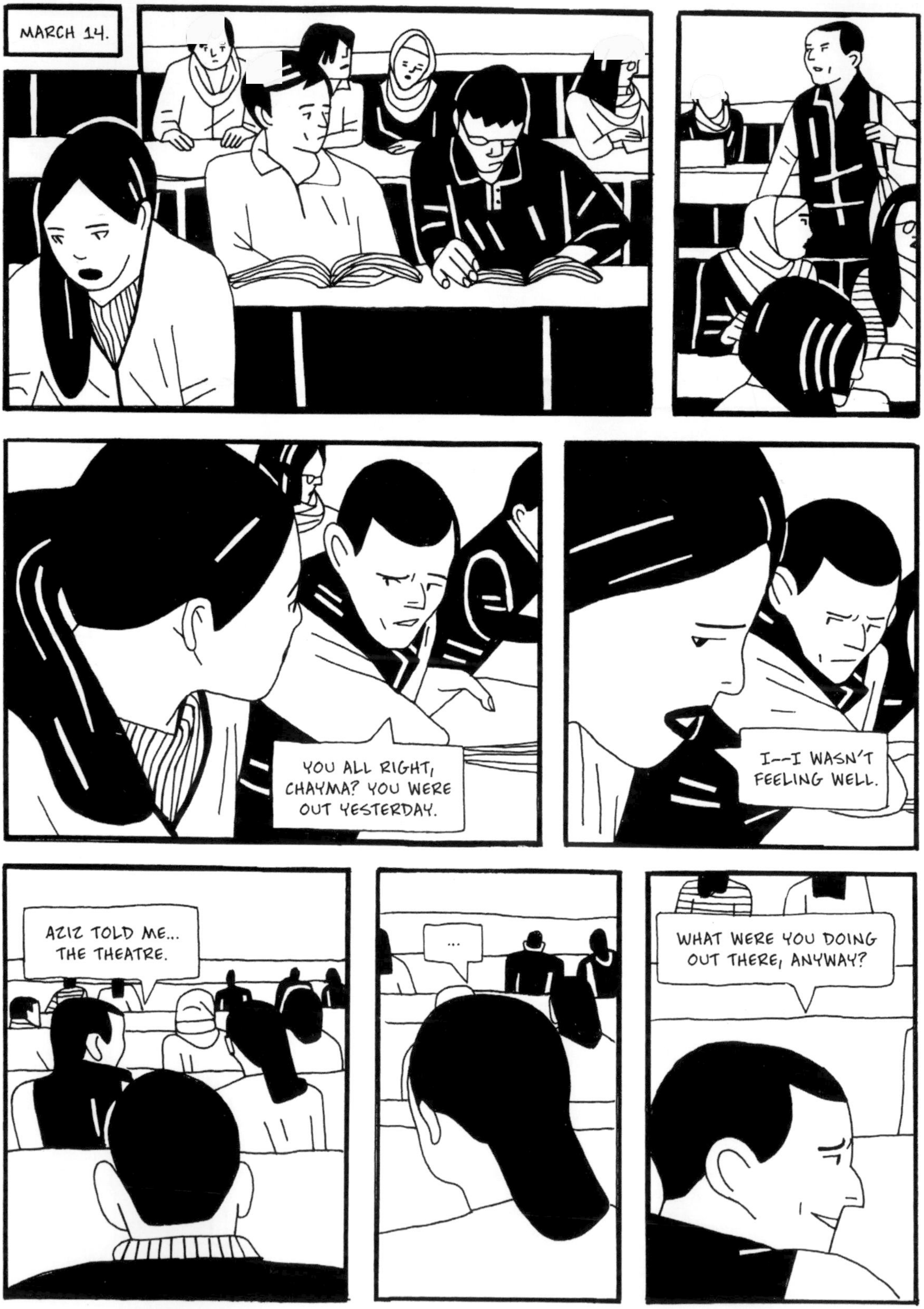
MARCH 14.
YOU ALL RIGHT, CHAYMA? YOU WERE OUT YESTERDAY.
I--I WASN'T FEELING WELL.
AZIZ TOLD ME... THE THEATRE.
...
WHAT WERE YOU DOING OUT THERE, ANYWAY?

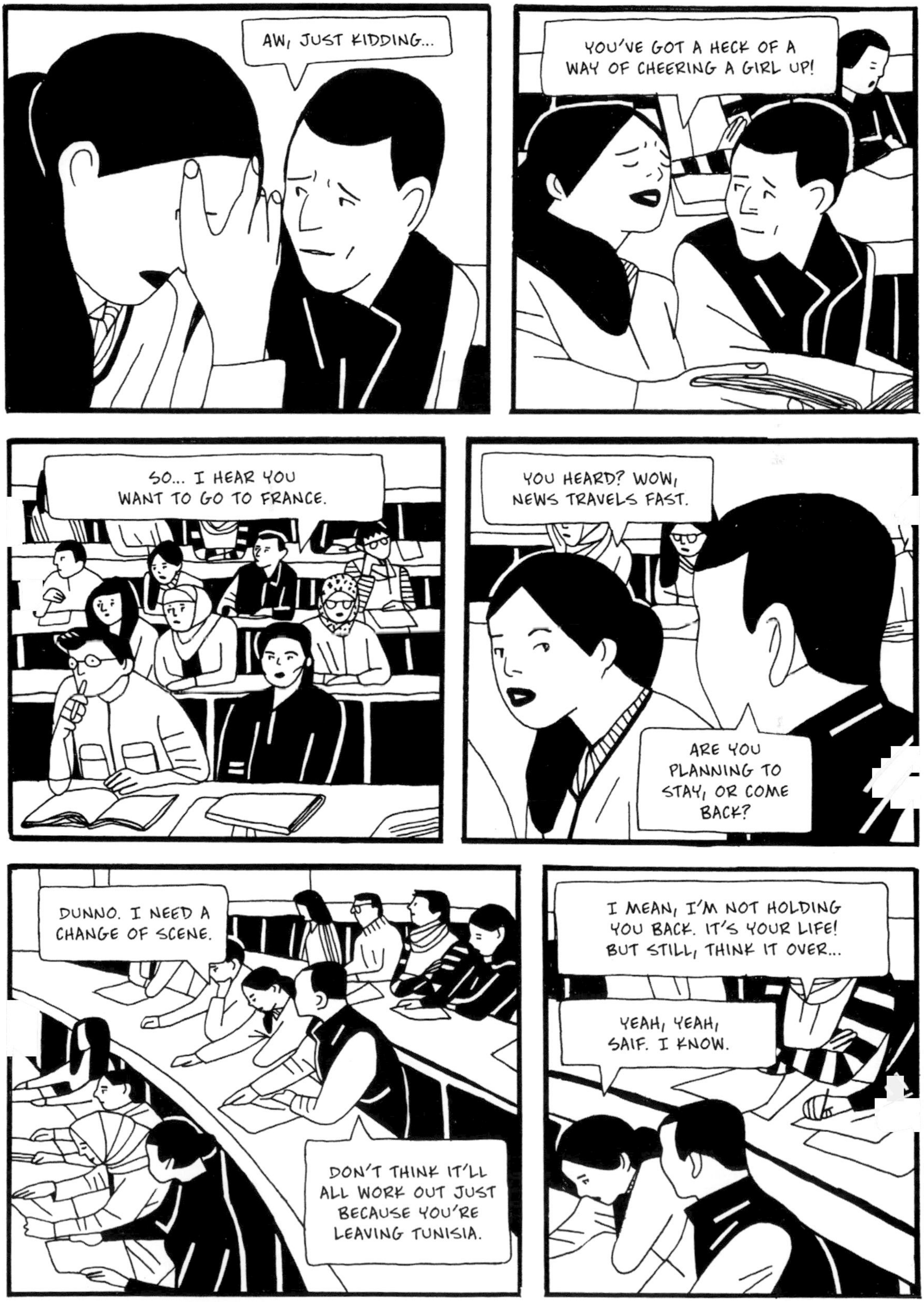
AW, JUST KIDDING...
YOU'VE GOT A HECK OF A WAY OF CHEERING A GIRL UP!
SO... I HEAR YOU WANT TO GO TO FRANCE.
YOU HEARD? WOW, NEWS TRAVELS FAST.
ARE YOU PLANNING TO STAY, OR COME BACK?
DUNNO. I NEED A CHANGE OF SCENE.
DON'T THINK IT'LL ALL WORK OUT JUST BECAUSE YOU'RE LEAVING TUNISIA.
I MEAN, I'M NOT HOLDING YOU BACK. IT'S YOUR LIFE! BUT STILL, THINK IT OVER...
YEAH, YEAH, SAIF. I KNOW.

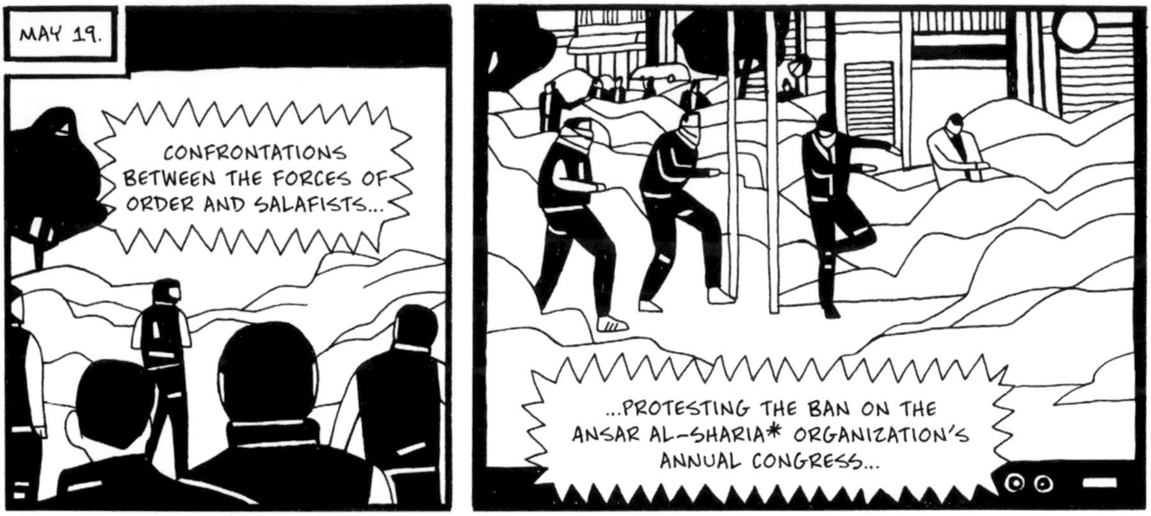
MAY 19.
CONFRONTATIONS BETWEEN THE FORCES OF ORDER AND SALAFISTS...
...PROTESTING THE BAN ON THE ANSAR AL-SHARIA* ORGANIZATION'S ANNUAL CONGRESS...

* SALAFIST ISLAMIST MILITIA GROUP

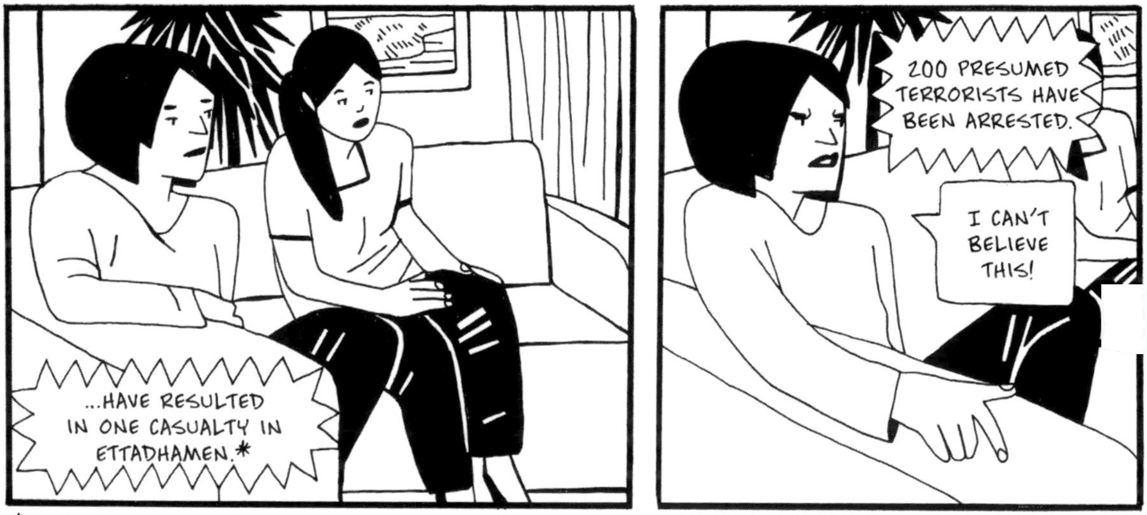
...HAVE RESULTED IN ONE CASUALTY IN ETTADHAMEN.*
200 PRESUMED TERRORISTS HAVE BEEN ARRESTED.
I CAN'T BELIEVE THIS!

* A WORKING-CLASS BOROUGH OF GREATER TUNIS

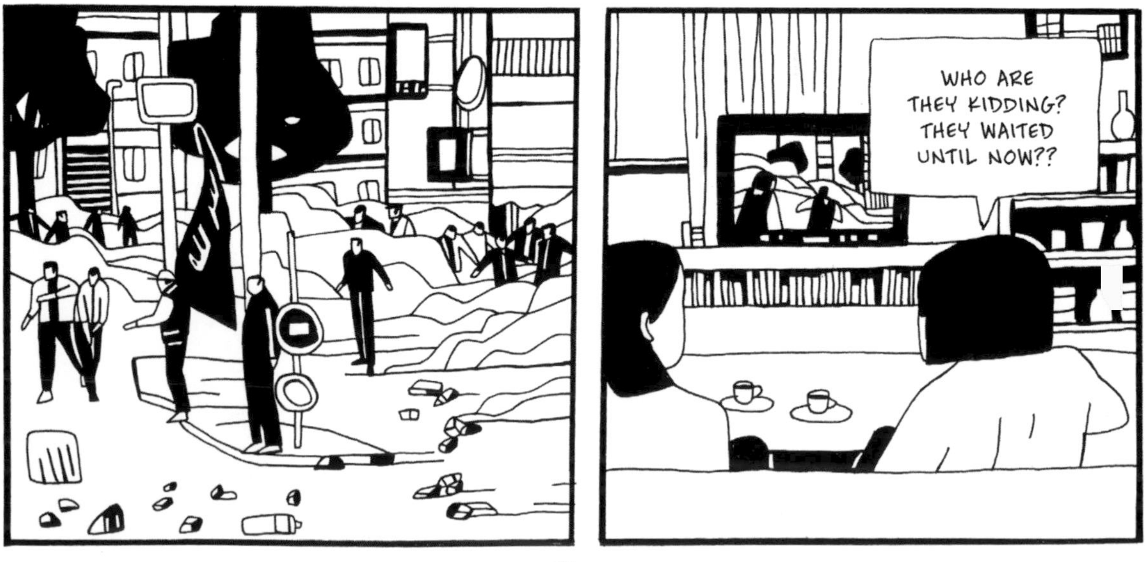
WHO ARE THEY KIDDING? THEY WAITED UNTIL NOW??

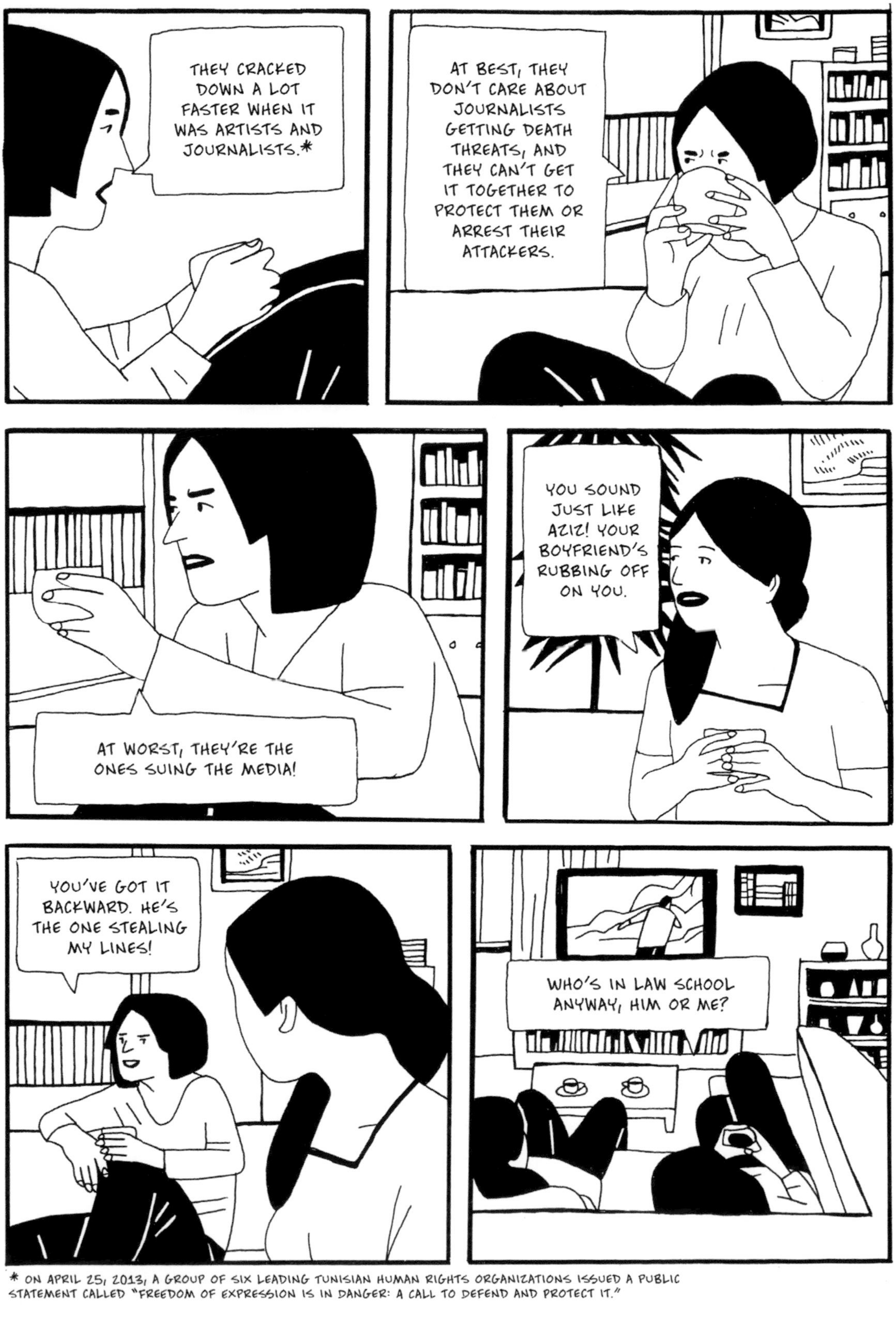
THEY CRACKED DOWN A LOT FASTER WHEN IT WAS ARTISTS AND JOURNALISTS.*
AT BEST, THEY DON'T CARE ABOUT JOURNALISTS GETTING DEATH THREATS, AND THEY CAN'T GET IT TOGETHER TO PROTECT THEM OR ARREST THEIR ATTACKERS.
AT WORST, THEY'RE THE ONES SUING THE MEDIA!
YOU SOUND JUST LIKE AZIZ! YOUR BOYFRIEND'S RUBBING OFF ON YOU.
YOU'VE GOT IT BACKWARD. HE'S THE ONE STEALING MY LINES!
WHO'S IN LAW SCHOOL ANYWAY, HIM OR ME?

* ON APRIL 25, 2013, A GROUP OF SIX LEADING TUNISIAN HUMAN RIGHTS ORGANIZATIONS ISSUED A PUBLIC STATEMENT CALLED "FREEDOM OF EXPRESSION IS IN DANGER: A CALL TO DEFEND AND PROTECT IT."

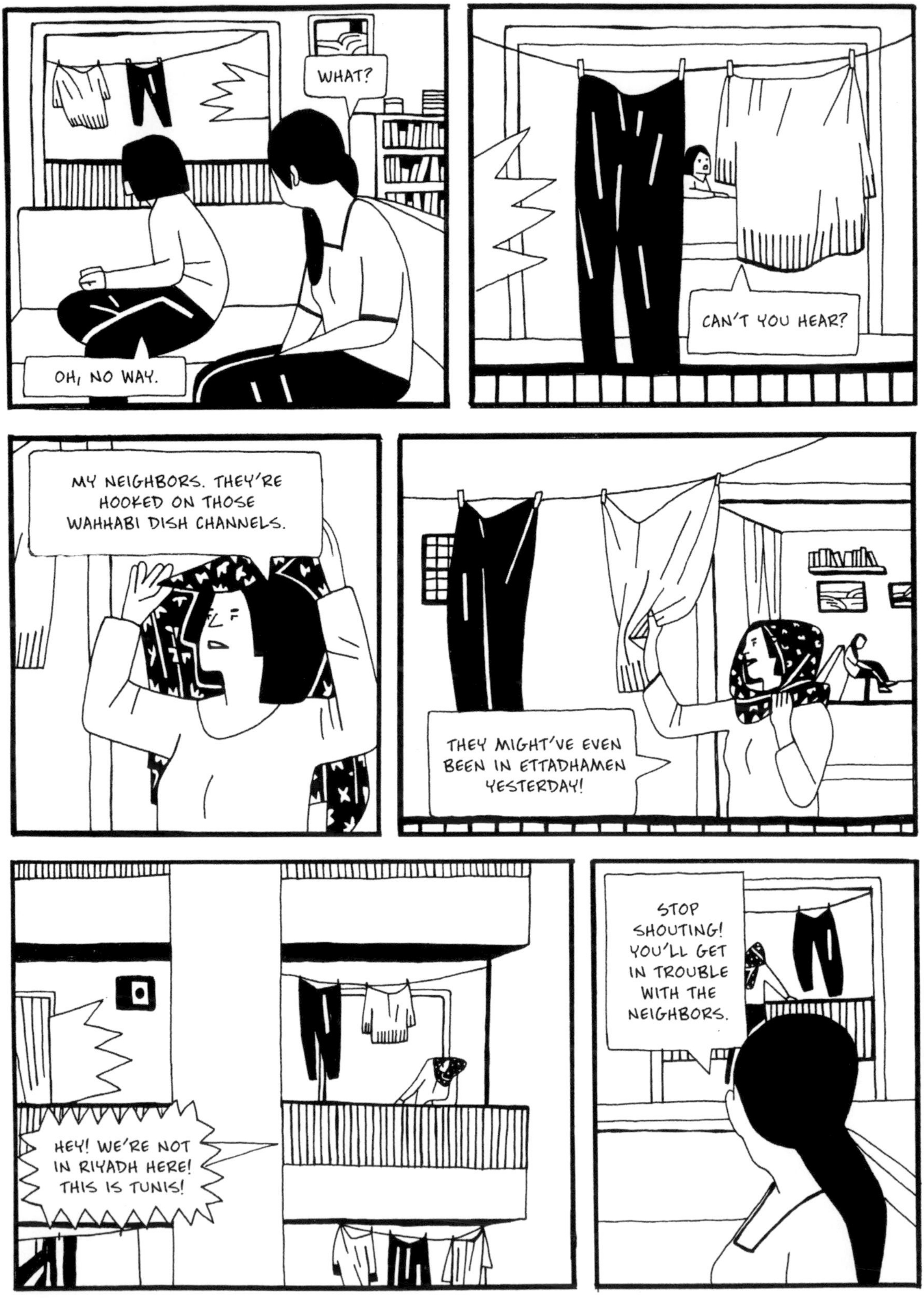
WHAT?
OH, NO WAY.
CAN'T YOU HEAR?
MY NEIGHBORS. THEY'RE HOOKED ON THOSE WAHHABI DISH CHANNELS.
THEY MIGHT'VE EVEN BEEN IN ETTADHAMEN YESTERDAY!
HEY! WE'RE NOT IN RIYADH HERE! THIS IS TUNIS!
STOP SHOUTING! YOU'LL GET IN TROUBLE WITH THE NEIGHBORS.

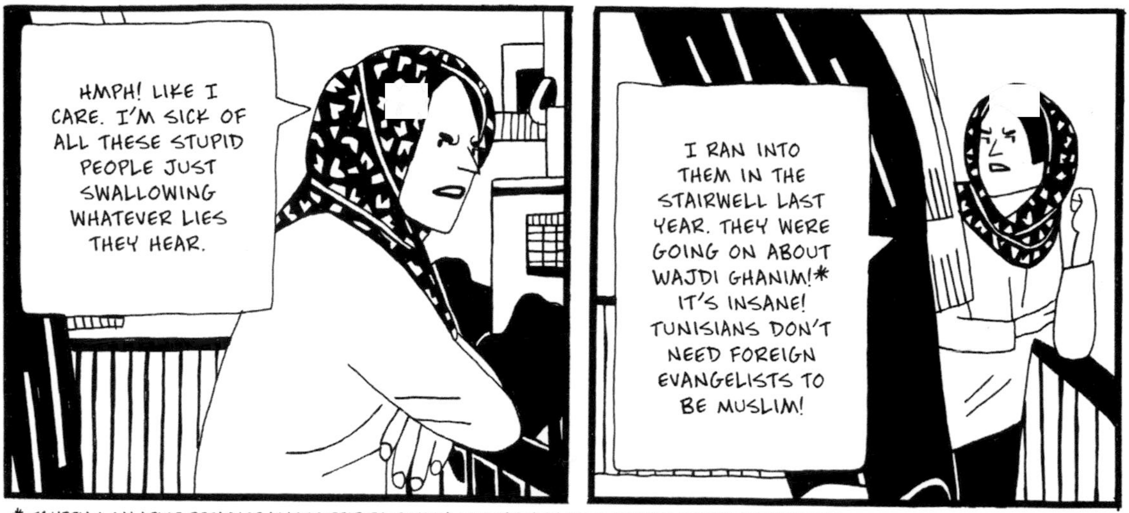
HMPH! LIKE I CARE. I'M SICK OF ALL THESE STUPID PEOPLE JUST SWALLOWING WHATEVER LIES THEY HEAR.
I RAN INTO THEM IN THE STAIRWELL LAST YEAR. THEY WERE GOING ON ABOUT WAJDI GHANIM!* IT'S INSANE! TUNISIANS DON'T NEED FOREIGN EVANGELISTS TO BE MUSLIM!

* EGYPTIAN SALAFIST PREACHER WHOSE TRIP TO TUNISIA IN FEBRUARY 2012 STIRRED GREAT CONTROVERSY

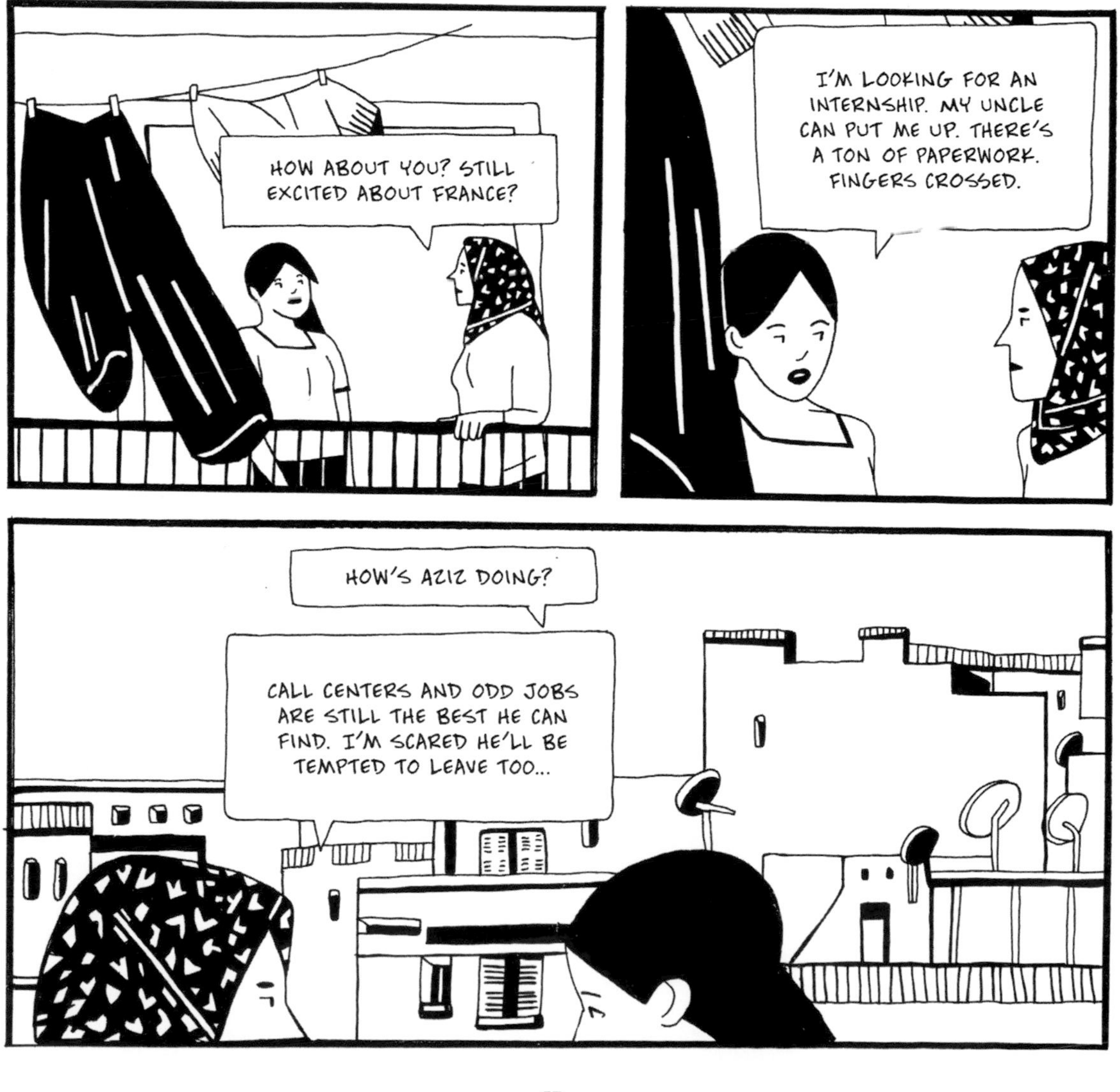
HOW ABOUT YOU? STILL EXCITED ABOUT FRANCE?
I'M LOOKING FOR AN INTERNSHIP. MY UNCLE CAN PUT ME UP. THERE'S A TON OF PAPERWORK. FINGERS CROSSED.
HOW'S AZIZ DOING?
CALL CENTERS AND ODD JOBS ARE STILL THE BEST HE CAN FIND. I'M SCARED HE'LL BE TEMPTED TO LEAVE TOO...

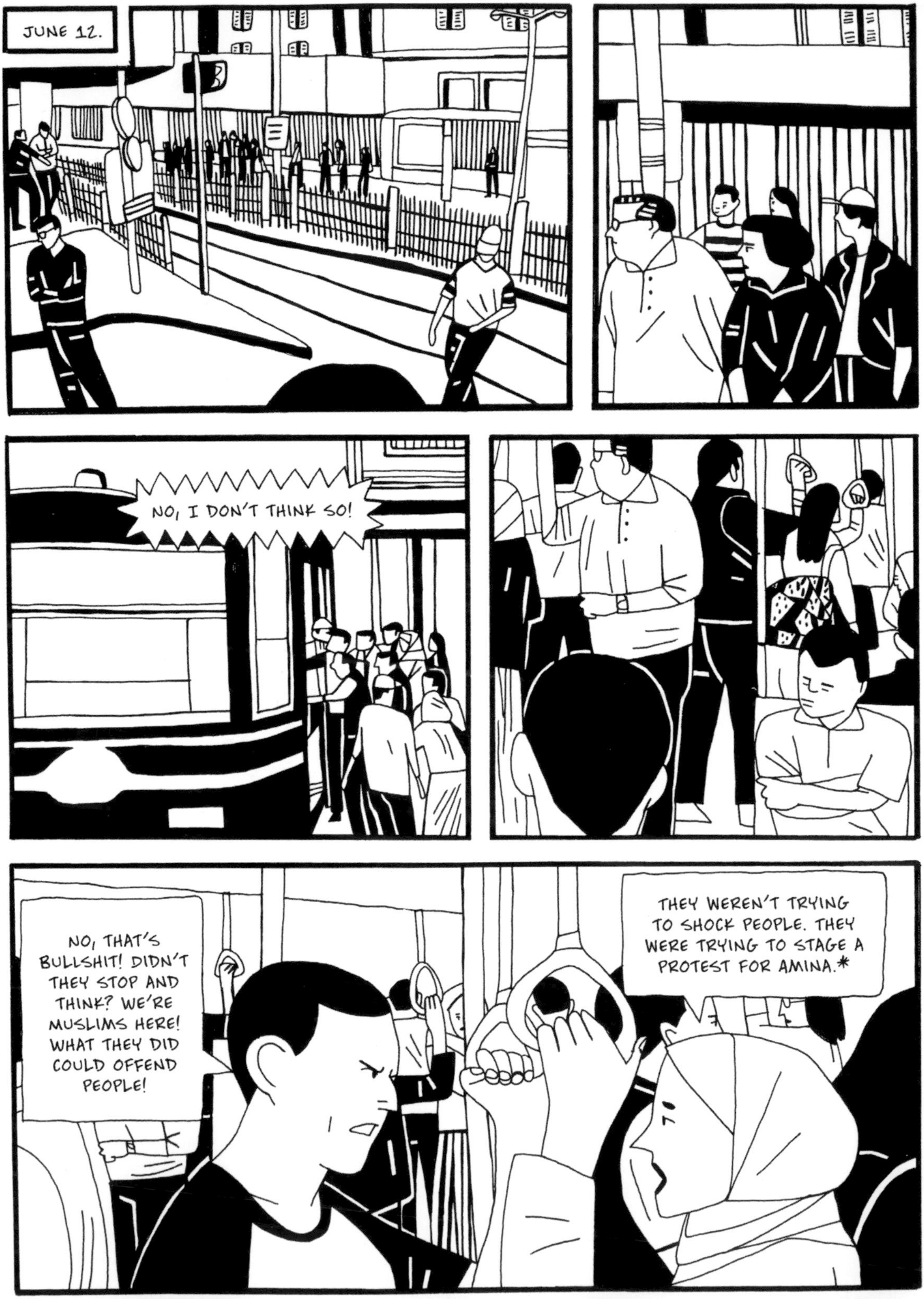
JUNE 12.
NO, I DON'T THINK SO!
NO, THAT'S BULLSHIT! DIDN'T THEY STOP AND THINK? WE'RE MUSLIMS HERE! WHAT THEY DID COULD OFFEND PEOPLE!
THEY WEREN'T TRYING TO SHOCK PEOPLE. THEY WERE TRYING TO STAGE A PROTEST FOR AMINA.*

* THREE MEMBERS OF THE ACTIVIST GROUP FEMEN--TWO FRENCH AND ONE GERMAN--WERE SENTENCED TO 4 MONTHS IN PRISON, BUT WERE FREED IN LATE JUNE. THEY HAD STAGED A TOPLESS PROTEST IN TUNIS ON BEHALF OF FELLOW TUNISIAN ACTIVIST AMINA TYLER

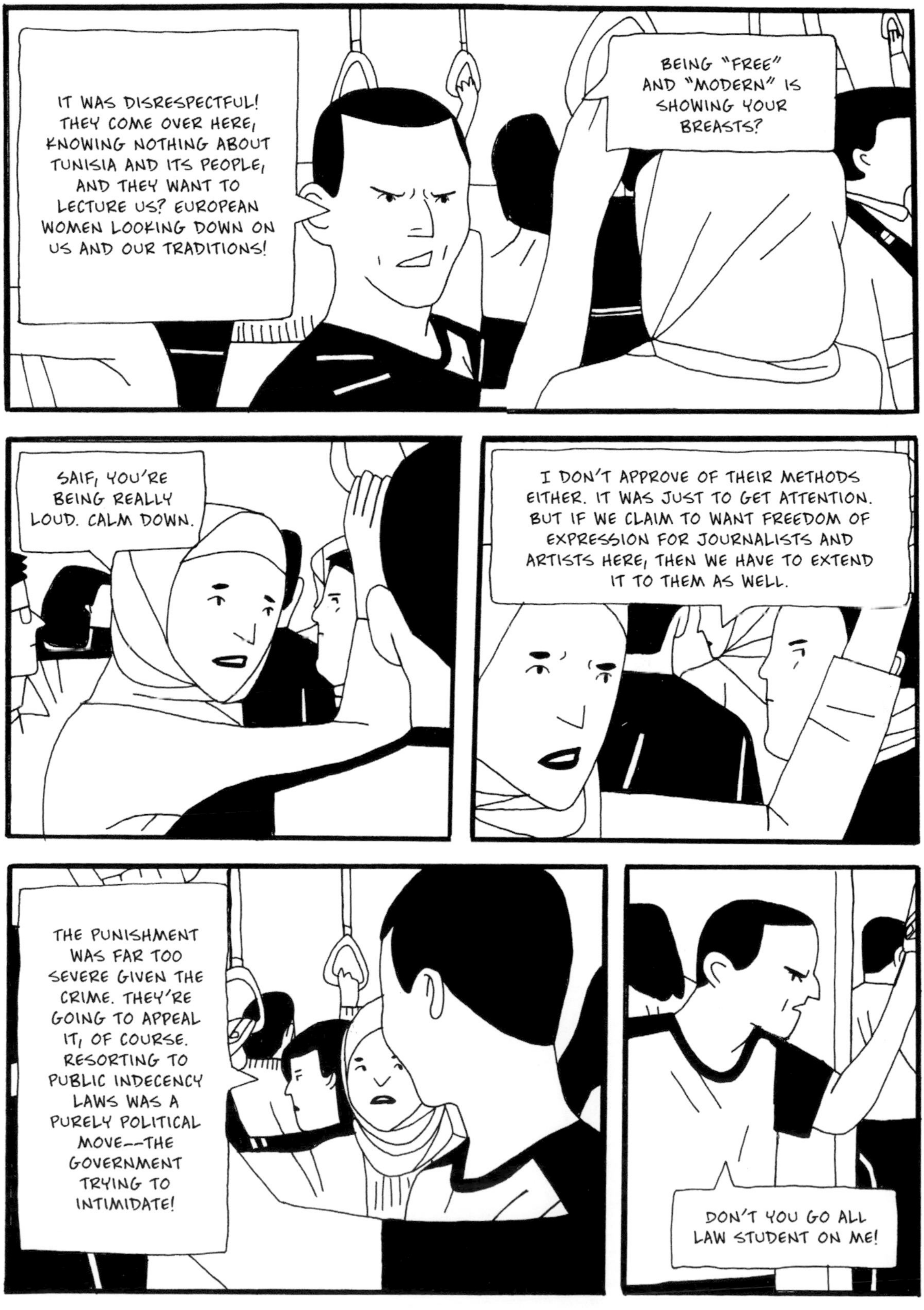
IT WAS DISRESPECTFUL! THEY COME OVER HERE, KNOWING NOTHING ABOUT TUNISIA AND ITS PEOPLE, AND THEY WANT TO LECTURE US? EUROPEAN WOMEN LOOKING DOWN ON US AND OUR TRADITIONS!
BEING "FREE" AND "MODERN" IS SHOWING YOUR BREASTS?
SAIF, YOU'RE BEING REALLY LOUD. CALM DOWN.
I DON'T APPROVE OF THEIR METHODS EITHER. IT WAS JUST TO GET ATTENTION. BUT IF WE CLAIM TO WANT FREEDOM OF EXPRESSION FOR JOURNALISTS AND ARTISTS HERE, THEN WE HAVE TO EXTEND IT TO THEM AS WELL.
THE PUNISHMENT WAS FAR TOO SEVERE GIVEN THE CRIME. THEY'RE GOING TO APPEAL IT, OF COURSE. RESORTING TO PUBLIC INDECENCY LAWS WAS A PURELY POLITICAL MOVE--THE GOVERNMENT TRYING TO INTIMIDATE!
DON'T YOU GO ALL LAW STUDENT ON ME!

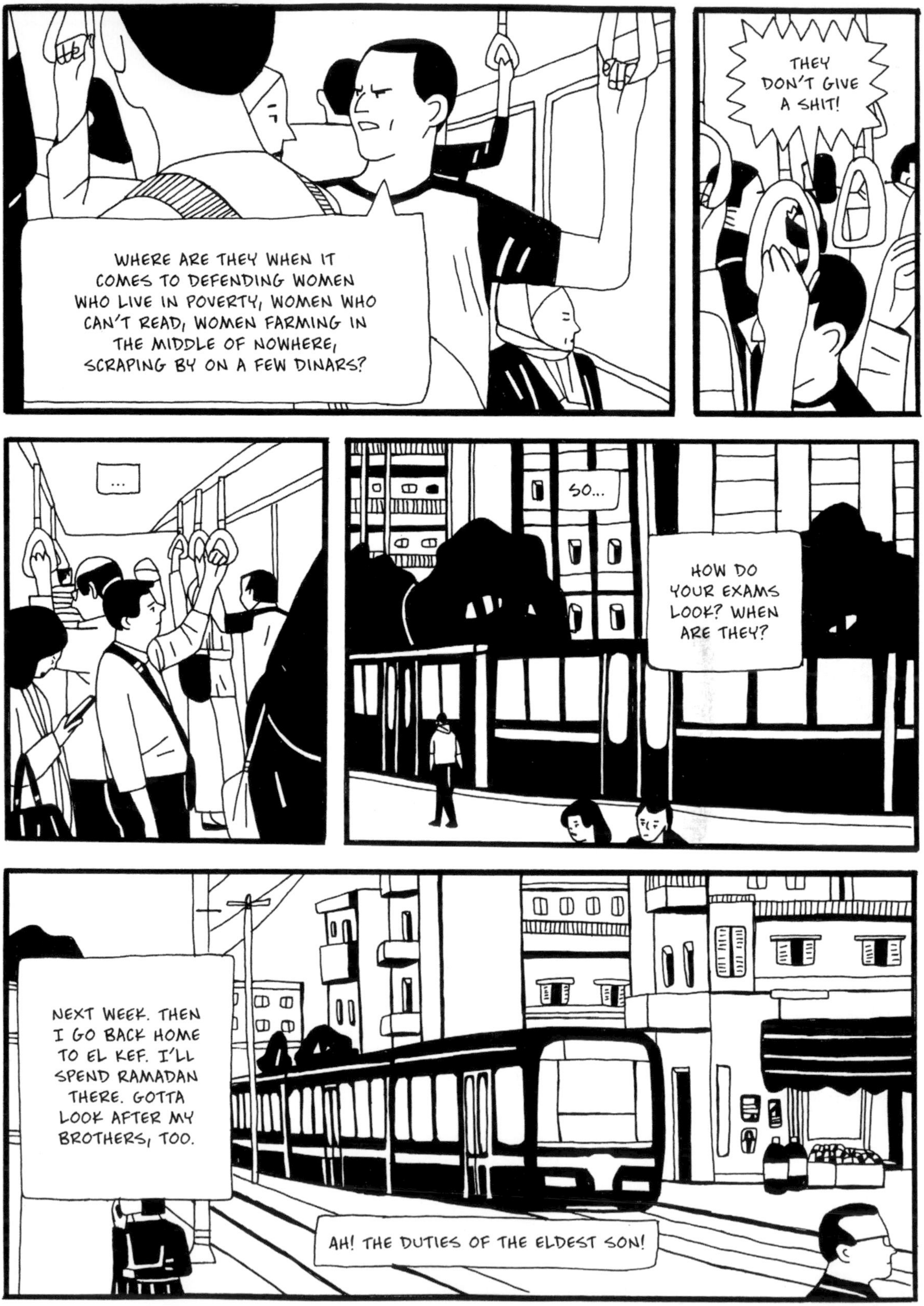

WHERE ARE THEY WHEN IT COMES TO DEFENDING WOMEN WHO LIVE IN POVERTY, WOMEN WHO CAN'T READ, WOMEN FARMING IN THE MIDDLE OF NOWHERE, SCRAPING BY ON A FEW DINARS?
THEY DON'T GIVE A SHIT!
...
SO...
HOW DO YOUR EXAMS LOOK? WHEN ARE THEY?
NEXT WEEK. THEN I GO BACK HOME TO EL KEF. I'LL SPEND RAMADAN THERE. GOTTA LOOK AFTER MY BROTHERS, TOO.
AH! THE DUTIES OF THE ELDEST SON!

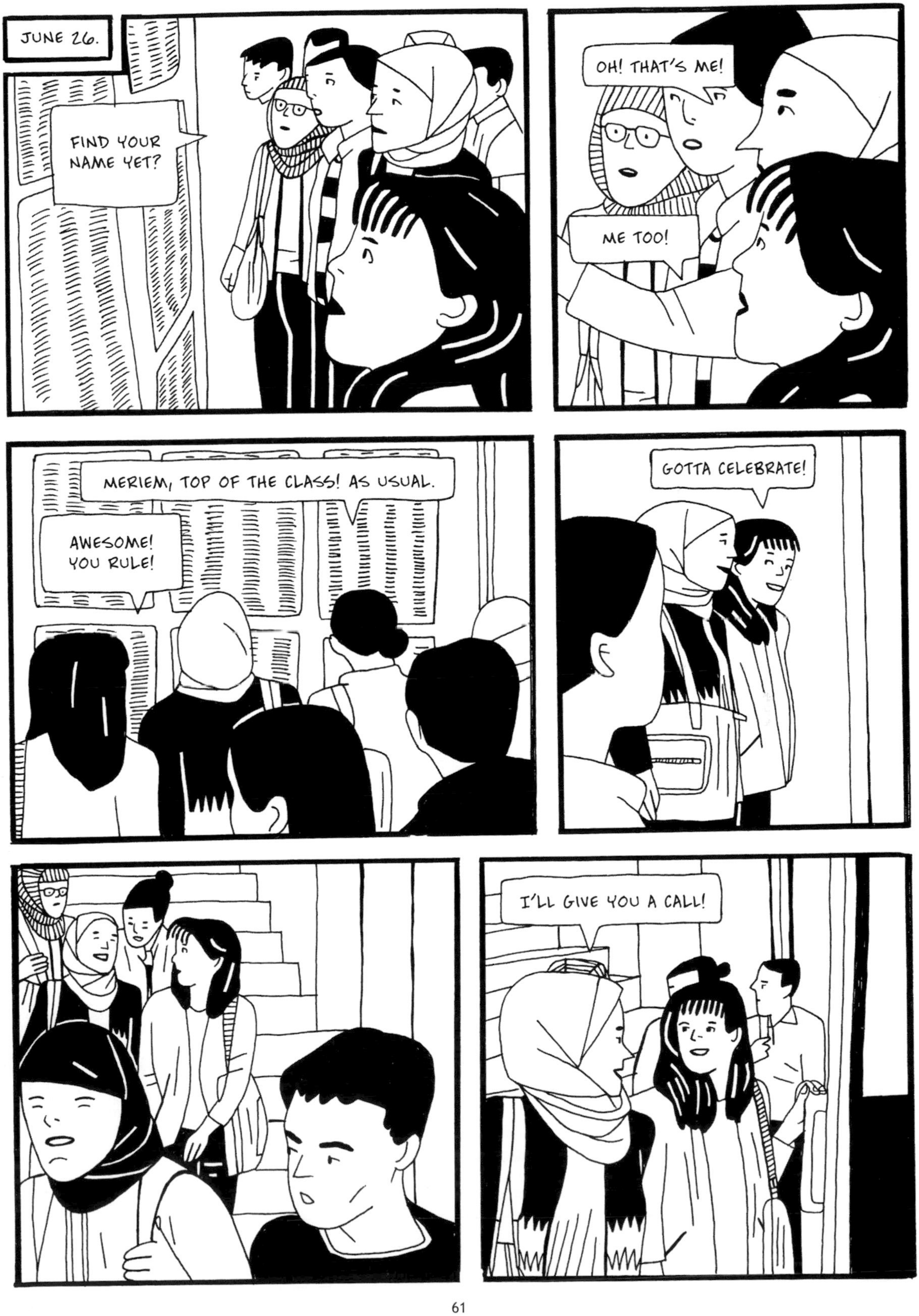
JUNE 26.
FIND YOUR NAME YET?
OH! THAT'S ME!
ME TOO!
MERIEM, TOP OF THE CLASS! AS USUAL.
AWESOME! YOU RULE!
GOTTA CELEBRATE!
I'LL GIVE YOU A CALL!

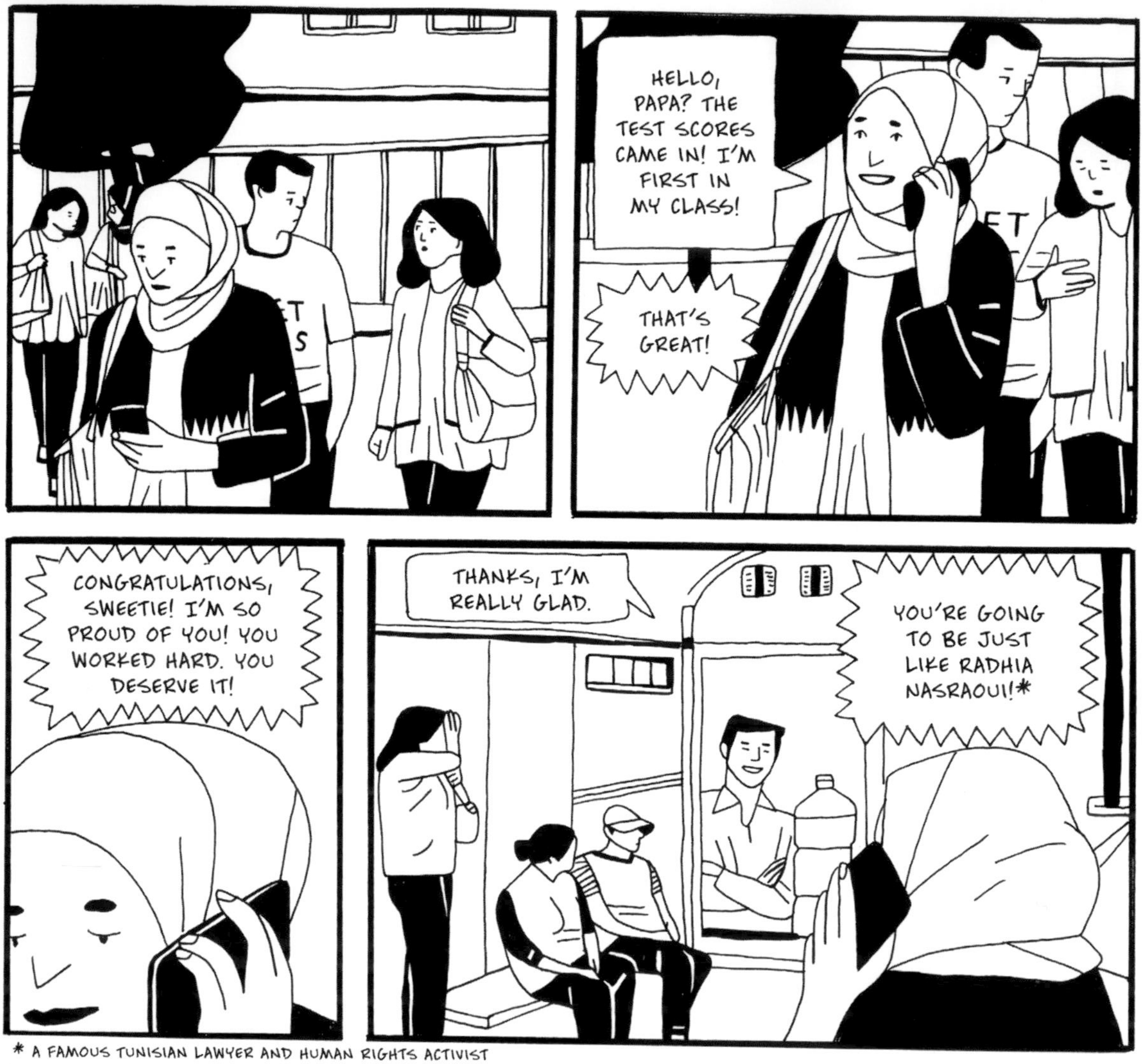
HELLO, PAPA? THE TEST SCORES CAME IN! I'M FIRST IN MY CLASS!
THAT'S GREAT!
CONGRATULATIONS, SWEETIE! I'M SO PROUD OF YOU! YOU WORKED HARD. YOU DESERVE IT!
THANKS, I'M REALLY GLAD.
YOU'RE GOING TO BE JUST LIKE RADHIA NASRAOUI!*

* A FAMOUS TUNISIAN LAWYER AND HUMAN RIGHTS ACTIVIST

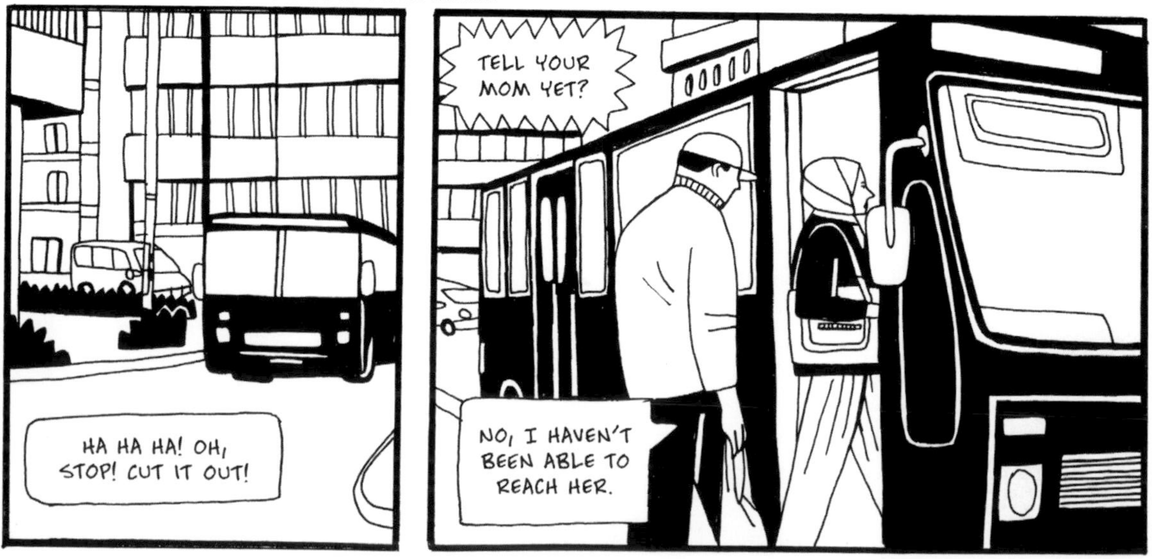
HA HA HA! OH, STOP! CUT IT OUT!
TELL YOUR MOM YET?
NO, I HAVEN'T BEEN ABLE TO REACH HER.

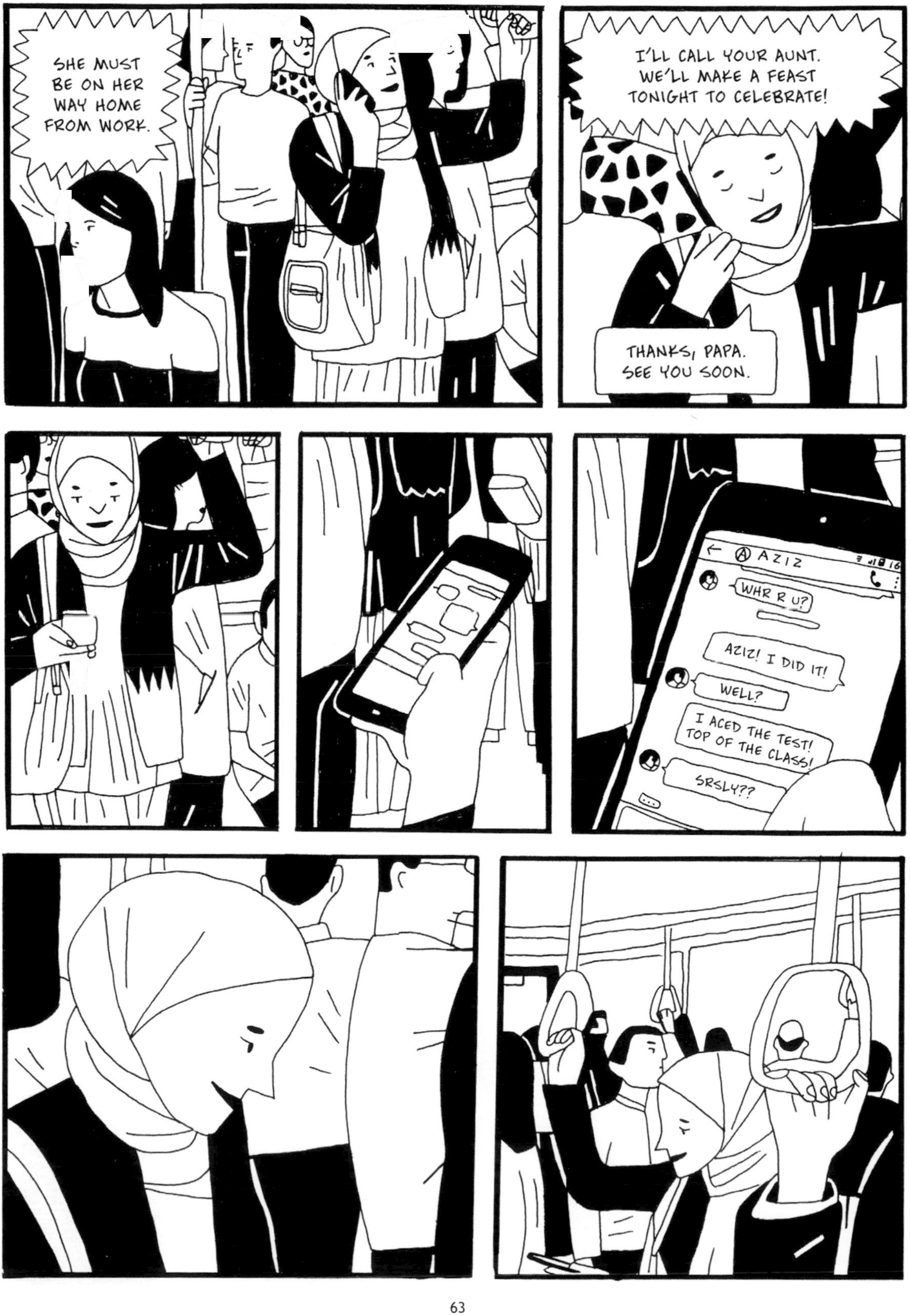
SHE MUST BE ON HER WAY HOME FROM WORK.
I'LL CALL YOUR AUNT. WE'LL MAKE A FEAST TONIGHT TO CELEBRATE!
THANKS, PAPA. SEE YOU SOON.
AZIZ
WHR R U?
AZIZ! I DID IT!
WELL?
I ACED THE TEST! TOP OF THE CLASS!
SRSLY??

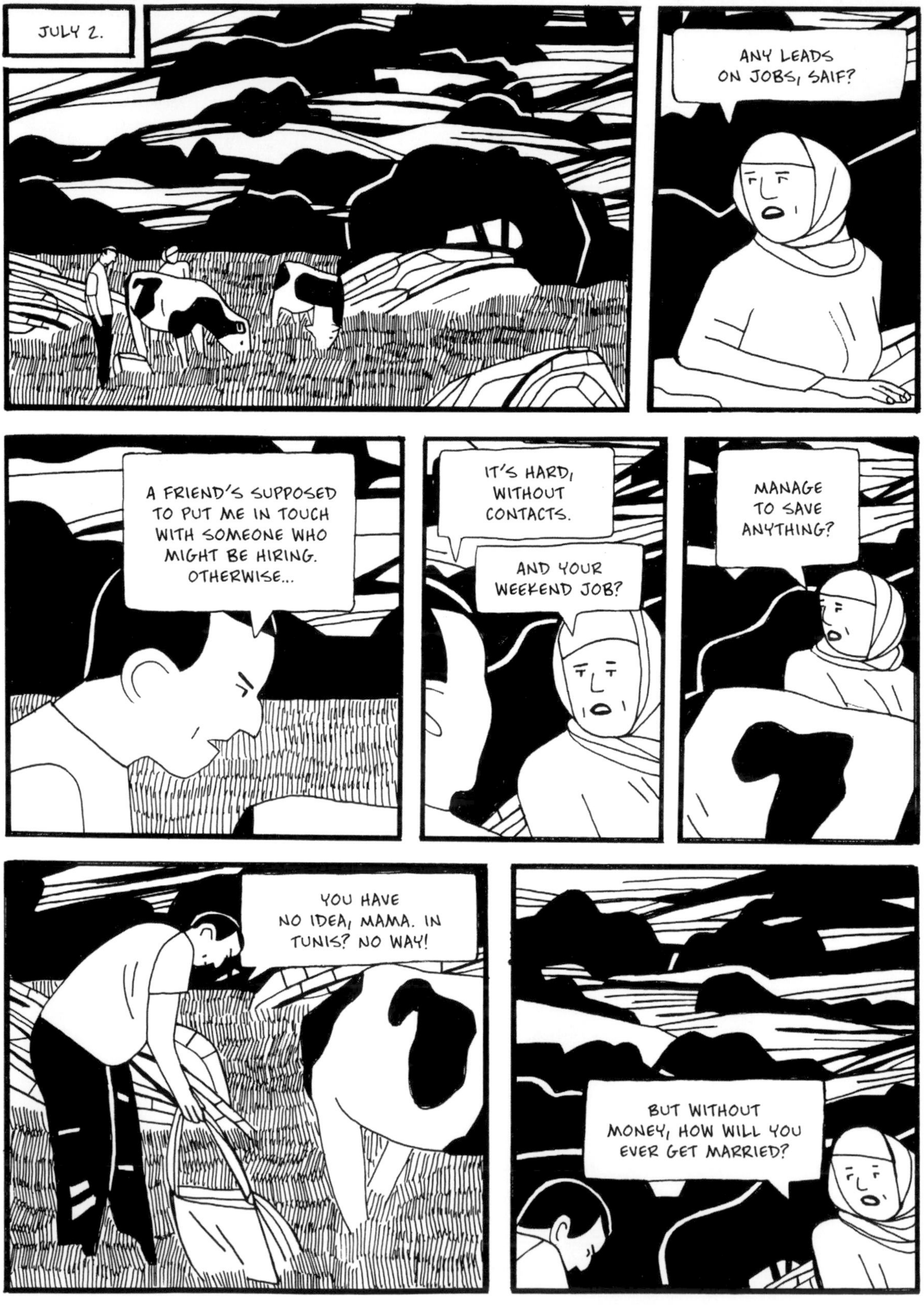
JULY 2.
ANY LEADS ON JOBS, SAIF?
A FRIEND'S SUPPOSED TO PUT ME IN TOUCH WITH SOMEONE WHO MIGHT BE HIRING. OTHERWISE...
IT'S HARD, WITHOUT CONTACTS.
AND YOUR WEEKEND JOB?
MANAGE TO SAVE ANYTHING?
YOU HAVE NO IDEA, MAMA. IN TUNIS? NO WAY!
BUT WITHOUT MONEY, HOW WILL YOU EVER GET MARRIED?

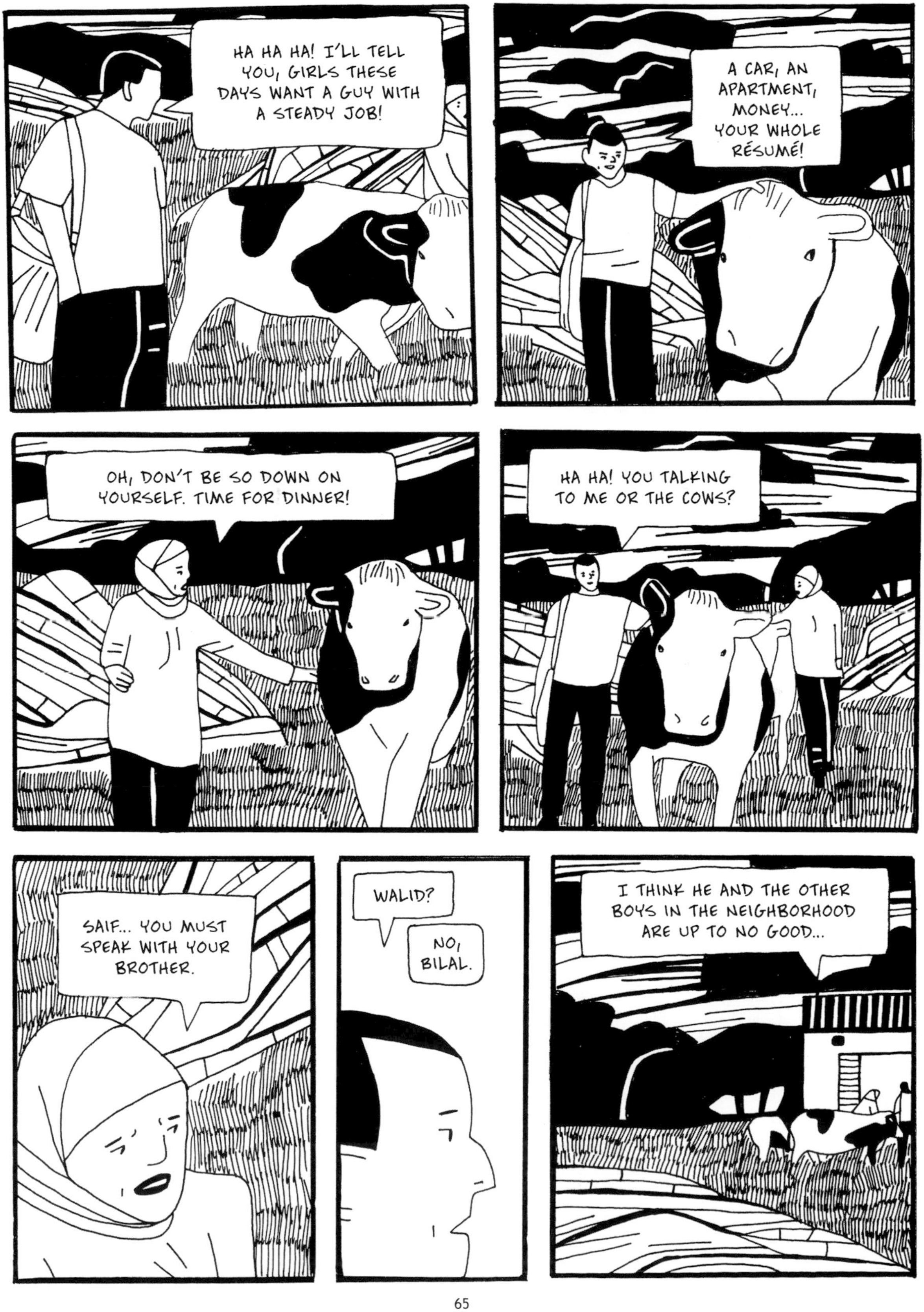
HA HA HA! I'LL TELL YOU, GIRLS THESE DAYS WANT A GUY WITH A STEADY JOB!
A CAR, AN APARTMENT, MONEY... YOUR WHOLE RÉSUMÉ!
OH, DON'T BE SO DOWN ON YOURSELF. TIME FOR DINNER!
HA HA! YOU TALKING TO ME OR THE COWS?
SAIF... YOU MUST SPEAK WITH YOUR BROTHER.
WALID?
NO, BILAL.
I THINK HE AND THE OTHER BOYS IN THE NEIGHBORHOOD ARE UP TO NO GOOD...

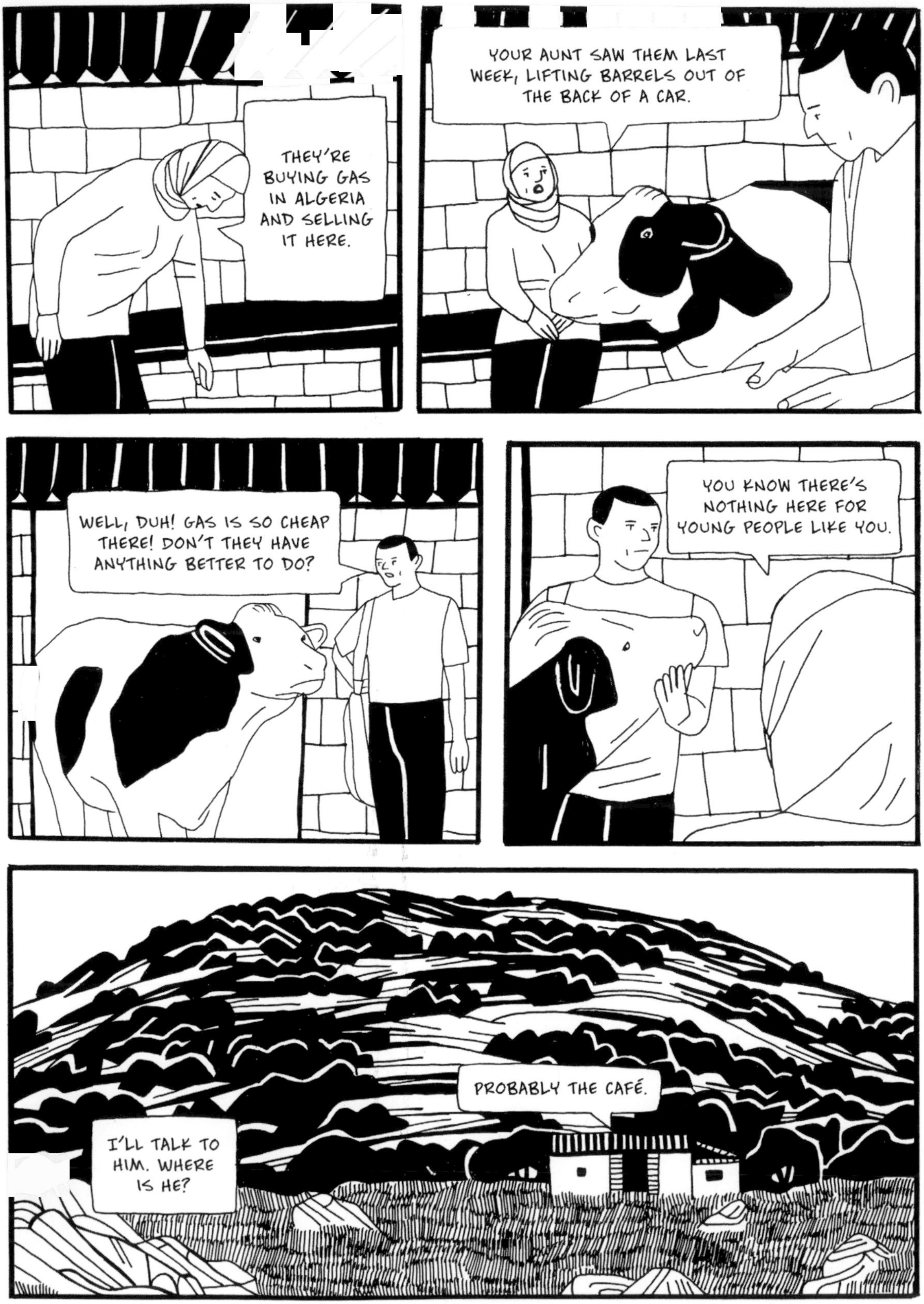
THEY'RE BUYING GAS IN ALGERIA AND SELLING IT HERE.
YOUR AUNT SAW THEM LAST WEEK, LIFTING BARRELS OUT OF THE BACK OF A CAR.
WELL, DUH! GAS IS SO CHEAP THERE! DON'T THEY HAVE ANYTHING BETTER TO DO?
YOU KNOW THERE'S NOTHING HERE FOR YOUNG PEOPLE LIKE YOU.
I'LL TALK TO HIM. WHERE IS HE?
PROBABLY THE CAFÉ.

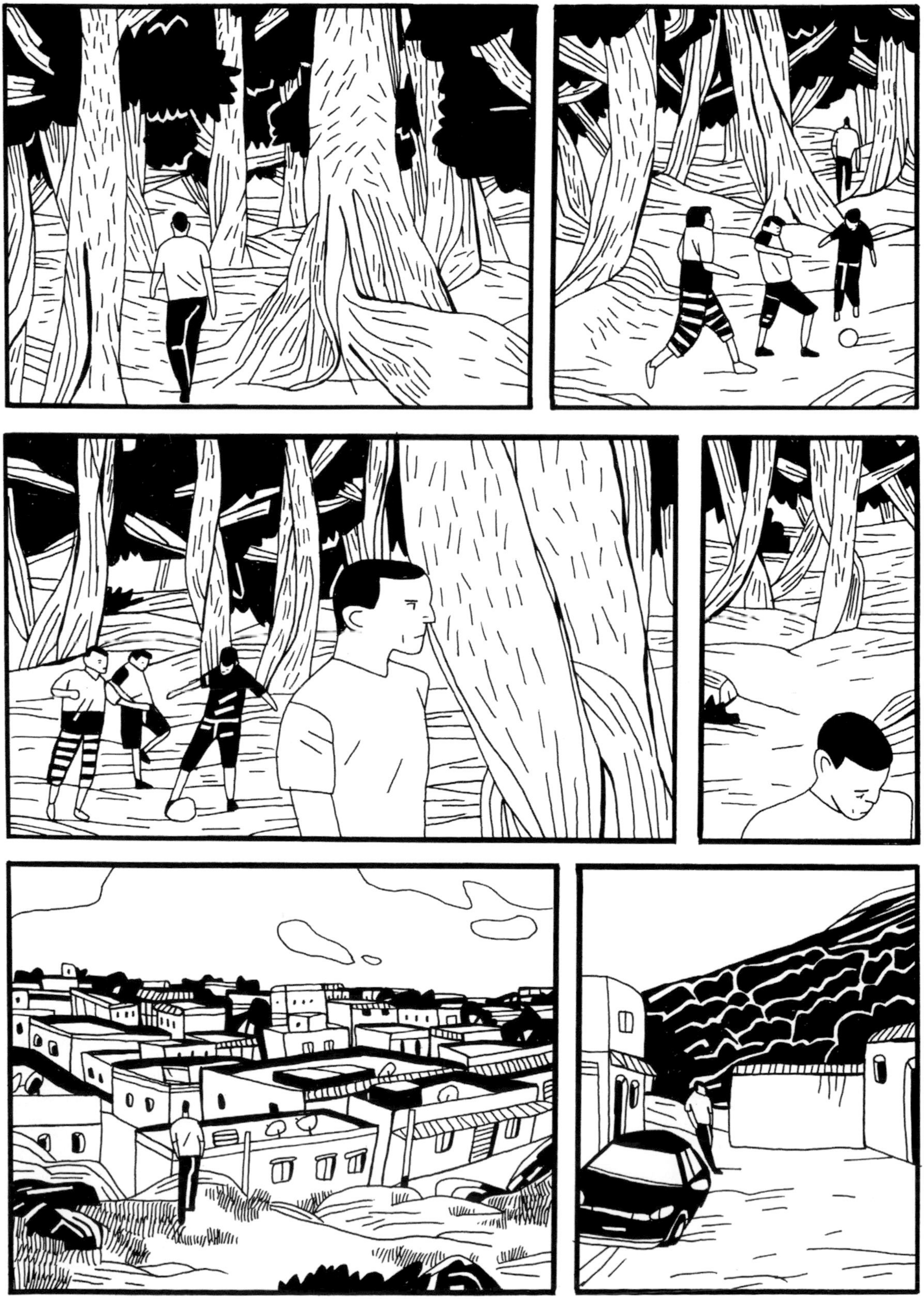

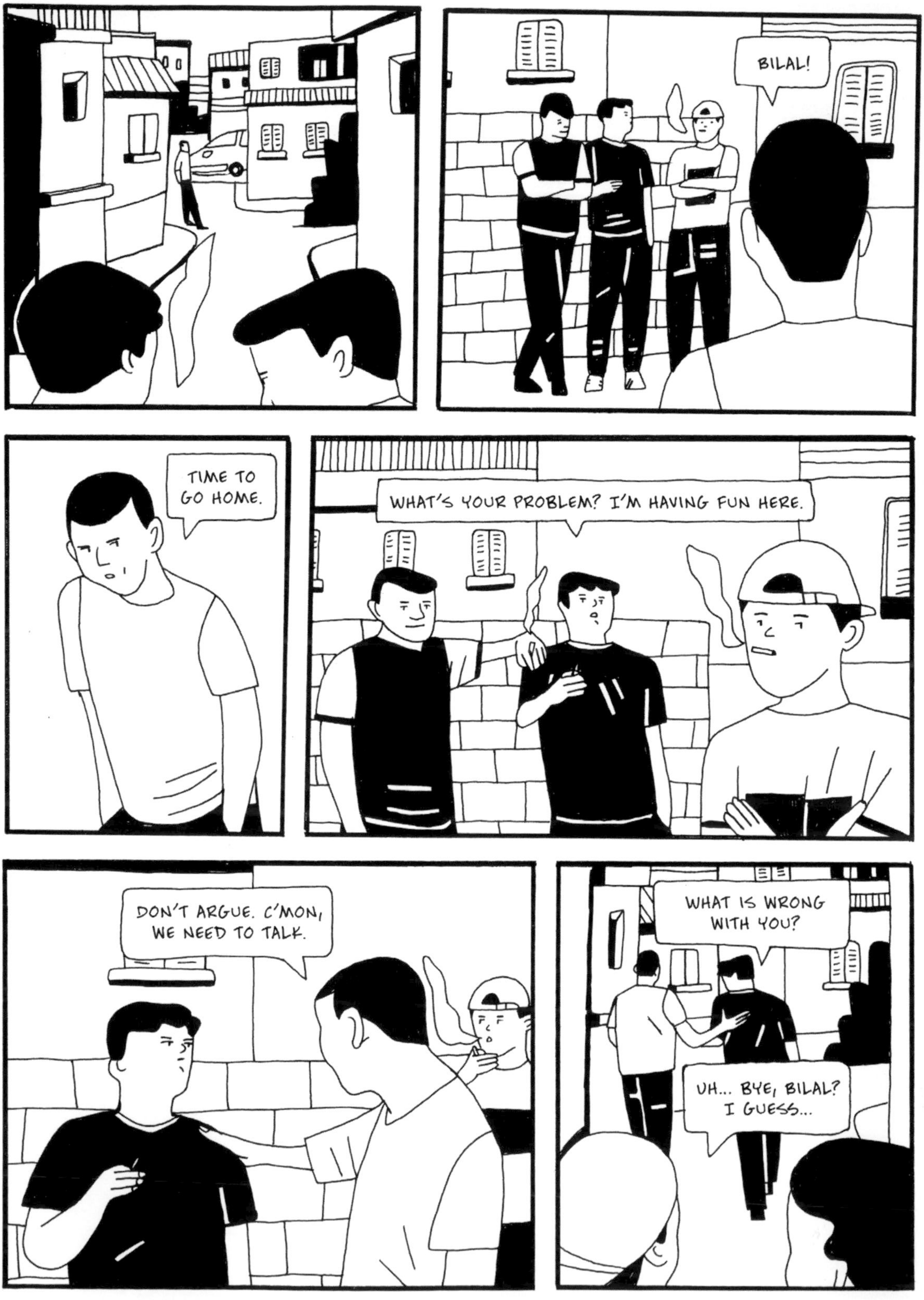
BILAL!
TIME TO GO HOME.
WHAT'S YOUR PROBLEM? I'M HAVING FUN HERE.
DON'T ARGUE. C'MON, WE NEED TO TALK.
WHAT IS WRONG WITH YOU?
UH... BYE, BILAL? I GUESS...

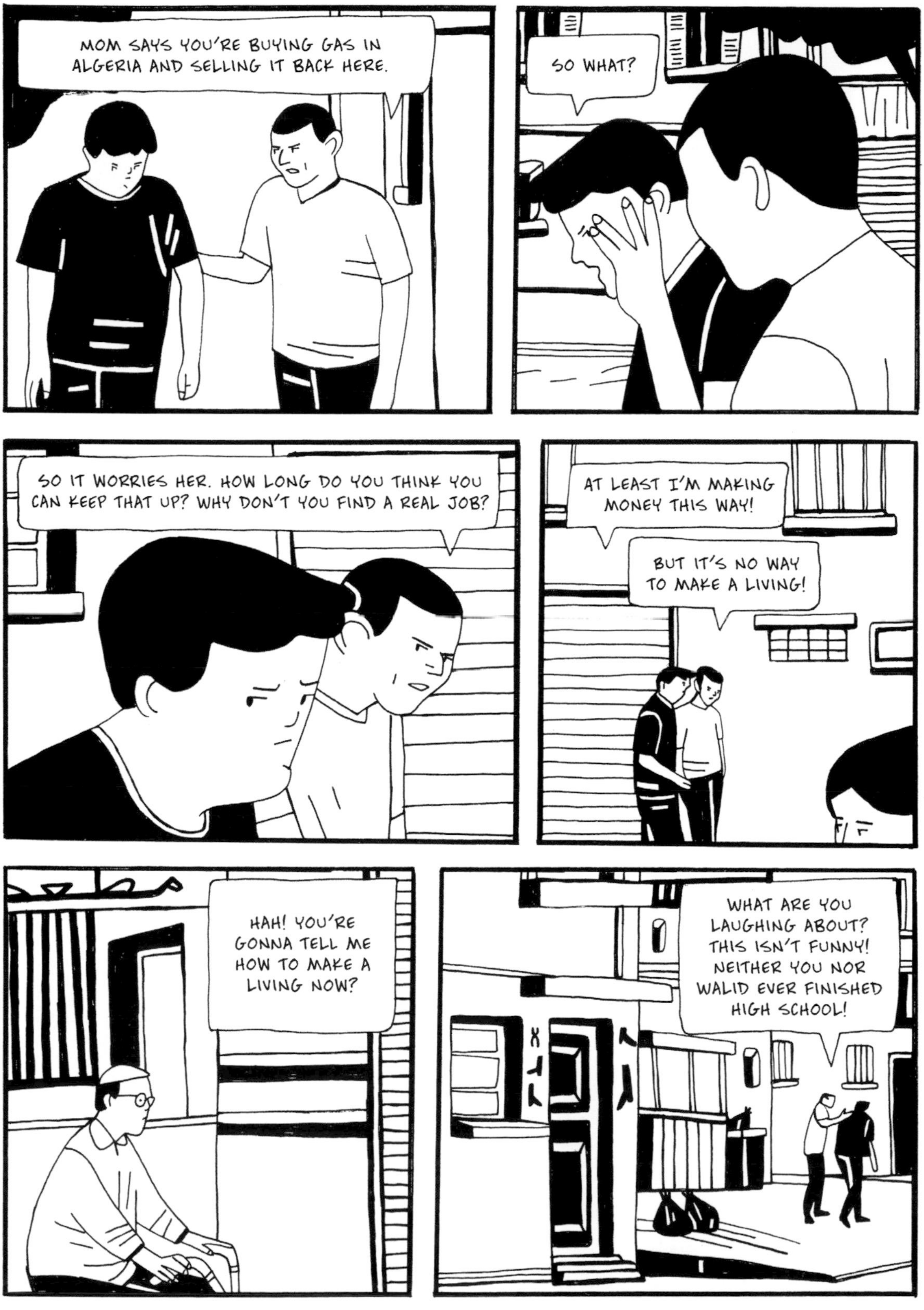
MOM SAYS YOU'RE BUYING GAS IN ALGERIA AND SELLING IT BACK HERE.
SO WHAT?
SO IT WORRIES HER. HOW LONG DO YOU THINK YOU CAN KEEP THAT UP? WHY DON'T YOU FIND A REAL JOB?
AT LEAST I'M MAKING MONEY THIS WAY!
BUT IT'S NO WAY TO MAKE A LIVING!
HAH! YOU'RE GONNA TELL ME HOW TO MAKE A LIVING NOW?
WHAT ARE YOU LAUGHING ABOUT? THIS ISN'T FUNNY! NEITHER YOU NOR WALID EVER FINISHED HIGH SCHOOL!

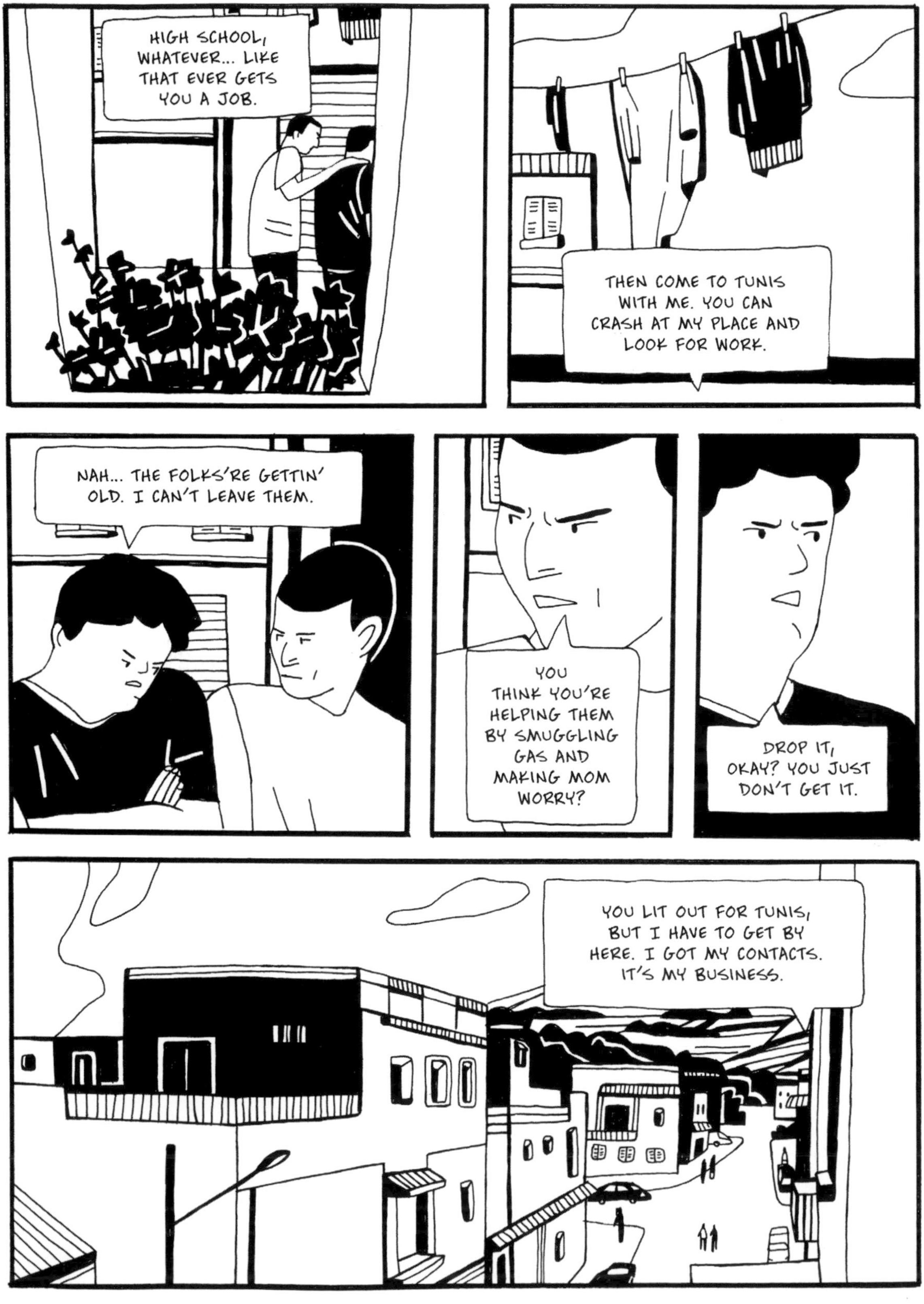
HIGH SCHOOL, WHATEVER... LIKE THAT EVER GETS YOU A JOB.
THEN COME TO TUNIS WITH ME. YOU CAN CRASH AT MY PLACE AND LOOK FOR WORK.
NAH... THE FOLKS'RE GETTIN' OLD. I CAN'T LEAVE THEM.
YOU THINK YOU'RE HELPING THEM BY SMUGGLING GAS AND MAKING MOM WORRY?
DROP IT, OKAY? YOU JUST DON'T GET IT.
YOU LIT OUT FOR TUNIS, BUT I HAVE TO GET BY HERE. I GOT MY CONTACTS. IT'S MY BUSINESS.

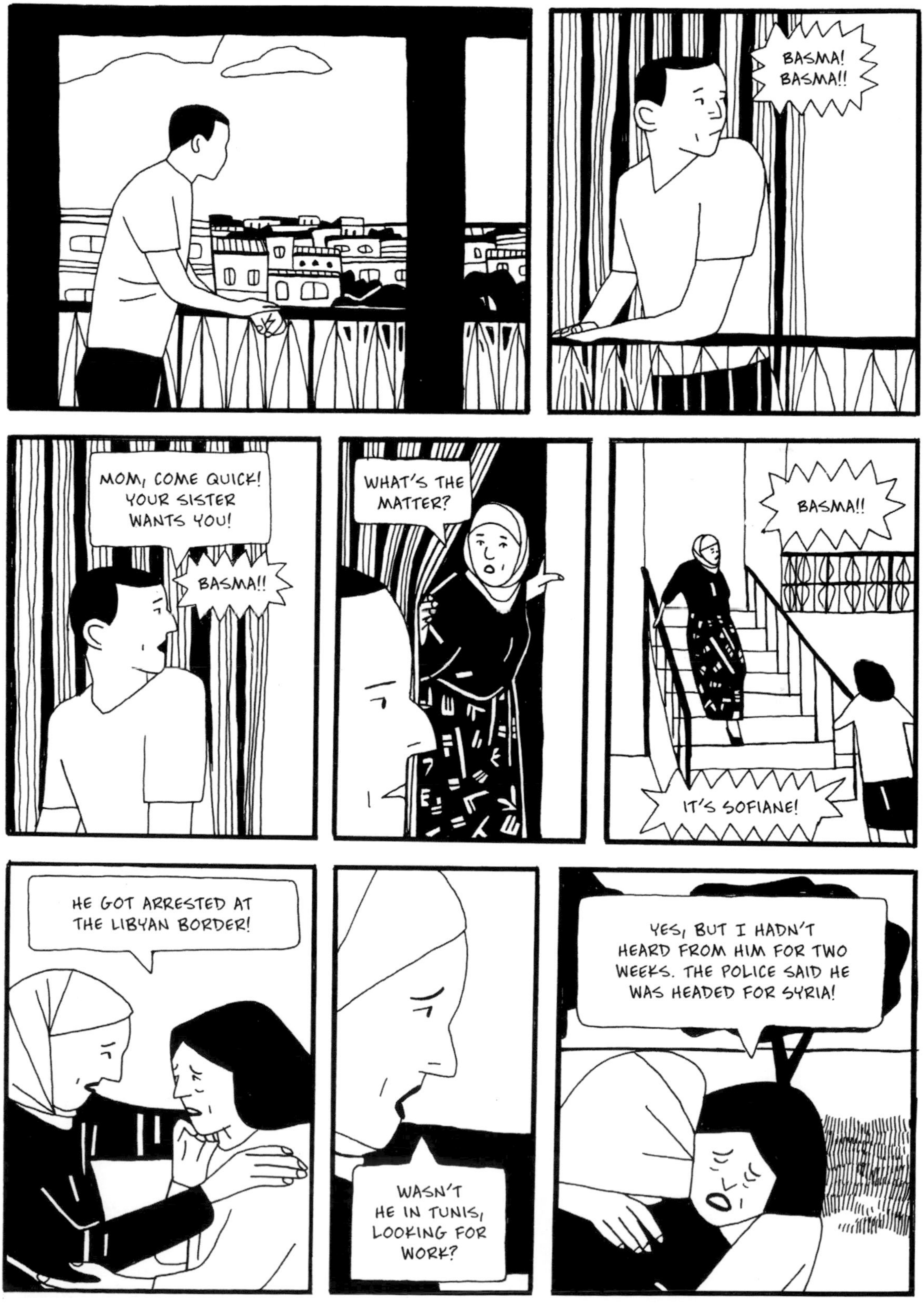
BASMA!
BASMA!!
MOM, COME QUICK! YOUR SISTER WANTS YOU!
BASMA!!
WHAT'S THE MATTER?
BASMA!!
IT'S SOFIANE!
HE GOT ARRESTED AT THE LIBYAN BORDER!
WASN'T HE IN TUNIS, LOOKING FOR WORK?
YES, BUT I HADN'T HEARD FROM HIM FOR TWO WEEKS. THE POLICE SAID HE WAS HEADED FOR SYRIA!

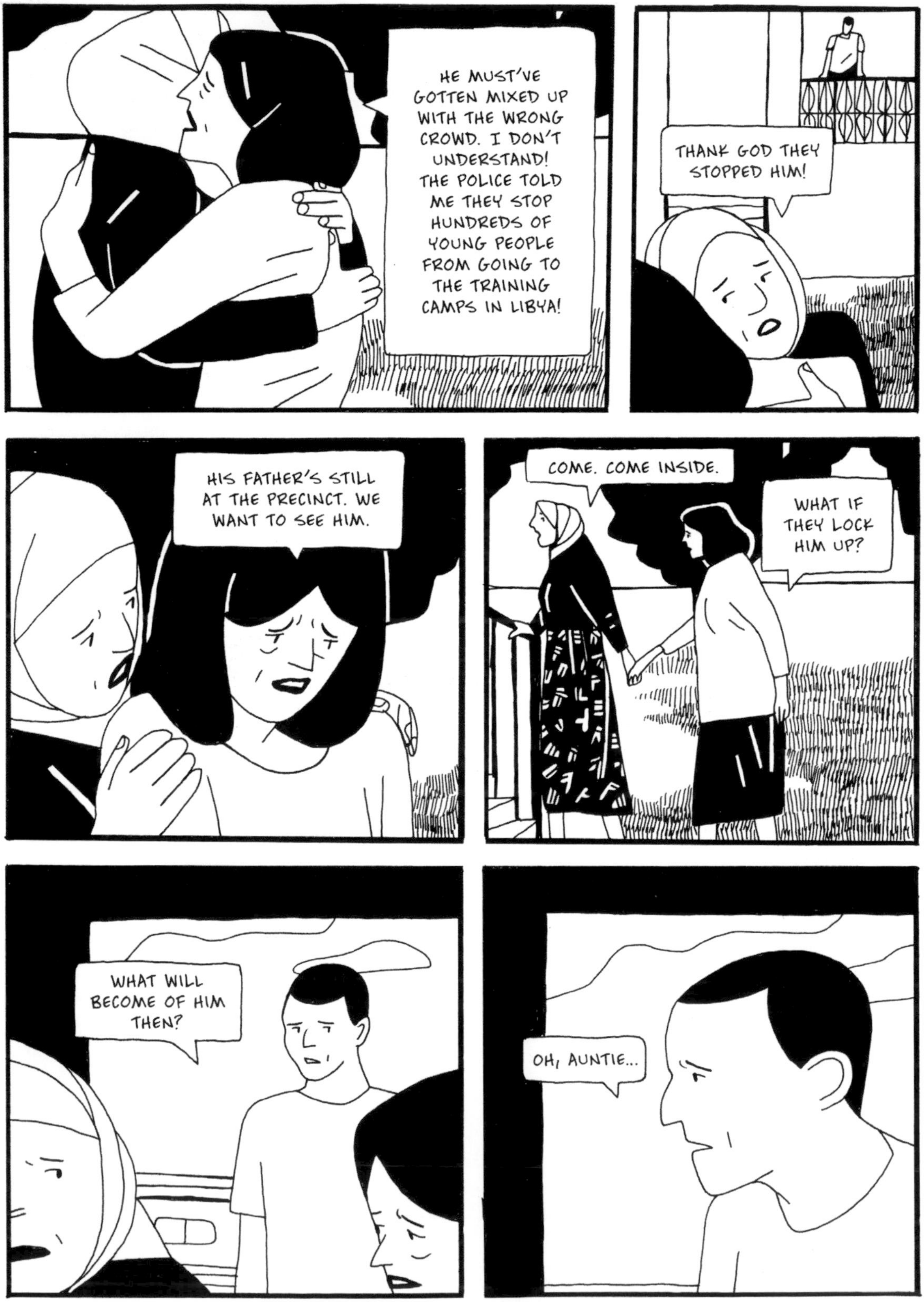
HE MUST'VE GOTTEN MIXED UP WITH THE WRONG CROWD. I DON'T UNDERSTAND! THE POLICE TOLD ME THEY STOP HUNDREDS OF YOUNG PEOPLE FROM GOING TO THE TRAINING CAMPS IN LIBYA!
THANK GOD THEY STOPPED HIM!
HIS FATHER'S STILL AT THE PRECINCT. WE WANT TO SEE HIM.
COME. COME INSIDE.
WHAT IF THEY LOCK HIM UP?
WHAT WILL BECOME OF HIM THEN?
OH, AUNTIE...

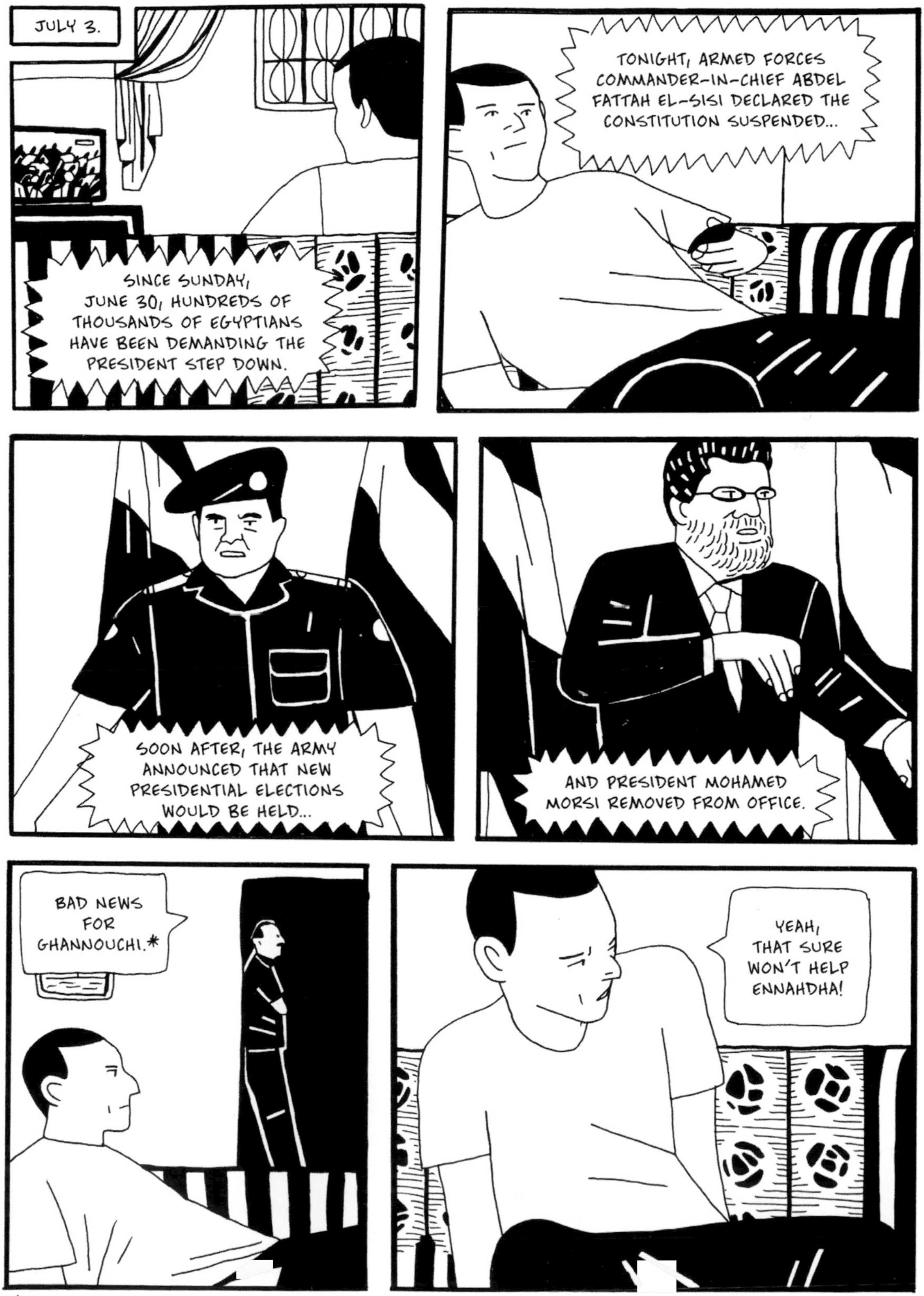
JULY 3.
SINCE SUNDAY, JUNE 30, HUNDREDS OF THOUSANDS OF EGYPTIANS HAVE BEEN DEMANDING THE PRESIDENT STEP DOWN.
TONIGHT, ARMED FORCES COMMANDER-IN-CHIEF ABDEL FATTAH EL-SISI DECLARED THE CONSTITUTION SUSPENDED...
SOON AFTER, THE ARMY ANNOUNCED THAT NEW PRESIDENTIAL ELECTIONS WOULD BE HELD...
AND PRESIDENT MOHAMED MORSI REMOVED FROM OFFICE.
BAD NEWS FOR GHANNOUCHI.*
YEAH, THAT SURE WON'T HELP ENNAHDHA!

* ENNAHDHA CO-FOUNDER

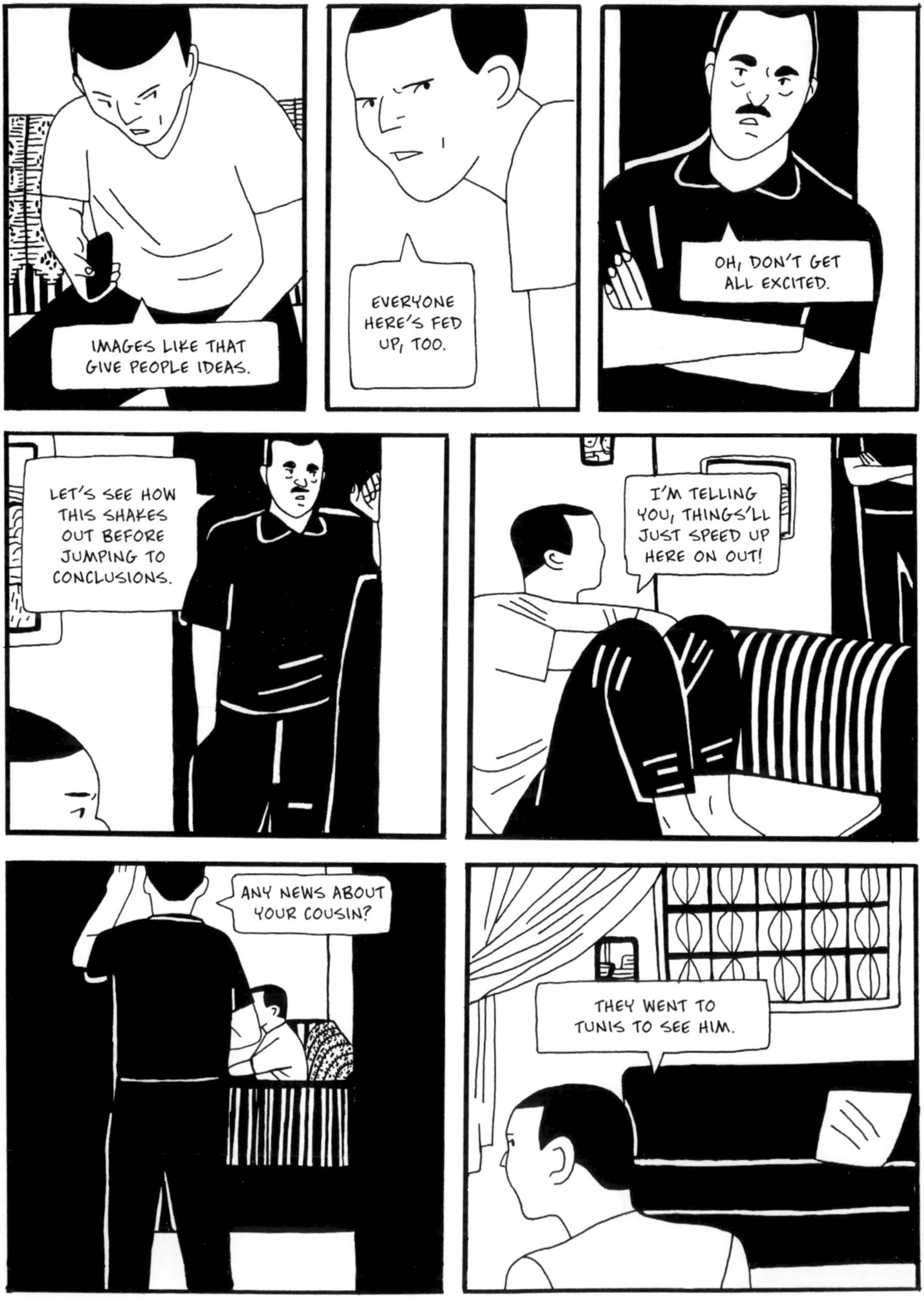
IMAGES LIKE THAT GIVE PEOPLE IDEAS.
EVERYONE HERE'S FED UP, TOO.
OH, DON'T GET ALL EXCITED.
LET'S SEE HOW THIS SHAKES OUT BEFORE JUMPING TO CONCLUSIONS.
I'M TELLING YOU, THINGS'LL JUST SPEED UP HERE ON OUT!
ANY NEWS ABOUT YOUR COUSIN?
THEY WENT TO TUNIS TO SEE HIM.

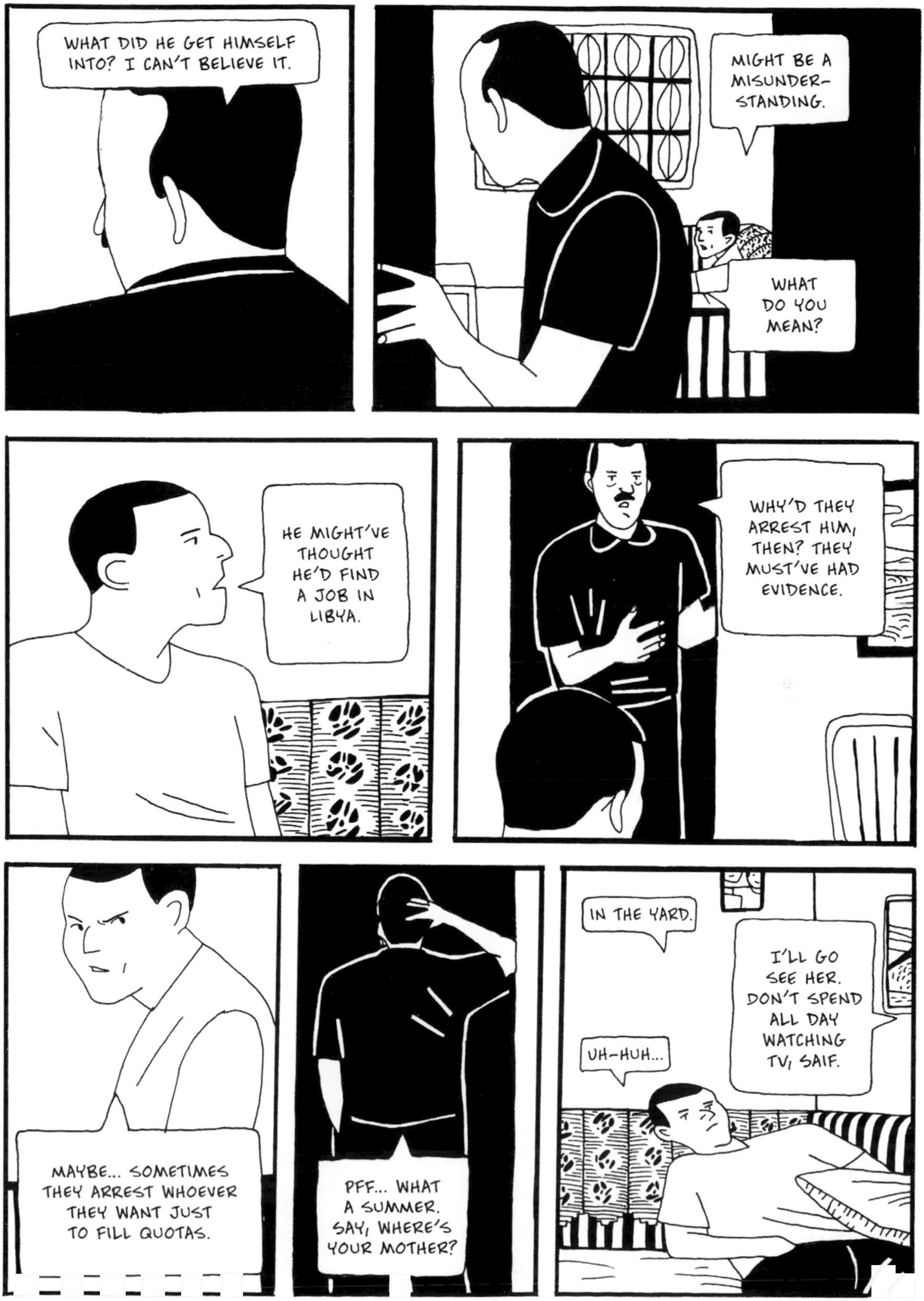
WHAT DID HE GET HIMSELF INTO? I CAN'T BELIEVE IT.
MIGHT BE A MISUNDER-STANDING.
WHAT DO YOU MEAN?
HE MIGHT'VE THOUGHT HE'D FIND A JOB IN LIBYA.
WHY'D THEY ARREST HIM, THEN? THEY MUST'VE HAD EVIDENCE.
MAYBE... SOMETIMES THEY ARREST WHOEVER THEY WANT JUST TO FILL QUOTAS.
PFF... WHAT A SUMMER. SAY, WHERE'S YOUR MOTHER?
IN THE YARD.
I'LL GO SEE HER. DON'T SPEND ALL DAY WATCHING TV, SAIF.
UH-HUH...

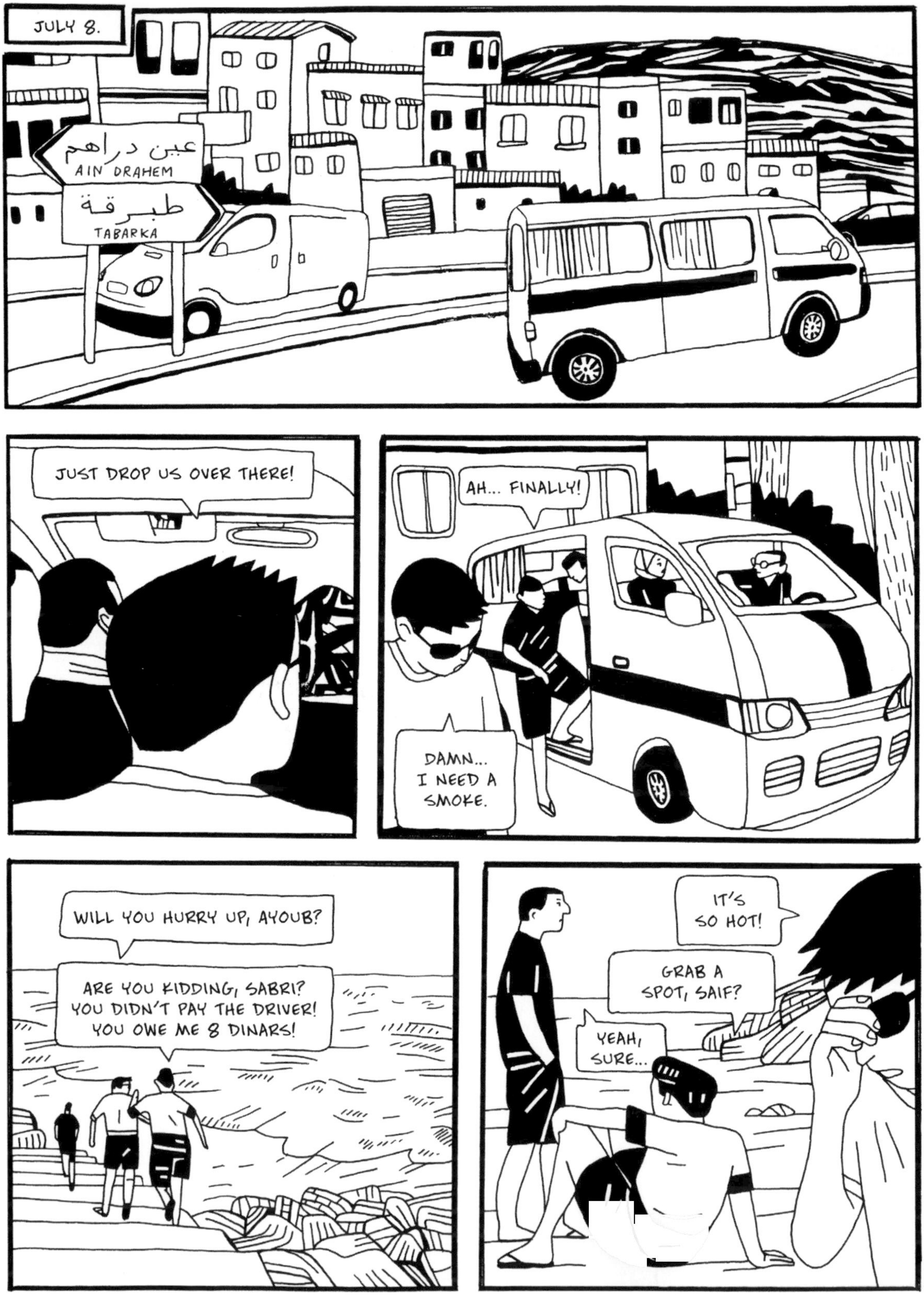
JULY 8.
عين دراهم
AIN DRAHEM
طبرقة
TABARKA
JUST DROP US OVER THERE!
AH... FINALLY!
DAMN... I NEED A SMOKE.
WILL YOU HURRY UP, AYOUB?
ARE YOU KIDDING, SABRI? YOU DIDN'T PAY THE DRIVER! YOU OWE ME 8 DINARS!
IT'S SO HOT!
GRAB A SPOT, SAIF?
YEAH, SURE...

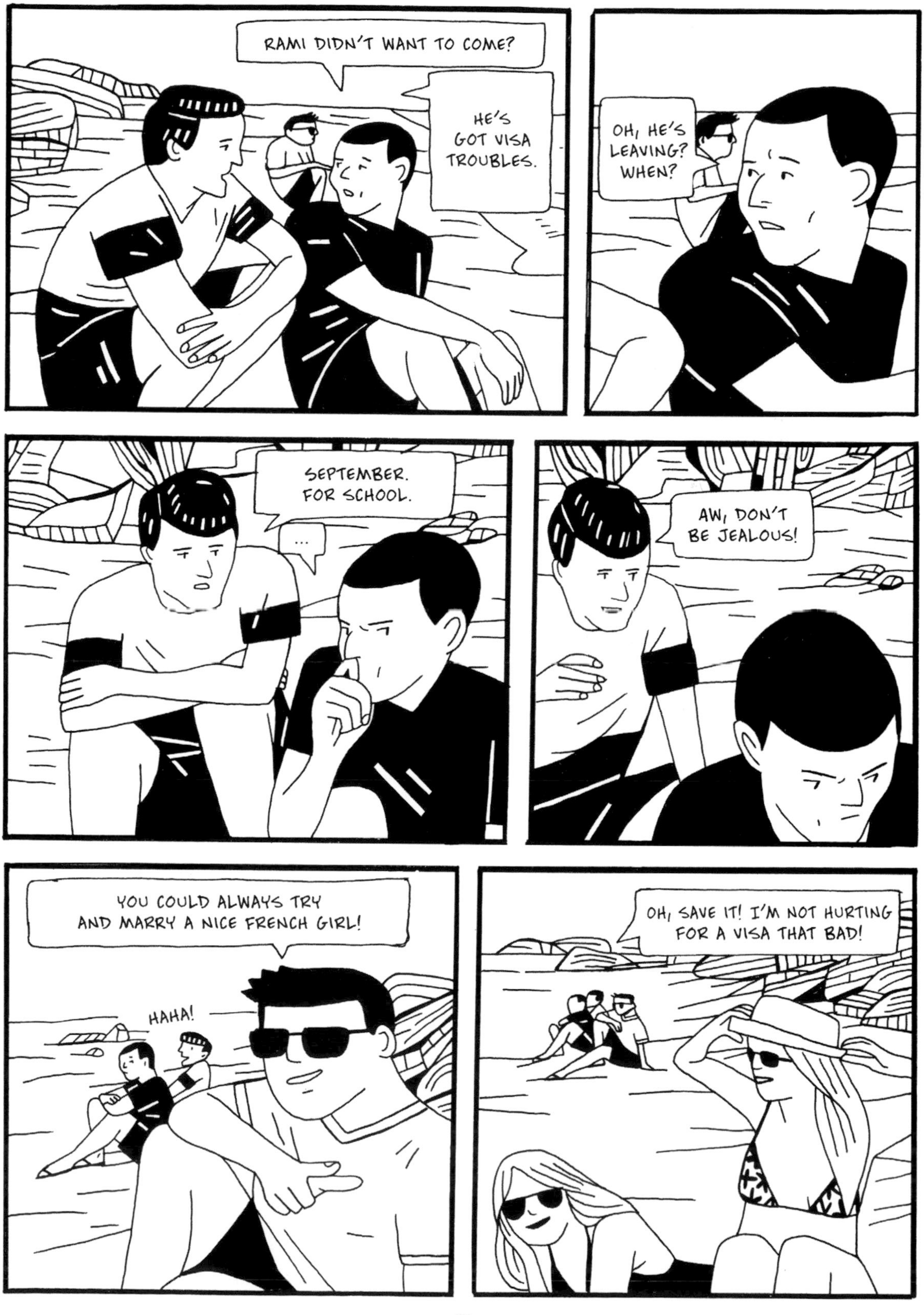
RAMI DIDN'T WANT TO COME?
HE'S GOT VISA TROUBLES.
OH, HE'S LEAVING? WHEN?
SEPTEMBER. FOR SCHOOL.
...
AW, DON'T BE JEALOUS!
YOU COULD ALWAYS TRY AND MARRY A NICE FRENCH GIRL!
HAHA!
OH, SAVE IT! I'M NOT HURTING FOR A VISA THAT BAD!

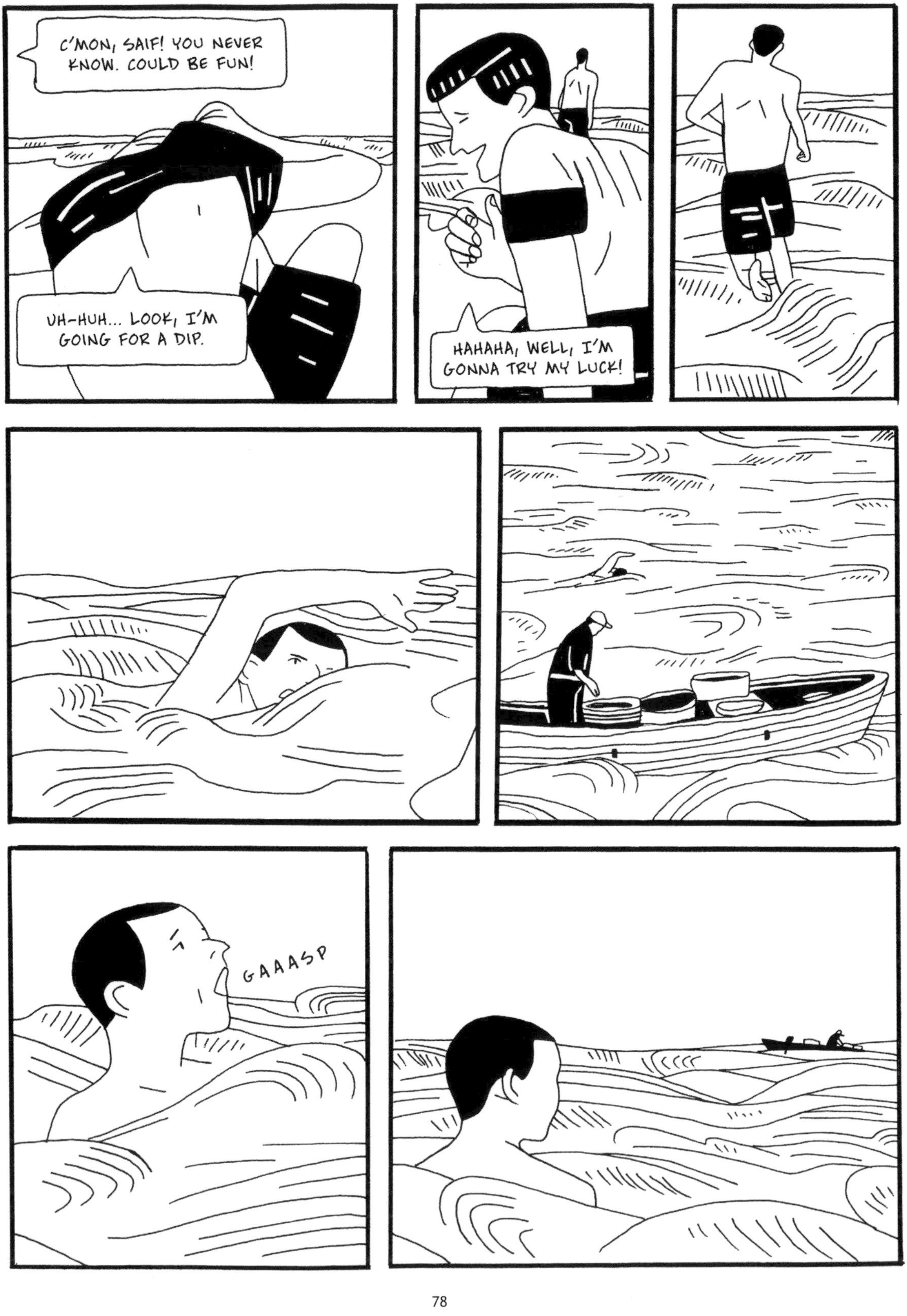
C'MON, SAIF! YOU NEVER KNOW. COULD BE FUN!
UH-HUH... LOOK, I'M GOING FOR A DIP.
HAHAHA, WELL, I'M GONNA TRY MY LUCK!
GAAASP

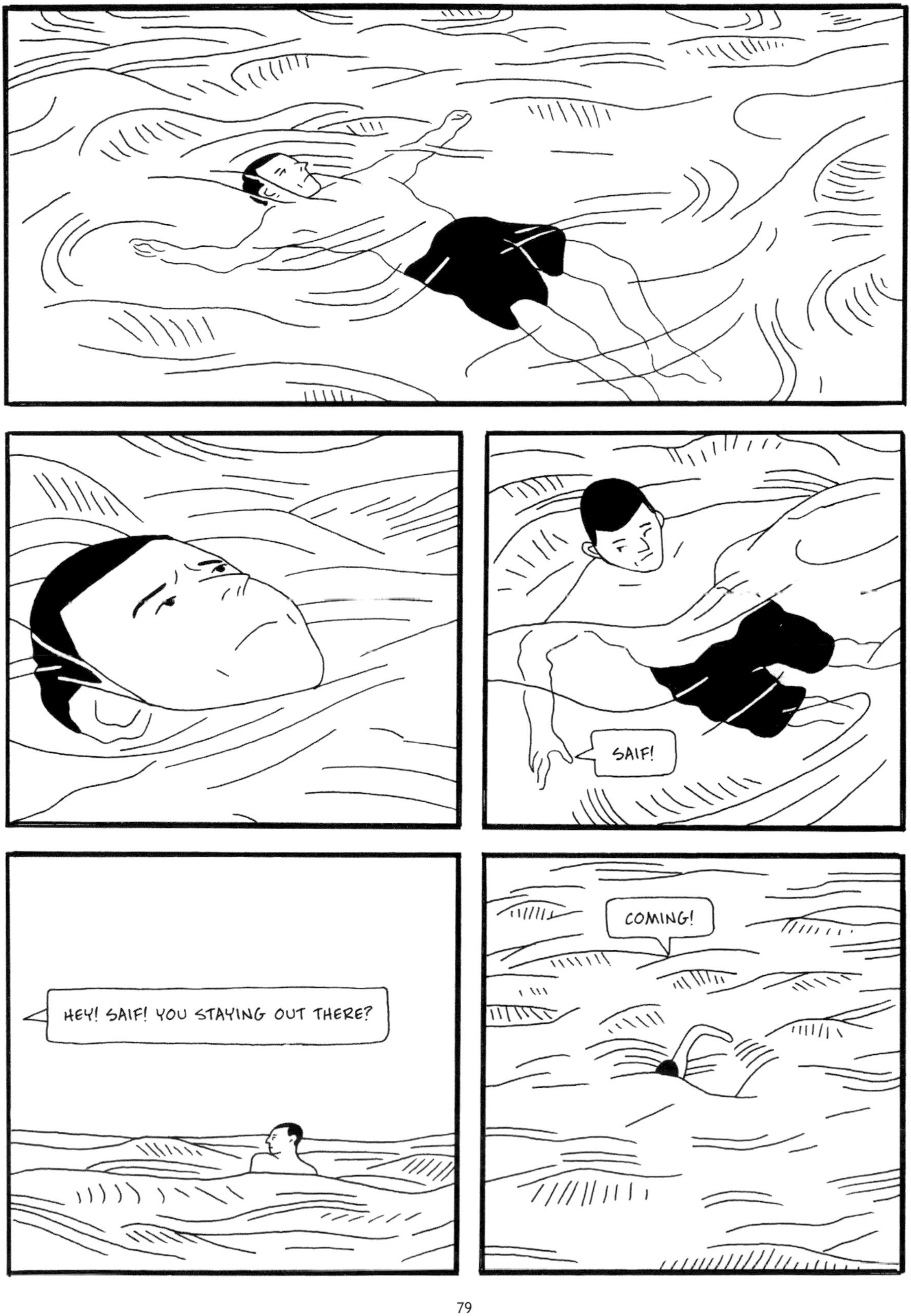
SAIF!
HEY! SAIF! YOU STAYING OUT THERE?
COMING!

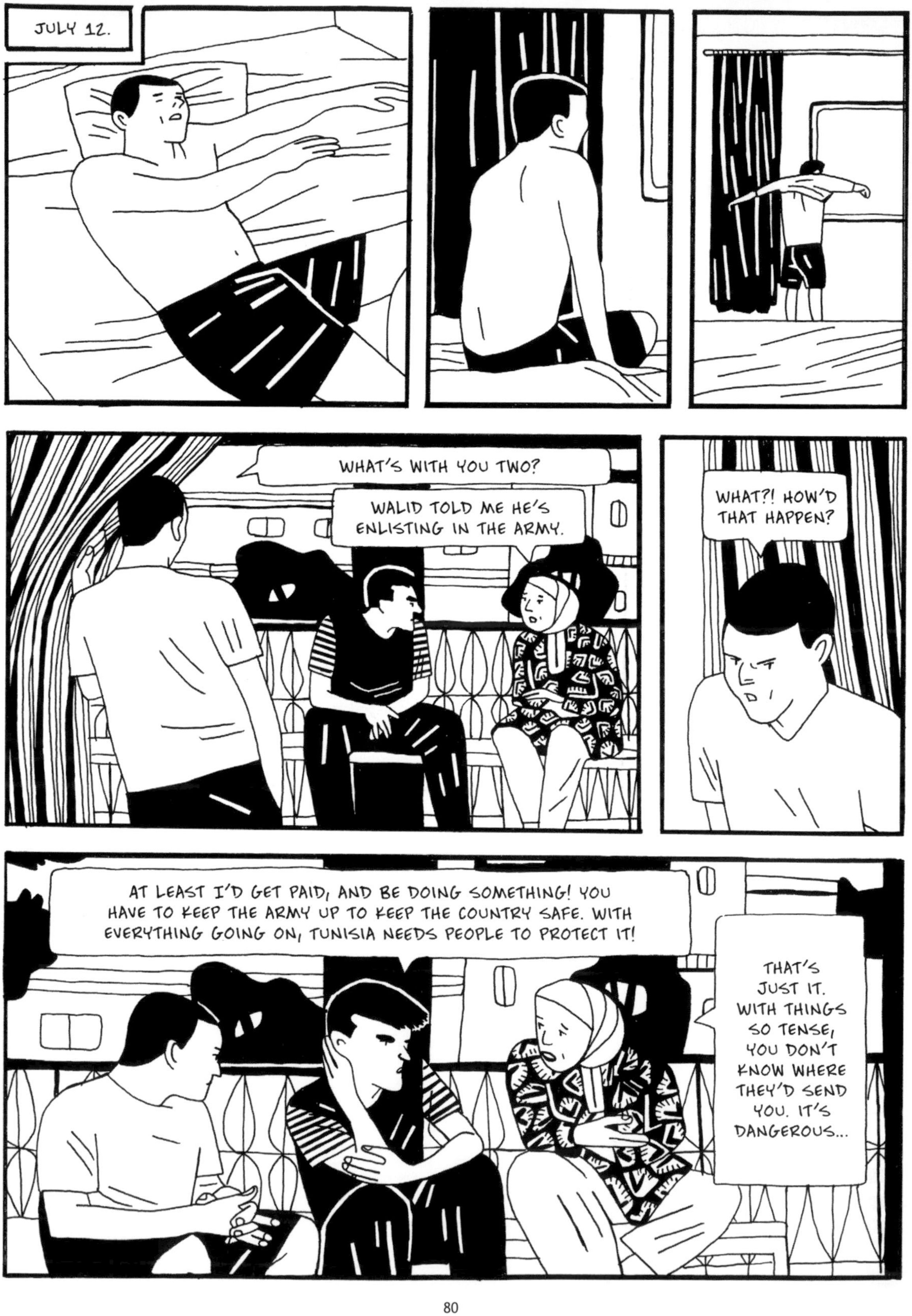
JULY 12.
WHAT'S WITH YOU TWO?
WALID TOLD ME HE'S ENLISTING IN THE ARMY.
WHAT?! HOW'D THAT HAPPEN?
AT LEAST I'D GET PAID, AND BE DOING SOMETHING! YOU HAVE TO KEEP THE ARMY UP TO KEEP THE COUNTRY SAFE. WITH EVERYTHING GOING ON, TUNISIA NEEDS PEOPLE TO PROTECT IT!
THAT'S JUST IT. WITH THINGS SO TENSE, YOU DON'T KNOW WHERE THEY'D SEND YOU. IT'S DANGEROUS...

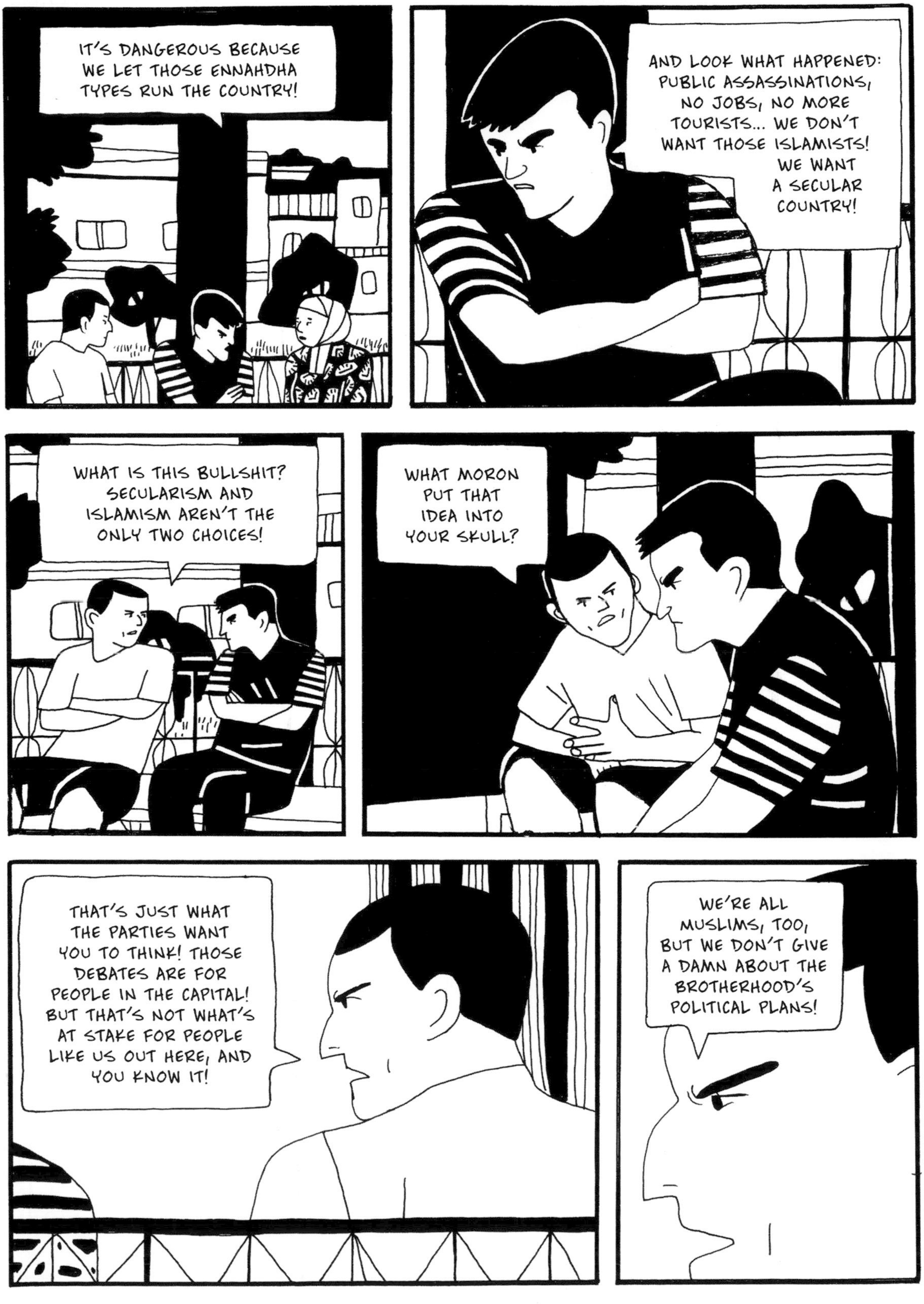
IT'S DANGEROUS BECAUSE WE LET THOSE ENNAHDHA TYPES RUN THE COUNTRY!
AND LOOK WHAT HAPPENED: PUBLIC ASSASSINATIONS, NO JOBS, NO MORE TOURISTS... WE DON'T WANT THOSE ISLAMISTS! WE WANT A SECULAR COUNTRY!
WHAT IS THIS BULLSHIT? SECULARISM AND ISLAMISM AREN'T THE ONLY TWO CHOICES!
WHAT MORON PUT THAT IDEA INTO YOUR SKULL?
THAT'S JUST WHAT THE PARTIES WANT YOU TO THINK! THOSE DEBATES ARE FOR PEOPLE IN THE CAPITAL! BUT THAT'S NOT WHAT'S AT STAKE FOR PEOPLE LIKE US OUT HERE, AND YOU KNOW IT!
WE'RE ALL MUSLIMS, TOO, BUT WE DON'T GIVE A DAMN ABOUT THE BROTHERHOOD'S POLITICAL PLANS!

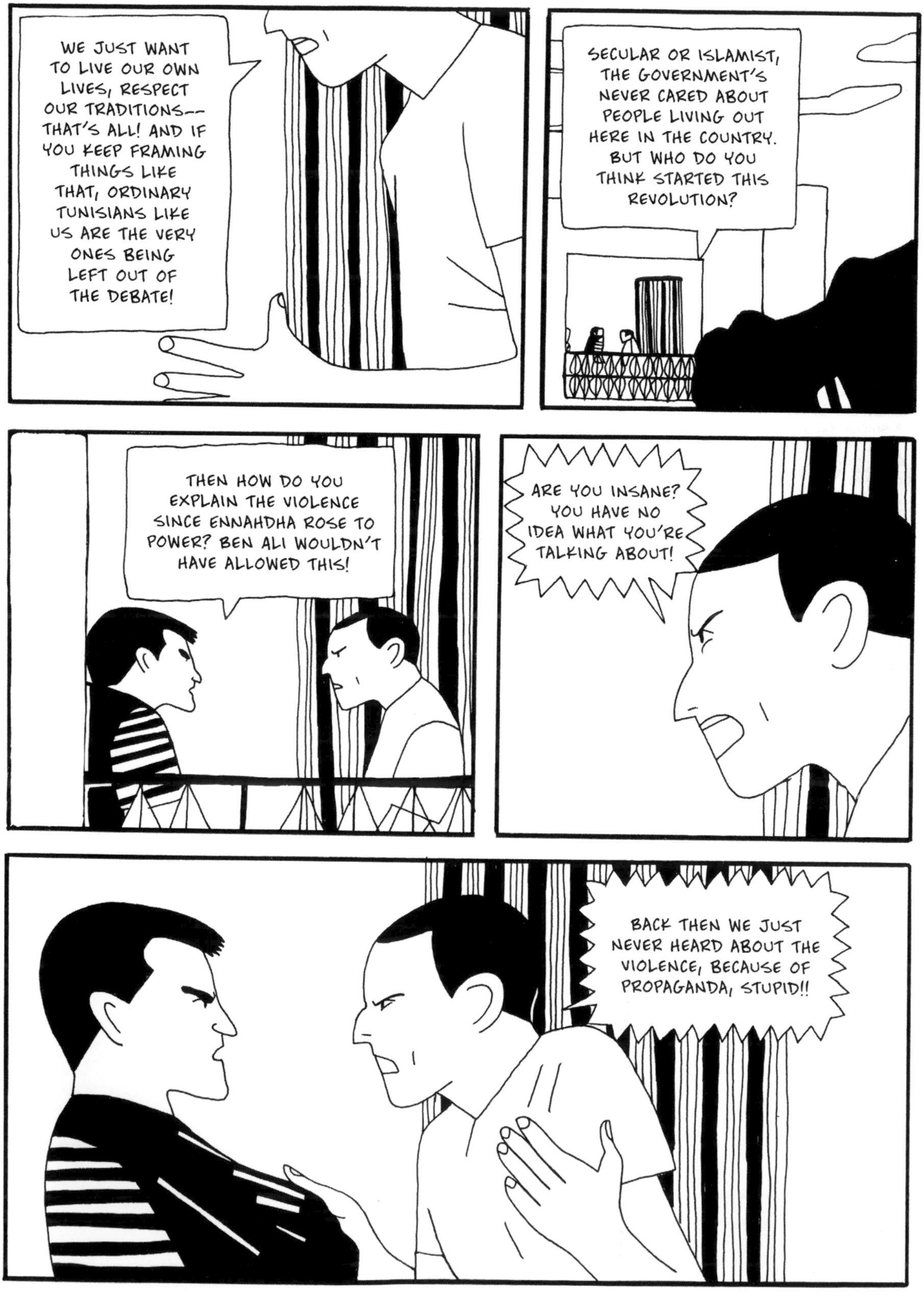
WE JUST WANT TO LIVE OUR OWN LIVES, RESPECT OUR TRADITIONS-- THAT'S ALL! AND IF YOU KEEP FRAMING THINGS LIKE THAT, ORDINARY TUNISIANS LIKE US ARE THE VERY ONES BEING LEFT OUT OF THE DEBATE!
SECULAR OR ISLAMIST, THE GOVERNMENT'S NEVER CARED ABOUT PEOPLE LIVING OUT HERE IN THE COUNTRY. BUT WHO DO YOU THINK STARTED THIS REVOLUTION?
THEN HOW DO YOU EXPLAIN THE VIOLENCE SINCE ENNAHDHA ROSE TO POWER? BEN ALI WOULDN'T HAVE ALLOWED THIS!
ARE YOU INSANE? YOU HAVE NO IDEA WHAT YOU'RE TALKING ABOUT!
BACK THEN WE JUST NEVER HEARD ABOUT THE VIOLENCE, BECAUSE OF PROPAGANDA, STUPID!!

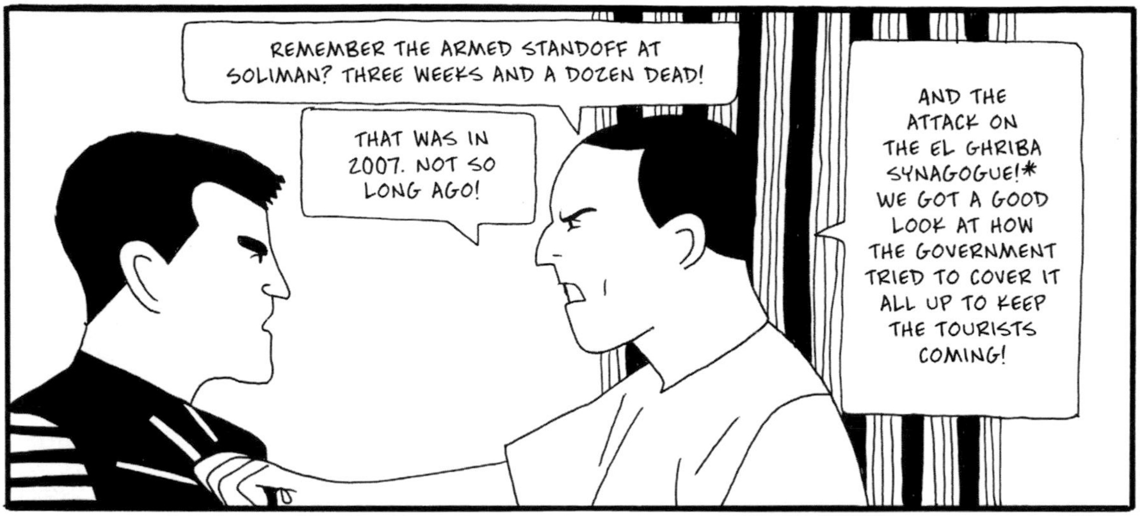
REMEMBER THE ARMED STANDOFF AT SOLIMAN? THREE WEEKS AND A DOZEN DEAD!
THAT WAS IN 2007. NOT SO LONG AGO!
AND THE ATTACK ON THE EL GHRIBA SYNAGOGUE!* WE GOT A GOOD LOOK AT HOW THE GOVERNMENT TRIED TO COVER IT ALL UP TO KEEP THE TOURISTS COMING!

* SUICIDE TRUCK BOMBING ON APRIL 11, 2012, IN DJERBA. 19 DEAD

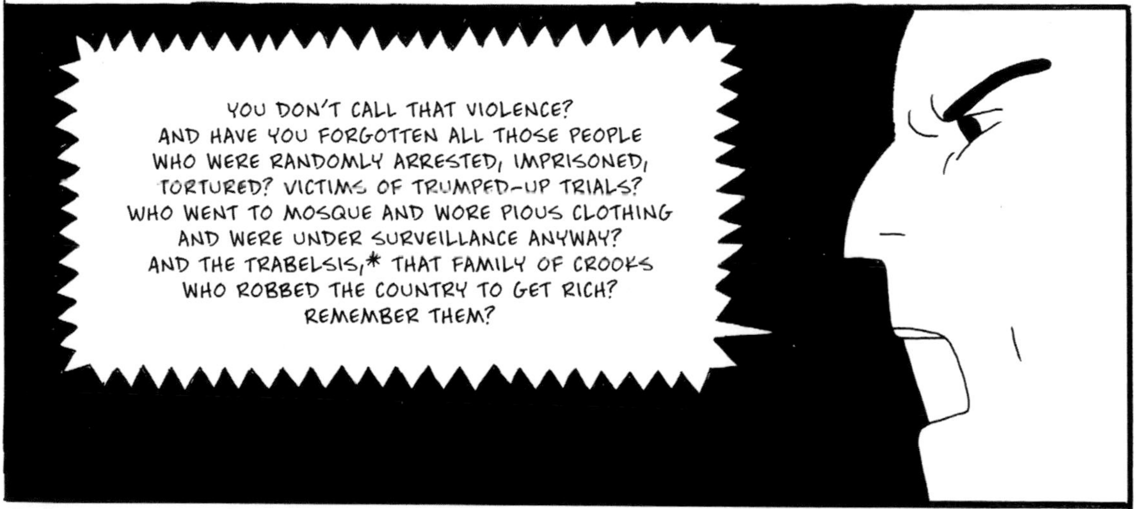
YOU DON'T CALL THAT VIOLENCE? AND HAVE YOU FORGOTTEN ALL THOSE PEOPLE WHO WERE RANDOMLY ARRESTED, IMPRISONED, TORTURED? VICTIMS OF TRUMPED-UP TRIALS? WHO WENT TO MOSQUE AND WORE PIOUS CLOTHING AND WERE UNDER SURVEILLANCE ANYWAY? AND THE TRABELSIS,* THAT FAMILY OF CROOKS WHO ROBBED THE COUNTRY TO GET RICH? REMEMBER THEM?

* LEÏLA TRABELSI, BEN ALI'S SECOND WIFE, AND HER FAMILY, OFTEN REFERRED TO AS THE "TRABELSI MAFIA"

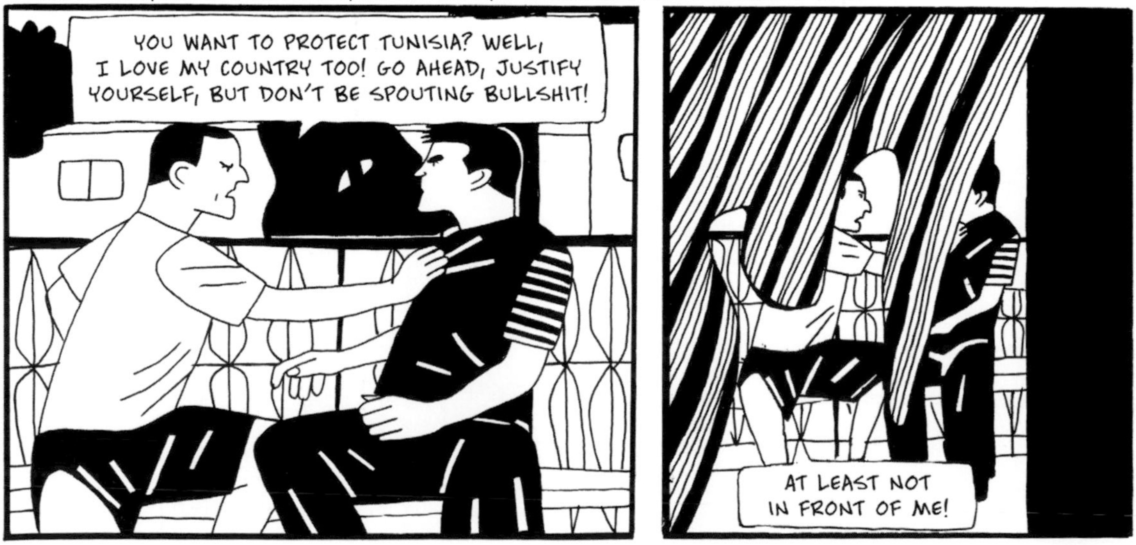
YOU WANT TO PROTECT TUNISIA? WELL, I LOVE MY COUNTRY TOO! GO AHEAD, JUSTIFY YOURSELF, BUT DON'T BE SPOUTING BULLSHIT!
AT LEAST NOT IN FRONT OF ME!

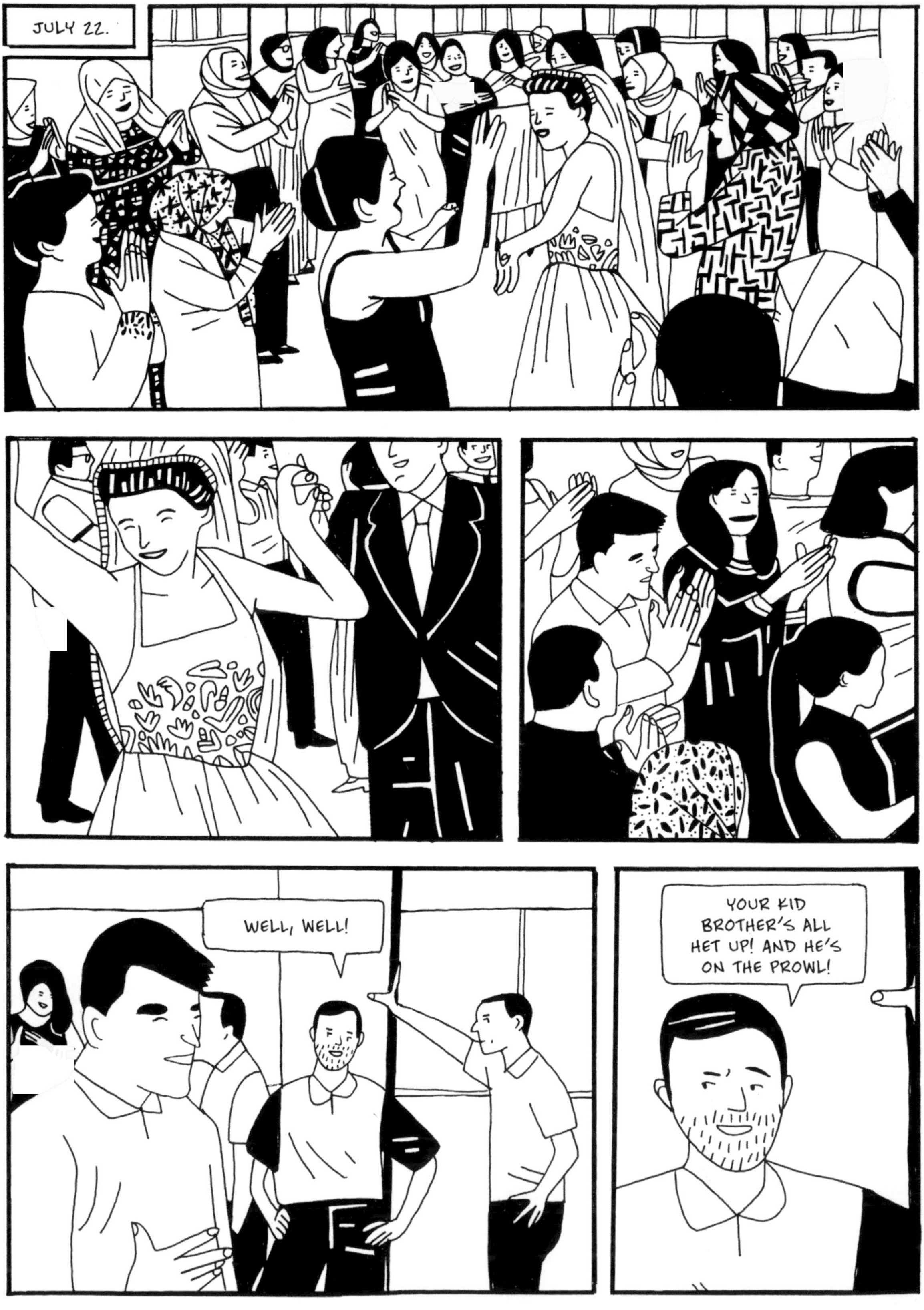
JULY 22.
WELL, WELL!
YOUR KID BROTHER'S ALL HET UP! AND HE'S ON THE PROWL!

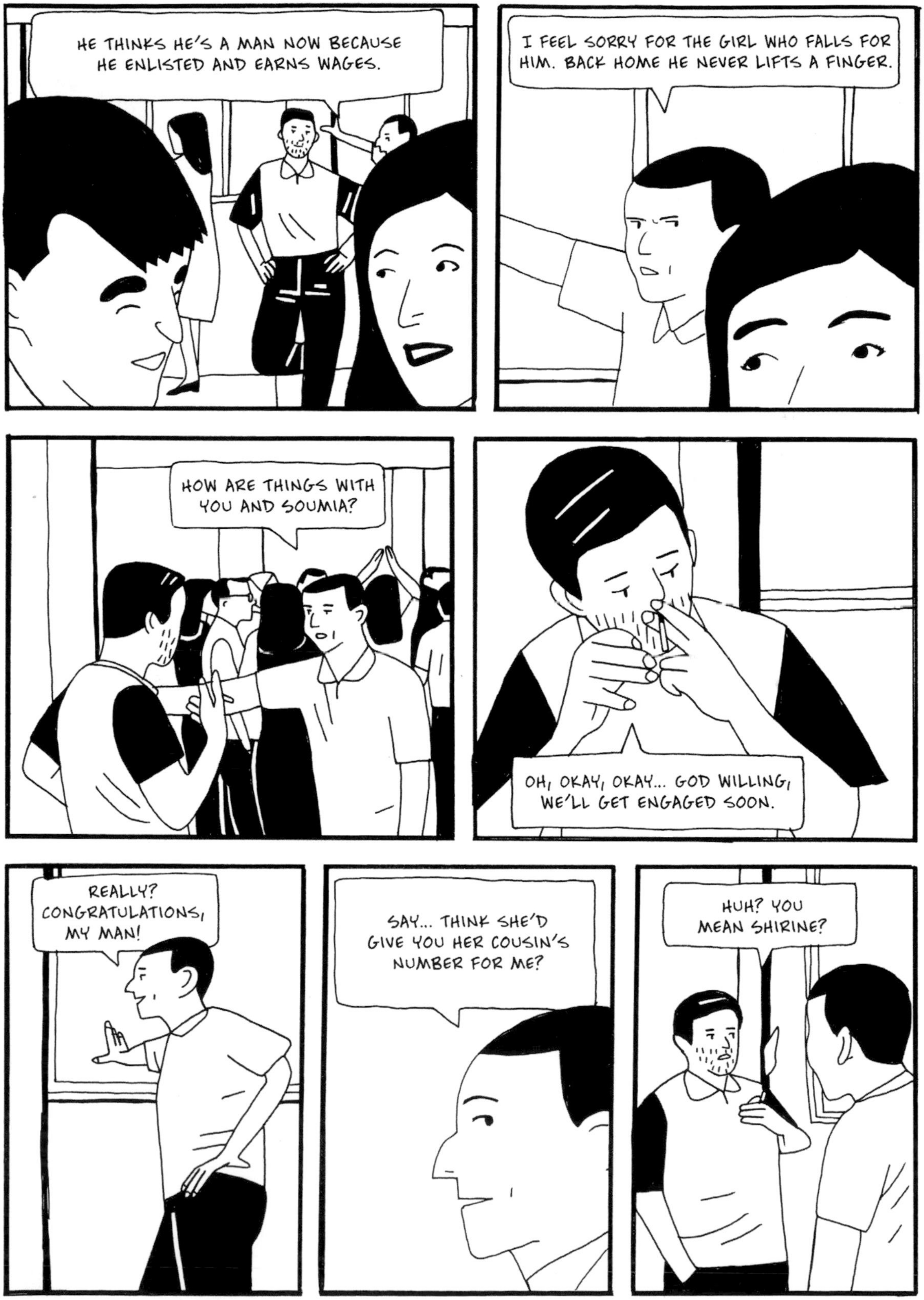
HE THINKS HE'S A MAN NOW BECAUSE HE ENLISTED AND EARNS WAGES.
I FEEL SORRY FOR THE GIRL WHO FALLS FOR HIM. BACK HOME HE NEVER LIFTS A FINGER.
HOW ARE THINGS WITH YOU AND SOUMIA?
OH, OKAY, OKAY... GOD WILLING, WE'LL GET ENGAGED SOON.
REALLY? CONGRATULATIONS, MY MAN!
SAY... THINK SHE'D GIVE YOU HER COUSIN'S NUMBER FOR ME?
HUH? YOU MEAN SHIRINE?

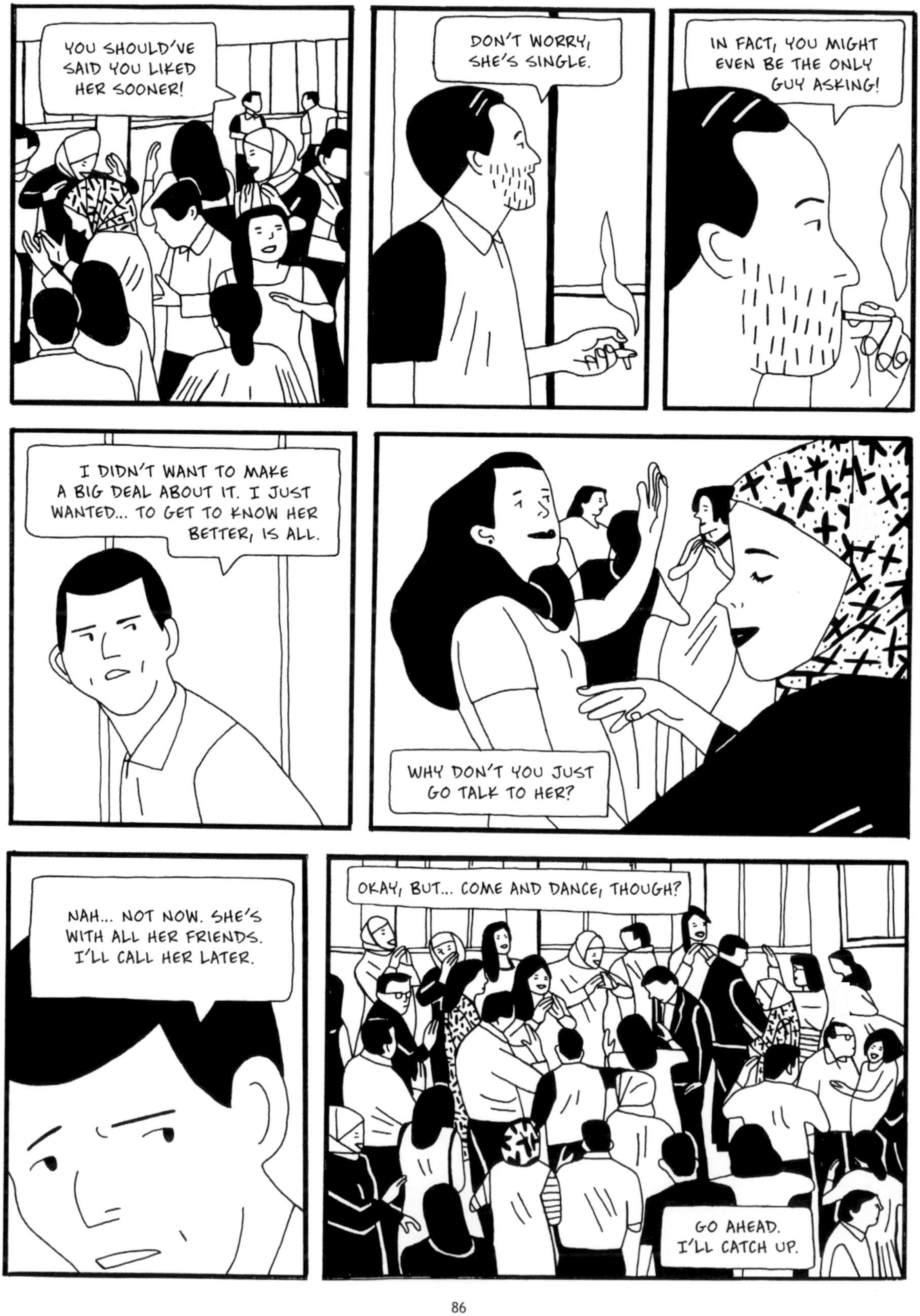
YOU SHOULD'VE SAID YOU LIKED HER SOONER!
DON'T WORRY, SHE'S SINGLE.
IN FACT, YOU MIGHT EVEN BE THE ONLY GUY ASKING!
I DIDN'T WANT TO MAKE A BIG DEAL ABOUT IT. I JUST WANTED... TO GET TO KNOW HER BETTER, IS ALL.
WHY DON'T YOU JUST GO TALK TO HER?
NAH... NOT NOW. SHE'S WITH ALL HER FRIENDS. I'LL CALL HER LATER.
OKAY, BUT... COME AND DANCE, THOUGH?
GO AHEAD. I'LL CATCH UP.

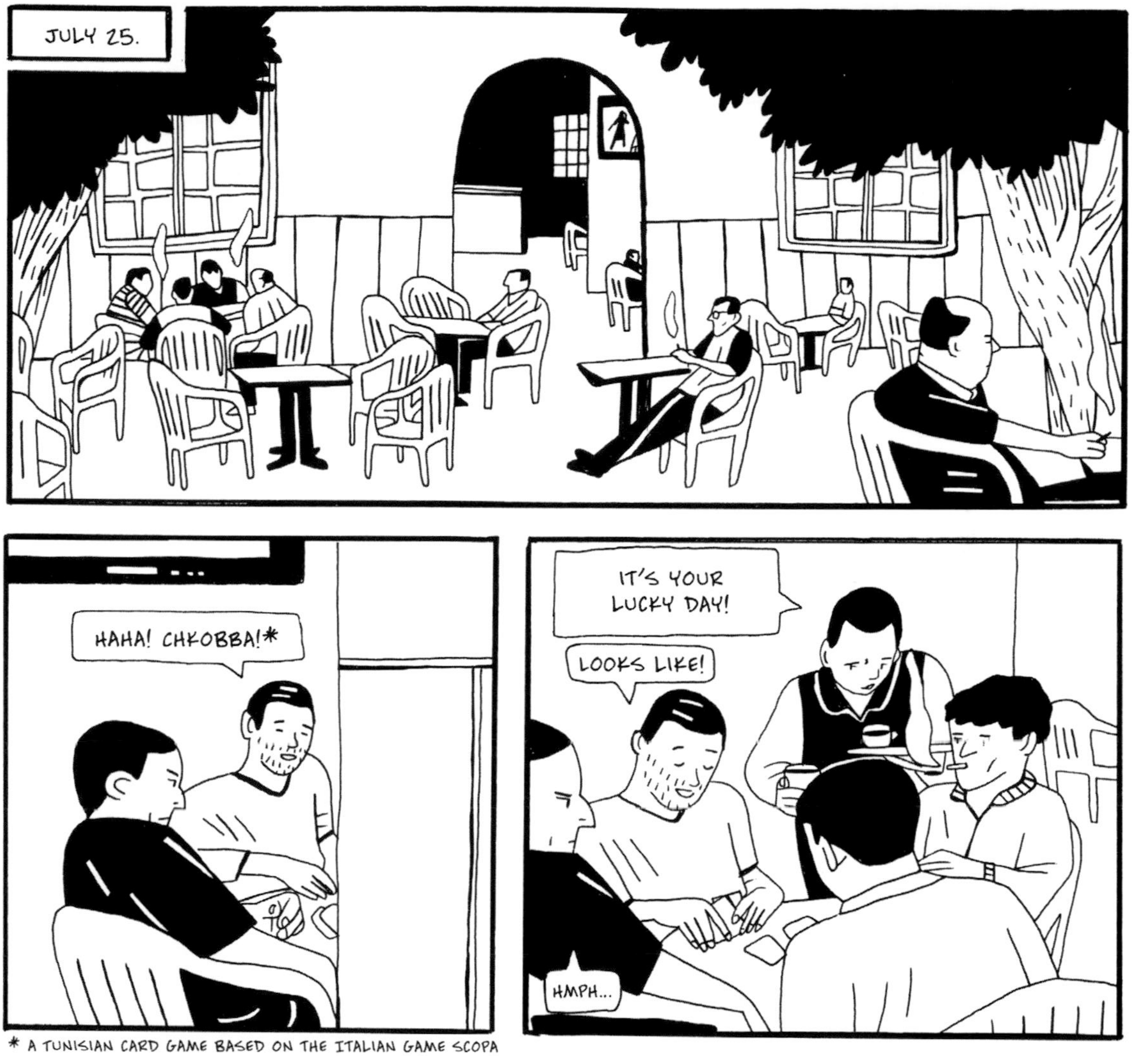
JULY 25.
HAHA! CHKOBBA!*
IT'S YOUR LUCKY DAY!
LOOKS LIKE!
HMPH...

* A TUNISIAN CARD GAME BASED ON THE ITALIAN GAME SCOPA

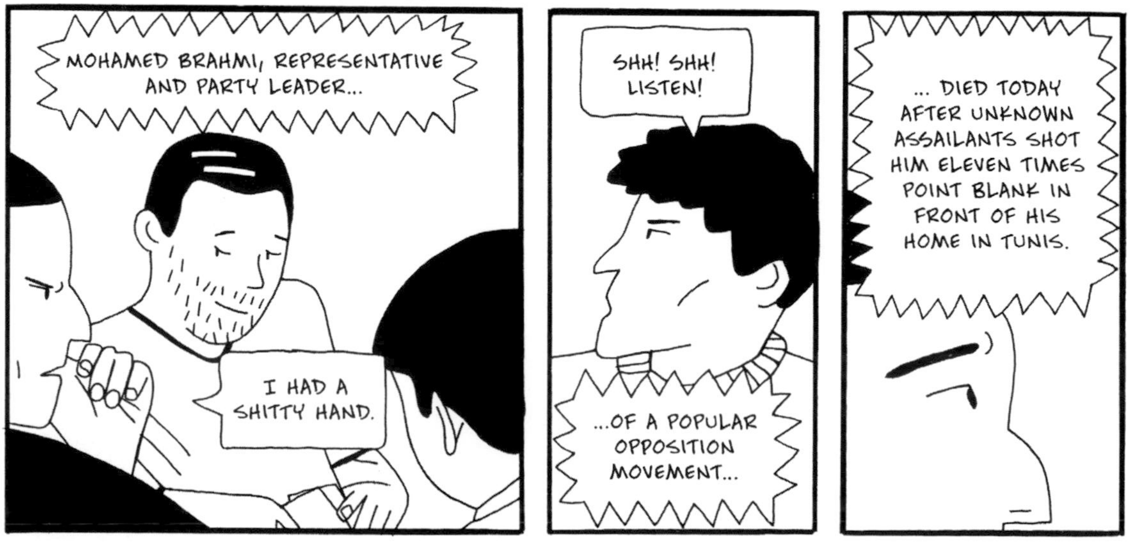
MOHAMED BRAHMI, REPRESENTATIVE AND PARTY LEADER...
I HAD A SHITTY HAND.
SHH! SHH! LISTEN!
...OF A POPULAR OPPOSITION MOVEMENT...
... DIED TODAY AFTER UNKNOWN ASSAILANTS SHOT HIM ELEVEN TIMES POINT BLANK IN FRONT OF HIS HOME IN TUNIS.

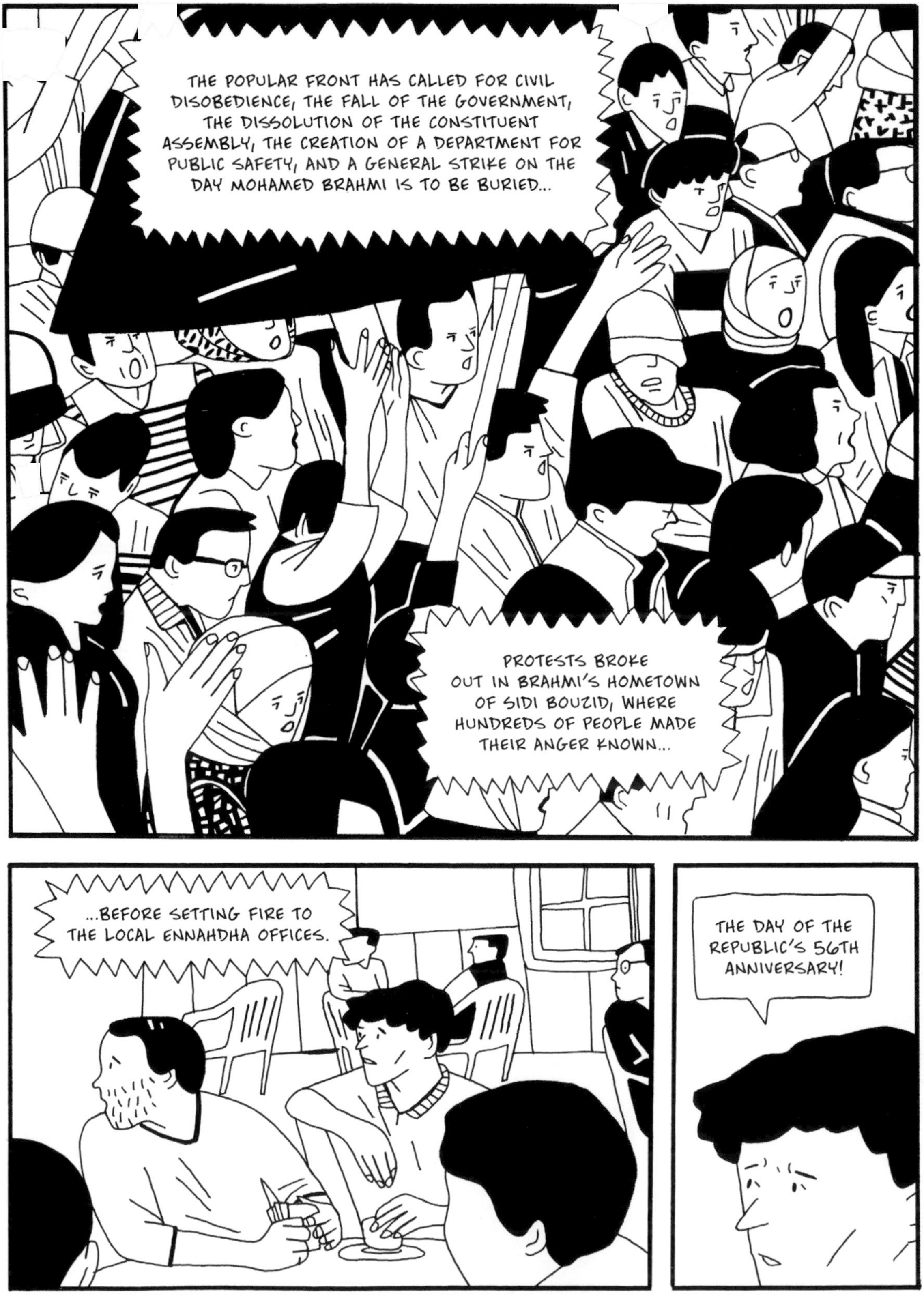
THE POPULAR FRONT HAS CALLED FOR CIVIL DISOBEDIENCE, THE FALL OF THE GOVERNMENT, THE DISSOLUTION OF THE CONSTITUENT ASSEMBLY, THE CREATION OF A DEPARTMENT FOR PUBLIC SAFETY, AND A GENERAL STRIKE ON THE DAY MOHAMED BRAHMI IS TO BE BURIED...
PROTESTS BROKE OUT IN BRAHMI'S HOMETOWN OF SIDI BOUZID, WHERE HUNDREDS OF PEOPLE MADE THEIR ANGER KNOWN...
...BEFORE SETTING FIRE TO THE LOCAL ENNAHDHA OFFICES.
THE DAY OF THE REPUBLIC'S 56TH ANNIVERSARY!

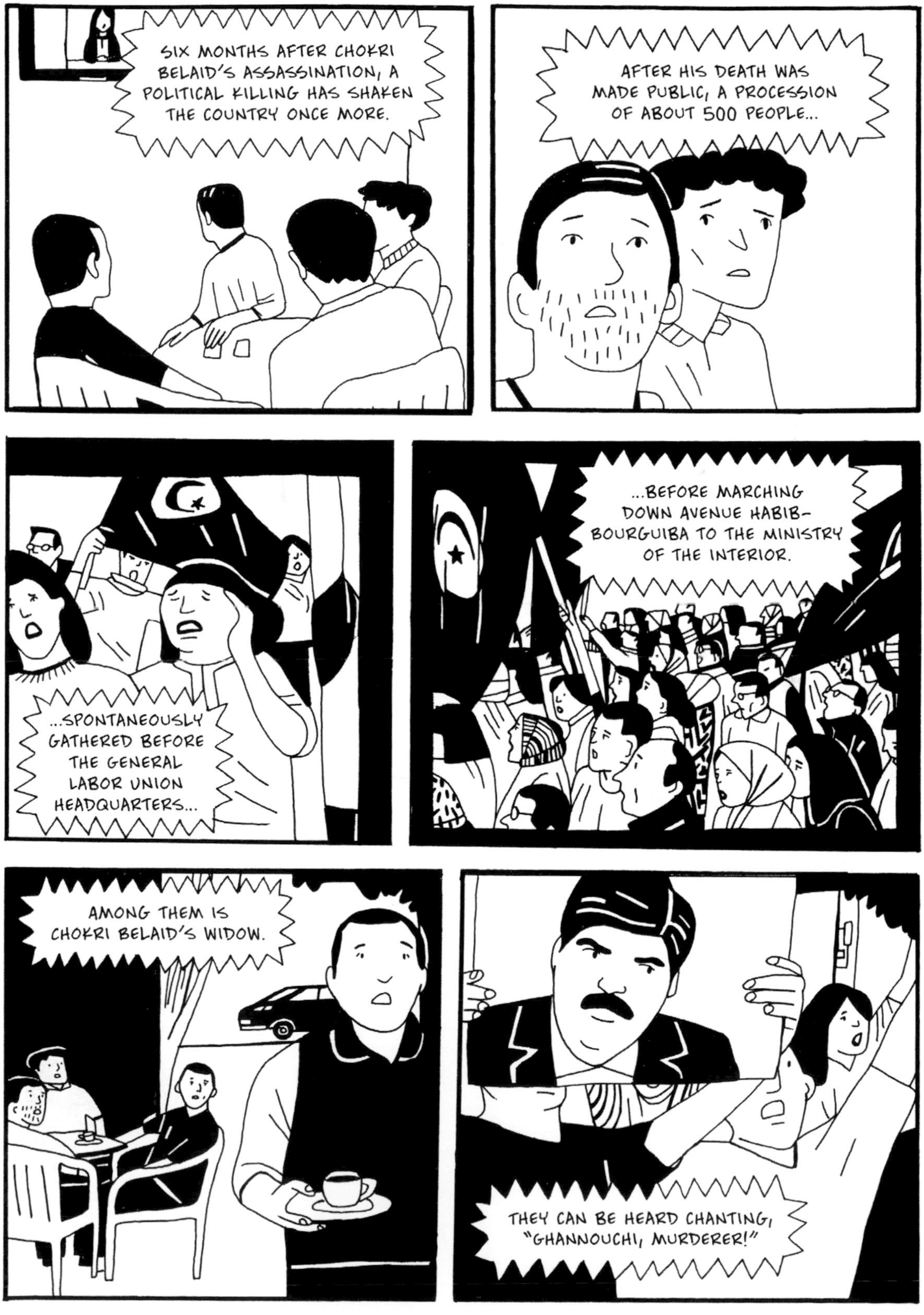
SIX MONTHS AFTER CHOKRI BELAID'S ASSASSINATION, A POLITICAL KILLING HAS SHAKEN THE COUNTRY ONCE MORE.
AFTER HIS DEATH WAS MADE PUBLIC, A PROCESSION OF ABOUT 500 PEOPLE...
...SPONTANEOUSLY GATHERED BEFORE THE GENERAL LABOR UNION HEADQUARTERS...
...BEFORE MARCHING DOWN AVENUE HABIB-BOURGUIBA TO THE MINISTRY OF THE INTERIOR.
AMONG THEM IS CHOKRI BELAID'S WIDOW.
THEY CAN BE HEARD CHANTING, "GHANNOUCHI, MURDERER!"

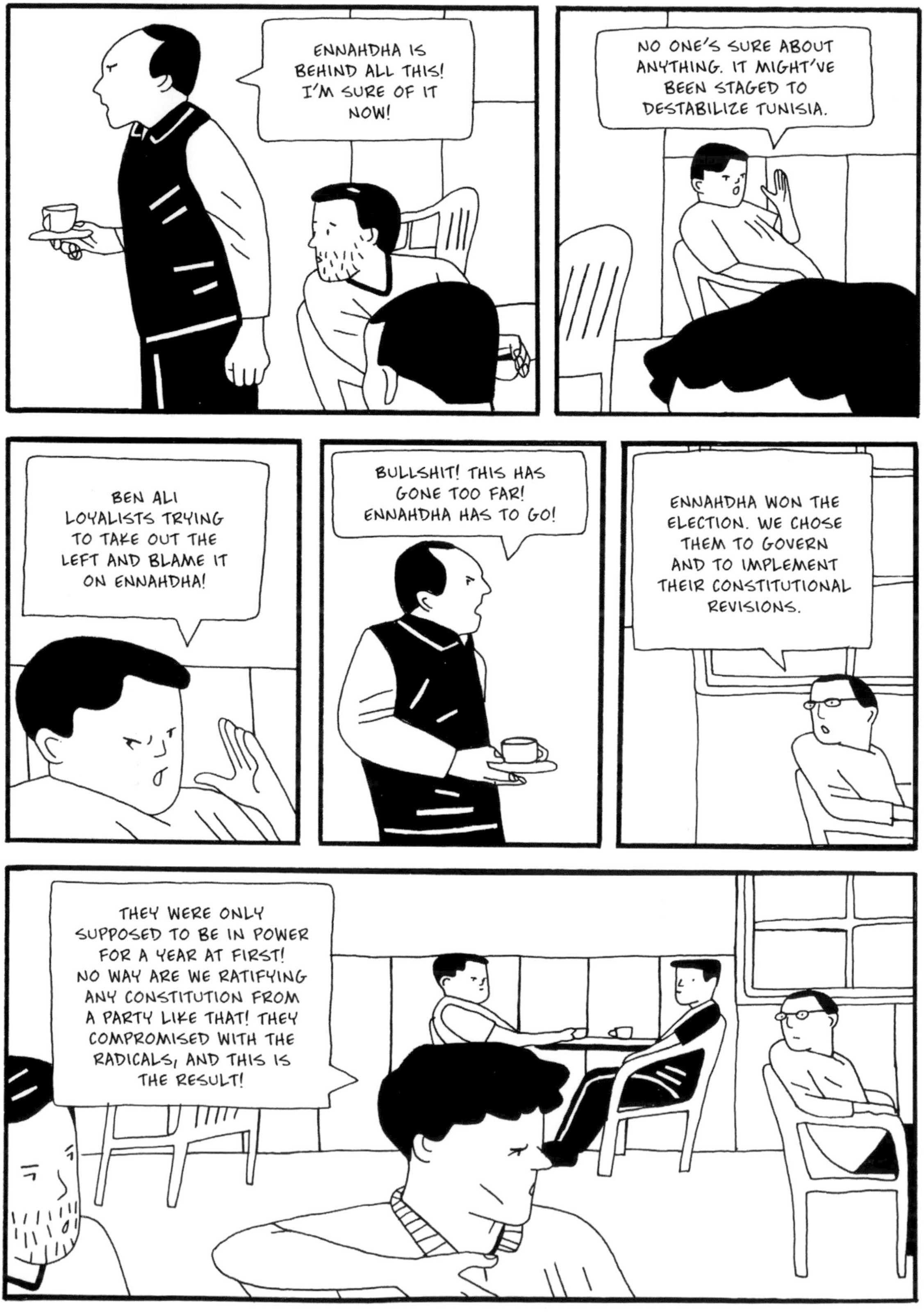
ENNAHDHA IS BEHIND ALL THIS! I'M SURE OF IT NOW!
NO ONE'S SURE ABOUT ANYTHING. IT MIGHT'VE BEEN STAGED TO DESTABILIZE TUNISIA.
BEN ALI LOYALISTS TRYING TO TAKE OUT THE LEFT AND BLAME IT ON ENNAHDHA!
BULLSHIT! THIS HAS GONE TOO FAR! ENNAHDHA HAS TO GO!
ENNAHDHA WON THE ELECTION. WE CHOSE THEM TO GOVERN AND TO IMPLEMENT THEIR CONSTITUTIONAL REVISIONS.
THEY WERE ONLY SUPPOSED TO BE IN POWER FOR A YEAR AT FIRST! NO WAY ARE WE RATIFYING ANY CONSTITUTION FROM A PARTY LIKE THAT! THEY COMPROMISED WITH THE RADICALS, AND THIS IS THE RESULT!

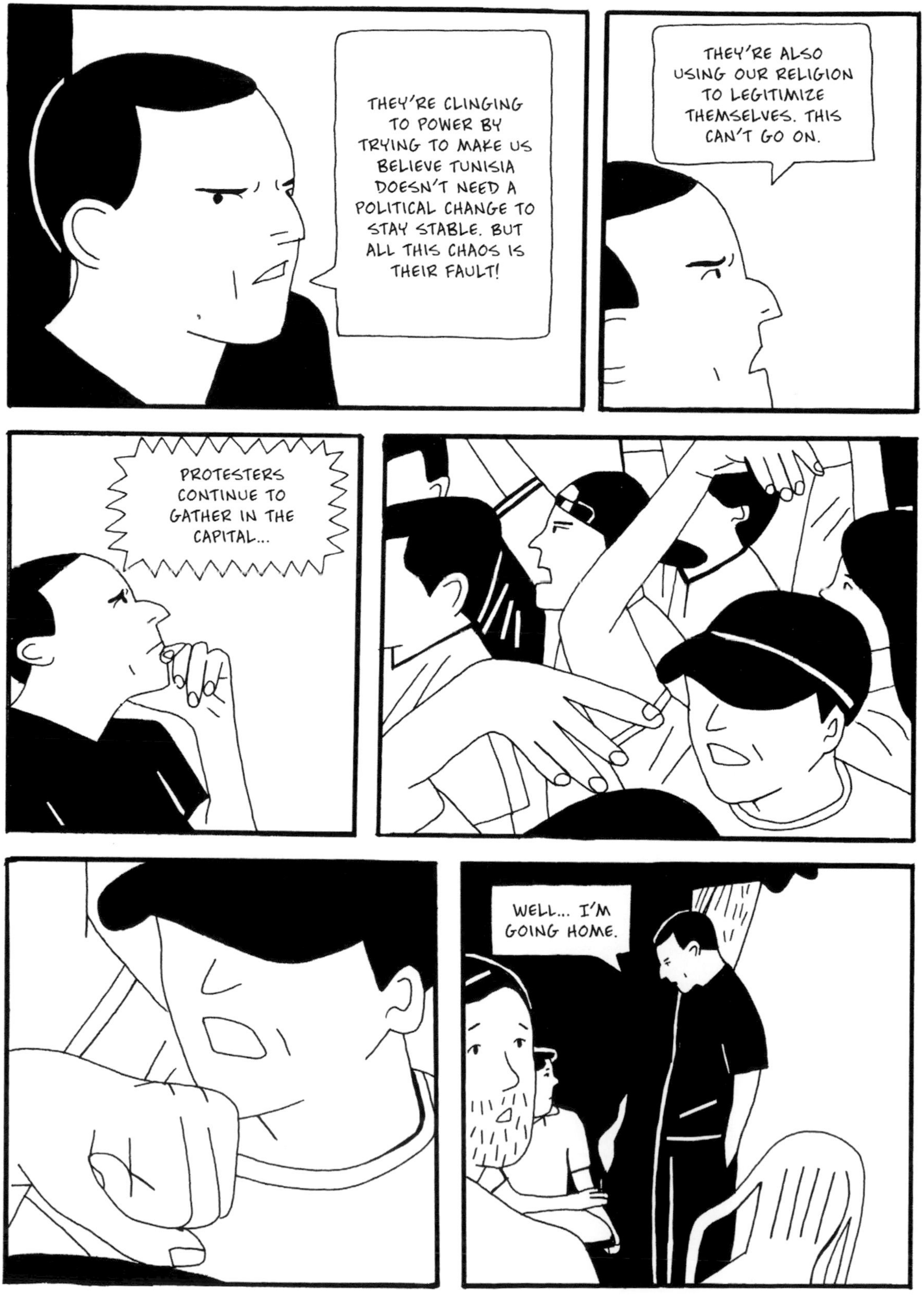
THEY'RE CLINGING TO POWER BY TRYING TO MAKE US BELIEVE TUNISIA DOESN'T NEED A POLITICAL CHANGE TO STAY STABLE. BUT ALL THIS CHAOS IS THEIR FAULT!
THEY'RE ALSO USING OUR RELIGION TO LEGITIMIZE THEMSELVES. THIS CAN'T GO ON.
PROTESTERS CONTINUE TO GATHER IN THE CAPITAL...
WELL... I'M GOING HOME.

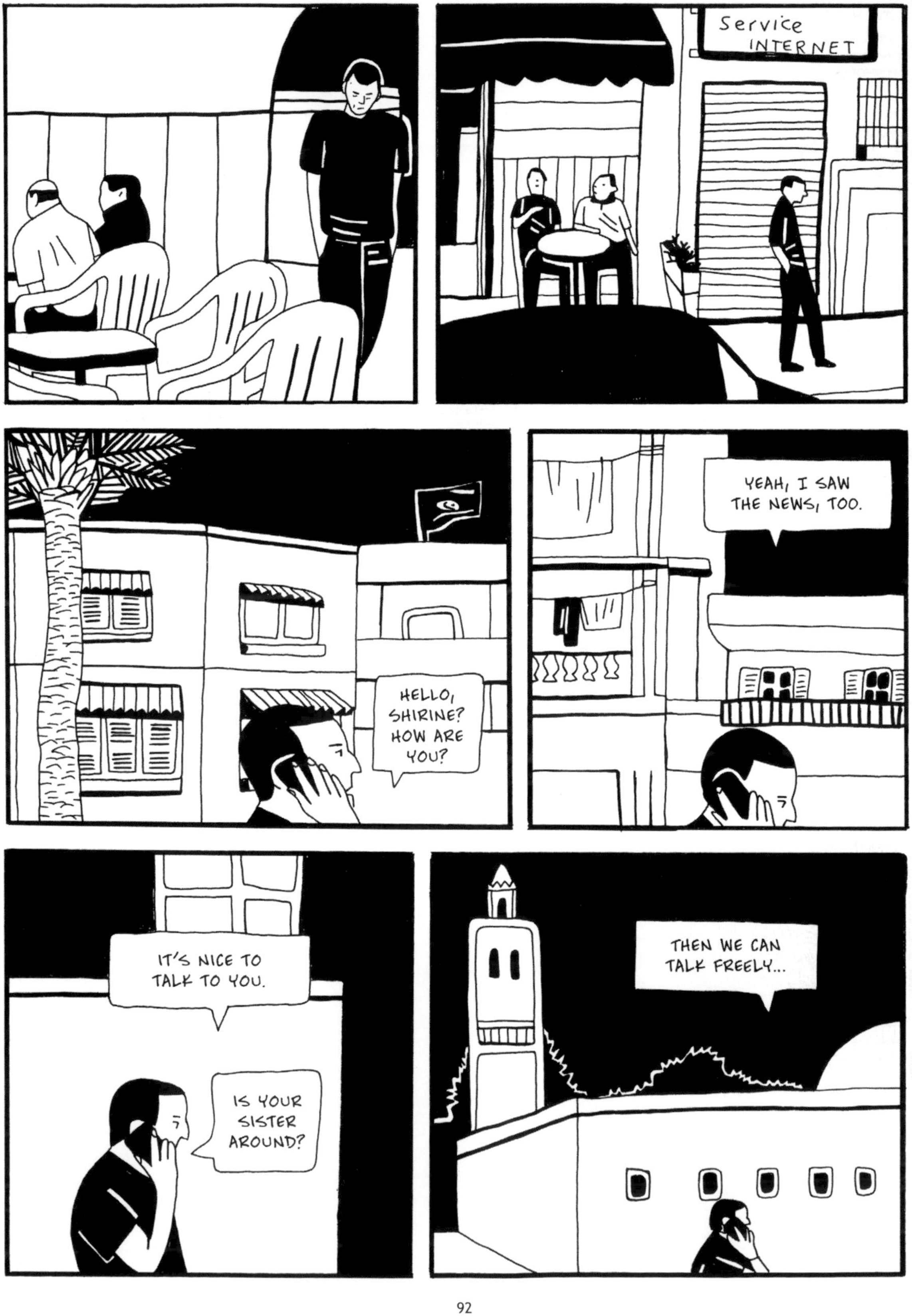
Service
INTERNET
HELLO, SHIRINE? HOW ARE YOU?
YEAH, I SAW THE NEWS, TOO.
IT'S NICE TO TALK TO YOU.
IS YOUR SISTER AROUND?
THEN WE CAN TALK FREELY...

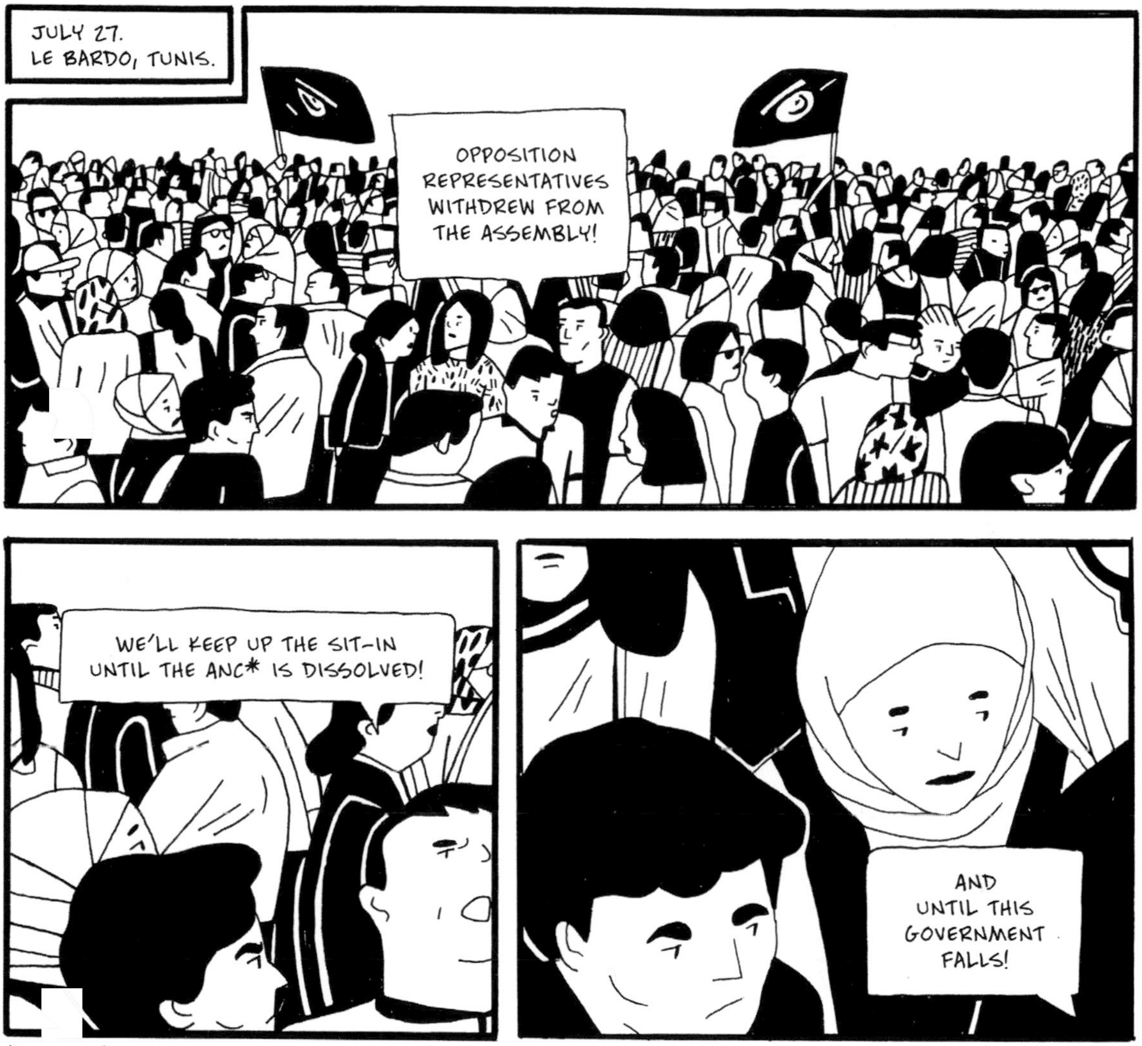
JULY 27.
LE BARDO, TUNIS.
OPPOSITION REPRESENTATIVES WITHDREW FROM THE ASSEMBLY!
WE'LL KEEP UP THE SIT-IN UNTIL THE ANC* IS DISSOLVED!
AND UNTIL THIS GOVERNMENT FALLS!

* ASSEMBLÉE NATIONALE CONSTITUANTE: NATIONAL CONSTITUENT ASSEMBLY, THE BODY IN CHARGE OF DEVISING A NEW TUNISIAN CONSTITUTION

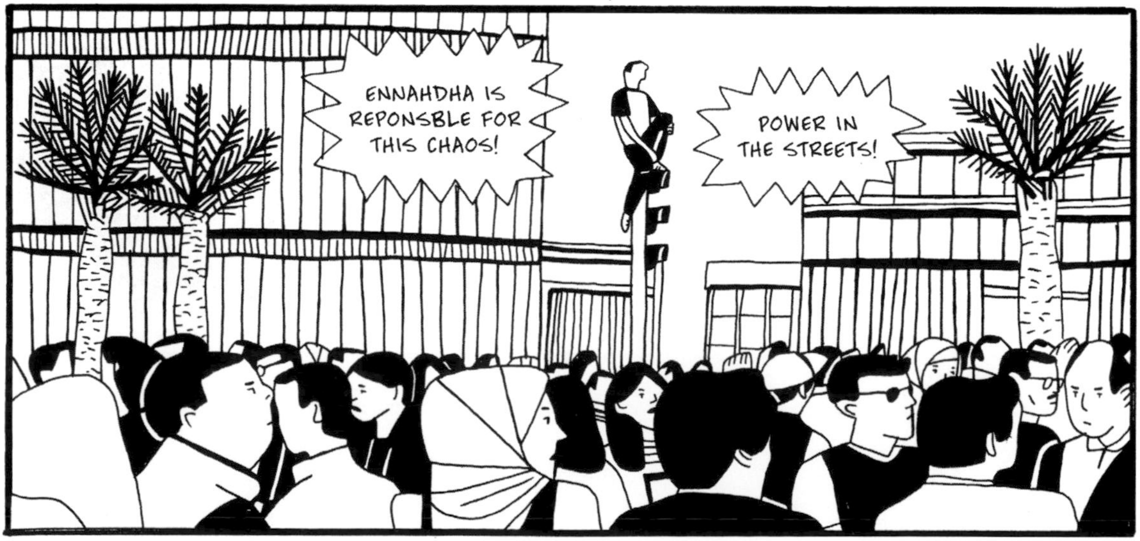
ENNAHDHA IS REPONSBLE FOR THIS CHAOS!
POWER IN THE STREETS!

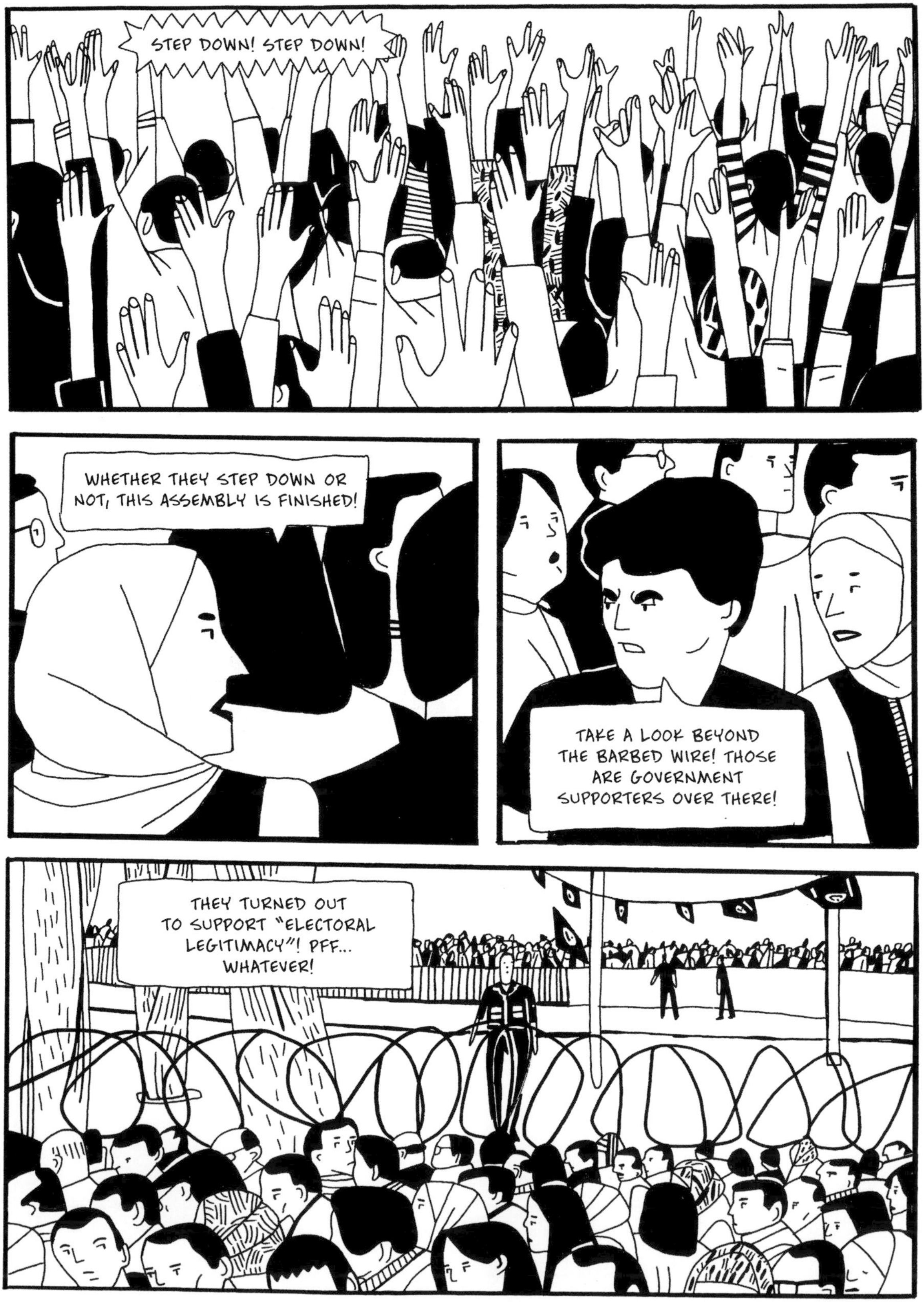
STEP DOWN! STEP DOWN!
WHETHER THEY STEP DOWN OR NOT, THIS ASSEMBLY IS FINISHED!
TAKE A LOOK BEYOND THE BARBED WIRE! THOSE ARE GOVERNMENT SUPPORTERS OVER THERE!
THEY TURNED OUT TO SUPPORT "ELECTORAL LEGITIMACY"! PFF... WHATEVER!

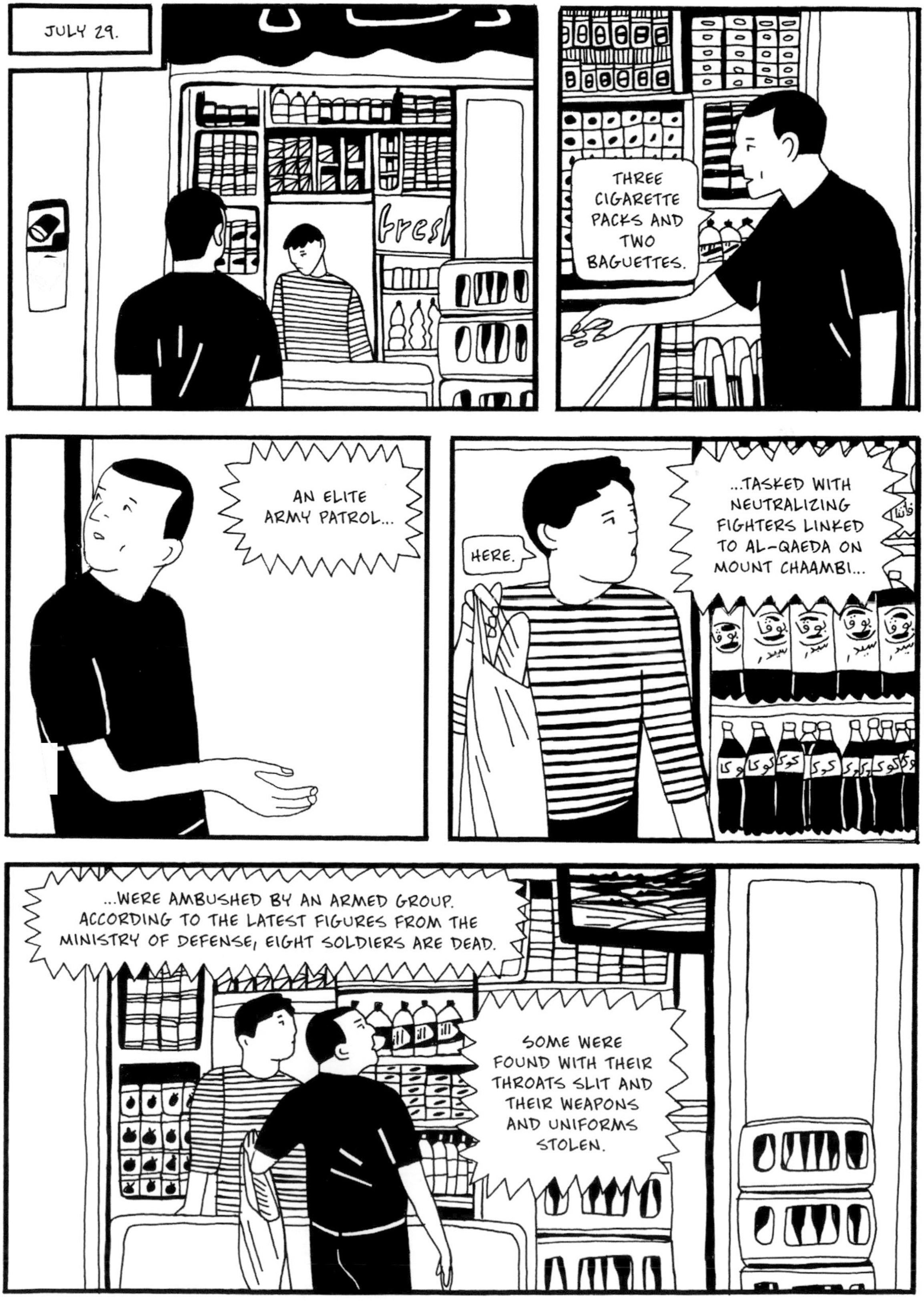
JULY 29.
THREE CIGARETTE PACKS AND TWO BAGUETTES.
AN ELITE ARMY PATROL...
HERE.
...TASKED WITH NEUTRALIZING FIGHTERS LINKED TO AL-QAEDA ON MOUNT CHAAMBI...
...WERE AMBUSHED BY AN ARMED GROUP. ACCORDING TO THE LATEST FIGURES FROM THE MINISTRY OF DEFENSE, EIGHT SOLDIERS ARE DEAD.
SOME WERE FOUND WITH THEIR THROATS SLIT AND THEIR WEAPONS AND UNIFORMS STOLEN.

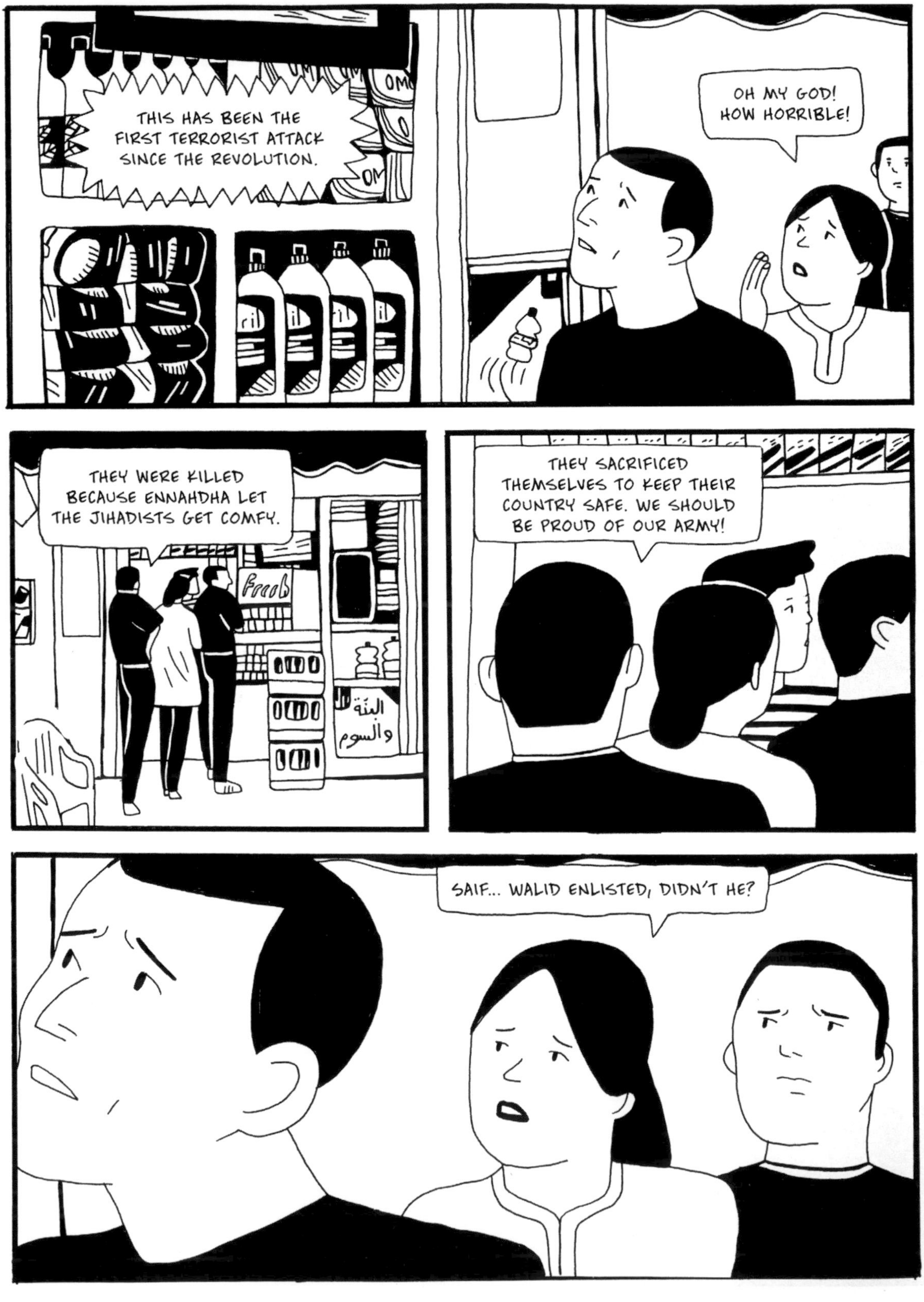
THIS HAS BEEN THE FIRST TERRORIST ATTACK SINCE THE REVOLUTION.
OH MY GOD! HOW HORRIBLE!
THEY WERE KILLED BECAUSE ENNAHDHA LET THE JIHADISTS GET COMFY.
البنَة
والسوم
THEY SACRIFICED THEMSELVES TO KEEP THEIR COUNTRY SAFE. WE SHOULD BE PROUD OF OUR ARMY!
SAIF... WALID ENLISTED, DIDN'T HE?

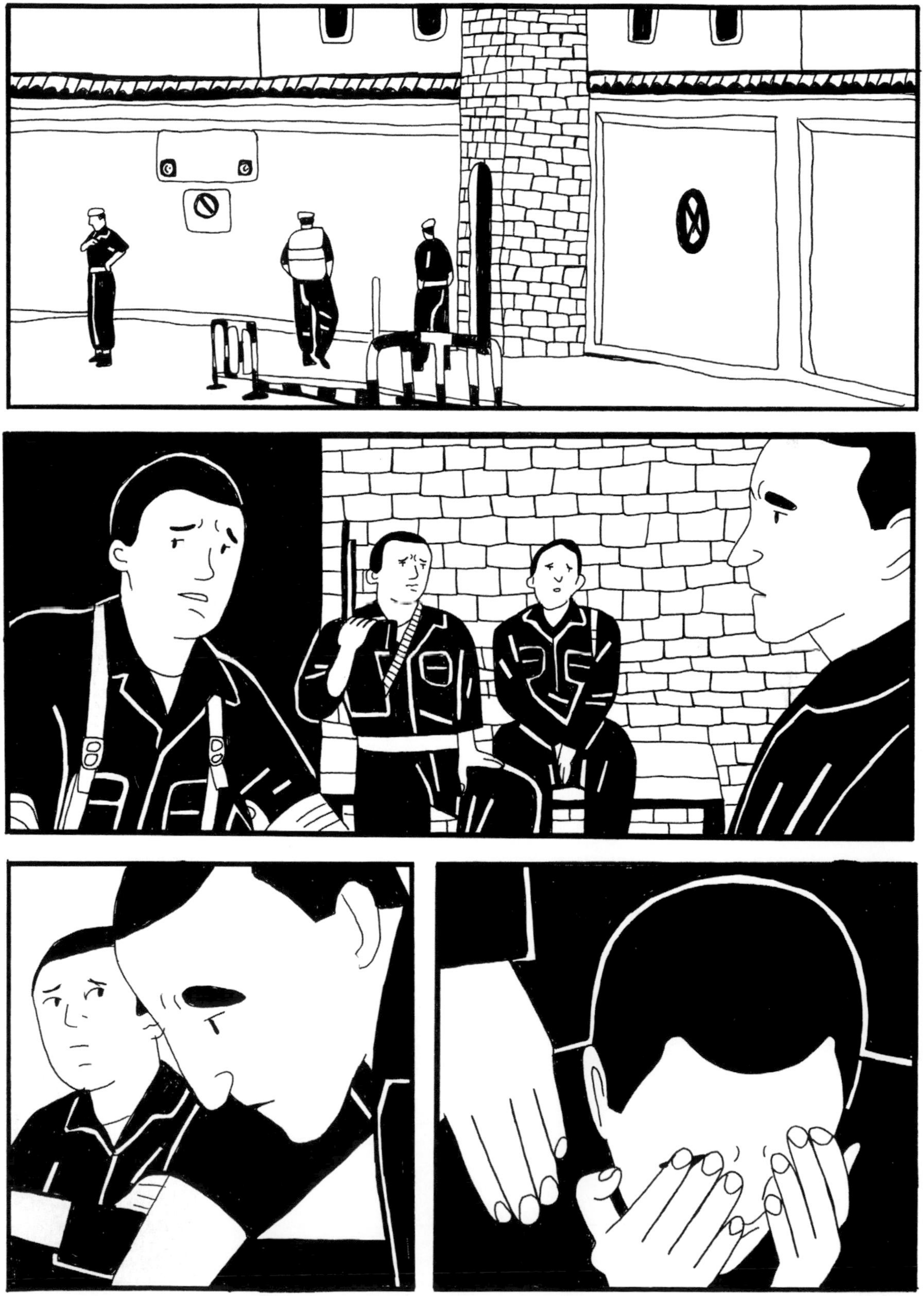

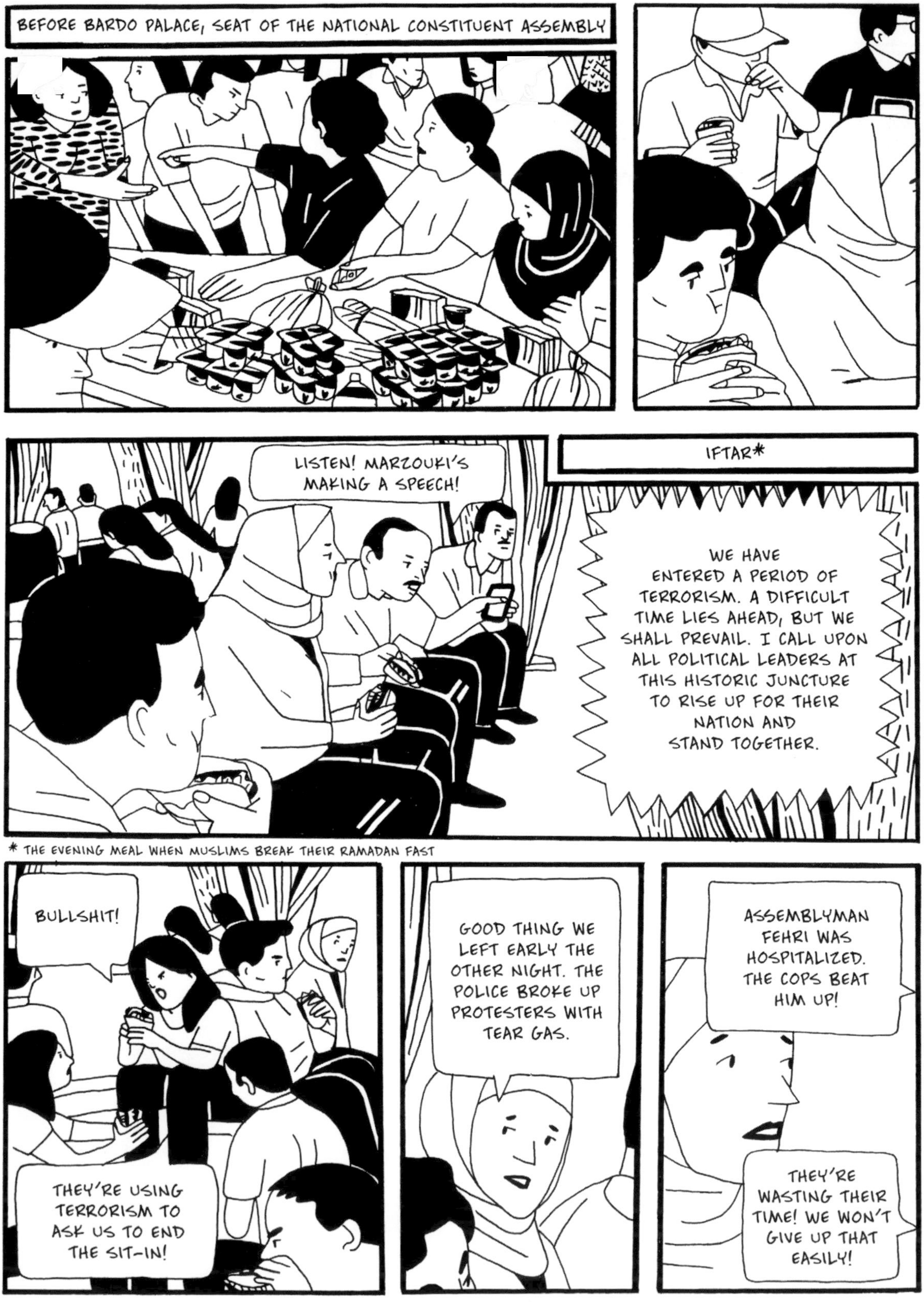

BEFORE BARDO PALACE, SEAT OF THE NATIONAL CONSTITUENT ASSEMBLY
LISTEN! MARZOUKI'S MAKING A SPEECH!
IFTAR*
WE HAVE ENTERED A PERIOD OF TERRORISM. A DIFFICULT TIME LIES AHEAD, BUT WE SHALL PREVAIL. I CALL UPON ALL POLITICAL LEADERS AT THIS HISTORIC JUNCTURE TO RISE UP FOR THEIR NATION AND STAND TOGETHER.
* THE EVENING MEAL WHEN MUSLIMS BREAK THEIR RAMADAN FAST
BULLSHIT!
THEY'RE USING TERRORISM TO ASK US TO END THE SIT-IN!
GOOD THING WE LEFT EARLY THE OTHER NIGHT. THE POLICE BROKE UP PROTESTERS WITH TEAR GAS.
ASSEMBLYMAN FEHRI WAS HOSPITALIZED. THE COPS BEAT HIM UP!
THEY'RE WASTING THEIR TIME! WE WON'T GIVE UP THAT EASILY!

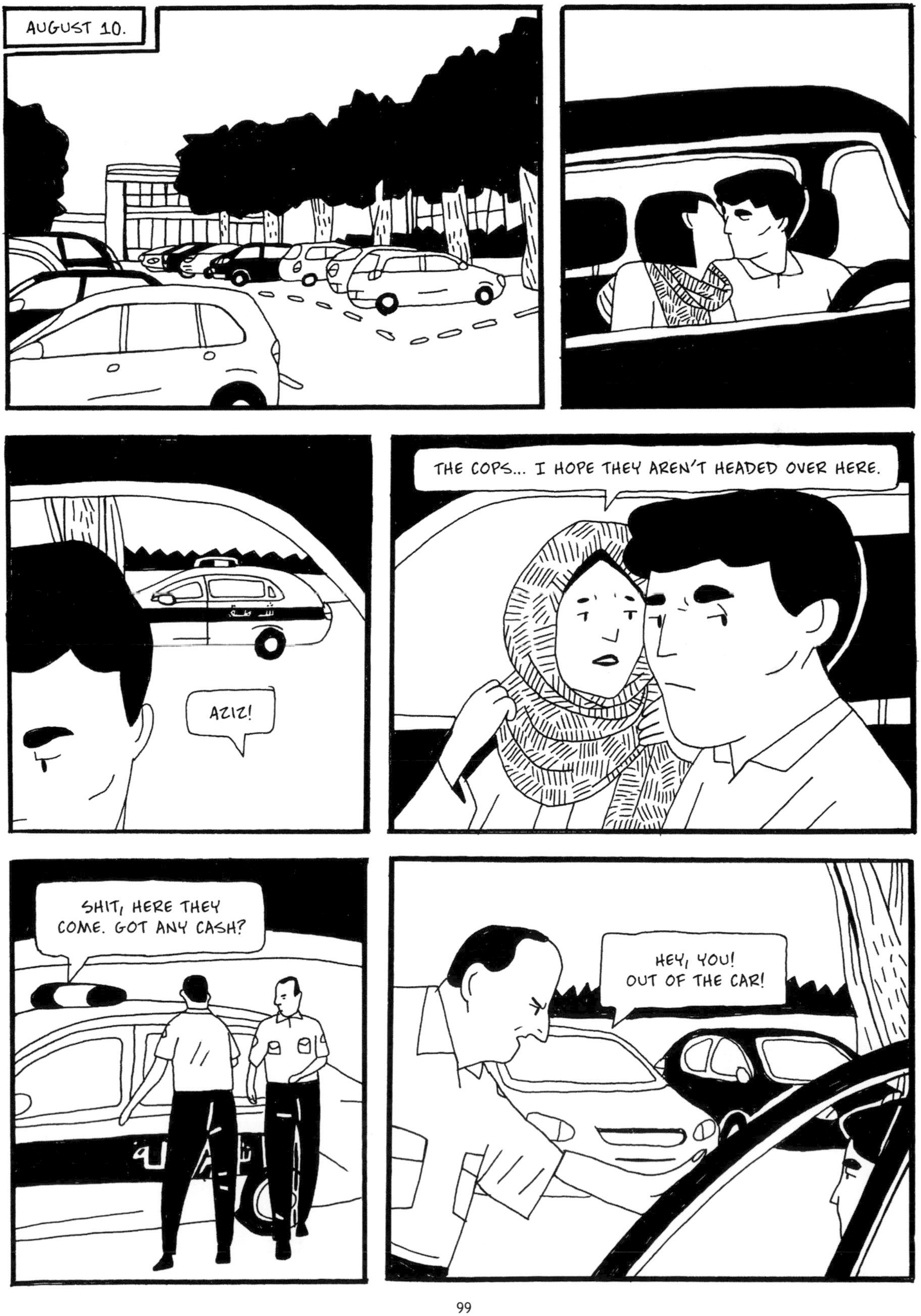
AUGUST 10.
THE COPS... I HOPE THEY AREN'T HEADED OVER HERE.
AZIZ!
SHIT, HERE THEY COME. GOT ANY CASH?
HEY, YOU! OUT OF THE CAR!

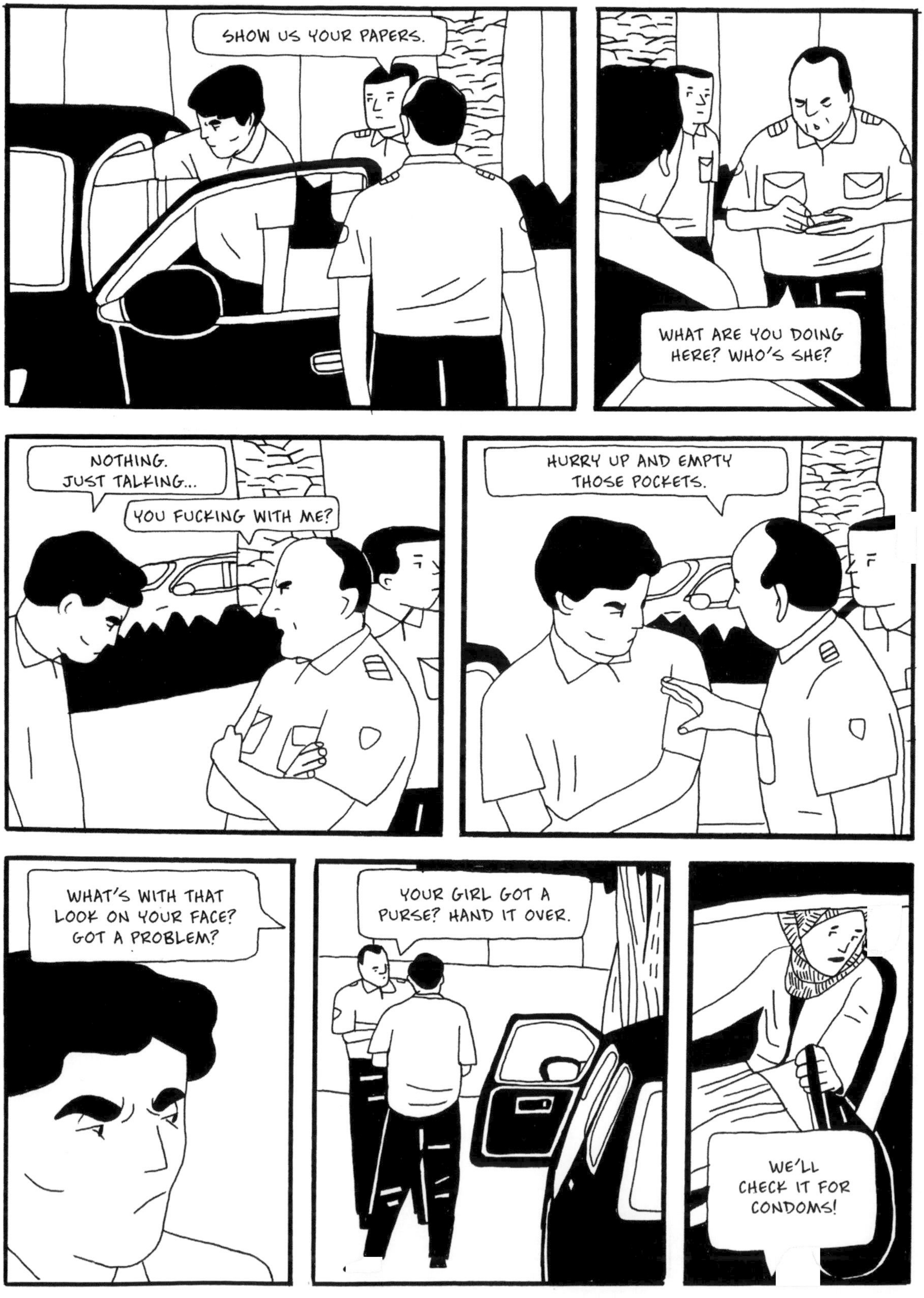
SHOW US YOUR PAPERS.
WHAT ARE YOU DOING HERE? WHO'S SHE?
NOTHING. JUST TALKING...
YOU FUCKING WITH ME?
HURRY UP AND EMPTY THOSE POCKETS.
WHAT'S WITH THAT LOOK ON YOUR FACE? GOT A PROBLEM?
YOUR GIRL GOT A PURSE? HAND IT OVER.
WE'LL CHECK IT FOR CONDOMS!

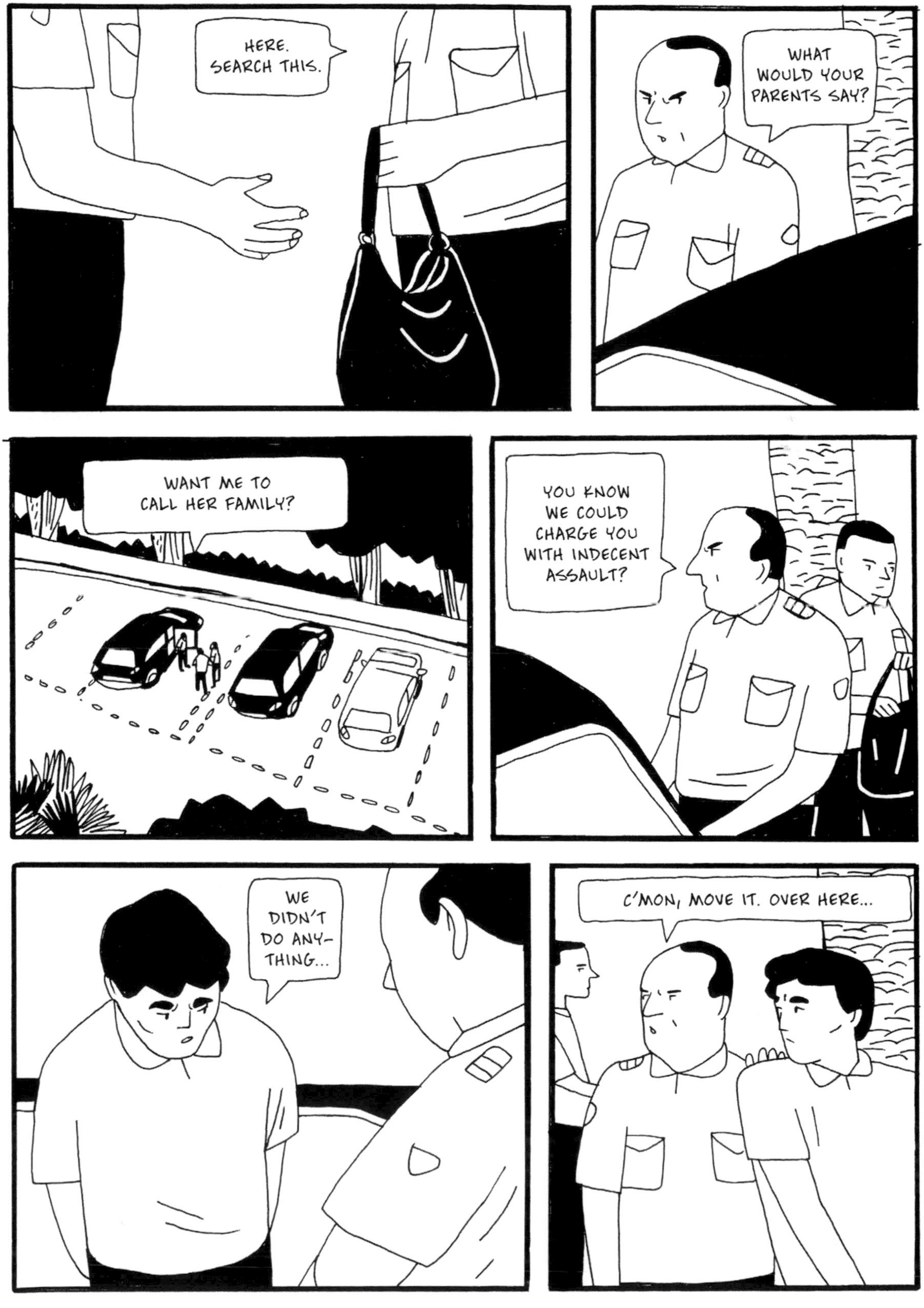
HERE. SEARCH THIS.
WHAT WOULD YOUR PARENTS SAY?
WANT ME TO CALL HER FAMILY?
YOU KNOW WE COULD CHARGE YOU WITH INDECENT ASSAULT?
WE DIDN'T DO ANY-THING...
C'MON, MOVE IT. OVER HERE...

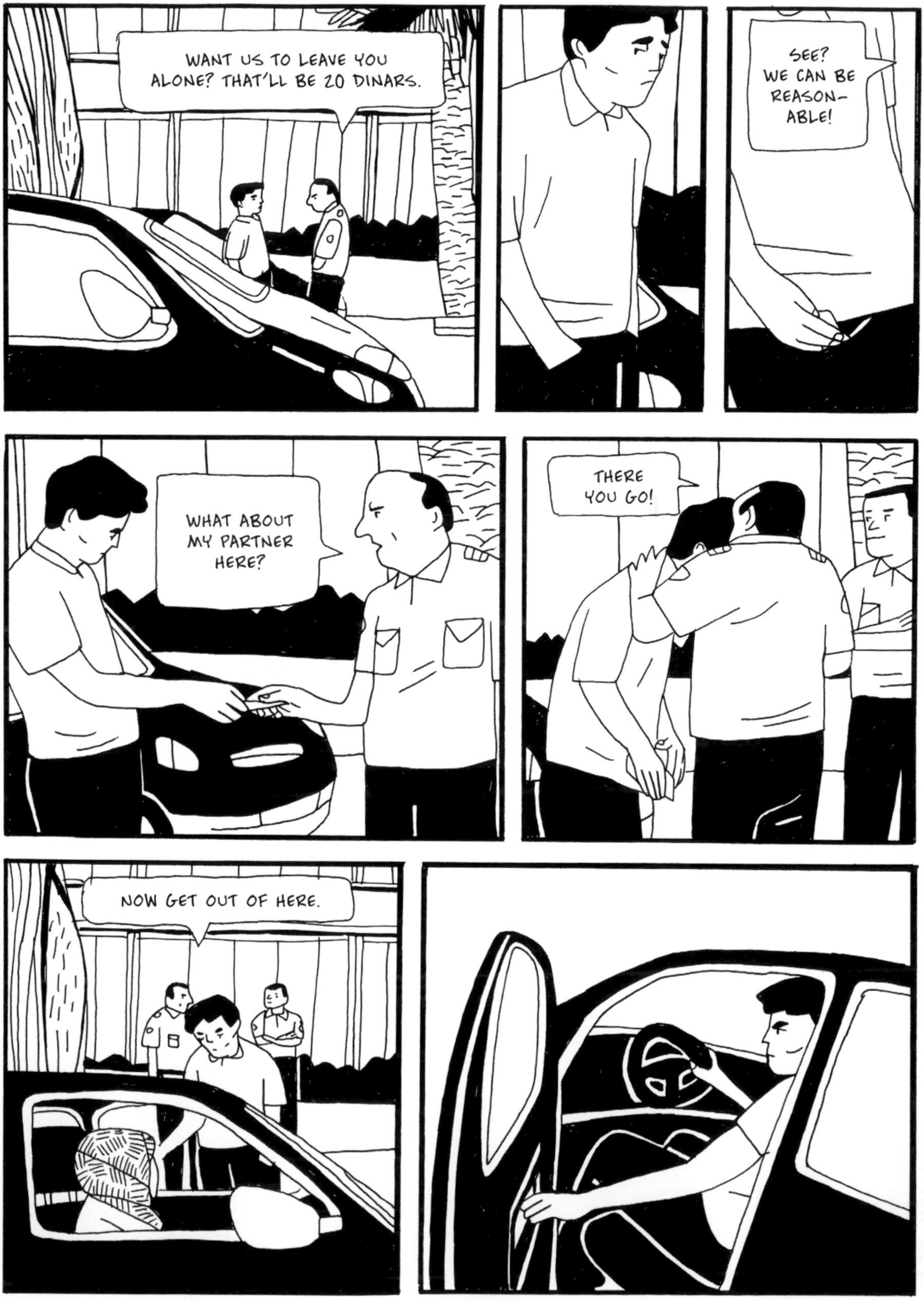

WANT US TO LEAVE YOU ALONE? THAT'LL BE 20 DINARS.
SEE? WE CAN BE REASON-ABLE!
WHAT ABOUT MY PARTNER HERE?
THERE YOU GO!
NOW GET OUT OF HERE.

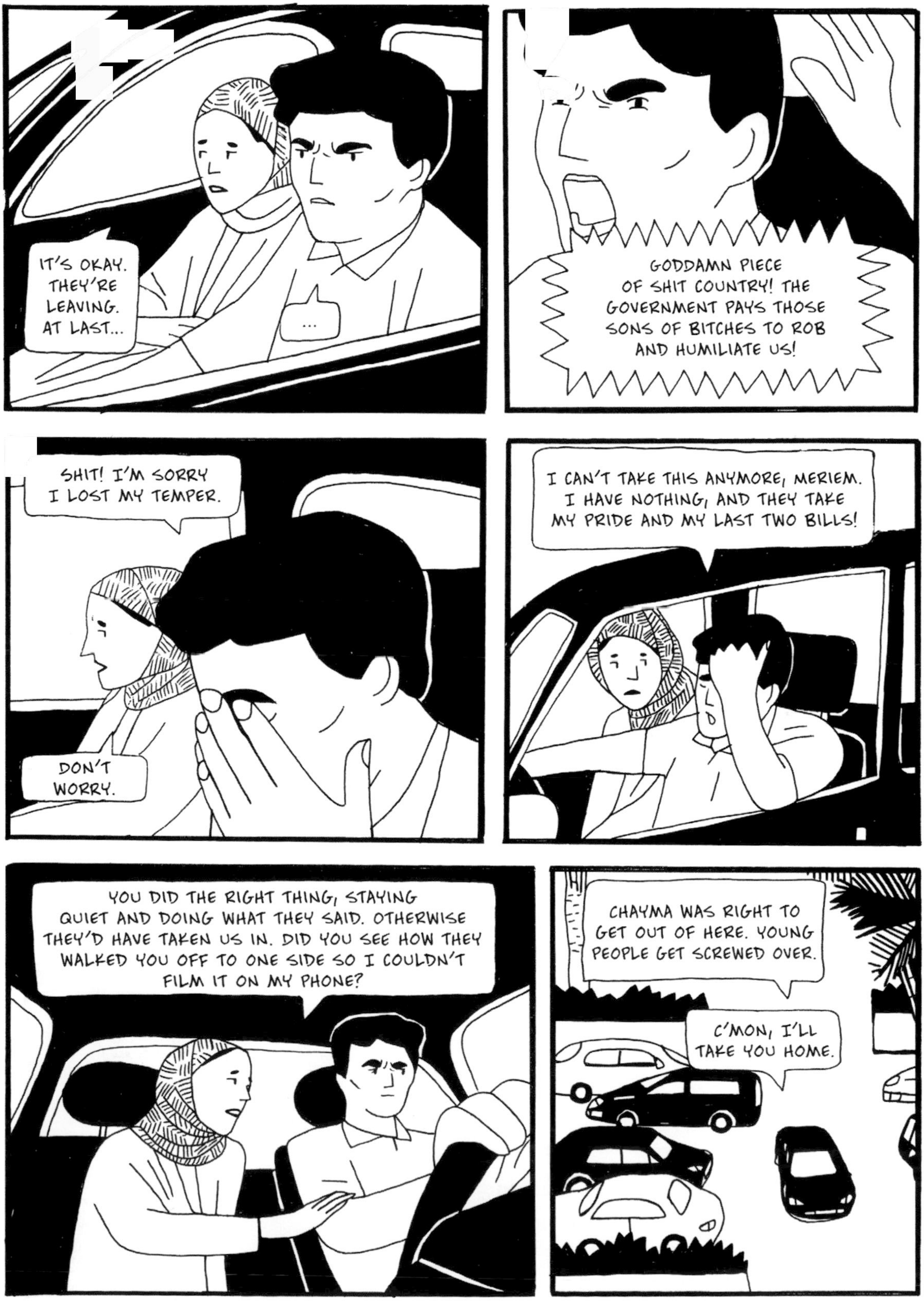
IT'S OKAY. THEY'RE LEAVING. AT LAST...
...
GODDAMN PIECE OF SHIT COUNTRY! THE GOVERNMENT PAYS THOSE SONS OF BITCHES TO ROB AND HUMILIATE US!
SHIT! I'M SORRY I LOST MY TEMPER.
DON'T WORRY.
I CAN'T TAKE THIS ANYMORE, MERIEM. I HAVE NOTHING, AND THEY TAKE MY PRIDE AND MY LAST TWO BILLS!
YOU DID THE RIGHT THING, STAYING QUIET AND DOING WHAT THEY SAID. OTHERWISE THEY'D HAVE TAKEN US IN. DID YOU SEE HOW THEY WALKED YOU OFF TO ONE SIDE SO I COULDN'T FILM IT ON MY PHONE?
CHAYMA WAS RIGHT TO GET OUT OF HERE. YOUNG PEOPLE GET SCREWED OVER.
C'MON, I'LL TAKE YOU HOME.

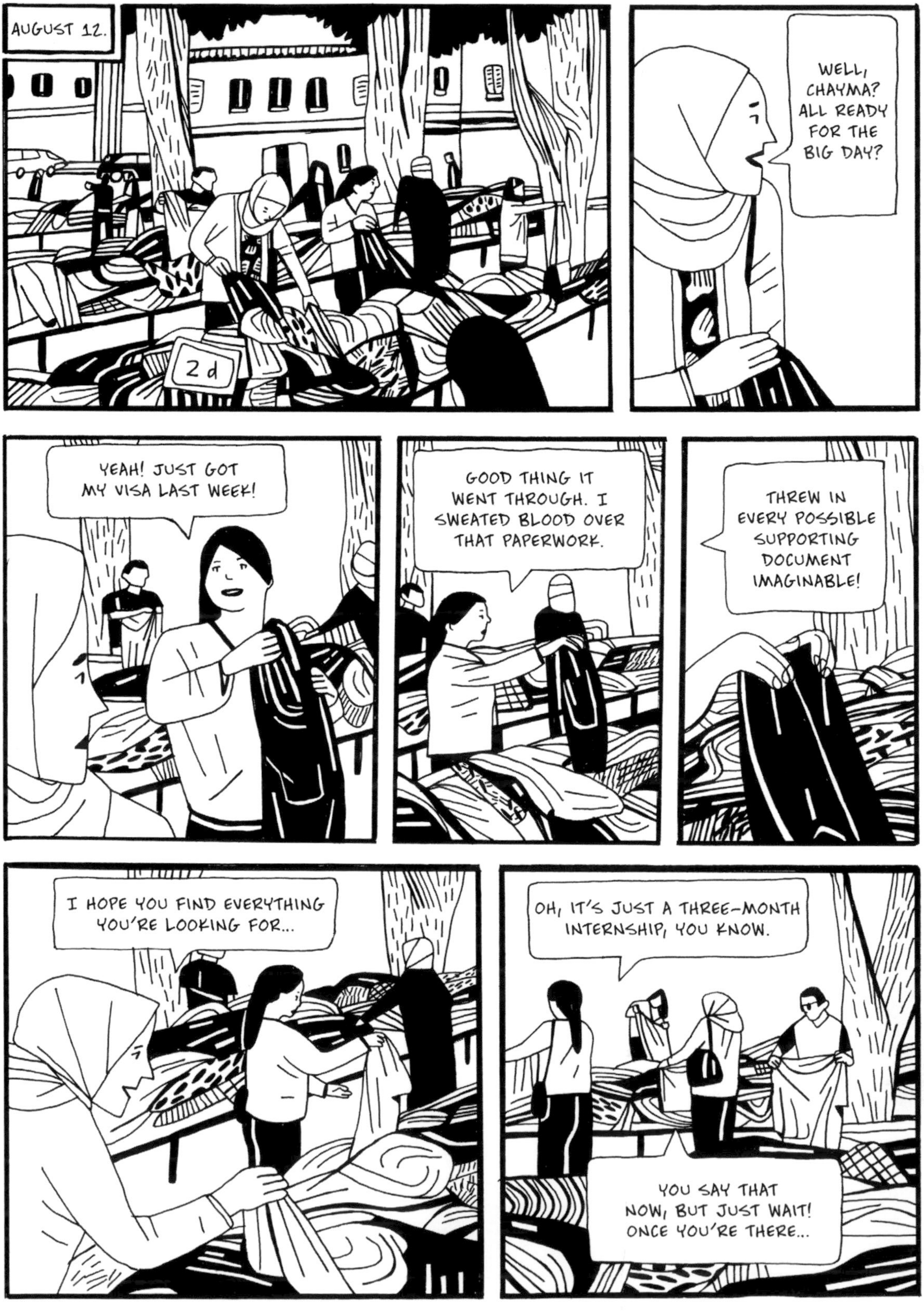
AUGUST 12.
2 d
WELL, CHAYMA? ALL READY FOR THE BIG DAY?
YEAH! JUST GOT MY VISA LAST WEEK!
GOOD THING IT WENT THROUGH. I SWEATED BLOOD OVER THAT PAPERWORK.
THREW IN EVERY POSSIBLE SUPPORTING DOCUMENT IMAGINABLE!
I HOPE YOU FIND EVERYTHING YOU'RE LOOKING FOR...
OH, IT'S JUST A THREE-MONTH INTERNSHIP, YOU KNOW.
YOU SAY THAT NOW, BUT JUST WAIT! ONCE YOU'RE THERE...

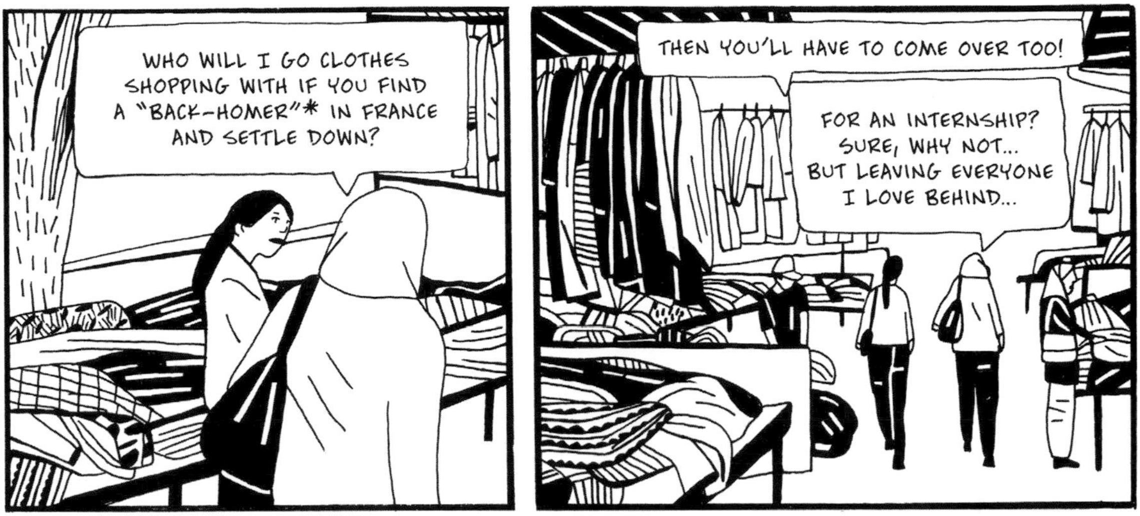
WHO WILL I GO CLOTHES SHOPPING WITH IF YOU FIND A "BACK-HOMER"* IN FRANCE AND SETTLE DOWN?
THEN YOU'LL HAVE TO COME OVER TOO!
FOR AN INTERNSHIP? SURE, WHY NOT... BUT LEAVING EVERYONE I LOVE BEHIND...

* NICKNAME FOR FRANCO-TUNISIANS WHO, WHILE ON VACATION IN TUNISIA, OFTEN SAY, "BACK HOME IN FRANCE"...

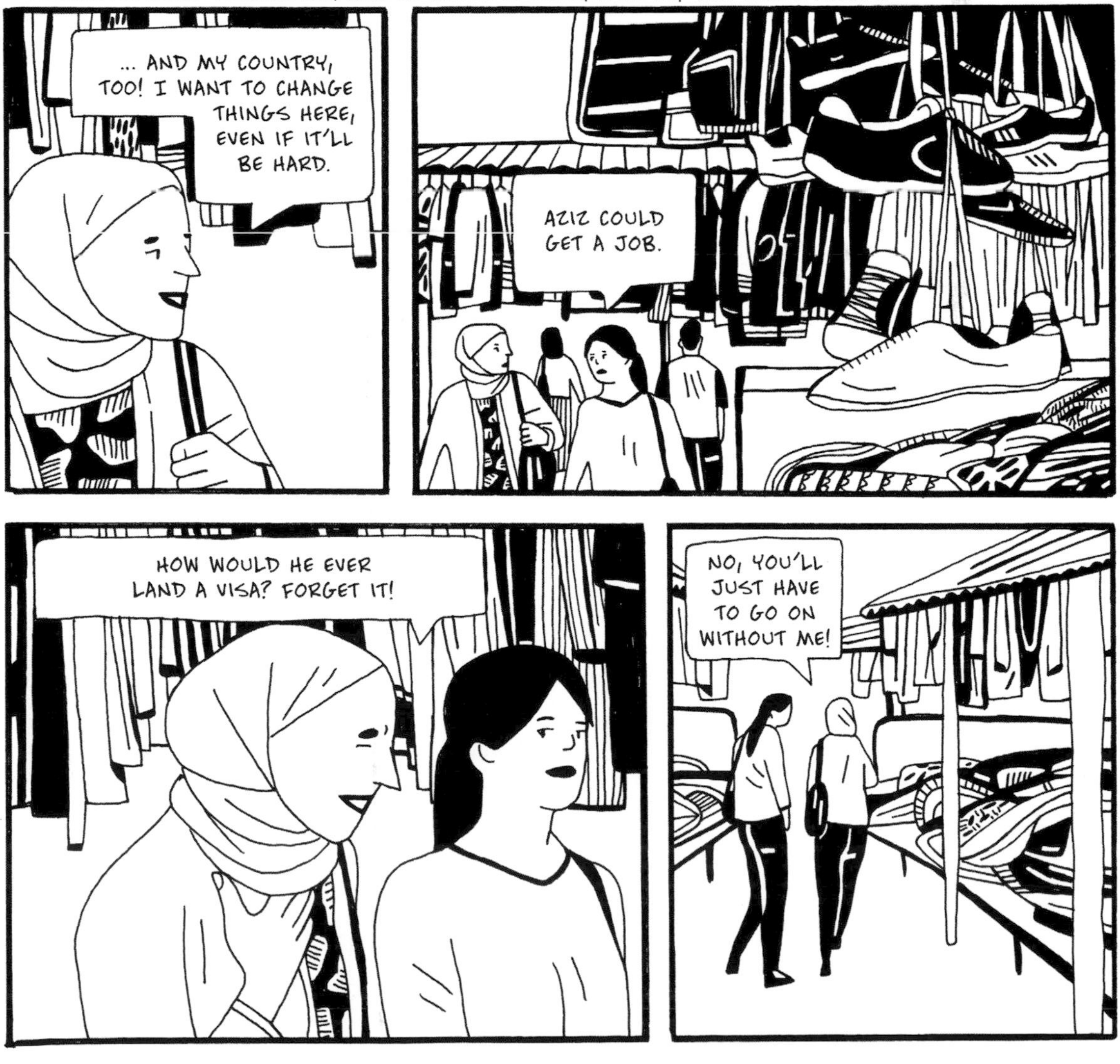
... AND MY COUNTRY, TOO! I WANT TO CHANGE THINGS HERE, EVEN IF IT'LL BE HARD.
AZIZ COULD GET A JOB.
HOW WOULD HE EVER LAND A VISA? FORGET IT!
NO, YOU'LL JUST HAVE TO GO ON WITHOUT ME!

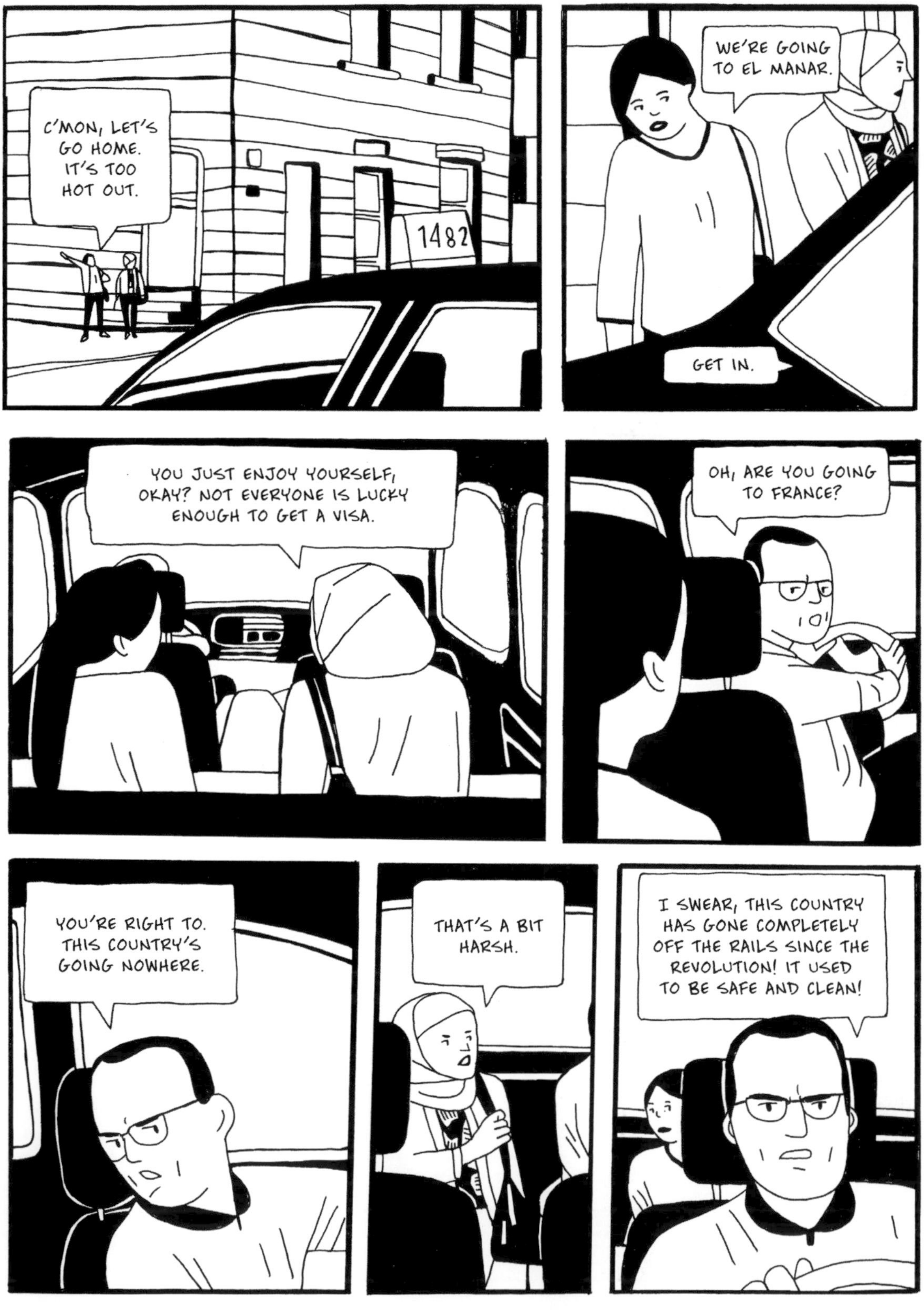
C'MON, LET'S GO HOME. IT'S TOO HOT OUT.
1482
WE'RE GOING TO EL MANAR.
GET IN.
YOU JUST ENJOY YOURSELF, OKAY? NOT EVERYONE IS LUCKY ENOUGH TO GET A VISA.
OH, ARE YOU GOING TO FRANCE?
YOU'RE RIGHT TO. THIS COUNTRY'S GOING NOWHERE.
THAT'S A BIT HARSH.
I SWEAR, THIS COUNTRY HAS GONE COMPLETELY OFF THE RAILS SINCE THE REVOLUTION! IT USED TO BE SAFE AND CLEAN!

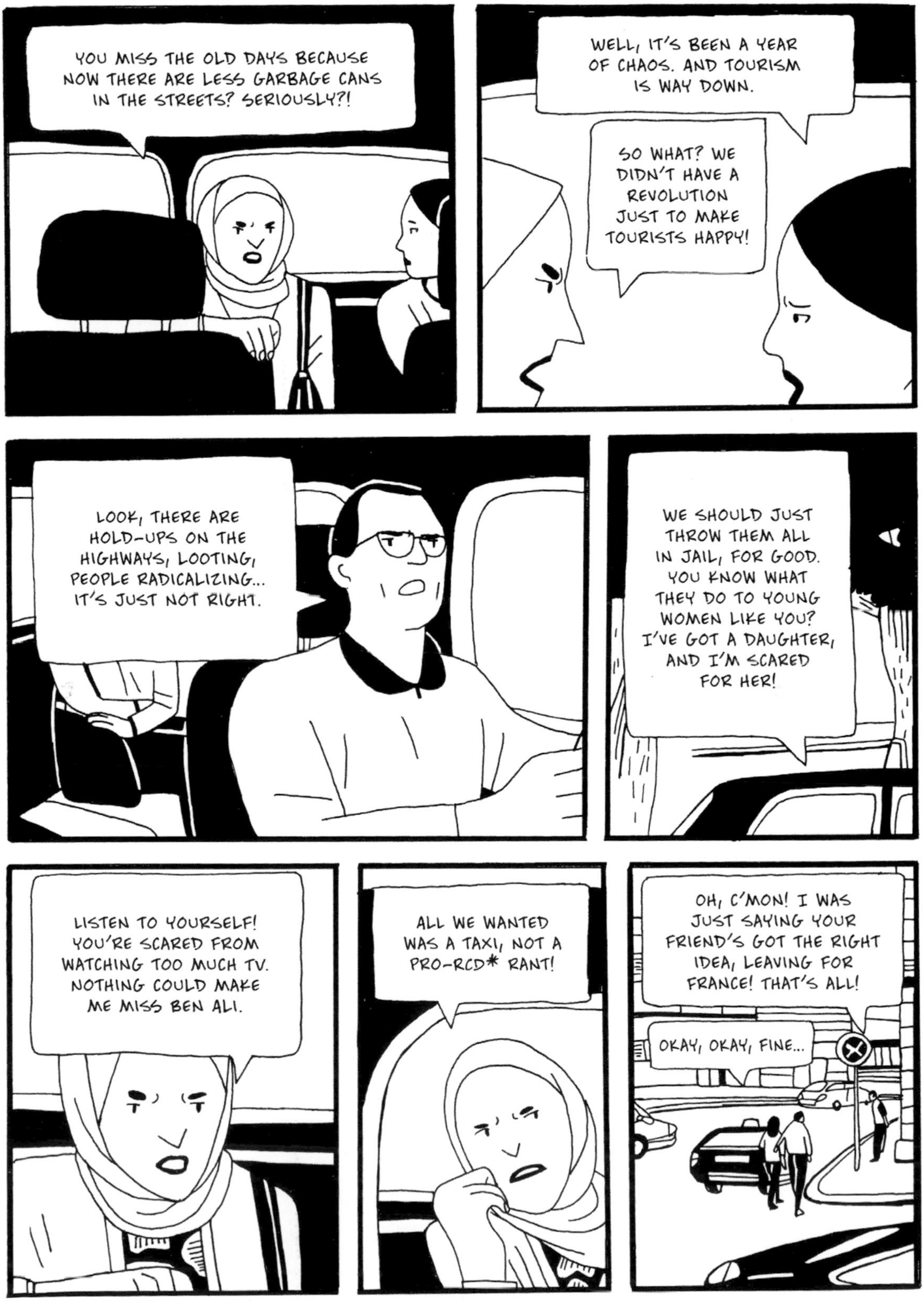
YOU MISS THE OLD DAYS BECAUSE NOW THERE ARE LESS GARBAGE CANS IN THE STREETS? SERIOUSLY?!
WELL, IT'S BEEN A YEAR OF CHAOS. AND TOURISM IS WAY DOWN.
SO WHAT? WE DIDN'T HAVE A REVOLUTION JUST TO MAKE TOURISTS HAPPY!
LOOK, THERE ARE HOLD-UPS ON THE HIGHWAYS, LOOTING, PEOPLE RADICALIZING... IT'S JUST NOT RIGHT.
WE SHOULD JUST THROW THEM ALL IN JAIL, FOR GOOD. YOU KNOW WHAT THEY DO TO YOUNG WOMEN LIKE YOU? I'VE GOT A DAUGHTER, AND I'M SCARED FOR HER!
LISTEN TO YOURSELF! YOU'RE SCARED FROM WATCHING TOO MUCH TV. NOTHING COULD MAKE ME MISS BEN ALI.
ALL WE WANTED WAS A TAXI, NOT A PRO-RCD* RANT!
OH, C'MON! I WAS JUST SAYING YOUR FRIEND'S GOT THE RIGHT IDEA, LEAVING FOR FRANCE! THAT'S ALL!
OKAY, OKAY, FINE...

* RASSEMBLEMENT CONSTITUTIONNEL DÉMOCRATIQUE, OR DEMOCRATIC CONSTITUTIONAL RALLY, A POLITICAL PARTY BEN ALI FOUNDED IN 1988

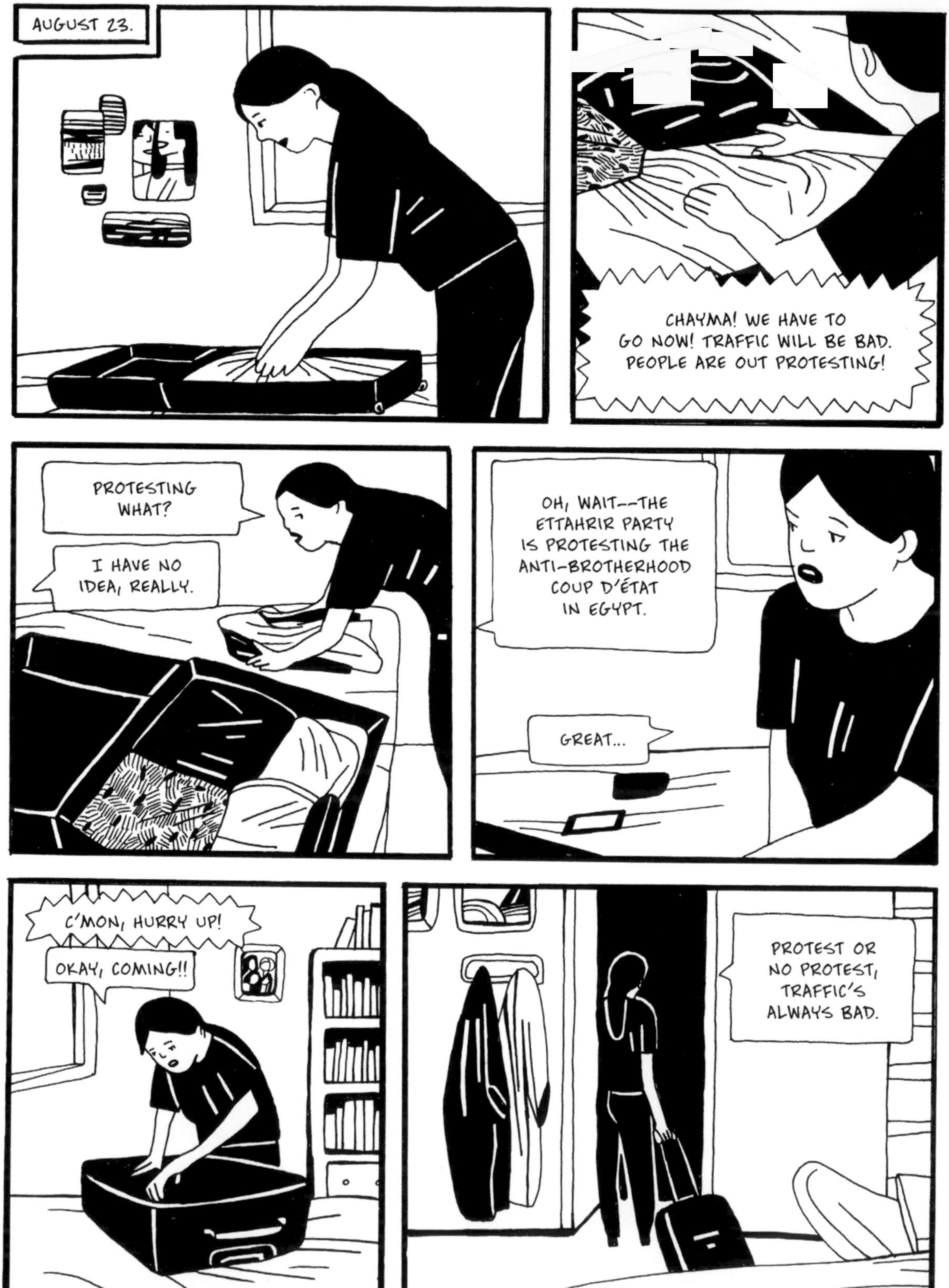
AUGUST 23.
CHAYMA! WE HAVE TO GO NOW! TRAFFIC WILL BE BAD. PEOPLE ARE OUT PROTESTING!
PROTESTING WHAT?
I HAVE NO IDEA, REALLY.
OH, WAIT--THE ETTAHRIR PARTY IS PROTESTING THE ANTI-BROTHERHOOD COUP D'ÉTAT IN EGYPT.
GREAT...
C'MON, HURRY UP!
OKAY, COMING!!
PROTEST OR NO PROTEST, TRAFFIC'S ALWAYS BAD.

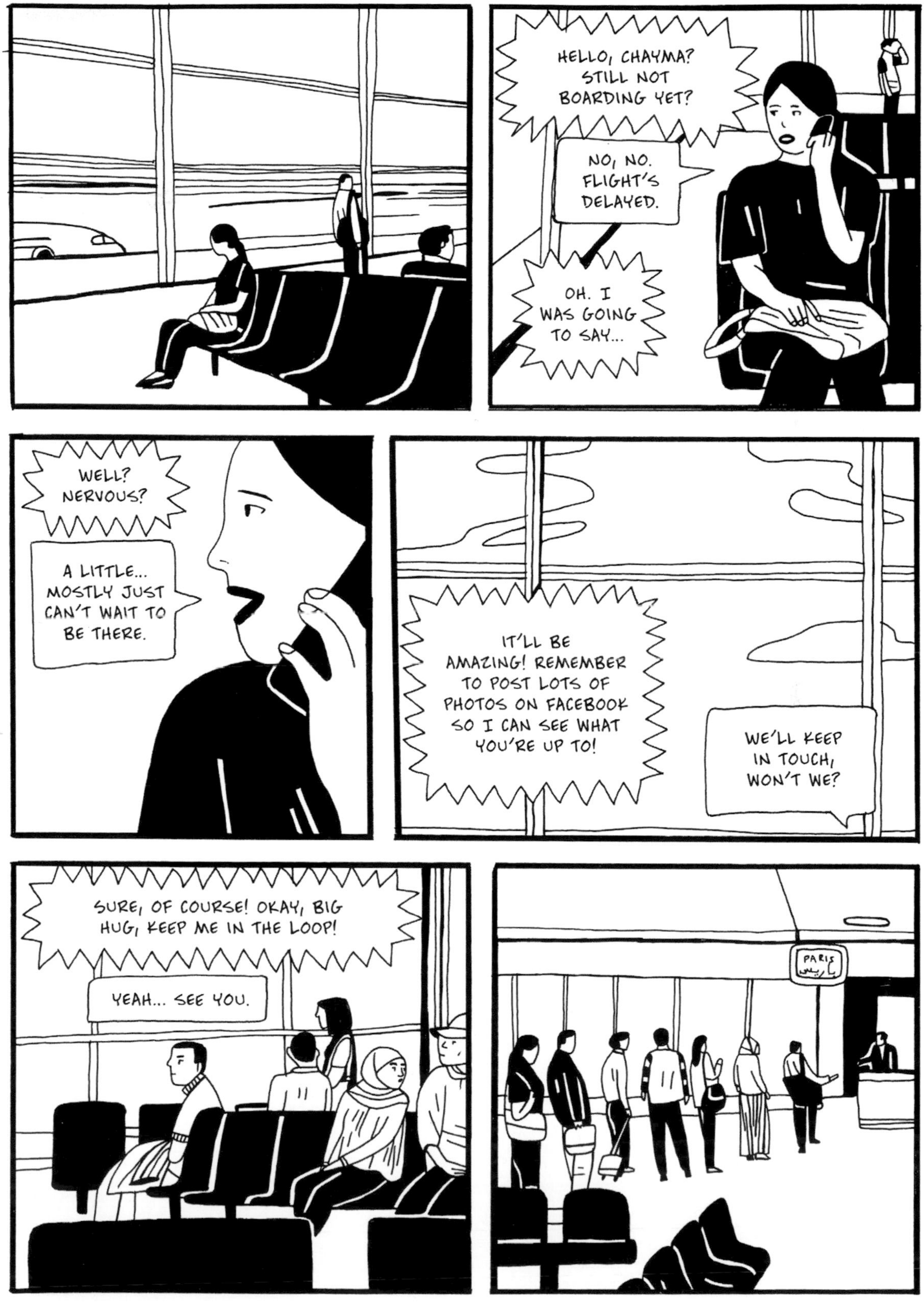
HELLO, CHAYMA? STILL NOT BOARDING YET?
NO, NO. FLIGHT'S DELAYED.
OH. I WAS GOING TO SAY...
WELL? NERVOUS?
A LITTLE... MOSTLY JUST CAN'T WAIT TO BE THERE.
IT'LL BE AMAZING! REMEMBER TO POST LOTS OF PHOTOS ON FACEBOOK SO I CAN SEE WHAT YOU'RE UP TO!
WE'LL KEEP IN TOUCH, WON'T WE?
SURE, OF COURSE! OKAY, BIG HUG, KEEP ME IN THE LOOP!
YEAH... SEE YOU.
PARIS

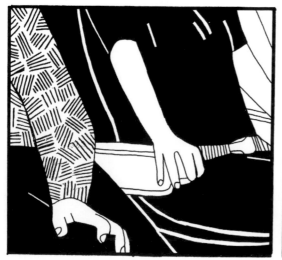

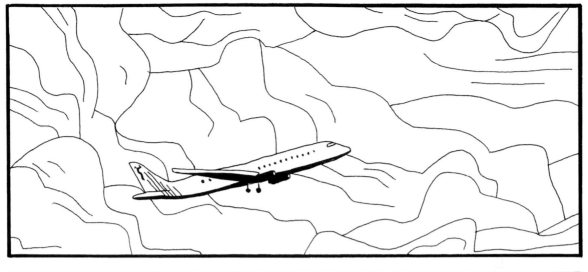

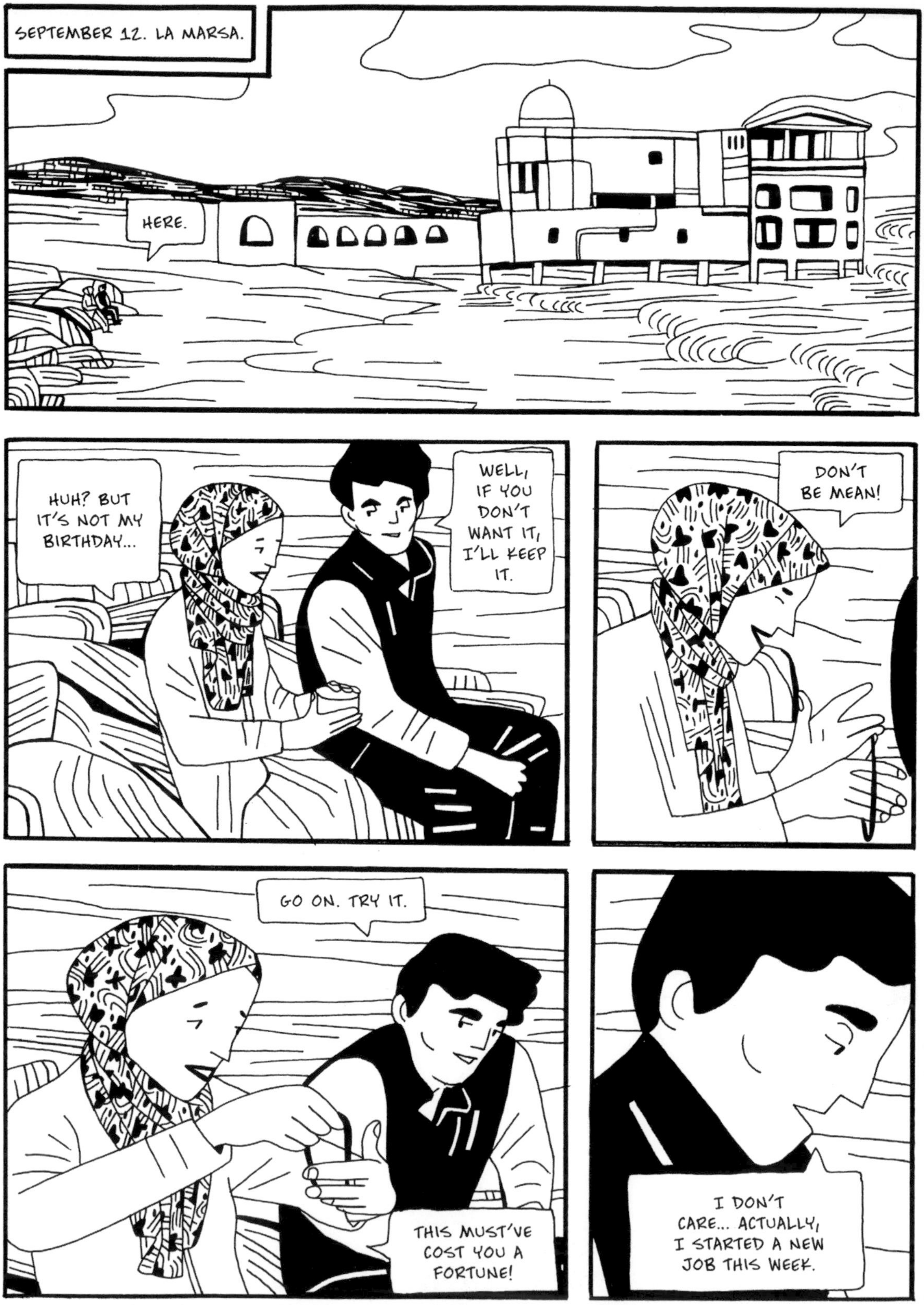
SEPTEMBER 12. LA MARSA.
HERE.
HUH? BUT IT'S NOT MY BIRTHDAY...
WELL, IF YOU DON'T WANT IT, I'LL KEEP IT.
DON'T BE MEAN!
GO ON. TRY IT.
THIS MUST'VE COST YOU A FORTUNE!
I DON'T CARE... ACTUALLY, I STARTED A NEW JOB THIS WEEK.

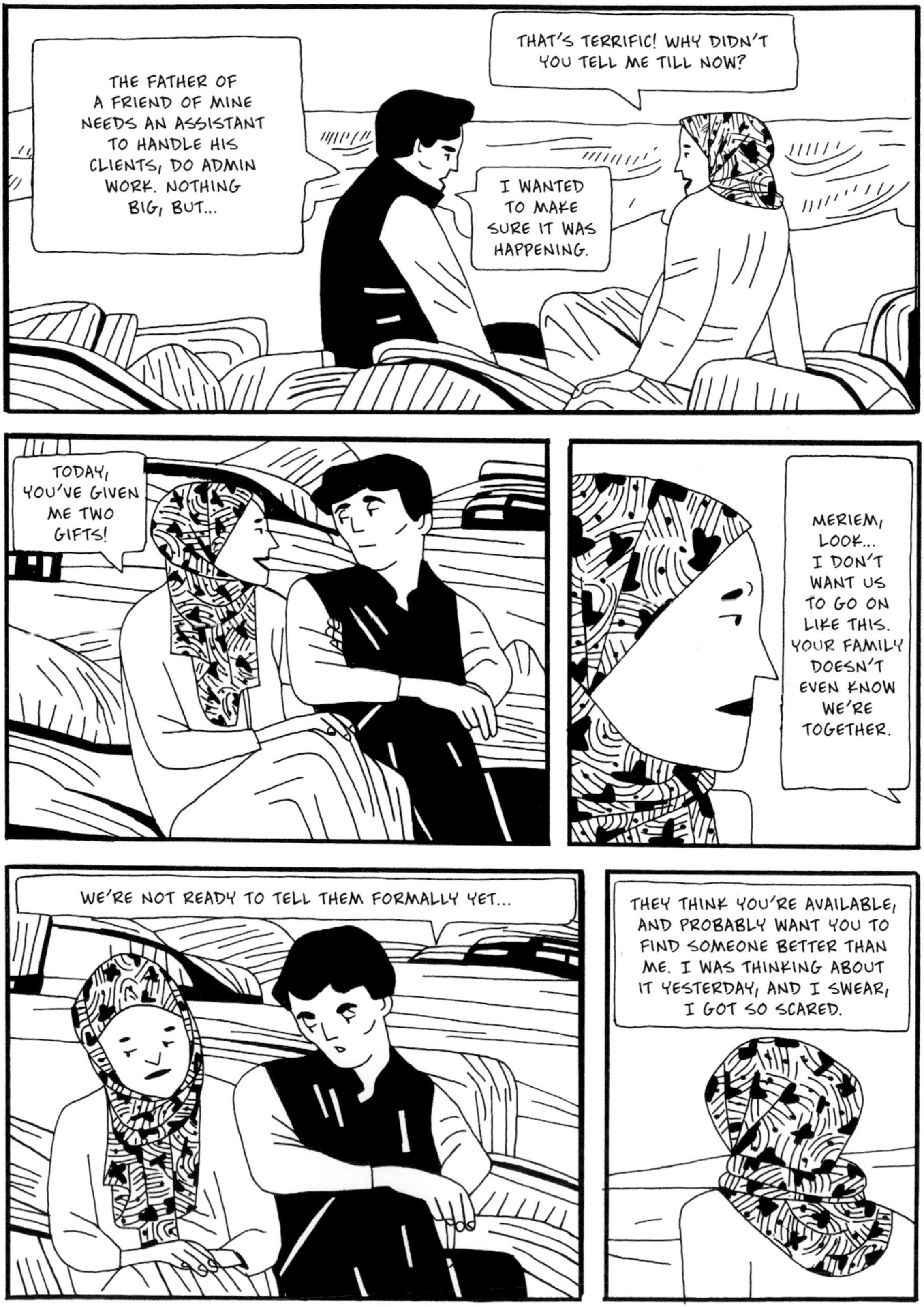
THE FATHER OF A FRIEND OF MINE NEEDS AN ASSISTANT TO HANDLE HIS CLIENTS, DO ADMIN WORK. NOTHING BIG, BUT...
THAT'S TERRIFIC! WHY DIDN'T YOU TELL ME TILL NOW?
I WANTED TO MAKE SURE IT WAS HAPPENING.
TODAY, YOU'VE GIVEN ME TWO GIFTS!
MERIEM, LOOK... I DON'T WANT US TO GO ON LIKE THIS. YOUR FAMILY DOESN'T EVEN KNOW WE'RE TOGETHER.
WE'RE NOT READY TO TELL THEM FORMALLY YET...
THEY THINK YOU'RE AVAILABLE, AND PROBABLY WANT YOU TO FIND SOMEONE BETTER THAN ME. I WAS THINKING ABOUT IT YESTERDAY, AND I SWEAR, I GOT SO SCARED.

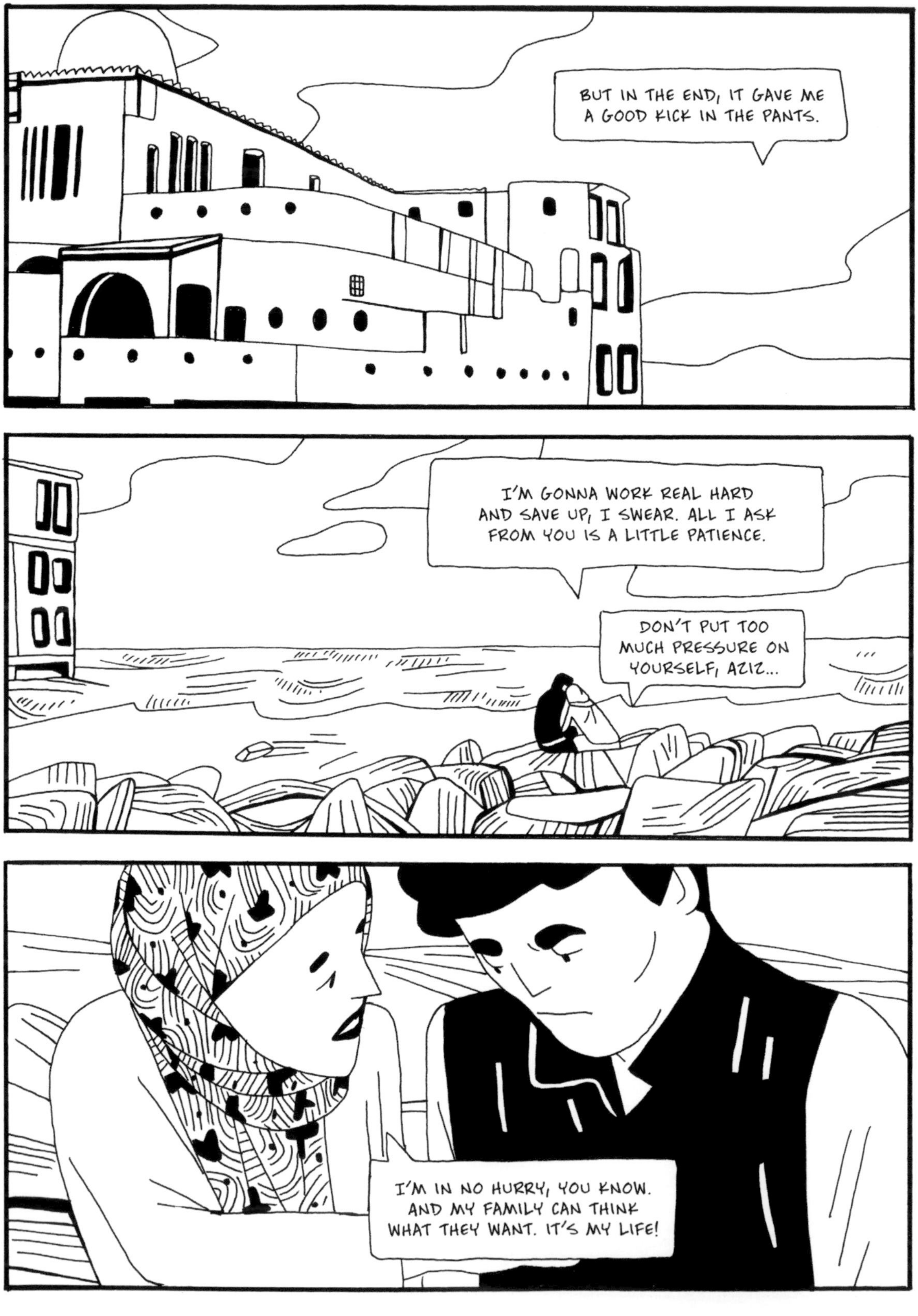

BUT IN THE END, IT GAVE ME A GOOD KICK IN THE PANTS.
I'M GONNA WORK REAL HARD AND SAVE UP, I SWEAR. ALL I ASK FROM YOU IS A LITTLE PATIENCE.
DON'T PUT TOO MUCH PRESSURE ON YOURSELF, AZIZ...
I'M IN NO HURRY, YOU KNOW. AND MY FAMILY CAN THINK WHAT THEY WANT. IT'S MY LIFE!

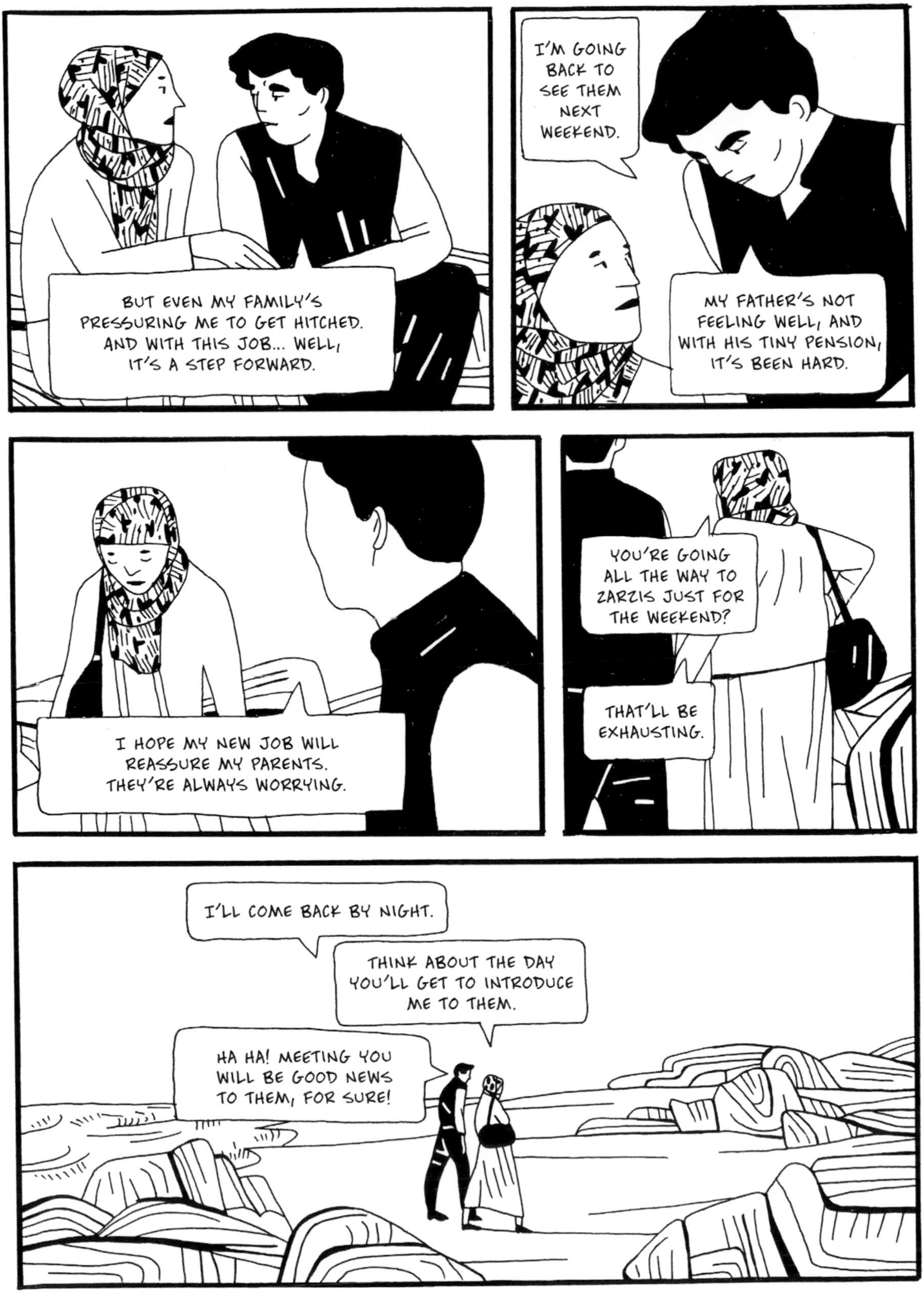
BUT EVEN MY FAMILY'S PRESSURING ME TO GET HITCHED. AND WITH THIS JOB... WELL, IT'S A STEP FORWARD.
I'M GOING BACK TO SEE THEM NEXT WEEKEND.
MY FATHER'S NOT FEELING WELL, AND WITH HIS TINY PENSION, IT'S BEEN HARD.
I HOPE MY NEW JOB WILL REASSURE MY PARENTS. THEY'RE ALWAYS WORRYING.
YOU'RE GOING ALL THE WAY TO ZARZIS JUST FOR THE WEEKEND?
THAT'LL BE EXHAUSTING.
I'LL COME BACK BY NIGHT.
THINK ABOUT THE DAY YOU'LL GET TO INTRODUCE ME TO THEM.
HA HA! MEETING YOU WILL BE GOOD NEWS TO THEM, FOR SURE!

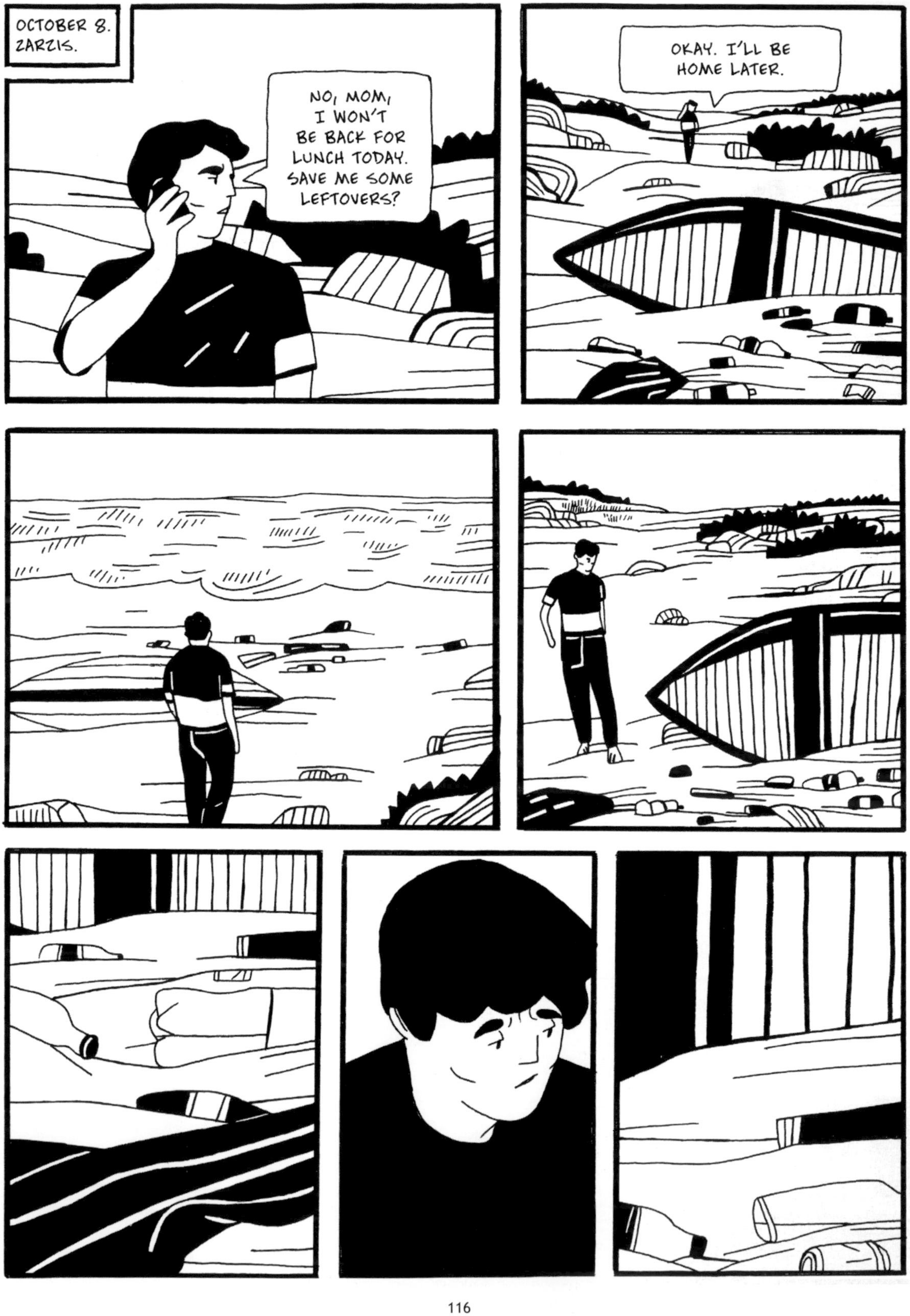
OCTOBER 8. ZARZIS.
NO, MOM, I WON'T BE BACK FOR LUNCH TODAY. SAVE ME SOME LEFTOVERS?
OKAY. I'LL BE HOME LATER.

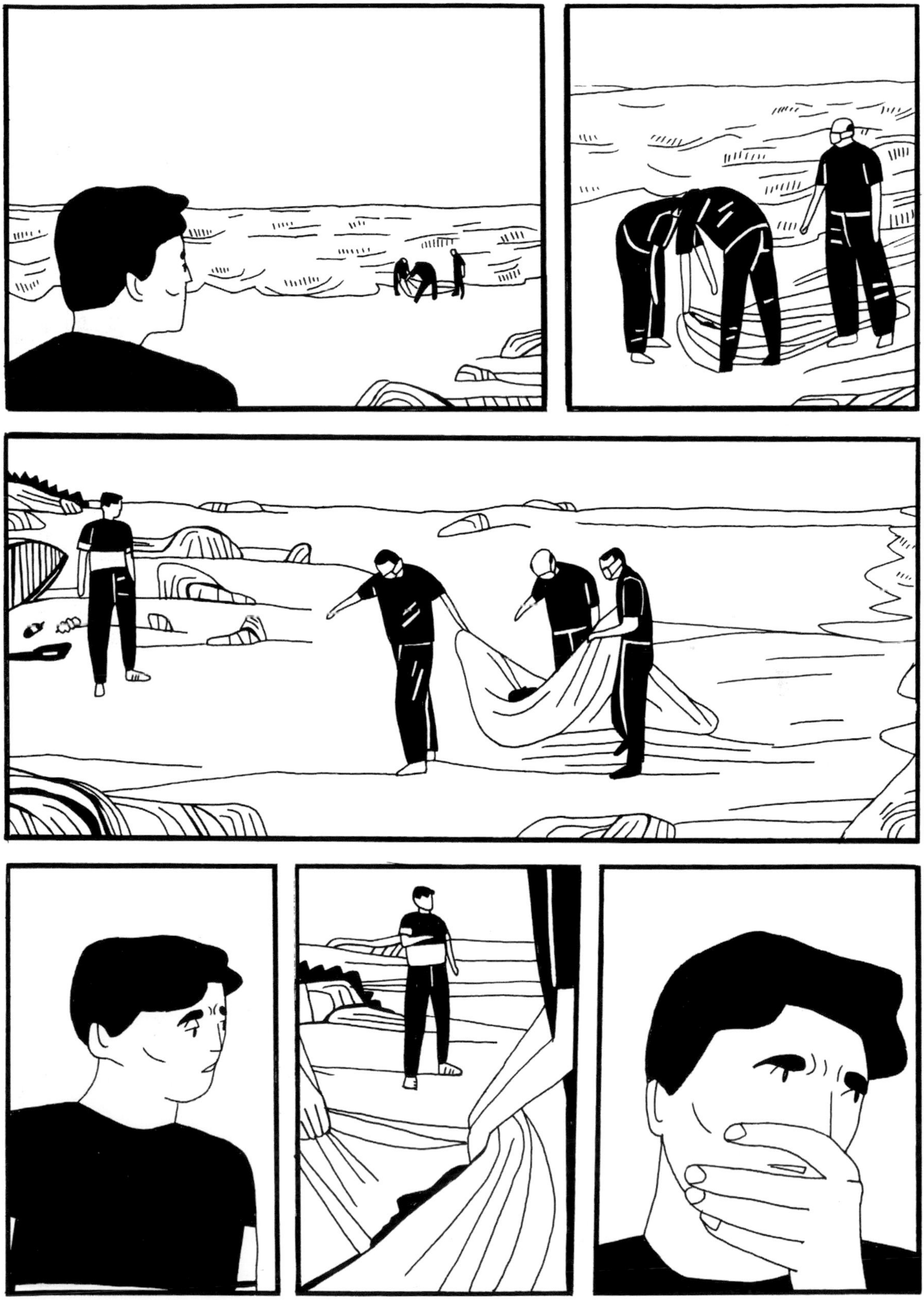

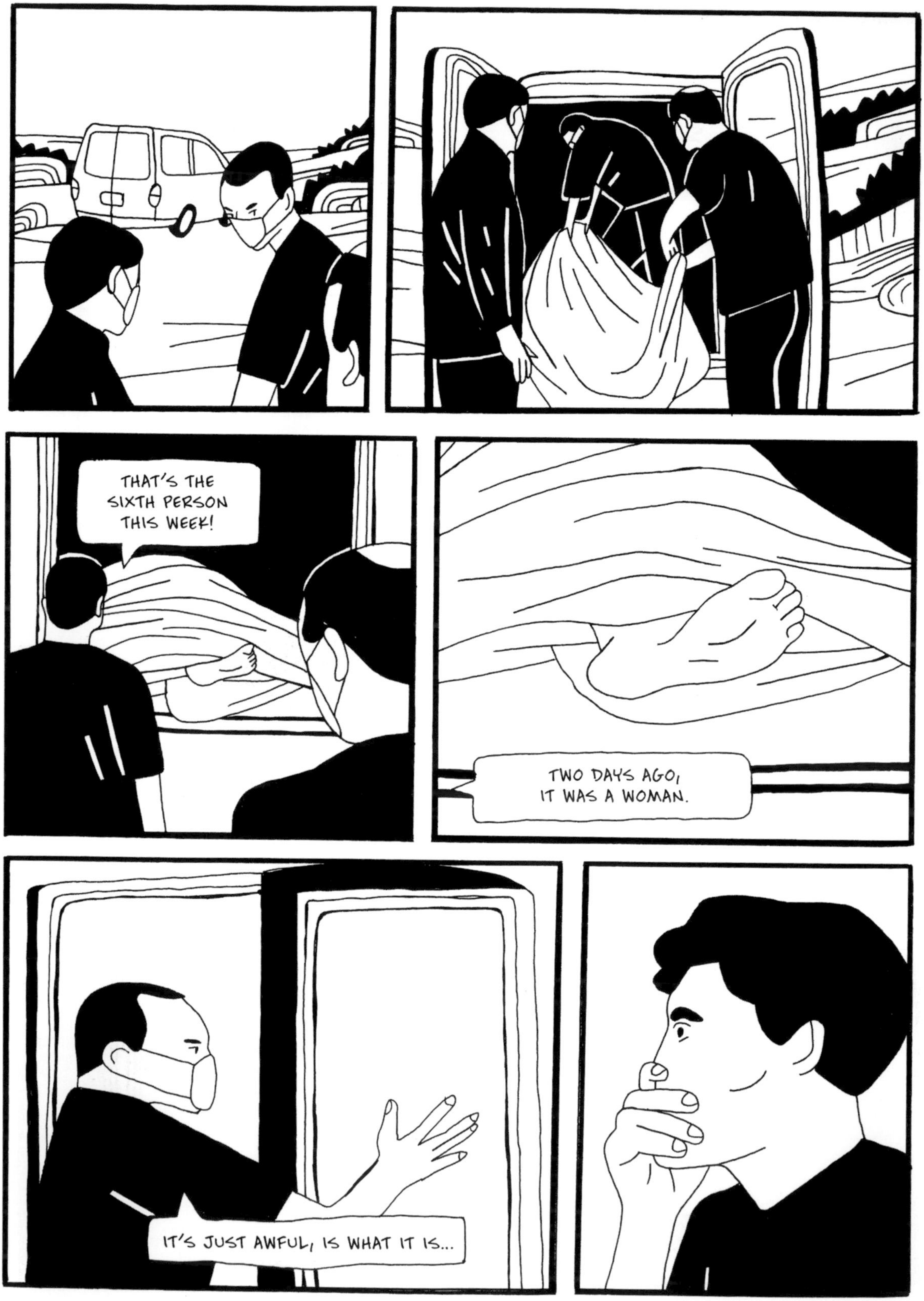
THAT'S THE SIXTH PERSON THIS WEEK!
TWO DAYS AGO, IT WAS A WOMAN.
IT'S JUST AWFUL, IS WHAT IT IS...

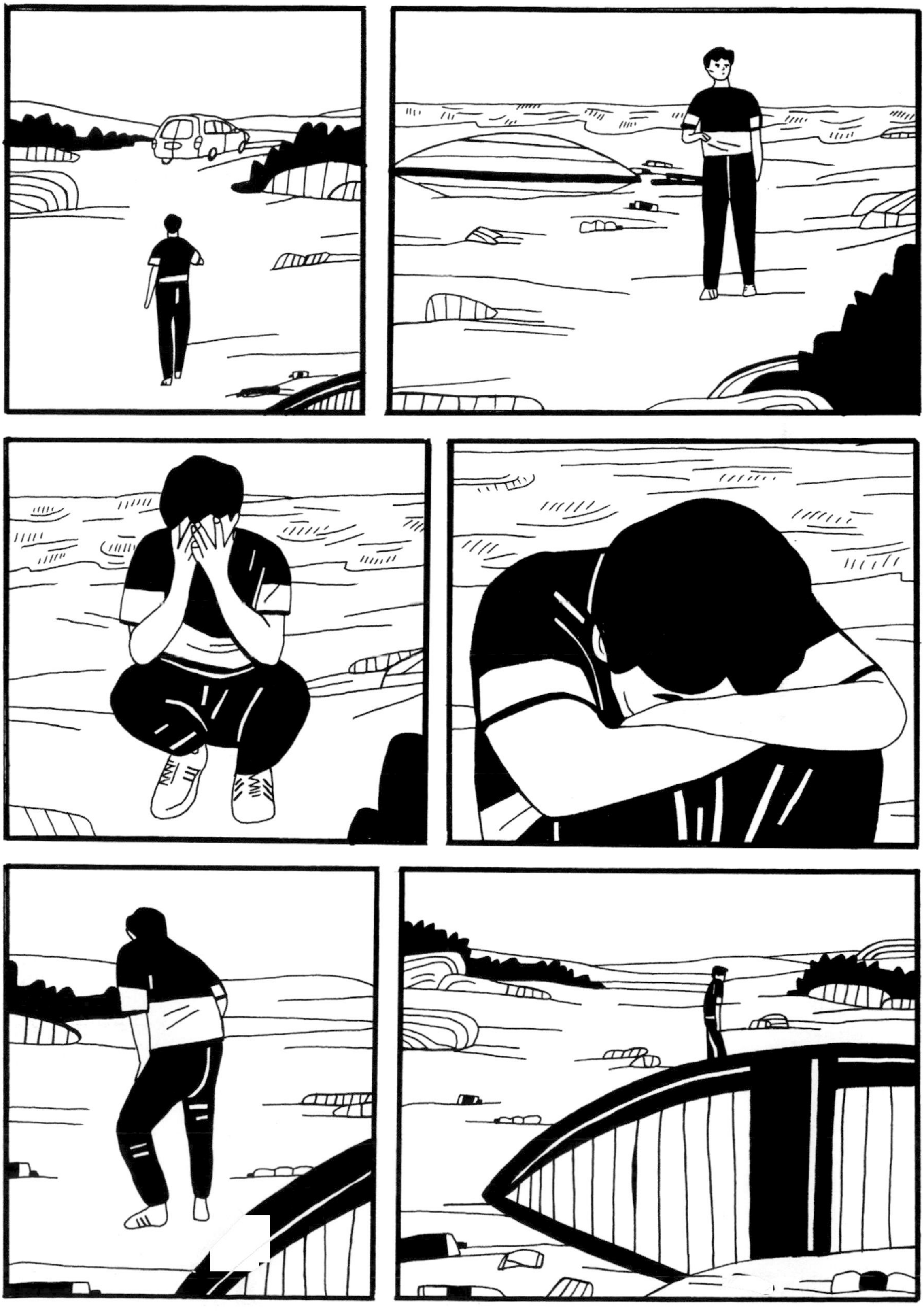

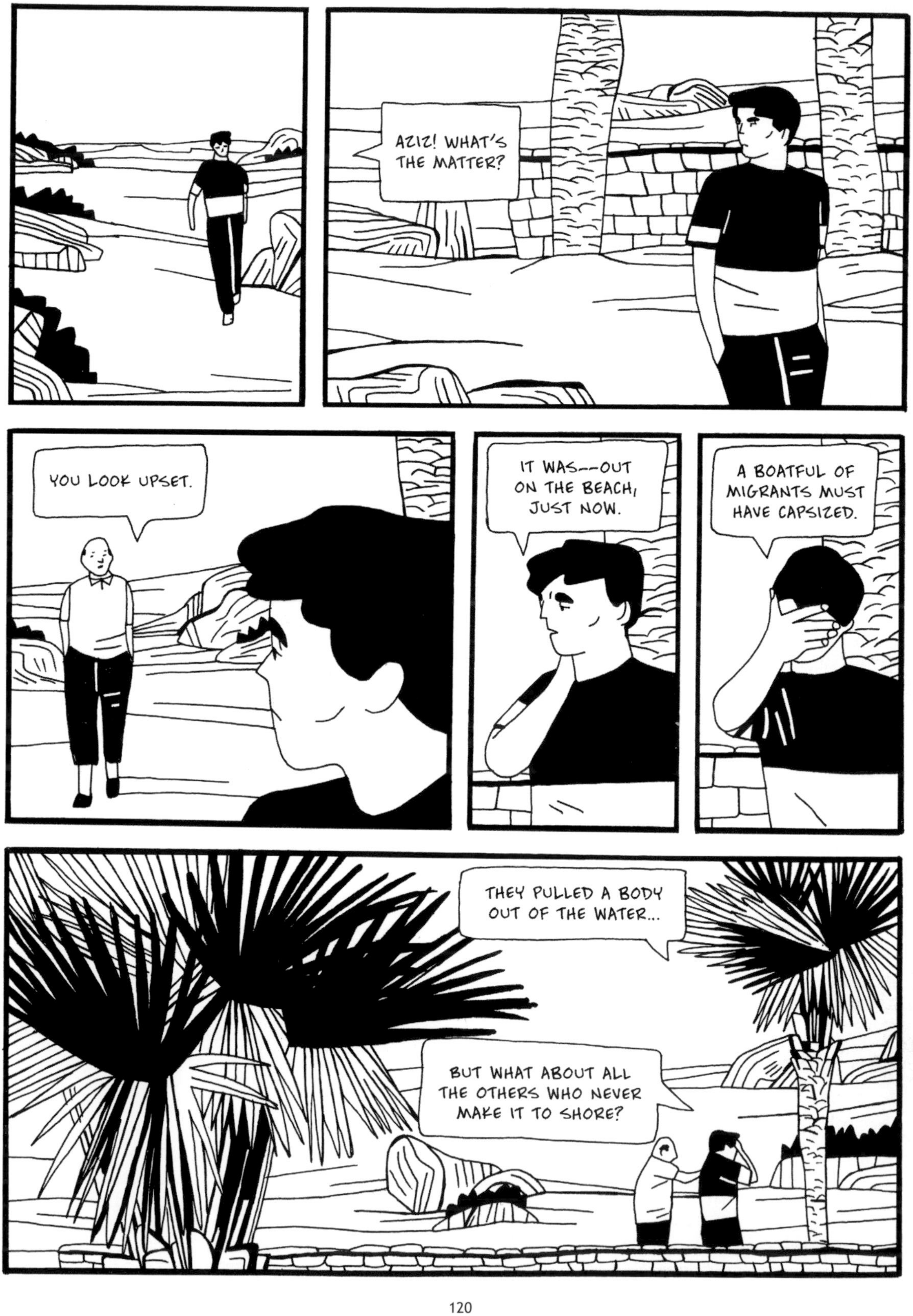
AZIZ! WHAT'S THE MATTER?
YOU LOOK UPSET.
IT WAS--OUT ON THE BEACH, JUST NOW.
A BOATFUL OF MIGRANTS MUST HAVE CAPSIZED.
THEY PULLED A BODY OUT OF THE WATER...
BUT WHAT ABOUT ALL THE OTHERS WHO NEVER MAKE IT TO SHORE?

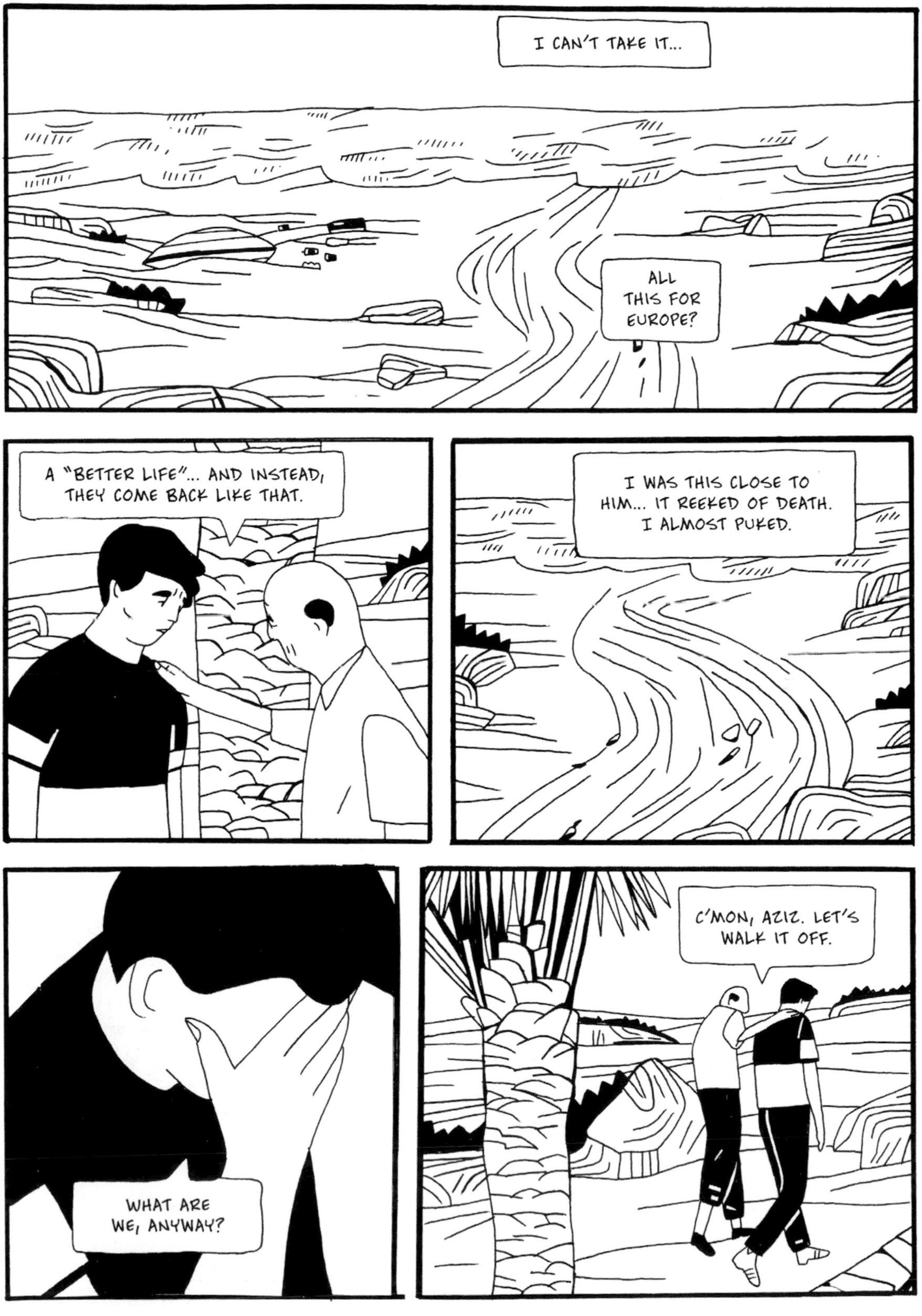
I CAN'T TAKE IT...
ALL THIS FOR EUROPE?
A "BETTER LIFE"... AND INSTEAD, THEY COME BACK LIKE THAT.
I WAS THIS CLOSE TO HIM... IT REEKED OF DEATH. I ALMOST PUKED.
WHAT ARE WE, ANYWAY?
C'MON, AZIZ. LET'S WALK IT OFF.

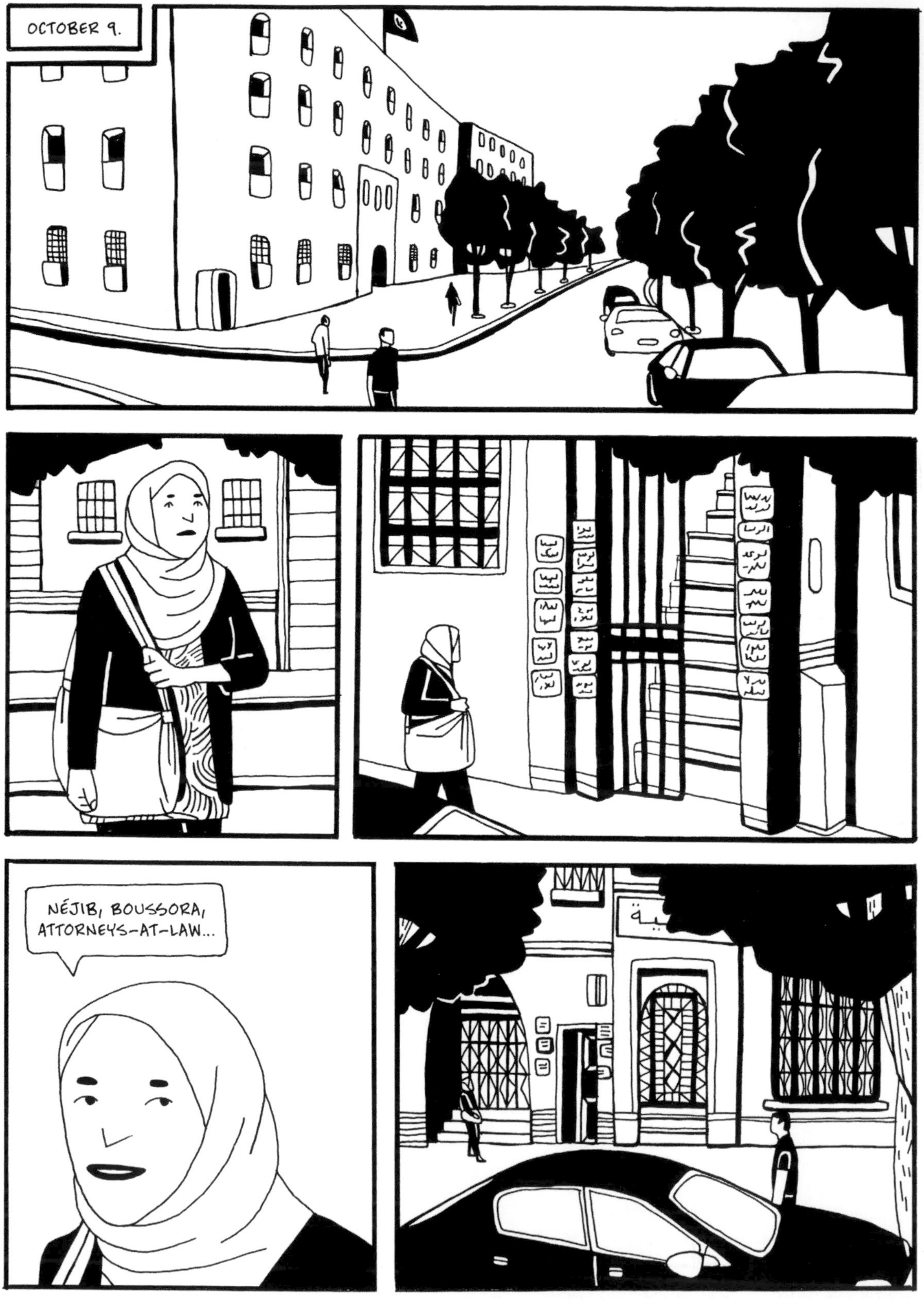
OCTOBER 9.
NÉJIB, BOUSSORA, ATTORNEYS-AT-LAW...

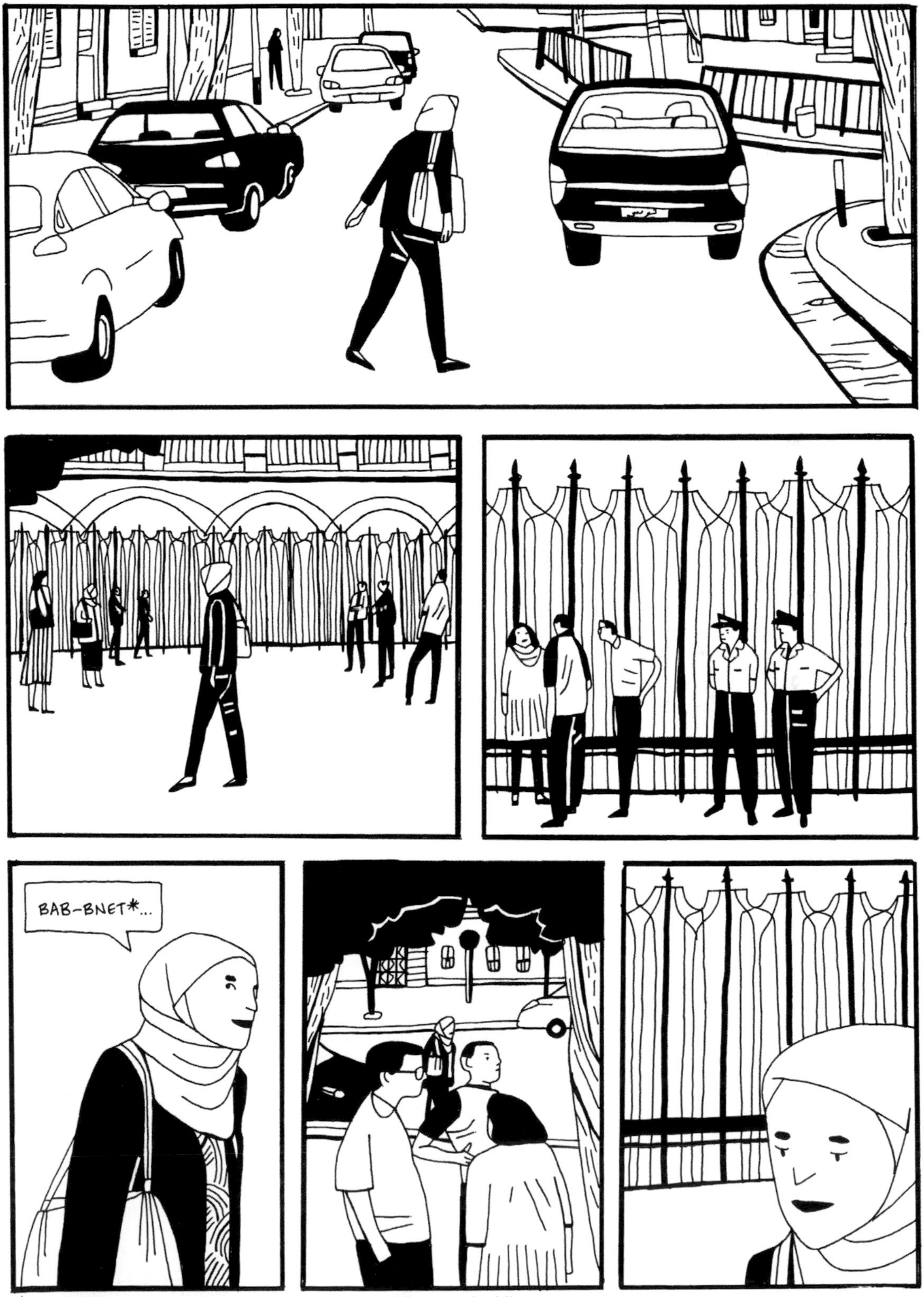
BAB-BNET*...

* THE TUNISIAN ORDER OF LAWYERS AND THE COURTHOUSE ARE ON BOULEVARD BAB BNET, OR THE GATE OF DAUGHTERS, NAMED FOR AN ANCIENT TALE

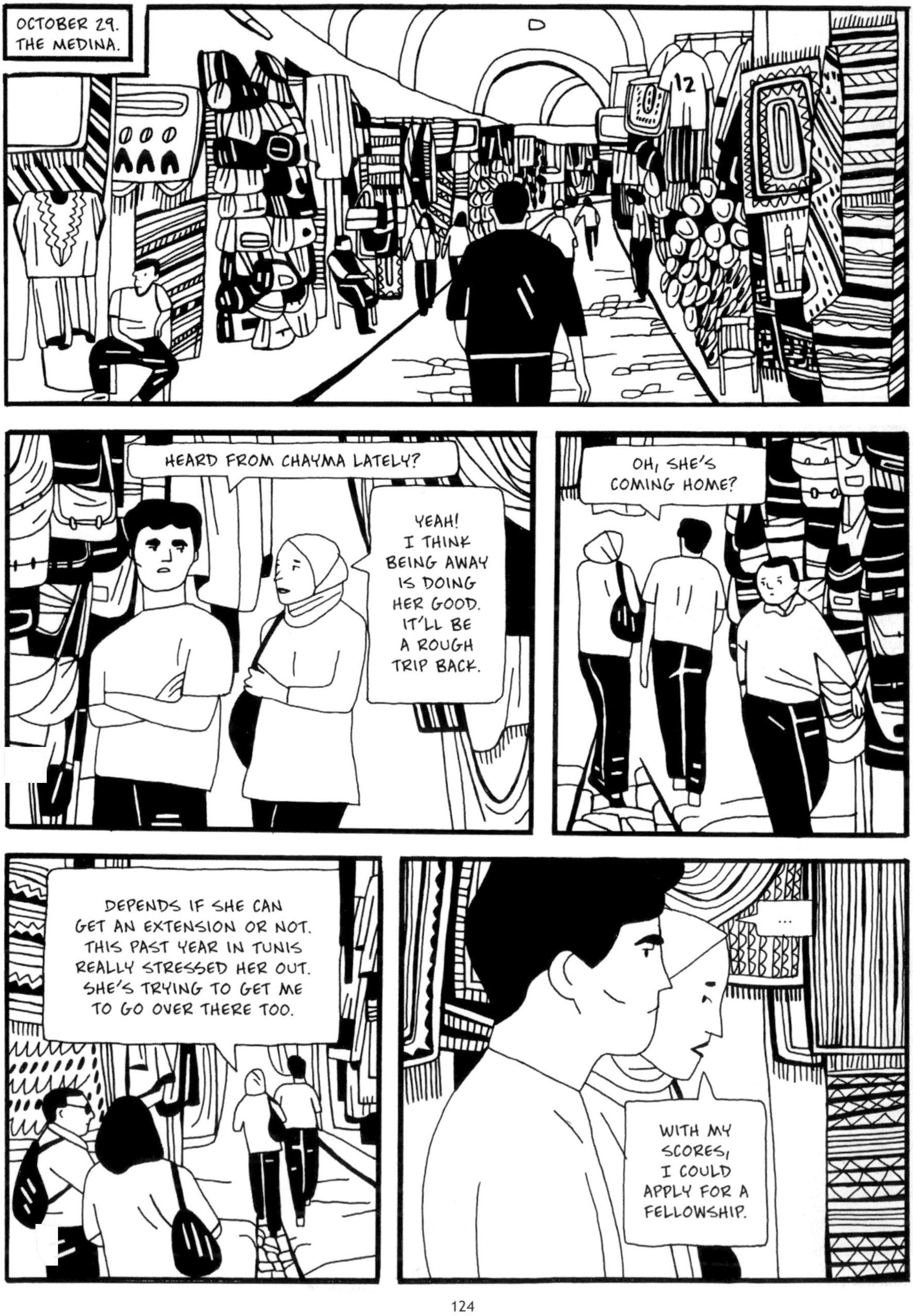
OCTOBER 29. THE MEDINA.
HEARD FROM CHAYMA LATELY?
YEAH! I THINK BEING AWAY IS DOING HER GOOD. IT'LL BE A ROUGH TRIP BACK.
OH, SHE'S COMING HOME?
DEPENDS IF SHE CAN GET AN EXTENSION OR NOT. THIS PAST YEAR IN TUNIS REALLY STRESSED HER OUT. SHE'S TRYING TO GET ME TO GO OVER THERE TOO.
...
WITH MY SCORES, I COULD APPLY FOR A FELLOWSHIP.

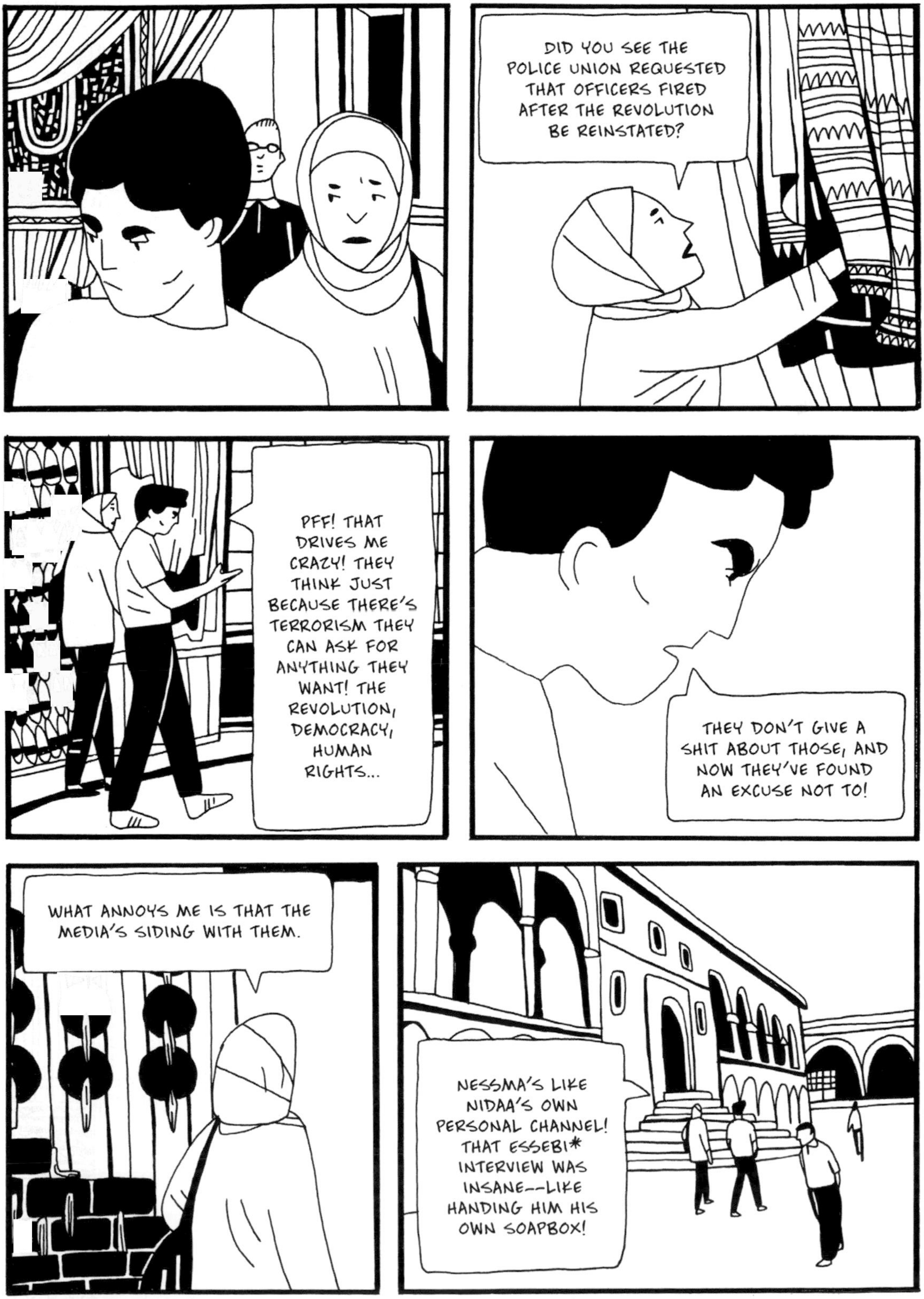
DID YOU SEE THE POLICE UNION REQUESTED THAT OFFICERS FIRED AFTER THE REVOLUTION BE REINSTATED?
PFF! THAT DRIVES ME CRAZY! THEY THINK JUST BECAUSE THERE'S TERRORISM THEY CAN ASK FOR ANYTHING THEY WANT! THE REVOLUTION, DEMOCRACY, HUMAN RIGHTS...
THEY DON'T GIVE A SHIT ABOUT THOSE, AND NOW THEY'VE FOUND AN EXCUSE NOT TO!
WHAT ANNOYS ME IS THAT THE MEDIA'S SIDING WITH THEM.
NESSMA'S LIKE NIDAA'S OWN PERSONAL CHANNEL! THAT ESSEBI* INTERVIEW WAS INSANE--LIKE HANDING HIM HIS OWN SOAPBOX!

* MOHAMED BEJI CAID ESSEBSI, FOUNDER OF NIDAA TOUNES, OR THE "CALL OF TUNISIA" PARTY, TUNISIAN PRESIDENT STARTING IN DECEMBER 2014, AFTER THE EVENTS DEPICTED IN THIS BOOK

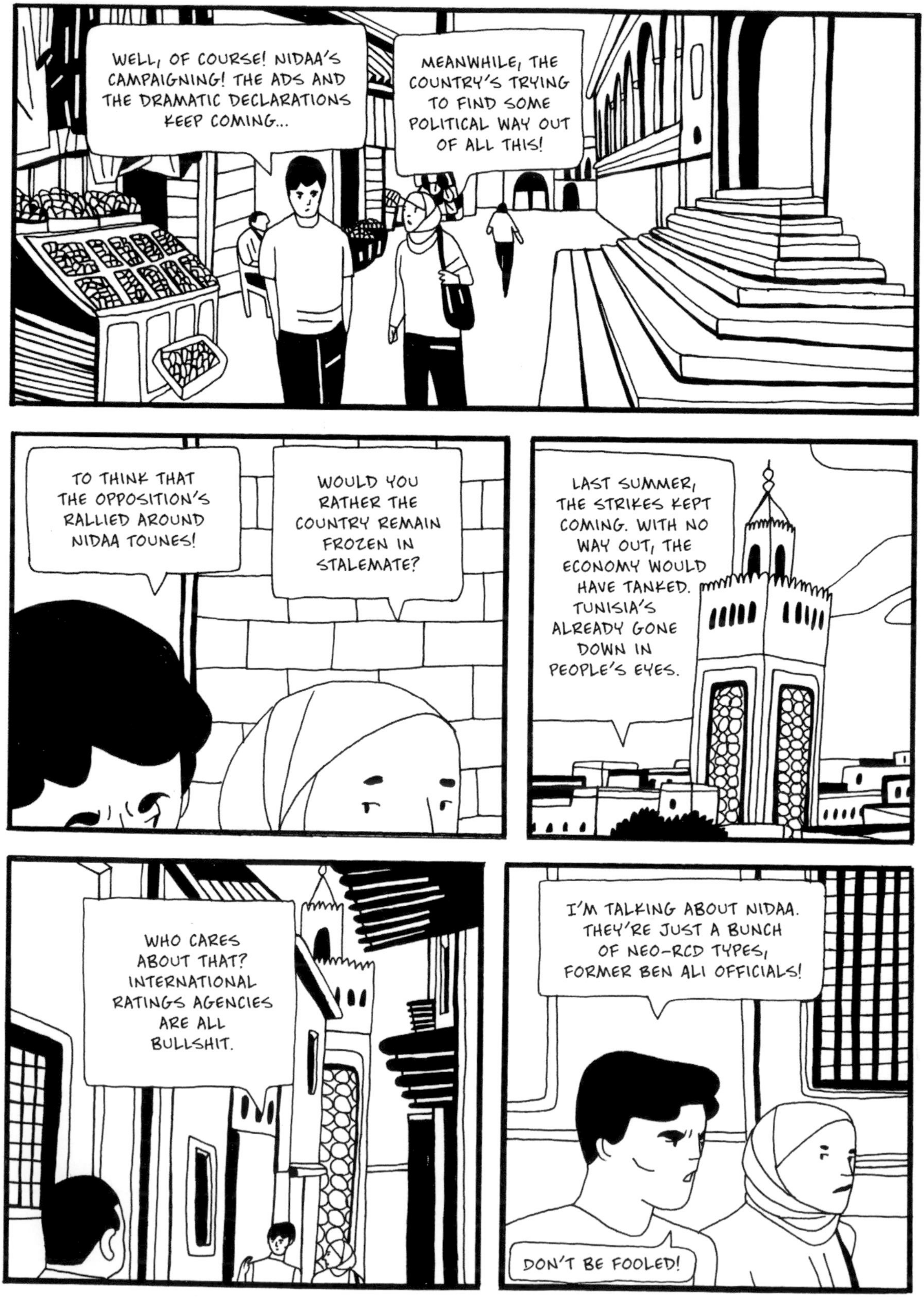
WELL, OF COURSE! NIDAA'S CAMPAIGNING! THE ADS AND THE DRAMATIC DECLARATIONS KEEP COMING...
MEANWHILE, THE COUNTRY'S TRYING TO FIND SOME POLITICAL WAY OUT OF ALL THIS!
TO THINK THAT THE OPPOSITION'S RALLIED AROUND NIDAA TOUNES!
WOULD YOU RATHER THE COUNTRY REMAIN FROZEN IN STALEMATE?
LAST SUMMER, THE STRIKES KEPT COMING. WITH NO WAY OUT, THE ECONOMY WOULD HAVE TANKED. TUNISIA'S ALREADY GONE DOWN IN PEOPLE'S EYES.
WHO CARES ABOUT THAT? INTERNATIONAL RATINGS AGENCIES ARE ALL BULLSHIT.
I'M TALKING ABOUT NIDAA. THEY'RE JUST A BUNCH OF NEO-RCD TYPES, FORMER BEN ALI OFFICIALS!
DON'T BE FOOLED!

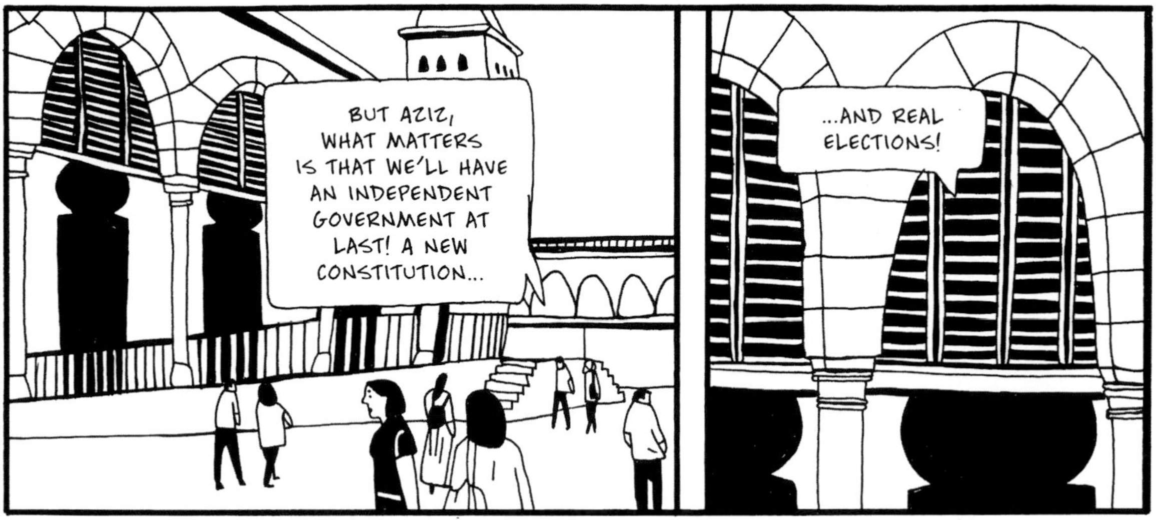
BUT AZIZ, WHAT MATTERS IS THAT WE'LL HAVE AN INDEPENDENT GOVERNMENT AT LAST! A NEW CONSTITUTION...
...AND REAL ELECTIONS!

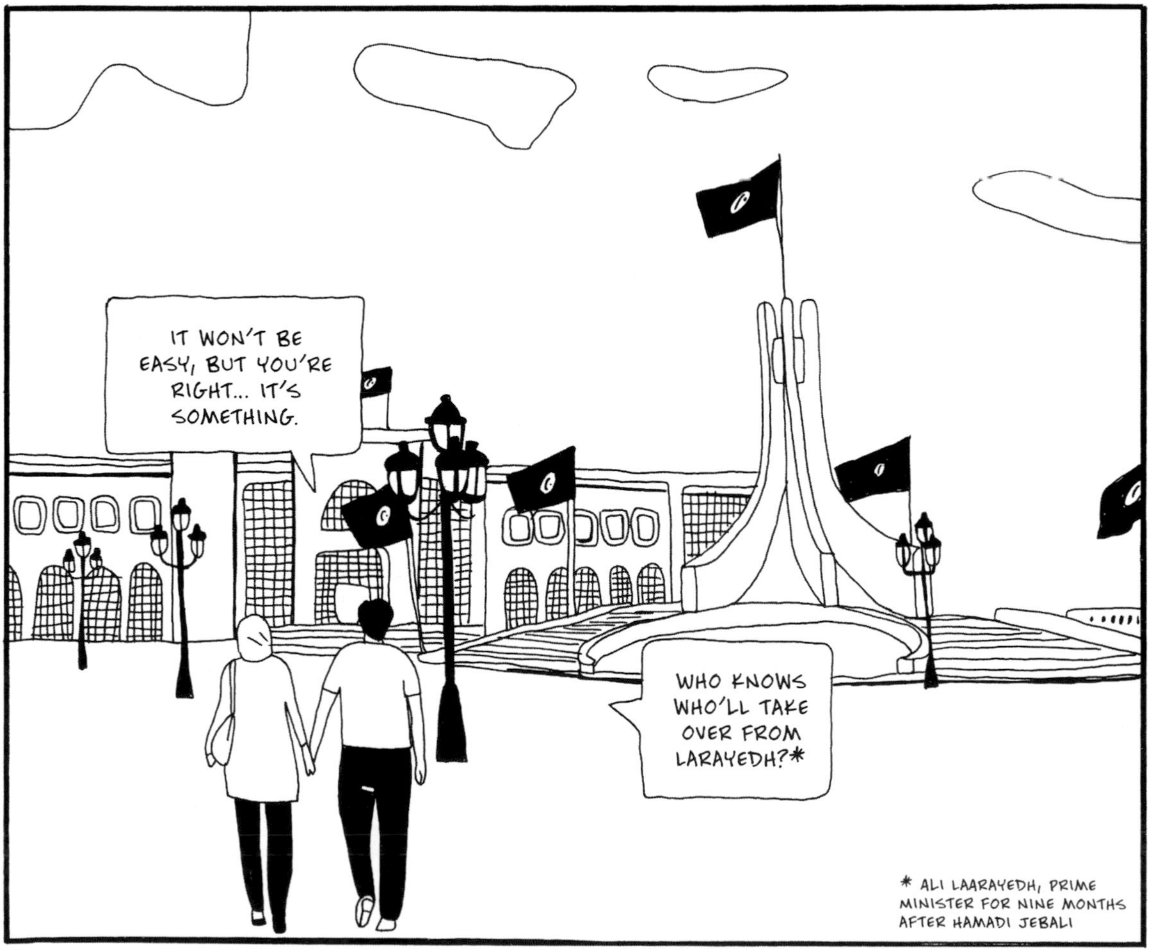
IT WON'T BE EASY, BUT YOU'RE RIGHT... IT'S SOMETHING.
WHO KNOWS WHO'LL TAKE OVER FROM LARAYEDH?*
* ALI LAARAYEDH, PRIME MINISTER FOR NINE MONTHS AFTER HAMADI JEBALI

ON DECEMBER 14, MEHDI JOMAA, FORMER MINISTER OF INDUSTRY IN THE ENNAHDHA ADMINISTRATION, BUT A POLITICAL INDEPENDENT, BECAME INTERIM PRIME MINISTER AND HAD TO ASSEMBLE A NEW GOVERNMENT BEFORE HIS TERM BEGAN IN EARLY 2014. THE CONSTITUTION WOULD FINALLY BE RATIFIED IN TOTO ON JANUARY 26, 2014, AND THREE DAYS LATER, THE NEW GOVERNMENT TOOK OFFICE.

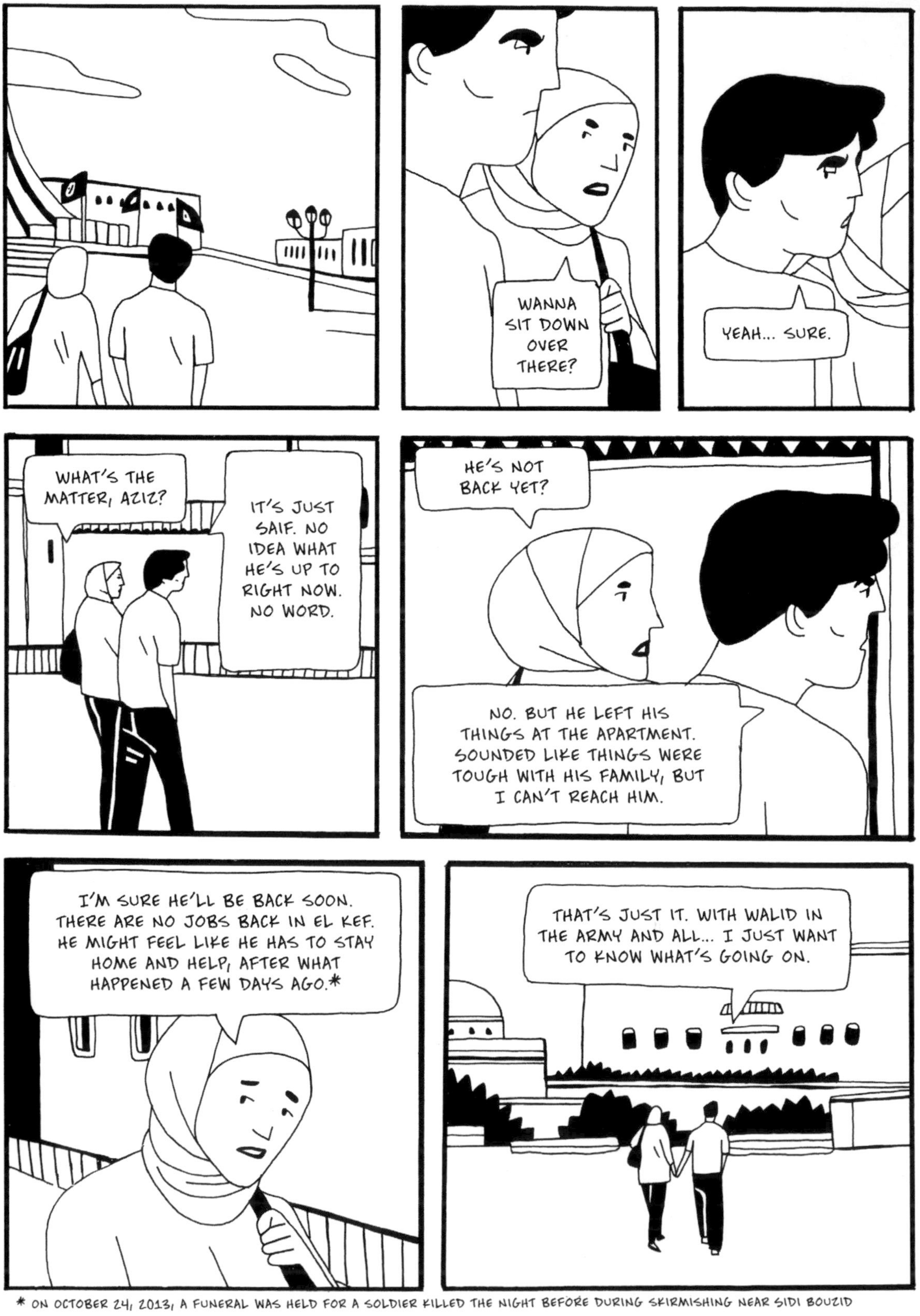
WANNA SIT DOWN OVER THERE?
YEAH... SURE.
WHAT'S THE MATTER, AZIZ?
IT'S JUST SAIF. NO IDEA WHAT HE'S UP TO RIGHT NOW. NO WORD.
HE'S NOT BACK YET?
NO. BUT HE LEFT HIS THINGS AT THE APARTMENT. SOUNDED LIKE THINGS WERE TOUGH WITH HIS FAMILY, BUT I CAN'T REACH HIM.
I'M SURE HE'LL BE BACK SOON. THERE ARE NO JOBS BACK IN EL KEF. HE MIGHT FEEL LIKE HE HAS TO STAY HOME AND HELP, AFTER WHAT HAPPENED A FEW DAYS AGO.*
THAT'S JUST IT. WITH WALID IN THE ARMY AND ALL... I JUST WANT TO KNOW WHAT'S GOING ON.

* ON OCTOBER 24, 2013, A FUNERAL WAS HELD FOR A SOLDIER KILLED THE NIGHT BEFORE DURING SKIRMISHING NEAR SIDI BOUZID

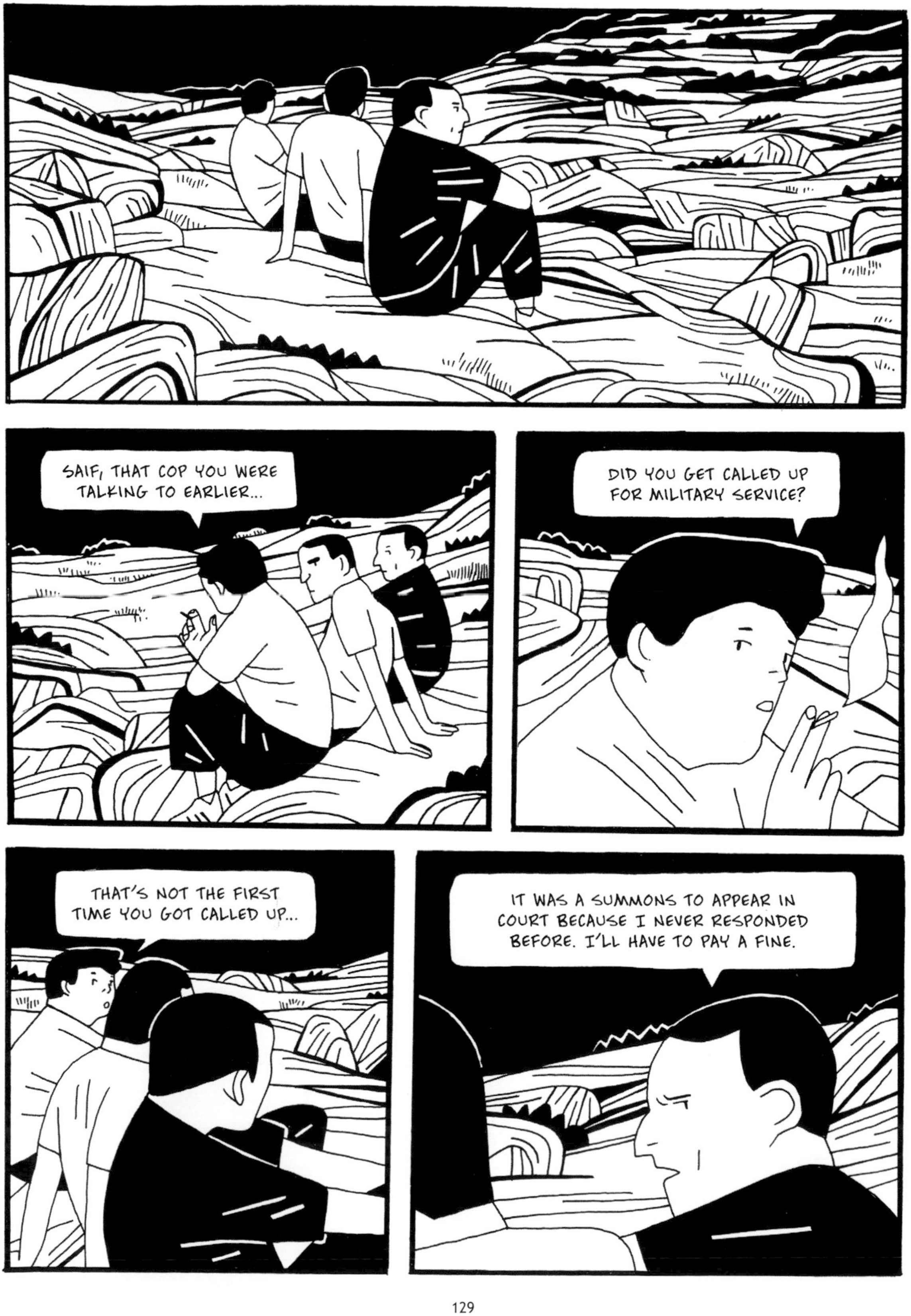
SAIF, THAT COP YOU WERE TALKING TO EARLIER...
DID YOU GET CALLED UP FOR MILITARY SERVICE?
THAT'S NOT THE FIRST TIME YOU GOT CALLED UP...
IT WAS A SUMMONS TO APPEAR IN COURT BECAUSE I NEVER RESPONDED BEFORE. I'LL HAVE TO PAY A FINE.

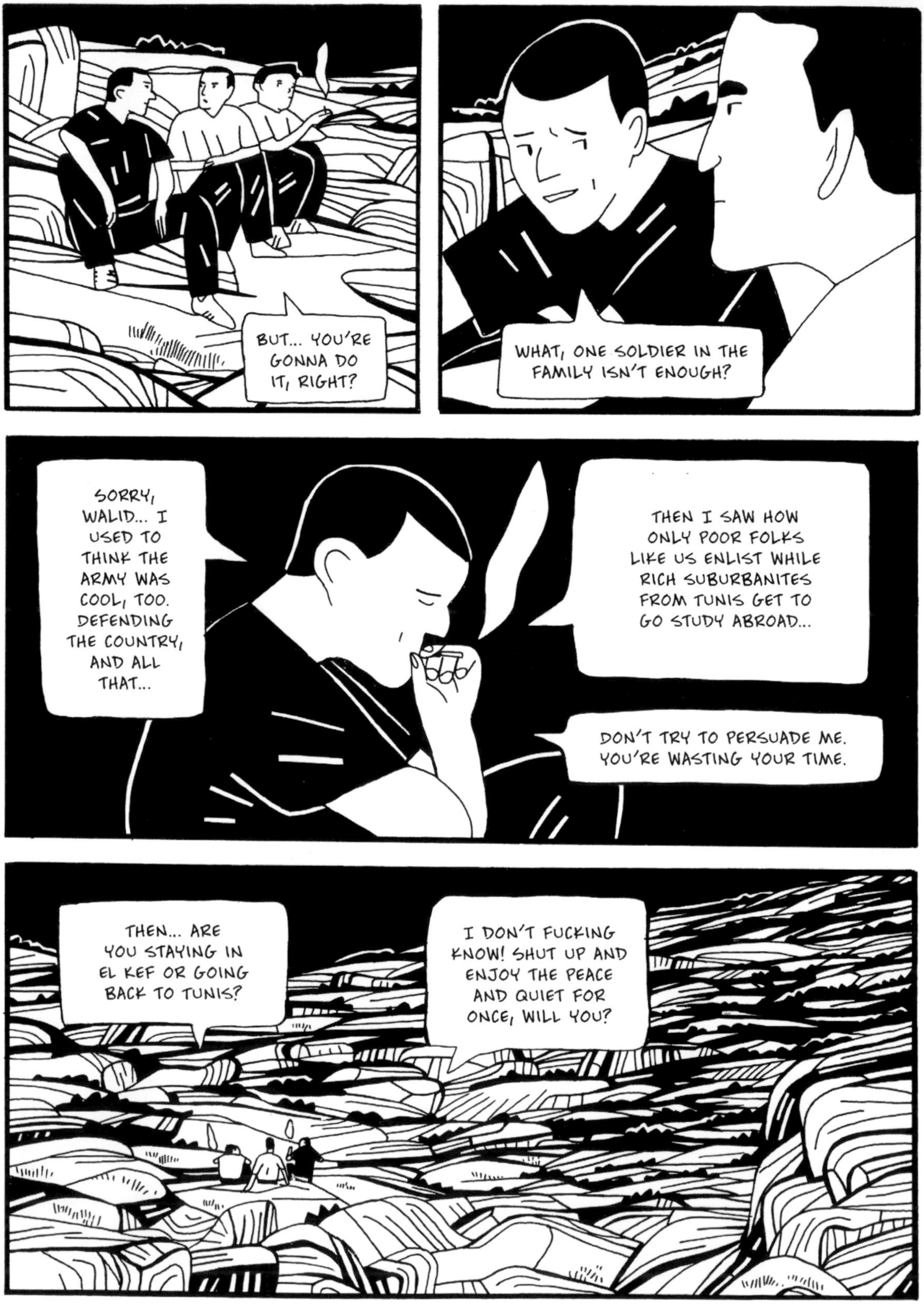
BUT... YOU'RE GONNA DO IT, RIGHT?
WHAT, ONE SOLDIER IN THE FAMILY ISN'T ENOUGH?
SORRY, WALID... I USED TO THINK THE ARMY WAS COOL, TOO. DEFENDING THE COUNTRY, AND ALL THAT...
THEN I SAW HOW ONLY POOR FOLKS LIKE US ENLIST WHILE RICH SUBURBANITES FROM TUNIS GET TO GO STUDY ABROAD...
DON'T TRY TO PERSUADE ME. YOU'RE WASTING YOUR TIME.
THEN... ARE YOU STAYING IN EL KEF OR GOING BACK TO TUNIS?
I DON'T FUCKING KNOW! SHUT UP AND ENJOY THE PEACE AND QUIET FOR ONCE, WILL YOU?

After
the spring

A Story of Tunisian Youth

TUNISIA'S POLITICAL LANDSCAPE IN 2013

Ennahdha ("renaissance") begins as a movement and becomes a conservative Islamist political party, founded by its president, Rached Ghannouchi. It was banned under Ben Ali's dictatorship, and the authorities cracked down on its activists until it was legalized in March 2011 (Ghannouchi lived in exile in London until the revolution).

Moncef Marzouki, who opposed Ben Ali's dictatorship, was arrested several times, then exiled to France. He was president of the LTDH (Tunisian League for Human Rights) from 1989 to 1994 and then, in 2001, founded the CPR, a center-left secular party.

After the revolution, the number of Tunisian political parties multiplied.

Nidaa Tounes (Call of Tunisia) self-identifies as a "modernist" party founded in June 2012 by Beji Caid Essebsi, a former minister under Habib Bourguiba. Nidaa Tounes gathers former cadres and leading figures from the RCD (Democratic Constitutional Rally), the party of fallen dictator Ben Ali.

Ej-Jabha (Popular Front for the Realization of the Objectives of the Revolution), is a leftist political and electoral alliance founded in October 2012, that brings together, among others, the Workers' Party (formerly the Tunisian Workers' Communist Party), led by Hamma Hammami (spokesperson for the Popular Front); the People's Current, led by Mohamed Brahmi; the Democratic Patriots' Unified Party, led by Chokri Belaid; and also the Workers' Left League, the Tunisian Ba'ath Movement, and the Green Tunisia Party.

Tunisia In 2013
Political Context
And Timeline

Having won a plurality in the Tunisian Constituent Assembly, the Ennahdha party formed a coalition called the "Troïka" with the Congress for the Republic (CPR, a party founded by Moncef Marzouki, who became Interim President of the Republic) and Ettakatol (founded by Mustapha Ben Jafar, who became President of the Assembly). Ennahdha's secretary-general Hamadi Jebali became the Prime Minister.

Timeline of Events

JANUARY 2013

El Kef is a city in a mountainous region in northwestern Tunisia, capital of the Kef governorate. The government had concluded a series of accords with the URT (El Kef Regional Workers' Union) to combat unemployment in the region. On January 8, young unemployed college graduates blocked road access to El Kef to protest the government's failure to uphold these accords. Following these actions, the URT called for a regional strike on January 16.

Northwestern Tunisia is a rural and agricultural region where the unemployment rate for recent college graduates has reached 40 percent. Since the revolution, various social movements have risen up to condemn the marginalization of the country's heartland in favor of coastal areas, to call for greater investment in that heartland, and to give voice to its overlooked citizenry, which consists largely of often illiterate farmers laboring for very low wages to support their households.

FEBRUARY

The regional convention of the Democratic Patriots' Unified Party (a far-left opposition party) takes place in El Kef on February 2nd. Armed militias attack this meeting. In a February 5th appearance on the Nessma TV network, the party's secretary-general Chokri Belaid openly holds Ennahdha responsible for the attack: "We held a meeting for the people during our party's annual regional convention [...] Just as I was finishing my speech, a group rushed into the hall and began attacking those gathered. We had not expected or even imagined that anyone would dare commit such an act, especially in El Kef. Our party's younger members rose to the occasion and drove them out of the hall. Once outside, our attackers began to throw stones. Our younger members tried to stop a few of them and turn them over to the police, but they were wounded in the hail of stones. Meanwhile, the police looked on, not lifting a finger. They only intervened when our attackers scattered! Some Ennahdha followers had warned us we'd never be allowed to hold our convention, but we didn't take them seriously enough. [...] These are not isolated acts that can be blamed on a small group, but rather actions planned by a central institution, aimed at diverse governorates and diverse political forces. [...] Whenever this government is confronted with a paralyzing crisis; whenever it tries to adopt unpopular measures like a price hike, as is the case right now; whenever the Ennahdha movement faces a crisis [...] we flee our problems through the use of violence. Who is behind this violence? In my view, a wing of the Ennahdha movement." Though he refrains from naming them, Chokri Belaid seems to be pointing a finger at the Leagues for the Protection of the Revolution (LPR), organizations that appeared on the public scene in 2012 and consist largely of Ennahdha sympathizers and radicals. Active throughout the entirety of Tunisia, they have resorted to several acts of violence (the October 18, 2012 assassination of Lotfi Nagdh, regional coordinator for the Nidaa Tounes party in Tataouine, is attributed to them).

The day after his interview, Chokri Belaid is murdered, shot to death right outside his home in El Menzah 6 (a neighborhood in northern Tunis). His loved ones, as well as segments of the intelligentsia and citizenry, hold the government responsible for being too indulgent with radical groups. Hamma Hammami, one of the leaders of the Popular Front, declares that the assassination was "planned and carried out by professionals."

On the night of February 6th, in response to these accusations and general indignation, Prime Minister Hamadi Jebali announces the formation of a government with national jurisdiction but no political affiliation, but his proposal, backed by his ally Ettakatol, is rejected the next day by Ennahdha (the party that had brought him to power) and its other ally, the CPR.

There is a rise in protests across the country. The Ennahdha offices in Siliana (northwest) are burned; protestors clash with the police in Gafsa (central-south) and several other regions. The opposition parties and the Tunisian General Labour Union call for a general strike on Friday, February 8, the day of Chokri Belaid's funeral, which is attended by 40,000 people.

On February 19, Hamadi Jebali resigns, and three days later, Moncef Marzouki appoints former Minister of the Interior Ali Laarayedh to form a new government.

MARCH

On March 2, the ANC (National Constituent Assembly) ratifies the new government by a vote of 137 out of 217. Where sovereign ministers are concerned, the government is filled out with leading independent figures, but it fails to include any parties besides those of the troika. Ennahdha, the CPR, and Ettakatol thus renew their alliance and maintain their control of executive power. Despite the people's wishes, the LPRs are maintained as well.

A clip from Weld El 15's song "Boulicia Kleb" ("Cops are dogs") goes live online on March 3. Alaa Eddine Yacoubi, a.k.a. Weld El 15, is a Tunisian rapper who spent nine months in prison in 2012 for cannabis consumption, as per "Law 52," an instrument of state repression that has put many young people behind bars. The song tells of the circumstances of his arrest. For three months, he evaded police before showing up for his trial, which ended in a two-year sentence without parole. The verdict outraged the rapper's many supporters present at the trial, who compared it to justice under Ben Ali's dictatorship. They are violently broken up by the police. Other Tunisian rappers—spokespeople for angry youth—also fall victim to the draconian Tunisian justice system: in the fall, Klay BBJ, accused of lyrics offensive to the authorities, is sentenced to a year and nine months in prison without parole for insulting a public official (though he would be acquitted on appeal).

Cases of self-immolation multiply throughout a country faced with economic decline and rising unemployment. On March 12 in Tunis, 27-year-old cigarette vendor Adel Khedri sets himself on fire in front of the municipal theatre on Avenue Habib Bourguiba. The funeral turns into a protest for locals and ambulatory, unlicensed street vendors like Khedri himself, driven to peddling by unemployment. On March 17, another young man, from an underprivileged housing development, sets himself on fire. From the revolution through the spring of 2013, there are between 150 and 200 cases of self-immolation in Tunisia.

APRIL

The Tunisian General Labour Union rebukes the government for supporting the LPRs and for seeking to limit the right to strike under the new constitution. Civil society rallies to defend the freedoms of expression and the press in the face of proposed legislation to curb them.

These freedoms, already abused by several lawsuits brought against journalists in 2011 and 2012, are once more put to the test in 2013: in July, 19 artists are arrested for "indecent exposure" during a street performance in El Kef; in September, cameraman Mourad Meherzi faces charges of "conspiring to commit violence against a government official" and "defamation," among others, for videotaping the Minister of Culture getting egged; the editorial director of the French language daily newspaper *La Presse* is arbitrarily brought up on charges.

The creation of HAICA (High Independent Authority for Audiovisual Communication), a constitutional commission mandated with organizing the audiovisual sector and regulating, among other things, media time allocated to electoral campaigns, is pushed back yet again, this time until the month of May.

MAY

The government acknowledges the presence of groups with ties to AQIM (Al-Qaeda in the Islamic Maghreb) along the Algerian border in the area near El Kef and around Mount Chaambi (by the Kasserine governorate) and attempts to allay fears by implementing security measures.

The Salafist movement Ansar Al-Sharia is banned from setting up prayer meeting tents in several Tunisian cities. This decision is followed by clashes between Salafists and the forces of law and order. On May 19, the government bans the movement's conference in Kairouan, deploying significant security forces around the city, capital, and roads. Confrontations break out in Ettadhamen, a working-class neighborhood in Tunis, and the government makes several arrests.

The security situation bogs down, and on May 31, in the face of popular pressure, the government declares without tangible proof that certain members of Ansar Al-Sharia are involved in the events on Mount Chaambi, classifying the movement as a "terrorist group".

JUNE

Tunisian high-school student Amina Sboui (now Amina Tyler) had been arrested and detained as of May 19 for spray-painting "Femen" on a cemetery wall near the Great Mosque, and for possession of mace spray. Her loved ones and lawyers feared the verdict had been motivated by political considerations. Three Femen activists (two French women and a German woman) came to demonstrate topless before the Tunis court to show their support. They were arrested and, when brought before the examining magistrate, were charged with organized public indecency. On June 12, they are sentenced to prison without parole, but are freed at the end of the month. Amina, however, is given a fine of 300 dinars and released only in early August while awaiting her trial for desecrating a cemetery.

JULY

According to official figures, anywhere from 2,000 to 3,000 Tunisians left to fight in Syria between 2011 and 2013, while Tunisian authorities intercepted an estimated another 1,000. These figures continued to grow over the course of 2013. Tunisians who leave for Syria do not fit neatly into any one profile type, and their departures often remain shrouded in mystery, leaving loved ones, usually not informed of their decisions, distraught and bereft. However,

most who leave are young men likely influenced by movements such as Ansar Al-Sharia, often accused of urging them on and celebrating "martyrs".

On July 25, Mohamed Brahmi, an assemblyman highly critical of the government and founder of the People's Movement (a nationalist Nasserist party), is assassinated right outside his house. The Tunisian General Labour Union calls a general strike, and demonstrations take place throughout the country, demanding the government step down and the National Constituent Assembly be dissolved.

In the days that follow, hundreds and then thousands of demonstrators begin a sit-in before the Assembly's national headquarters in the city of Le Bardo. Pro-government demonstrators, albeit fewer in number, also set up shop there, divided from their opposition rivals by the police, who violently break up the peaceful demonstrators on the night of July 28th. Several people are wounded, including two Assemblymen (Noomane Fehri and Mongi Rahoui) and Popular Front activist Mohamed Mofti, who dies in Gafsa after being hit in the head by a tear gas canister. That night, demonstrators share iftar. The atmosphere is convivial. Dozens of assemblymen resign from opposition parties (the Popular Front, Nidaa Tounes...) to form the Front de salut national [Front for Saving the Nation]. On July 29, eight soldiers are killed on Mount Chaambi: in retaliation, the Ennahdha offices in Kasserine are vandalized.

AUGUST

Demonstrations continue as tens of thousands of people across the country demand the government step down. Ennahdha clings to power, calling for the legitimacy of the ballot box, and invoking a need for stability and cohesion during the anti-terrorist struggle. The party declares it will welcome a broader political coalition, but opposition parties see Mohamed Brahmi's assassination as marking the end of any legitimacy for the Assembly and the executive branch. Various attempts at mediation come to nothing.

Tunisian police are still largely seen as a repressive security force in the service of the powers that be. Corruption, humiliating and intimidating the public, abuse of power, violence and even acts of torture are still common practices among police officers. The resentment Tunisians feel toward the police, who seem to act with utter impunity and without respect for basic human rights, is further exacerbated by lawsuits brought forward after the revolution against activists, artists, journalists, and youth that police have sometimes assaulted during their arrest and/or detention. In late 2012, a young Tunisian raped by two officers was accused of "public indecency"; the officers claimed to have caught her in "immoral" circumstances with her fiancé. This affair scandalized the entire country, and a film was made from the book the victim wrote.

Also of note are the hundreds of young people who were hauled before the courts in 2014 for the misdemeanors of resisting arrest and acts of revolution—lawsuits begun in 2011 and 2012, often for similar reasons: disorderly conduct, defamation and violence against the police. Through the "Me too I torched a police station" campaign, public opinion rallied to denounce this persecution of revolutionary youth.

SEPTEMBER - OCTOBER
The UGTT (Tunisian General Labour Union), UTICA (Tunisian Union of Industry, Trade and Handicrafts, managerial department), the LTDH (Tunisian Human Rights League), and the Tunisian Order of Lawyers intercede as mediators to open a "national dialogue" and propose the adoption of a "road map" outlining three stages: forming the ISIE (Independent High Authority for Elections, in charge of organizing presidential elections and legislative referendums), nominating a Prime Minister and a new government of "technocrats" and accelerating the process of drafting a Constitution. On September 17, Ennahdha accepts this plan in principle but demands conditions regarding the adoption of the Constitution. Negotiations languish, and the implementation of the ISIE lags.

The month of October is marked by several clashes between armed groups, especially in northwestern and central Tunisia. On October 17, two Tunisian National Guardsmen are killed in Béja, and then on October 23, in the Sidi Bouzid region, six guardsmen and a police officer are killed during armed skirmishes. The next day, during a funeral for one of the guardsmen in El Kef, the Ennahdha offices are burned. The government proceeds with several arrests and raids. On October 30, a suicide attack in Sousse and another on the mausoleum of former president Habib Bourguiba in Monastir are foiled.

NOVEMBER - DECEMBER
Party leaders attempt to pick a new independent Prime Minister, but not until independent Mehdi Jomaa leaves his position as Minister of Industry in December is he appointed the new Prime Minister.

JANUARY 2014
After many delays during the drafting process, the new Constitution is finally adopted on January 26, 2014. The resulting regime reflects a mixed approach, partway between parliamentary and presidential. Despite Ennahdha's wishes, Sharia law is not integrated as a basis for the law, but the Constitution makes several references to Islam, especially in the first article. It recognizes such major principles as human rights; the freedoms of expression, the press, religion, and thought; as well as gender equality (despite Ennahdha's initial intentions of addressing "complementarity," which it abandoned in the face of uproar from the people and the political opposition).

Hélène Aldeguer

spent time in Tunis in October 2014, covering the parliamentary elections, living among the youth of the city and working alongside Tunisian journalists from Nawaat, an independent collective blog that provided a public platform for dissident voices and was blocked in Tunisia until 2011. Her work focuses on political and social issues related mainly to the Arab-Muslim world and includes the book *Un Chant d'Amour: Israel-Palestine, une histoire francaise* with writer Alain Gresh and illustrations for the website *Orient XXI*, which covers news events in countries from North Africa to the Middle East. She was selected for the Young Talent Contest at the Angoulême International Comics Festival in 2016 for her work, "2011–2016, Resume of a Revolution."